SELE_____NGS

HERBERT L_____

...wood, Nottinghamshire, the son of a coal mi_____
intelligence, determination, and the support first of his mother and
later of important literary mentors, he moved away from his origins,
gaining a foothold both in the world of the lower middle class and in
the world of artistic London. In 1908 he became a schoolmaster in
Croydon, and in 1911 his first novel, *The White Peacock*, was published.
Appearing set for steady progress towards literary and professional
respectability, Lawrence decisively halted this trajectory by eloping in
1912 with Frieda Weekley, the wife of one of his former professors, and
by publishing three years later an obscene book. *Sons and Lovers* (1913)
and a volume of short stories, *The Prussian Officer* (1914), had been well
received, but *The Rainbow* was banned on publication in 1915.
Lawrence had anticipated that this sexually candid and formally
experimental novel would cause a stir, but he was unprepared for the
campaign of vilification by certain reviewers. Lawrence's sense of
himself as an outlaw, and his frenzy at the militaristic fervour of the
war years, intensified his hatred of most aspects of English life and
sharpened the diagnostic probing of his next, and perhaps his greatest,
novel, *Women in Love* (1920). After the end of the war Lawrence
travelled restlessly—to Italy, Ceylon, Australia, America, Mexico, and
back to France and Italy—and despite steadily worsening health
embodied his experience prolifically in diverse genres. But though the
settings and plots of much of his later work are exotic, Lawrence was
always essentially concerned with what he saw as the death-in-life lived
by people in, the so-called advanced world, and for his last, and most
controversial, novel, *Lady Chatterley's Lover* (1928), he returned to the
English scene and the coal-mining Midlands which imaginatively still
possessed him. Lawrence died of tuberculosis on 2 March 1930.

MICHAEL HERBERT is Lecturer in English Language and Literature,
University of St Andrews. He has edited Lawrence's *Reflections on the
Death of a Porcupine and Other Essays* (Cambridge: Cambridge University
Press, 1988).

OXFORD WORLD'S CLASSICS

*For almost 100 years Oxford World's Classics have brought
readers closer to the world's great literature. Now with over 700
titles—from the 4,000-year-old myths of Mesopotamia to the
twentieth century's greatest novels—the series makes available
lesser-known as well as celebrated writing.*

*The pocket-sized hardbacks of the early years contained
introductions by Virginia Woolf, T. S. Eliot, Graham Greene, and
other literary figures which enriched the experience of reading.
Today the series is recognized for its fine scholarship and
reliability in texts that span world literature, drama and poetry,
religion, philosophy and politics. Each edition includes perceptive
commentary and essential background information to meet the
changing needs of readers.*

OXFORD WORLD'S CLASSICS

D. H. LAWRENCE

Selected Critical Writings

Edited with an Introduction and Notes by
MICHAEL HERBERT

Oxford   New York
OXFORD UNIVERSITY PRESS
1998

Oxford University Press, Great Clarendon Street, Oxford OX2 6DP

Oxford New York

Athens Auckland Bangkok Bogotá Buenos Aires Calcutta
Cape Town Chennai Dar es Salaam Delhi Florence Hong Kong Istanbul
Karachi Kuala Lumpur Madrid Melbourne Mexico City Mumbai
Nairobi Paris São Paulo Singapore Taipei Tokyo Toronto Warsaw
and associated companies in Berlin Ibadan

Oxford is a registered trade mark of Oxford University Press

British Library Cataloguing in Publication Data

Data available

Library of Congress Cataloging in Publication Data
Lawrence. D. H. (David Herbert), 1885–1930.
[Essays. Selections]
Selected critical writings/D.H. Lawrence; edited with an
introduction and notes by Michael Herbert.
(Oxford world's classics)
Includes bibliographical references and index.
1. Lawrence D. H. (David Herbert), 1885–1930—Aesthetics. 2. Literature—
History and criticism. 3. Art criticism. I. Herbert, Michael, 1949– .
II. Title. III. Series: Oxford world's classics (Oxford University Press)
PR6023.A93A6 1998 809—dc21 98–3286
ISBN 0-19-282364-7

1 3 5 7 9 10 8 6 4 2

Typeset by GCS, Leighton Buzzard, Bedfordshire
Printed in Great Britain by
The Bath Press,
Bath

CONTENTS

Contents

INTRODUCTION

LAWRENCE is one of the greatest critics, yet none of his critical works—not even the sustained achievement of *Studies in Classic American Literature* (1923)—would ever have been awarded a Ph.D. His examiners would say he is too personal, too casual and colloquial and chatty, too unsystematic, injudicious, undisciplined, aggressive, abusive... so the list would continue. True, he is also extremely perceptive and intelligent and sensible and sensitive and wide-ranging and lively and entertaining... Yet the instance is instructive. For Lawrence's critical writings are not only *un*academic but downright *anti*-academic, and his antipathy to academic critics is as forcefully expressed as that to any other of his perceived opponents:

All the critical twiddle-twaddle about style, and form, all this pseudo-scientific classifying and analysing of books in an imitation-botanical fashion, is mere impertinence, and mostly dull jargon.

That comes from the first paragraph of his hatchet-job on John Galsworthy. But the opening words of that paragraph put the positive case, what criticism can and should be about:

Literary Criticism can be no more than a reasoned account of the feeling produced upon the critic by the book he is criticising. Criticism can never be a science: it is, in the first place, much too personal, and in the second, it is concerned with values that science ignores. The touch-stone is emotion, not reason. We judge a work of art by its effect on our sincere and vital emotion, and nothing else.

These words are in essence the credo of Lawrence the critic, and not only the critic of literature, for, though that is his prime concern, his critical writings deal with a great range of subjects, from art to the Apocalypse. In all these areas, he gives 'a reasoned account' in the light of 'emotion, not reason'. The contradiction is typical, and highlights the characteristic tension between intelligent comprehension and emotional apprehension in all Lawrence's work: it is, to misapply his own words, 'much too personal', yet has enormous impact as a result. It is the completely individual—and therefore often idiosyncratic and sometimes wrong-headed—product of a completely independent and extra-ordinarily honest critical mind. Perhaps above all else it is *moral*, 'concerned with values that science ignores' and championing all that is 'sincere and vital'. His interests are philosophical, psychological, religious, sociological, historical, and cultural as well as literary and artistic, but they are all directed to a moral end: to the study of how we live and how to live, how the life of the individual relates to the life of society, and what it is about art that is significant in our lives.

'Moral' need not, of course, mean moralistic. This most sincere and vital of all critics is not trapped inside any moral straitjacket. Indeed, being morally straitjacketed is precisely one of the qualities he identifies as *im*moral in 'Morality and the Novel', because a novelist committed to any one line, even if it is a conventionally moral line, lacks the balance of opposing forces that true morality demands. This insistence on balance may seem surprising in one who is often criticized for being unbalanced; almost as surprising as the insistence on morality in one whose popular image is still that of a pornographer, as author of *Lady Chatterley's Lover*, probably the most notorious novel ever. These contradictions can be fruitfully explored in Lawrence's essays, where the expository nature of the writing is more easily responsive to straightforward analysis and understanding than in works that are more imaginative or creative—though the essays also possess these two attributes in abundance.

Why did he write them? The answers are probably as various as the essays themselves, though one of them, 'Climbing Down Pisgah', begins by rejecting some possible reasons for writing, including writing for the sake of humanity, or the Spirit, or Oneness and Wholeness. 'Adventure' is the only reason Lawrence readily accepts. Nevertheless, one of his rejected reasons, the financial, was clearly of importance to him. His reviews of whatever books were sent to him were written because he needed the money, and other pieces were placed by his agent with editors of periodicals in Britain and the United States for the same mundane reason. Sometimes, it is true, he did not actually make any money. For instance, the 'Study of Thomas Hardy' was commissioned by James Nisbet & Co. in 1914 for their series 'Writers of the Day', but outgrew the commission and remained unpublished in

Lawrence's lifetime. It became not only a short book on Hardy but also a kind of artistic manifesto, and a philosophical as well as critical counterpart to and commentary on *The Rainbow*, at which he was working contemporaneously. This is one of the cases, too, where Lawrence's creative and critical impulses overlap: so often, one feels he might have turned out a story or a poem on these subjects as readily as an essay. And despite the financial pressures behind the essays, they never come across as hack-work, for their subjects always arouse lively responses, whether positive or negative, or a mixture of both. The positive aspect here is perhaps best seen in those essays that were written—generally at Lawrence's own suggestion—as introductions to books, of which there are six examples in this selection: introductions are intended to help books sell, but, whether introducing his own creative work (paintings as well as poems), or the poems of Harry Crosby ('Chaos in Poetry'), or his own translation of a novel by Verga, or an astrological treatise on the Apocalypse, Lawrence's enthusiastic interests go far beyond 'normal' introductory commendations and any merely mercenary motive. In this critic's work there is a whole-hearted absorption in the act of creation: in the creations he is making as much as the creations he is discussing.

It is very common to think that creative writers who are also critics are likely to use their criticism to champion their own kind of writing, and this is probably as true of Lawrence as of T. S. Eliot, who is in many ways the polar opposite of Lawrence as both critic and artist. Eliot is formal, impersonal, and grandly authoritative where Lawrence is informal, personal, passionate, and very ungrand, though he can be assertive, even dogmatic, and in these and other characteristics he is more like Eliot's friend and mentor Ezra Pound. Eliot is one of a line of writers that, in the twentieth century, has come to be seen as dominant, and which Lawrence vehemently opposed. It is a line that starts with Flaubert and includes Thomas Mann, Joseph Conrad, Marcel Proust, and James Joyce—all of whom get savaged by Lawrence in the present volume. The line is essentially aesthetic, concerned with formal qualities and 'Art for art's sake', and is largely Continental and American, whereas Lawrence used to say 'Art for *my* sake' and is himself in a native English line going back at least to Hardy, one of the few living writers Lawrence admired. But perhaps one should say 'British', as he also had unqualified admiration for Robert Burns. And then again further qualifications are needed, as happens with almost any statement made about Lawrence, for he writes fiction with many 'Continental' qualities, drawn especially from the 'philosophic' novels of the Germans and the Russians, and his one book of criticism is about American writers, from whom he seems to have derived more pure pleasure than any other national grouping, and who influenced him profoundly. These writers—whether Hardy or Burns, Tolstoy or Dostoevsky, Whitman or Melville—have the kind of massive emotional directness that makes it very difficult to talk about them without using dangerously slippery words like 'honest' or 'sincere', words that would be anathema to the 'enemy', whose line has become the prevailing critical orthodoxy.

This volume begins (the essays are in chronological order of writing) with an onslaught on the 'enemy': Thomas Mann and the school of Flaubert, with their 'craving for form' and logic and control, their fanatical desire for 'mastery of the medium', and the need to exclude rigorously everything that does not belong aesthetically in the work. 'But', says Lawrence, 'can the human mind fix absolutely the definite line of a book, any more than it can fix absolutely any definite line of action for a living being?' And then, showing his remarkable balance, he immediately turns round: 'Thomas Mann, however, is personal, almost painfully so, in his subject-matter.' This could also be said of Eliot, whose 'impersonal' theory of poetry is startlingly belied by the 'almost painfully' personal nature of his own poems; Lawrence, of course, wanted *his* own poems to be read with some knowledge of his life. Most of this first essay is taken up by retelling the story of *Death in Venice*. Here, something of Lawrence's journalistic qualities shows through, not unattractively: he wants to interest and inform, and one way a book review (which this essay is) can do this is to tell the prospective reader something about the plot or other contents. Similar examples recur in other reviews, and in introductions to books. The review ends with a return to the attack on Mann and Flaubert for their 'dead' qualities, their lack of a 'living rhythm'.

Living qualities are what drew Lawrence to his next author. Dealing with Flaubert and Mann, he can admire even when

attacking, and he does not like to carp: as he says in a discussion of
the defects of the realistic method in *Madame Bovary* in his Introduction to *Mastro-don Gesualdo*, 'I hate talking about flaws in great
books.' But with his 'Study of Thomas Hardy' there was added to
admiration qualities such as fellow-feeling and even love. It is by
far the longest work he devoted to a single author—though
'devoted' is not entirely accurate. He himself said, in a letter of 5
September 1914 to his agent, J. B. Pinker, 'it will be about anything
but Thomas Hardy',[1] and the subjects dealt with range extraordinarily widely to include not only a great number of writers
from Aeschylus and Euripides, Horace and Virgil, Shakespeare and
Spenser to Shelley and Swinburne, Dickens and Dostoevsky,
Tolstoy and Turgenev, but also flowers, Women's Suffrage, money,
work and leisure, Renaissance painting, mythology, Futurism, God,
male and female, Love and Law, Lesh and Spirit, and many other
favourite topics. This would seem to lend support to the idea that
critics write about themselves rather than the author they are supposed to be criticizing, and there is some truth in that here, as
Lawrence reads all his authors in the light of what his own art was
aiming to do. All the same, much of the 'Study' *is* about Hardy, and
the extracts chosen here are largely of that 'relevant' kind. The
'Study' turned on its head many conventional responses to such
things as Hardy's morality, characterization, and fondness for co-
incidences, so that Lawrence's insights into the older novelist's
psychological explorations—which he learnt from and took further
in his own fictions—have remained valuable for students of Hardy
as well as of Lawrence.

This psychological approach marks a turning point in the
critical treatment of Hardy, and it is especially fascinating to see
how one great writer is analysed by another with similar artistic
aims. No longer is the apparent malevolence of 'fate' the prime
interest, or Hardy's 'pessimism'. The 'Study' focuses rather on the
importance of Hardy as an explorer of the world of the unconscious, that great submerged Freudian iceberg of which
characters' external qualities of appearance and 'personality' and
possessions and class and social relations are merely the visible tip.
The visible tip is of course what conventional novelists present,

---

[1] *The Letters of D. H. Lawrence*, ii, ed. George T. Zytaruk and James T. Boulton
(Cambridge: Cambridge University Press, 1982), 212.

and Lawrence is like Virginia Woolf in rejecting that form of 'realism'. In Hardy, as in himself, the interest lies in what is of essence in the characters, which he memorably terms 'explosive'. Characters in Hardy's novels

explode out of the convention. They are people each with a real, vital, potential self, even the apparently wishy-washy heroines of the earlier books, and this self suddenly bursts the shell of manner and convention and commonplace opinion, and acts independently, absurdly, without mental knowledge or acquiescence.

This, rather than 'fate', is the explanation for so much that seems improbable in such masterpieces as *Tess of the d'Urbervilles*, and Lawrence has done a great service in helping us to understand the psychology of his predecessor's creations.

When Lawrence does turn to outside forces in relation to Hardy's characters, he turns to the landscape rather than fate, that 'great background, vital and vivid, which matters more than the people who move upon it', as they act out their 'little human morality play', and which is 'the wonder of Hardy's novels, and gives them their beauty'. Hardy shares with great writers such as Shakespeare and Sophocles and Tolstoy 'this setting behind the small action of his protagonists the terrific action of unfathomed nature, setting a smaller system of morality ... within the vast, uncomprehended and incomprehensible morality of nature or of life itself'. Fate may punish transgressions in Shakespeare or Sophocles, but Lawrence shows that in Hardy and Tolstoy the characters are victims of society and its codes, rather than 'the unfathomed moral forces of nature', and that is their tragedy.

Lawrence's views on tragedy, often going back to the Greeks, are prominent in his 'Study of Thomas Hardy' and remind us that many of his critical opinions on such topics are scattered in many different places. His complete critical writings would stretch to many volumes, with thousands of critical comments in his letters alone. In the Preface to Lawrence's play *Touch and Go*, he maintains that tragedy is not 'disaster' but 'the working out of some immediate passional problem within the soul of man', its essence being 'that a man should go through with his fate, and not dodge it and go bumping into an accident'.[2] The accidental, as Lawrence demonstrates in the case of Hardy, is probably not an accident, but determined psychologically, and that is to him a tragedy in the way an accident is not, whether in life or in novels and plays.

Poetry, though, is the subject of 'Poetry of the Present' and 'Whitman', and a reminder that Lawrence can speak not only as a great prose writer but also as a great poet. 'Poetry of the Present' is a defence of the kind of free verse that Lawrence turned to in *Look! We Have Come Through!* (1917) after the formal rhymed verse of his earlier poems. He brought it to its highest pitch of perfection in *Birds, Beasts and Flowers* (1923) and the posthumously collected *Last Poems*—but 'perfection' is a word he does not himself wish to apply to this new kind of poetry, for it smacks of the finished-off, in the sense of dead as well as perfect, whereas the new poetry is not of the past or the future but of the immediate present, where there is 'no perfection, no consummation, nothing finished'. Lawrence hated art that was 'finished', that you could walk round, as in a museum, and here he mounts an eloquent defence of art that is alive rather than dead, restless and groping rather than fixed and achieved, of the moment rather than permanent. Permanent value, however, is exactly what his free verse poems achieve, *because* they are so alive. As he says, the essence of free verse is that it should be 'direct utterance from the instant, whole man', and he shows that this is possible. But he also generously acknowledges Whitman as his inspiration, for Whitman's is 'the best poetry of this kind'.

The essay on Whitman is reproduced here in a version of 1920 that was later revised and extended for *Studies in Classic American Literature*, when it lost much of its balance and sympathy, and became rather staccato, declamatory, and jeering. In the earlier version, Lawrence balances his quarrels with Whitman's self-consciousness and overdoneness and 'Democracy, En Masse, One Identity, and so on' against the great positives of 'the greatest of the Americans'. Whitman has gone further, it seems to his follower,

---

[2] *Phoenix II: Uncollected, Unpublished and Other Prose Works by D. H. Lawrence*, ed. Warren Roberts and Harry T. Moore (London: William Heinemann, 1968), 291 and 293.

'in actual living expression, than any man'; he has advanced in 'life-knowledge' and attained 'a degree of extensive consciousness greater, perhaps, than any man in the modern world'; and in so doing he has 'opened a new field of living'. Lawrence does not deal only in grand generalizations, however: one way in which he does follow modern critical trends is to pay a lot of attention to the 'words on the page', with both short and lengthy quotations from his authors. From the 'unforgettable loveliness of Whitman's lines', as well as those showing his 'falsity' and 'merging', is drawn evidence for the general statements. Lawrence is particularly fascinated, at this stage of his life, with Whitman's presentation of the friendship between man and man, something as sacred as the marriage of man and woman. This essay was written at the same time as Lawrence moved to his 'leadership' novels, with a change of emphasis from 'love' (as in even the titles of such novels as *Sons and Lovers* and *Women in Love*) to 'power' in *Aaron's Rod* (1922), *Kangaroo* (1923), and *The Plumed Serpent* (1926). Whitman captures the 'pure sensual body of man' and shows, 'alone of all moderns', that man at his deepest 'acts womanless'. This 'love between comrades' is something to which Lawrence returns in his American essays.

'The Spirit of Place', and three other essays from *Studies in Classic American Literature*, on Fenimore Cooper's Leatherstocking novels, Melville's *Typee* and *Omoo*, and his *Moby Dick*, give a flavour of the humorous, rapid-fire, informal later style. This style is clearly related to Lawrence's residence in America between 1922 and 1925, when the predominantly 'serious' rhetoric of his wartime and immediately post-war essay-writing gives way to a typically more American, 'popular', and lighter humorous mode. It is not only a case of writing for a new audience, with many essays being published in periodicals in the United States, for he also keeps his British audience in mind. Indeed, his *Studies in Classic American Literature* seem designed to introduce their subjects to British audiences as much as to their fellow-countrymen. In both countries they have been of seminal importance. It took many years before American literature became a subject of 'respectable' study in Britain, but Lawrence did much of the groundwork in introducing it, and in the United States itself his book has been regarded by a roll-call of distinguished critics (among them, Edmund Wilson,

Lionel Trilling, Edward Dahlberg, Leslie Fiedler, Irving Howe, Alfred Kazin, and Eugene Goodheart) as providing the most fundamental and penetrating insights into their national literature ever made. This level of response distinguishes the *Studies* from Lawrence's other critical writings, most of which have not been given much attention. This is partly to be accounted for by the nature of publication: the American essays form a book, whereas other essays either appeared in periodicals, which are not reviewed in the way books are, or in books where they are in competition with other contributions.

Apart from its style, 'The Spirit of Place' has another claim in its final form: it is the source of a number of sentences that have had a celebrated career in the academic world that has otherwise so often scorned their originator. 'Art-speech is the only truth'; 'Never trust the artist. Trust the tale. The proper function of a critic is to save the tale from the artist who created it'; 'Every continent has its own great spirit of place.'

What comes over strongly in the essay on Cooper's Leatherstocking novels is a great love for the books, which Lawrence reads not as realism but as wish-fulfilment and 'lovely myth', while also deriving much humour from such things as the two 'monsters' in Cooper's world, his wife and his work. And the acute perceptiveness of this writing about Cooper has been praised even by the 'enemy', with T. S. Eliot's generous recognition that Lawrence is responsible for 'probably the most brilliant of critical essays'[3] on this novelist.

The first essay on Melville is also enthusiastic, but contains nothing on that admired author as unforgettable as its devastating comment on Conrad: 'Snivel in a wet hanky'. The essay presents Melville as the 'greatest seer and poet of the sea', dismissing competition from Swinburne as well as Conrad. It analyses the effects of the view of the South Seas as paradisal, leading Lawrence into a very personal response to beautiful 'savages' and why he cannot 'commingle' with them, and the argument that Melville's longed-for 'perfect' relationship is neither possible nor desirable.

[3] 'American Literature and the American Language', a talk at the University of Washington, 9 June 1953, reprinted in *To Criticize the Critic* (London: Faber & Faber, 1965), 52.

Lawrence suspects Melville's 're-birth myth' in 'the green Eden of the Golden Age, the valley of the cannibal savages', is unconscious, because his 'underconsciousness was always mystical and symbolical'.

Novels and novelists naturally form the largest single category in this novelist's critical writings. The earliest piece is on 'The Future of the Novel', in which—in the title supplied by the periodical in which it first appeared—Lawrence offers 'Surgery for the Novel—or a Bomb'. He dissects or blows up both the 'serious' novelists like Joyce and Proust and Dorothy Richardson, all of whom he finds self-consciously absorbed in minute analysis of feelings as they 'strip their smallest emotions to the finest threads' ('Did I feel a twinge in my little toe, or didn't I?'), and the popular bestsellers with titles such as *The Sheik* and their 'shaky' morals. In their place the future of the novel must be 'to present us with new, really new feelings, a whole line of new emotion, which will get us out of the emotional rut'. The moral aspects are taken up again in 'Morality and the Novel', with the most sustainedly brilliant and memorable series of summings-up:

Morality in the novel is the trembling instability of the balance. When the novelist puts his thumb in the scale, to pull down the balance to his own predilection, that is immorality.

If a novel reveals true and vivid relationships, it is a moral work, no matter what the relationships may consist in.

The novel is a perfect medium for revealing to us the changing rainbow of our living relationships. The novel can help us to live, as nothing else can: no didactic Scripture, anyhow.

'The Novel' is more aggressive than this, more irritable and derisive, as it lays into novelists with a 'didactic purpose' and didactically prescribes three essential qualities for the novel: that it be 'quick' or alive, organically interrelated in all its parts, and 'honorable'. 'You can't fool the novel', which knows that 'Everything is relative', even though the novelist may be a 'dribbling liar' (in the final typescript this was originally 'masturbating liar'), like Tolstoy with his 'absolute'. 'Why the Novel Matters' is calmer and less combative, though no less feelingly expressed, as the novel is seen as 'the one bright book of life' and the novelist 'superior to the saint, the scientist, the philosopher and the poet, who are all great masters of different bits of man-alive, but never get the whole hog'.

Other treatments of novelists include the review of *Hadrian the Seventh*, which shows the range of the critical sensibility at play in these writings, for who could have imagined the *poseur* 'Fr. Rolfe' or 'Baron Corvo' appealing to the champion of the true, the real, the genuine? Yet Lawrence is able to see the pretensions and affectations and preciosities and also to recognize that this book lives, that it is in fact 'extraordinarily alive', and to pay enthusiastic tribute to its 'extraordinary and daring' achievement, for 'if some of it is caviare, at least it came out of the belly of a live fish'. This is the kind of review that sends readers rushing out to get the book.

Even the 'hatchet-job' on John Galsworthy can put readers *on* to Galsworthy rather than off him, as Auden noticed:

He is often quite dotty, he does not make the faintest pretense at being objective, but he is so passionately interested in the work he is talking about and so little interested in his reputation as a critic that even when he is violently and quite unfairly attacking an author, he makes him sound far more exciting and worth reading than most critics make one sound whom they are professing to praise.[4]

If not exactly dotty, the Galsworthy essay is certainly unobjective and at times unfair, with some wonderfully abrasive and dismissive strokes, usually at the expense of his characters rather than the novelist himself, for 'The Forsytes are all parasites', 'not full human individuals, but social beings, fallen to a lower level of life'. In so far as Galsworthy satirizes his characters, he impresses his critic, but he misses greatness by courting popularity when he sentimentalizes them, particularly in what Lawrence calls their 'doggy' sexuality, which he illustrates to devastating effect.

The Introduction to Verga's novel *Mastro-don Gesualdo* draws the prospective reader in by the opposite and more normal technique of praising Verga and giving information about his life and work, with some interesting comparisons between him and other Italian writers as well as Flaubert and—in a bold contrasting of the Sicilian and Russian attitudes to heroism—Chekhov, Tolstoy, and especially Dostoevsky.

---

[4] 'Some Notes on D. H. Lawrence', *Nation* (New York), 26 Apr. 1947, 482.

The essays on poetry are more heterogeneous than those on the novel. One of the funniest things Lawrence wrote is the review of an anthology of American verse in which minor contemporary poets are lampooned and their banal utterances unfavourably contrasted with those of classic predecessors like Byron, Gray, Keats, and of course Whitman. The reviewer even stoops to cheap jokes at the expense of (along with the unknowns) a friend among the contributors, Amy Lowell. All the same, the review does make some serious points in its comical way, as when Lawrence quotes

> Why do I think of stairways
> With a rush of hurt surprise?

and equally hilariously replies 'Heaven knows, my dear, unless you once fell down.' As W. H. Auden notes in an essay, Lawrence's own poetry never 'puts on an act'[5] like that of the unfortunate poetess he mocks; there is value, therefore, in making a stand for genuineness in poetry, even if it involves mockery of the false and can therefore be rather cruel. On the other hand, written out of kindness to a friend, 'Chaos in Poetry' is an introduction to a book: *Chariot of the Sun*, by Harry Crosby, published after the poet's suicide. But it is mainly interesting as another statement about the kind of poetry Lawrence himself was writing, and what he thought poetry could do, especially as expressed in this famous sentence: 'The essential quality of poetry is that it makes a new effort of attention, and "discovers" a new world within the known world.' Poets need to accept the chaos of life and light it up with their visions. Men do not like chaos, and erect umbrellas to shelter under, until the poet comes and makes a slit in the umbrella, 'a window to the sun'. We must go back to the sun—one of Lawrence's favourite tropes.

The poetry of sunless chaos is already a bore. The poetry of a regulated cosmos is nothing but a wire bird-cage. Because in all living poetry the living chaos stirs, sun-suffused and sun-impulsive, and most subtly chaotic.

The last essay on poetry in this selection is also an introduction to a book: to Lawrence's last collection of poems to be published in

---

[5] *The Dyer's Hand and Other Essays* (London: Faber & Faber, 1963), 288.

his lifetime, *Pansies*, which had been seized in the mail. The introduction is both a defence of these little poems as thoughts, or soothings of wounds, and a wider argument about taboos in literature, especially regarding the use of 'obscene' words. Lawrence's plea is for lifting the taboos in the name of sanity.

That introduction is serious if not solemn, but comedy is never far away in his critical writings, even when the writer is in deadly earnest. Consider the case of 'The Proper Study', with its good-humoured exploration of the phrase 'Know thyself' and its necessary extension to presuming God to scan; or how a favourite Biblical reversal in the title of 'Climbing Down Pisgah' alerts the reader to its humorous tone, as Lawrence tries to answer the question as to why he writes 'novels, stories, essays'. As we have seen, he rejects the usual answers, and comes up with 'the sense of adventure', which is highly appropriate for this most adventurous of writers, making a new 'venture in consciousness' in so many areas. He likewise rejects any monolithic absolute, and insists on 'relationship' and a relative and pluralistic vision of the world, in 'Him With His Tail in His Mouth', a jocularly-written (for 'Solemnity is a sign of fraud') meditation on 'life, or life-energy', starting from the serpent of eternity, beginnings and endings, and illustrated by reference to cave-paintings and ancient and modern sculpture as well as some of the denizens of Lawrence's ranch in New Mexico, his cow and his chickens.

The composite review of four books that were published in 1928 is included here to show the professional side of the reviewer's life, responding to whatever eclectic assortment he happened to be sent. Typically, he responded warmly to them all: encouragingly and glowingly to the young Robert Byron, and with a fellow feeling for the hot crusading fire of Clough Williams-Ellis, a fellow campaigner against the desecration of the countryside by the 'developer', but with withering heat turned on the inanities of Maurice Baring and the faked puppeteering of a rancidly ill-humoured Somerset Maugham.

'Art and Morality' is the first of Lawrence's essays primarily—as opposed to incidentally—about painting, and it repeats the insistence on relationship as the basis of morality as well as the basis of design in art, which is 'a recognition of the relation between various things':

What art has got to do, and will go on doing, is to reveal things in their different relationships.
There is nothing to do, but to maintain a true relationship to the things we move with and amongst and against.
A new relationship between ourselves and the universe means a new morality.

Far from the usual idea that 'art is immoral', Lawrence finds artists much more moral than the supposedly moral bourgeoisie who object to them on moral grounds. He mounts here the first of his passionate defences of Cézanne and his new way of seeing, which is not what the camera sees. His apples are not 'nailed-down' but 'unsteady'; his vision is not wrong but different.

Cézanne reappears in 'Introduction to These Paintings' , which does not in fact deal with Lawrence's own pictures so much as the mental attitude that has infected responses to art since the end of the sixteenth century, when 'a horror of sexual life' took hold of 'the northern consciousness', because of the fear of syphilis. Lawrence traces these original ideas of his through the centuries with reference to a great number of painters, in their national schools, and with particular attention to the comparatively poor showing of the English, except in landscape. The essay then moves to another impassioned but more sustained defence of his hero, Cézanne, before concluding with hopes for a new age of artistic expression by the young in England.

If one might have expected that essay to be a defence of his own paintings, 'Making Pictures' *is* an account—a very personal account—of Lawrence's own painting, conveying the joy it has given him, 'a form of delight that words can never give', but it leaves the question of the censorship of his pictures to the long, deeply felt and finely argued essay on 'Pornography and Obscenity'. Lawrence objects to objections that pornography 'arouses sexual feelings', for there is nothing wrong with that. Yet he would himself censor genuine pornography 'rigorously', explaining that it can be recognised by its secrecy and its attempt to 'insult sex, to do dirt on it', and that one of its effects is to provoke masturbation. We must fight 'the purity-lie' and do away with 'the dirty little secret', bringing sex healthily into the open.

Movingly, in the last essay included here, as in such related late works as *Apocalypse* and *Last Poems*, the dying writer is not embittered or whining, irritably aggressive or defensively self-justificatory, but calm, accepting, and grateful, yet as full of enthusiasm and wonder and 'life-energy' as ever. The phrase he used of Melville, 'mystical and symbolical', could define much of Lawrence's own approach throughout his life, and his earlier review of John Oman's *The Book of Revelation* testifies to his interest in both mysticism and symbolism. He is surprised that Dr Oman seems reluctant to accept astrological interpretations, and the main message of the review is that symbols have many meanings that can never be finally explained or exhausted. This short review looks forward to the much longer response to his favourite last book of the Bible at the end of Lawrence's life, his Introduction to Frederick Carter's *Dragon of the Apocalypse*, which vividly depicts how this astrological account of Revelation gave his imagination a 'marvellous release' and 'a whole great sky to move in'—something astronomy or scholastic works could not do. The Apocalypse itself matters to Lawrence only in so far as it also 'gives us imaginative release into another world'. He revels in its symbolism and its language, which have been part of his life since early childhood, and played such an important role in his own writing, with its symbols and Bible-inspired phrasings. It 'comes to life with a great new life', as Lawrence himself does.

This great critic cannot accept the Apocalypse as only a 'star-myth', for it is 'altogether too full of fierce feeling, fierce and moral'. And this perhaps sums up the reason why we cannot accept Lawrence's critical writings as 'only' criticism. They are not the sterile wastes that so much criticism wanders into, and which Lawrence rightly exposes by explicit condemnation as well as implicit examples of other, more vital ways of doing things. His criticism is always alive and feeling and real, never deadened, stale, factitious, or phoney. It does not give itself 'superior' airs by floating in some abstract intellectual vacuum, but is about the relationship of art and literature to life. Though he has his critical feet very much on the ground and can be as 'earthy' as any, he can also soar to challenging heights of intellectual as well as imaginative and emotional exploration and adventure. And he does all this in an extraordinarily varied number of ways. He knows when to arouse and enthuse and when to restrain and moderate, when to be facetious and when to be earnest, when to explain and explore and when to leave something temptingly unelaborated. Moreover, his range of styles and approaches is seemingly infinite: in this selection alone there is everything from the most beautifully controlled expression of achieved serenity in effortlessly detailed, soberly cogent analyses to the most rapid and wildly raking machine-gun staccato of splenetic frenzy and shrill abuse. But above all, Lawrence pays the subjects of his criticism—whether admired heroes or detested victims—the compliment of his full attention. And in his case this does not mean only an attentive intellect, but, as he says of thinking in the poem 'Thought',

> a man in his wholeness, wholly attending.

The whole man speaks in these critical writings, and if we hear 'holy' in that 'wholly' that, too, is appropriate for one in whom the religious and moral sense was so alive.

NOTE ON THE TEXTS

TEXTS for the essays in this edition are based on their first publication, as listed below, with clearly inadvertent errors corrected.

'Thomas Mann': *Blue Review*, July 1913.

'Study of Thomas Hardy': *Phoenix: The Posthumous Papers of D. H. Lawrence*, ed. Edward D. McDonald (New York: Viking Press, 1936).

'Poetry of the Present': *Playboy*, 4 and 5 (1919).

'Whitman': *Nation and Athenaeum*, 23 July 1921.

'The Spirit of Place', 'Fenimore Cooper's Leatherstocking Novels', 'Herman Melville's *Typee and Omoo*' and 'Herman Melville's *Moby Dick*': *Studies in Classic American Literature* (New York: Thomas Seltzer, 1923).

'The Future of the Novel': *International Book Review*, Apr. 1923, under the editorial title 'Surgery for the Novel—or a Bomb'.

Review of *A Second Contemporary Verse Anthology*: *Evening Post Literary Review*, 29 Sept. 1923.

'The Proper Study': *Adelphi*, Dec. 1923.

Review of *The Book of Revelation*: *Adelphi*, Apr. 1924.

'Climbing Down Pisgah': *Phoenix: The Posthumous Papers of D. H. Lawrence*, ed. Edward D. McDonald (New York: Viking Press, 1936).

'Art and Morality': *Calendar of Modern Letters*, Nov. 1925.

'Morality and the Novel': *Calendar of Modern Letters*, Dec. 1925.

'The Novel': *Reflections on the Death of a Porcupine and Other Essays* (Philadelphia: Centaur Press, 1925).

'Him With His Tail in His Mouth': *Reflections on the Death of a Porcupine and Other Essays* (Philadelphia: Centaur Press, 1925).

Review of *Hadrian the Seventh*: *Adelphi*, Dec. 1925.

'Why the Novel Matters': *Phoenix: The Posthumous Papers of D. H. Lawrence*, ed. Edward D. McDonald (New York: Viking Press, 1936).

'John Galsworthy': *Scrutinies by Various Writers*, collected by Edgell Rickword (London: Wishart & Co., 1928).

Introduction: Giovanni Verga, *Mastro-don Gesualdo*, trans. D. H.
  Lawrence (London: Jonathan Cape, 1928).
'Chaos in Poetry': *Échanges*, Dec. 1929.
Review of Four Contemporary Books: *Vogue*, 20 July 1928.
'Introduction to These Paintings': *The Paintings of D. H. Lawrence*
  (London: Mandrake Press, 1929).
Introduction: *Pansies* (London: P. R. Stephensen, 1929).
'Making Pictures': *Creative Art*, July 1929.
'Pornography and Obscenity': *This Quarter*, July–Sept. 1929.
Introduction to *The Dragon of the Apocalypse*: *London Mercury*, July
  1930.

SELECT BIBLIOGRAPHY

Lawrence has attracted a great deal of criticism and any bibliography of studies of his overall achievement would be very long. This reading list focuses selectively on Lawrence as critic.

Editions of D. H. Lawrence's Critical Writings

Studies in Classic American Literature (New York: Thomas Seltzer, 1923; London: Martin Seeker, 1924).

Reflections on the Death of a Porcupine and Other Essays (Philadelphia: Centaur Press, 1925).

Assorted Articles (London: Martin Seeker, 1930).

Phoenix: The Posthumous Papers of D. H. Lawrence, ed. Edward D. McDonald (New York: Viking Press; London: William Heinemann, 1936).

Selected Essays, ed. Richard Aldington (Harmondsworth: Penguin, 1950).

Selected Literary Criticism, ed. Anthony Beal (London: William Heinemann, 1956).

The Symbolic Meaning: The Uncollected Versions of Studies in Classic American Literature, ed. Armin Arnold (Arundel: Centaur Press, 1962; New York: Viking Press, 1964).

Phoenix II: Uncollected, Unpublished and Other Prose Works by D. H. Lawrence, ed. Warren Roberts and Harry T. Moore (London: Heinemann, 1968).

Apocalypse and the Writings on Revelation, ed. Mara Kalnins (Cambridge: Cambridge University Press, 1980).

Study of Thomas Hardy and Other Essays, ed. Bruce Steele (Cambridge: Cambridge University Press, 1985).

Reflections on the Death of a Porcupine and Other Essays, ed. Michael Herbert (Cambridge: Cambridge University Press, 1988).

Letters

The Letters of D. H. Lawrence, ed. James T. Boulton and others, 7 vols. (Cambridge: Cambridge University Press, 1979–93).

Biography

Worthen, John, *D. H. Lawrence: The Early Years 1885–1912* (Cambridge: Cambridge University Press, 1991).

Kinkead-Weekes, Mark, *D. H. Lawrence: Triumph to Exile 1912–1922* (Cambridge: Cambridge University Press, 1996).

Ellis, David, *D. H. Lawrence: Dying Game 1922–1930* (Cambridge University Press, 1998).

Criticism

Arnold, Armin, 'D. H. Lawrence, the Russians, and Giovanni Verga', *Comparative Literature Studies*, 2 (1965), 249–57.

Auden, W. H., 'Some Notes on D. H. Lawrence', *Nation* (New York), 26 Apr. 1947, 482–4.

—— 'D. H. Lawrence', in *The Dyer's Hand and Other Essays* (London: Faber & Faber, 1963), 277–95.

Bien, Peter, 'The Critical Philosophy of D. H. Lawrence', *D. H. Lawrence Review*, 17 (Summer 1984), 127–34.

Coombes, H. (ed.), *D. H. Lawrence: A Critical Anthology* (Harmondsworth: Penguin, 1973).

Daleski, H. M., *The Forked Flame: A Study of D. H. Lawrence* (London: Faber & Faber, 1965).

Deakin, William, 'Lawrence's Attack on Joyce and Proust', *Essays in Criticism* (Oct. 1957), 383–403.

Draper, R. P. (ed.), *D. H. Lawrence: The Critical Heritage* (London: Routledge & Kegan Paul, 1970).

Ellis, David (ed.), *D. H. Lawrence: Critical Assessments*, vol. iv (Robertsbridge: Helm, 1992).

—— and Mills, Howard, *D. H. Lawrence's Non-fiction: Art, Thought and Genre* (Cambridge: Cambridge University Press, 1988).

Fernihough, Anne, *D. H. Lawrence: Aesthetics and Ideology* (Oxford: Clarendon Press, 1993).

Foster, Richard, 'Criticism as Rage', in Harry T. Moore (ed.), *A D. H. Lawrence Miscellany* (London: William Heinemann, 1959), 312–25.

Goodheart, Eugene, *The Utopian Vision of D. H. Lawrence* (Chicago: Chicago University Press, 1963).

Gordon, David J., *D. H. Lawrence as a Literary Critic* (New Haven: Yale University Press, 1966).

Journet, Debra, 'D. H. Lawrence's Criticism of Modern Literature', *D. H. Lawrence Review*, 17 (Spring 1984), 29–47.

Klingopulos, G. D., Review of *D. H. Lawrence: Selected Literary Criticism*, in *Essays in Criticism* (July 1957), 294–303.

Leavis, F. R., Reviews of *Phoenix: The Posthumous Papers of D. H. Lawrence*, in *Scrutiny* (Dec. 1937), 352–8, and (of a reissue) in *Spectator*, 24 Mar. 1961, 412 and 414.

Pinion, F. B., *A D. H. Lawrence Companion* (London: Macmillan, 1978).

Rees, Richard, *Brave Men: A Study of D. H. Lawrence and Simone Weil* (Carbondale: Southern Illinois University Press, 1959).

Salgado, Gamini, 'D. H. Lawrence as Literary Critic', *London Magazine* (Feb. 1960), 49–57.

Swigg, Richard, *Lawrence, Hardy, and American Literature* (London: Oxford University Press, 1972).

Tindall, William York, *D. H. Lawrence and Susan His Cow* (New York: Columbia University Press, 1939).

Trilling, Diana, 'Letter to a Young Critic', introd. to *The Selected Letters of D. H. Lawrence* (New York: Doubleday Anchor, 1961).

Turnell, Martin, 'An Essay on Criticism', *Dublin Review*, 444 (1948), 72–95.

Further Reading in Oxford World's Classics

Lawrence, D. H., *A Modern Lover and Other Stories*, ed. Antony Atkins.

—— *The Prussian Officer and Other Stories*, ed. Antony Atkins.

—— *The Rainbow*, ed. Kate Flint.

—— *Sons and Lovers*, ed. David Trotter.

—— *The White Peacock*, ed. David Bradshaw.

—— *Women in Love*, ed. David Bradshaw.

A CHRONOLOGY OF
D. H. LAWRENCE

1885 David Herbert Lawrence, born September in Eastwood, Nottinghamshire, son of coal miner.

1891 Begins education which leads from Board School through scholarship to Nottingham High School, and eventually, after a year spent as a clerk in a factory, to teacher training at Nottingham University College 1906–8.

1901 Begins friendship with Jessie Chambers, the 'Miriam' of *Sons and Lovers*.

1908 Appointed to staff of Davidson Road School, Croydon.

1909 First serious publication, five poems in *English Review*.

1910 Becomes engaged to Louie Burrows. Death of mother, Lydia Lawrence, 9 December. First novel published January 1911, *The White Peacock*.

1912 Breaks off engagement, February. Elopes in May to Germany with Frieda Weekley, wife of professor at Nottingham. Novel, *The Trespasser*, published.

1913 *Sons and Lovers* published.

1914 Marries Frieda. *The Prussian Officer* stories published.

1915 *The Rainbow* published and immediately banned. Lawrences, impoverished, spend rest of war years in Cornwall, where they are harassed by military authorities, then London, Berkshire, and Derbyshire. At war's end they leave for Italy. In 1919 Lawrence seriously ill with influenza.

1920 Publication of *Women in Love* in New York, and of *The Lost Girl*.

1922 Leaves Europe for Ceylon and Australia and eventually New Mexico. *Fantasia of the Unconscious* published, also a collection of stories *England, My England* and novel, *Aaron's Rod*.

1923 Major stories published, *The Ladybird*, *The Fox*, and *The Captain's Doll*, critical *Studies in Classic American Literature*, novel *Kangaroo*, and poems *Birds, Beasts and Flowers*.

1924 After time in England, France, and Germany, travels to New Mexico and Mexico. Death of father, John Arthur Lawrence, 10 September.

1925 After stay in England lives mainly in Italy. It is recognized that Lawrence has tuberculosis.

1926 Novel, *The Plumed Serpent*, published. Makes last visit to England.

1927 *Mornings in Mexico* published.

1928 *The Women Who Rode Away and Other stories* published and, privately in Florence, *Lady Chatterley's Lover* (unexpurgated text banned in Great Britain until 1960). *Collected Poems.* Lives in Switzerland and then mainly in France.

1929 Exhibition of paintings in London raided by police. Writes *Apocalypse*, published posthumously 1931.

1930 Dies 2 March, at Vence, Alpes Maritimes, France.

SELECTED CRITICAL
WRITINGS

Thomas Mann

THOMAS MANN is perhaps the most famous of German novelists now writing. He, and his elder brother, Heinrich Mann, with Jakob Wassermann,* are acclaimed the three artists in fiction of present-day Germany.

But Germany is now undergoing that craving for form in fiction, that passionate desire for the mastery of the medium of narrative, that will of the writer to be greater than and undisputed lord over the stuff he writes, which is figured to the world in Gustave Flaubert.*

Thomas Mann is over middle age, and has written three or four books: *Buddenbrooks*, a novel of the patrician life of Lübeck; *Tristan*, a collection of six *Novellen; Königliche Hoheit*, an unreal Court romance; various stories, and lastly, *Der Tod in Venedig*.* The author himself is the son of a Lübeck *Patrizier*.*

It is as an artist rather than as a story-teller that Germany worships Thomas Mann. And yet it seems to me, this craving for form is the outcome, not of artistic conscience, but of a certain attitude to life. For form is not a personal thing like style. It is impersonal like logic. And just as the school of Alexander Pope* was logical in its expressions, so it seems the school of Flaubert is, as it were, logical in its aesthetic form. 'Nothing outside the definite line of the book', is a maxim.* But can the human mind fix absolutely the definite line of a book, any more than it can fix absolutely any definite line of action for a living being?

Thomas Mann, however, is personal, almost painfully so, in his subject-matter. In 'Tonio Kröger', the long *Novelle* at the end of the *Tristan* volume, he paints a detailed portrait of himself as a youth and younger man, a careful analysis. And he expresses at some length the misery of being an artist. 'Literature is not a calling, it is a curse.' Then he says to the Russian painter girl:* 'There is no artist anywhere but longs again, my love, for the common life.' But any young artist might say that. It is because the stress of life in a young man, but particularly in an artist, is very strong, and has as yet found no outlet, so that it rages inside him in *Sturm und Drang*.* But the condition is the same, only more tragic, in the Thomas Mann of fifty-three.* He has never found any outlet for himself, save his art. He has never given himself to anything but his art. This is all well and good, if his art absorbs and satisfies him, as it has done some great men, like Corot.* But then there are the other artists, the more human, like Shakespeare and Goethe, who must give themselves to life as well as to art. And if these were afraid, or despised life, then with their surplus they would ferment and become rotten. Which is what ails Thomas Mann. He is physically ailing, no doubt. But his complaint is deeper: it is of the soul.

And out of this soul-ailment, this unbelief, he makes his particular art, which he describes, in 'Tonio Kröger', as *'Wählerisch, erlesen, kostbar, fein, reizbar gegen das Banale, und aufs höchste empfindlich in Fragen des Taktes und Geschmacks.'* * He is a disciple, in method, of the Flaubert who wrote: 'I worked sixteen hours yesterday, today the whole day, and have at last finished one page.' In writing of the *Leitmotiv** and its influence, he says: 'Now this method alone is sufficient to explain my slowness. It is the result neither of anxiety nor indigence, but of an overpowering sense of responsibility for the choice of every word, the coining of every phrase . . . a responsibility that longs for perfect freshness, and which, after two hours' work, prefers not to undertake an important sentence. For which sentence is important, and which not? Can one know before hand whether a sentence, or part of a sentence may not be called upon to appear again as *Motiv,* peg, symbol, citation or connexion? And a sentence which must be heard twice must be fashioned accordingly. It must—I do not speak of beauty—possess a certain high level, and symbolic suggestion, which will make it worthy to sound again in any epic future. So every point becomes a standing ground, every adjective a decision, and it is clear that such work is not to be produced off-hand.'

This, then, is the method. The man himself was always delicate in constitution. 'The doctors said he was too weak to go to school, and must work at home.' I quote from Aschenbach, in *Der Tod in Venedig.* 'When he fell, at the age of fifty-three, one of his closest observers said of him: "Aschenbach has always lived like this"— and he gripped his fist hard clenched; "never like this"—and he let his open hand lie easily on the arm of the chair.'

He* forced himself to write, and kept himself to the work. Speaking of one of his works, he says: 'It was pardonable, yea, it showed plainly the victory of his morality, that the uninitiated reader supposed the book to have come of a solid strength and one long breath; whereas it was the result of small daily efforts and hundreds of single inspirations.'

And he gives the sum of his experience in the belief: '*dass beinahe alles Grosse, was dastehe, als ein Trotzdem dastehe, trotz Kummer und Qual, Armut, Verlassenheit, Körperschwäche, Laster, Leidenschaft und tausend hemmnischen Zustände gekommen sei.*'* And then comes the final revelation, difficult to translate. He is speaking of life as it is written into his books:

'For endurance of one's fate, grace in suffering, does not only mean passivity, but is an active work, a positive triumph, and the Sebastian figure is the most beautiful symbol, if not of all art, yet of the art in question. If one looked into this portrayed world and saw the elegant self-control that hides from the eyes of the world to the last moment the inner undermining, the biological decay; saw the yellow ugliness which, sensuously at a disadvantage, could blow its choking heat of desire to a pure flame, and even rise to sovereignty in the kingdom of beauty; saw the pale impotence which draws out of the glowing depths of its intellect sufficient strength to subdue a whole vigorous people, bring them to the foot of the Cross, to the feet of impotence; saw the amiable bearing in the empty and severe service of Form; saw the quickly enervating longing and art of the born swindler: if one saw such a fate as this, and all the rest it implied, then one would be forced to doubt whether there were in reality any other heroism than that of weakness. Which heroism, in any case, is more of our time than this?'

Perhaps it is better to give the story of *Der Tod in Venedig*, from which the above is taken, and to whose hero it applies.

Gustav von Aschenbach, a fine, famous author, over fifty years of age, coming to the end of a long walk one afternoon, sees as he is approaching a burying place, near Munich, a man standing between the chimeric figures of the gateway. This man in the gate of the cemetery is almost the *Motiv* of the story. By him, Aschenbach is infected with a desire to travel. He examines himself minutely, in a way almost painful in its frankness, and one sees the whole soul of this author of fifty-three. And it seems, the artist has absorbed the man, and yet the man is there, like an exhausted organism on which a parasite has fed itself strong. Then begins a kind of Holbein *Totentanz*.* The story is quite natural in appearance, and yet there is the gruesome sense of symbolism throughout. The man near the burying ground has suggested travel—but whither? Aschenbach sets off to a watering place on the Austrian coast of the Adriatic, seeking some adventure, some passionate adventure, to which his sick soul and unhealthy body have been kindled. But finding himself on the Adriatic, he knows it is not thither that his desire draws him, and he takes ship for Venice. It is all real, and yet with a curious sinister unreality, like decay, the 'biological decay'. On board there is a man who reminds one of the man in the gateway, though there is no connexion. And then, among a crowd of young Poles who are crossing, is a ghastly fellow, whom Aschenbach sees is an old man dressed up as young, who capers unsuspected among the youths, drinks hilariously with them, and falls hideously drunk at last on the deck, reaching to the author, and slobbering about '*dem allerliebsten, dem schönsten Liebchen*'.* Suddenly the upper plate of his false teeth falls on his underlip.

Aschenbach takes a gondola to the Lido, and again the gondolier reminds one of the man in the cemetery gateway. He is, moreover, one who will make no concession, and, in spite of Aschenbach's demand to be taken back to St Mark's, rows him in his black craft to the Lido, talking to himself softly all the while. Then he goes without payment.

The author stays in a fashionable hotel on the Lido. The adventure is coming, there by the pallid sea. As Aschenbach comes down into the hall of the hotel, he sees a beautiful Polish boy of about fourteen, with honey-coloured curls clustering round his pale face, standing with his sisters and their governess.

Aschenbach loves the boy—but almost as a symbol. In him he loves life and youth and beauty, as Hyacinth* in the Greek myth. This, I suppose, is blowing the choking heat to pure flame, and raising it to the kingdom of beauty. He follows the boy, watches him all day long on the beach, fascinated by beauty concrete before him. It is still the *Künstler** and his abstraction: but there is also the 'yellow ugliness, sensually at a disadvantage', of the elderly man below it all. But the picture of the writer watching the folk on the beach gleams and lives with a curious, gold-phosphorescent light, touched with the brightness of Greek myth, and yet a modern seashore with folks on the sands, and a half-threatening, diseased sky.

Aschenbach, watching the boy in the hotel lift, finds him delicate, almost ill, and the thought that he may not live long fills the elderly writer with a sense of peace. It eases him to think the boy should die.

Then the writer suffers from the effect of the *sirocco*, and intends to depart immediately from Venice. But at the station he finds with joy that his luggage has gone wrong, and he goes straight back to the hotel. There, when he sees Tadziu again, he knows why he could not leave Venice.

There is a month of hot weather, when Aschenbach follows Tadziu about, and begins to receive a look, loving, from over the lad's shoulder. It is wonderful, the heat, the unwholesomeness, the passion in Venice. One evening comes a street singer, smelling of carbolic acid, and sings beneath the veranda of the hotel. And this time, in gruesome symbolism, it is the man from the burying ground distinctly.

The rumour is, that the black cholera is in Venice. An atmosphere of secret plague hangs over the city of canals and palaces. Aschenbach verifies the report at the English bureau, but cannot bring himself to go away from Tadziu, nor yet to warn the Polish family. The secretly pest-smitten days go by. Aschenbach follows the boy through the stinking streets of the town and loses him. And on the day of the departure of the Polish family, the famous author dies of the plague.

It is absolutely, almost intentionally, unwholesome. The man is sick, body and soul. He portrays himself as he is, with wonderful skill and art, portrays his sickness. And since any genuine portrait is valuable, this book has its place. It portrays one man, one atmosphere, one sick vision. It claims to do no more. And we have to allow it. But we know it is unwholesome—it does not strike me as being morbid for all that, it is too well done—and we give it its place as such.

Thomas Mann seems to me the last sick sufferer from the complaint of Flaubert. The latter stood away from life as from a leprosy. And Thomas Mann, like Flaubert, feels vaguely that he has in him something finer than ever physical life revealed. Physical life is a disordered corruption, against which he can fight with only one weapon, his fine aesthetic sense, his feeling for beauty, for perfection, for a certain fitness which soothes him, and gives an inner pleasure, however corrupt the stuff of life may be. There he is, after all these years, full of disgusts and loathing of himself as Flaubert was, and Germany is being voiced, or partly so, by him. And so, with real suicidal intention, like Flaubert's, he sits, a last too-sick disciple, reducing himself grain by grain to the statement of his own disgust, patiently, self-destructively, so that his statement at least may be perfect in a world of corruption. But he is so late.

Already I find Thomas Mann, who, as he says, fights so hard against the banal in his work, somewhat banal. His expression may be very fine. But by now what he expresses is stale. I think we have learned our lesson, to be sufficiently aware of the fulsomeness of life. And even while he has a rhythm in style, yet his work has none of the rhythm of a living thing, the rise of a poppy, then the after uplift of the bud, the shedding of the calyx and the spreading wide of the petals, the falling of the flower and the pride of the seed-head. There is an unexpectedness in this such as does not come from their carefully plotted and arranged developments. Even *Madame Bovary** seems to me dead in respect to the living rhythm of the whole work. While it is there in *Macbeth* like life itself.

But Thomas Mann is old—and we are young. Germany does not feel very young to me.

from Study of Thomas Hardy

THIS is supposed to be a book about the people in Thomas Hardy's novels. But if one wrote everything they give rise to, it would fill the Judgment Book.

One thing about them is that none of the heroes and heroines care very much for money, or immediate self-preservation, and all of them are struggling hard to come into being. What exactly the struggle into being consists in, is the question. But most obviously, from the Wessex novels, the first and chiefest factor is the struggle into love and the struggle with love: by love, meaning the love of a man for a woman and a woman for a man. The *via media* to being, for man or woman, is love, and love alone. Having achieved and accomplished love, then the man passes into the unknown. He has become himself, his tale is told. Of anything that is complete there is no more tale to tell. The tale is about becoming complete, or about the failure to become complete.

It is urged against Thomas Hardy's characters that they do unreasonable things—quite, quite unreasonable things. They are always going off unexpectedly and doing something that nobody would do. That is quite true, and the charge is amusing. These people of Wessex are always bursting suddenly out of bud and taking a wild flight into flower, always shooting suddenly out of a tight convention, a tight, hide-bound cabbage state into something quite madly personal. It would be amusing to count the number of special marriage licenses taken out in Hardy's books. Nowhere, except perhaps in Jude, is there the slightest development of personal action in the characters: it is all explosive. Jude, however, does see more or less what he is doing, and acts from choice. He is more consecutive. The rest explode out of the convention. They are people each with a real, vital, potential self, even the apparently wishy-washy heroines of the earlier books, and this self suddenly bursts the shell of manner and convention and commonplace opinion, and acts independently, absurdly, without mental knowledge or acquiescence.

And from such an outburst the tragedy usually develops. For there does exist, after all, the great self-preservation scheme, and in

it we must all live. Now to live in it after bursting out of it was the
problem these Wessex people found themselves faced with. And
they never solved the problem, none of them except the comically,
insufficiently treated Ethelberta.*

This because they must subscribe to the system in themselves.
From the more immediate claims of self-preservation they could
free themselves: from money, from ambition for social success.
None of the heroes or heroines of Hardy cared much for these
things. But there is the greater idea of self-preservation, which is
formulated in the State, in the whole modelling of the community.
And from this idea, the heroes and heroines of Wessex, like the
heroes and heroines of almost anywhere else, could not free themselves. In the long run, the State, the Community, the established
form of life remained, remained intact and impregnable, the
individual, trying to break forth from it, died of fear, of exhaustion,
or of exposure to attacks from all sides, like men who have left the
walled city to live outside in the precarious open.

This is the tragedy of Hardy, always the same: the tragedy of
those who, more or less pioneers, have died in the wilderness,
whither they had escaped for free action, after having left the
walled security, and the comparative imprisonment, of the
established convention. This is the theme of novel after novel:
remain quite within the convention, and you are good, safe, and
happy in the long run, though you never have the vivid pang of
sympathy on your side: or, on the other hand, be passionate,
individual, wilful, you will find the security of the convention a
walled prison, you will escape, and you will die, either of your own
lack of strength to bear the isolation and the exposure, or by direct
revenge from the community, or from both. This is the tragedy,
and only this: it is nothing more metaphysical than the division of a
man against himself in such a way: first, that he is a member of the
community, and must, upon his honour, in no way move to
disintegrate the community, either in its moral or its practical
form; second, that the convention of the community is a prison to
his natural, individual desire, a desire that compels him, whether
he feel justified or not, to break the bounds of the community, lands
him outside the pale, there to stand alone, and say: 'I was right, my
desire was real and inevitable; if I was to be myself I must fulfil it,
convention or no convention,' or else, there to stand alone,

doubting, and saying: 'Was I right, was I wrong? If I was wrong, oh, let me die!'—in which case he courts death.

The growth and the development of this tragedy, the deeper and deeper realization of this division and this problem, the coming towards some conclusion, is the one theme of the Wessex novels.*

And therefore the books must be taken chronologically, to reveal the development and to advance towards the conclusion.

1. *Desperate Remedies.*

Springrove, the dull hero, fast within convention, dare not tell Cytherea that he is already engaged, and thus prepares the complication. Manston, represented as fleshily passionate, breaks the convention and commits murder, which is very extreme, under compulsion of his desire for Cytherea. He is aided by the darkly passionate, lawless Miss Aldclyffe. He and Miss Aldclyffe meet death, and Springrove and Cytherea are united to happiness and success.

2. *Under the Greenwood Tree.*

After a brief excursion from the beaten track in the pursuit of social ambition and satisfaction of the imagination, figured by the Clergyman, Fancy, the little school-mistress, returns to Dick, renounces imagination, and settles down to steady, solid, physically satisfactory married life, and all is as it should be. But Fancy will carry in her heart all her life many unopened buds that will die un-flowered; and Dick will probably have a bad time of it.

3. *A Pair of Blue Eyes.*

Elfride breaks down in her attempt to jump the first little hedge of convention, when she comes back after running away with Stephen. She cannot stand even a little alone. Knight, his conventional ideas backed up by selfish instinct, cannot endure Elfride when he thinks she is not virgin, though now she loves him beyond bounds. She submits to him, and owns the conventional idea entirely right, even whilst she is innocent. An aristocrat walks off with her whilst the two men hesitate, and she, poor innocent victim of passion not vital enough to overthrow the most banal conventional ideas, lies in a bright coffin, while the three confirmed lovers mourn, and say how great the tragedy is.

4. *Far from the Madding Crowd.*

The unruly Bathsheba, though almost pledged to Farmer

Boldwood, a ravingly passionate, middle-aged bachelor pretendant, who has suddenly started in mad pursuit of some unreal conception of woman, personified in Bathsheba, lightly runs off and marries Sergeant Troy, an illegitimate aristocrat, unscrupulous and yet sensitive in taking his pleasures. She loves Troy, he does not love her. All the time she is loved faithfully and persistently by the good Gabriel, who is like a dog that watches the bone and bides the time. Sergeant Troy treats Bathsheba badly, never loves her, though he is the only man in the book who knows anything about her. Her pride helps her to recover. Troy is killed by Boldwood; exit the unscrupulous, but discriminative, almost cynical young soldier and the mad, middle-aged pursuer of the Fata Morgana; enter the good, steady Gabriel, who marries Bathsheba because he will make her a good husband, and the flower of imaginative first love is dead for her with Troy's scorn of her.

5. *The Hand of Ethelberta.*

Ethelberta, a woman of character and of brilliant parts, sets out in pursuit of social success, finds that Julius, the only man she is inclined to love, is too small for her, hands him over to the good little Picotee, and she herself, sacrificing almost cynically what is called her heart, marries the old scoundrelly Lord Mountclerc, runs him and his estates and governs well, a sound, strong pillar of established society, now she has nipped off the bud of her heart. Moral: it is easier for the butler's daughter to marry a lord than to find a husband with her love, if she be an exceptional woman.

The Hand of Ethelberta is the one almost cynical comedy. It marks the zenith of a certain feeling in the Wessex novels, the zenith of the feeling that the best thing to do is to kick out the craving for 'Love' and substitute commonsense, leaving sentiment to the minor characters.

This novel is a shrug of the shoulders, and a last taunt to hope, it is the end of the happy endings, except where sanity and a little cynicism again appear in *The Trumpet Major*, to bless where they despise. It is the hard, resistant, ironical announcement of personal failure, resistant and half-grinning. It gives way to violent, angry passions and real tragedy, real killing of beloved people, self-killing. Till now, only Elfride among the beloved, has been killed; the good men have always come out on top.

6. *The Return of the Native.*

This is the first tragic and important novel. Eustacia, dark, wild, passionate, quite conscious of her desires and inheriting no tradition which would make her ashamed of them, since she is of a novelistic Italian* birth, loves, first, the unstable Wildeve, who does not satisfy her, then casts him aside for the newly returned Clym, whom she marries. What does she want? She does not know, but it is evidently some form of self-realization; she wants to be herself, to attain herself. But she does not know how, by what means, so romantic imagination says, Paris and the *beau monde.* As if that would have stayed her unsatisfaction.

Clym has found out the vanity of Paris and the *beau monde.* What, then, does he want? He does not know; his imagination tells him he wants to serve the moral system of the community, since the material system is despicable. He wants to teach little Egdon boys in school. There is as much vanity in this, easily, as in Eustacia's Paris. For what is the moral system but the ratified form of the material system? What is Clym's altruism but a deep, very subtle cowardice, that makes him shirk his own being whilst apparently acting nobly; which makes him choose to improve mankind rather than to struggle at the quick of himself into being. He is not able to undertake his own soul, so he will take a commission for society to enlighten the souls of others. It is a subtle equivocation. Thus both Eustacia and he sidetrack from themselves, and each leaves the other unconvinced, unsatisfied, unrealized. Eustacia, because she moves outside the convention, must die; Clym, because he identified himself with the community, is transferred from Paris to preaching. He had never become an integral man, because when faced with the demand to produce himself, he remained under cover of the community and excused by his altruism.

His remorse over his mother is adulterated with sentiment; it is exaggerated by the push of tradition behind it. Even in this he does not ring true. He is always according to pattern, producing his feelings more or less on demand, according to the accepted standard. Practically never is he able to act or even feel in his original self: he is always according to the convention. His punishment is his final loss of all his original self: he is left preaching, out of sheer emptiness.

Thomasin and Venn have nothing in them turbulent enough to push them to the bounds of the convention. There is always room for them inside. They are genuine people, and they get the prize within the walls.

Wildeve, shifty and unhappy, attracted always from outside and never driven from within, can neither stand with nor without the established system. He cares nothing for it, because he is unstable, has no positive being. He is an eternal assumption.

The other victim, Clym's mother, is the crashing-down of one of the old, rigid pillars of the system. The pressure on her is too great. She is weakened from the inside also, for her nature is non-conventional; it cannot own the bounds.

So, in this book, all the exceptional people, those with strong feelings and unusual characters, are reduced; only those remain who are steady and genuine, if commonplace. Let a man will for himself, and he is destroyed. He must will according to the established system.

The real sense of tragedy is got from the setting. What is the great, tragic power in the book? It is Egdon Heath. And who are the real spirits of the Heath? First, Eustacia, then Clym's mother, then Wildeve. The natives have little or nothing in common with the place.

What is the real stuff of tragedy in the book? It is the Heath. It is the primitive, primal earth, where the instinctive life heaves up. There, in the deep, rude stirring of the instincts, there was the reality that worked the tragedy. Close to the body of things, there can be heard the stir that makes us and destroys us. The heath heaved with raw instinct. Egdon, whose dark soil was strong and crude and organic as the body of a beast. Out of the body of this crude earth are born Eustacia, Wildeve, Mistress Yeobright, Clym, and all the others. They are one year's accidental crop. What matters if some are drowned or dead, and others preaching or married: what matter, any more than the withering heath, the red-dening berries, the seedy furze, and the dead fern of one autumn of Egdon? The Heath persists. Its body is strong and fecund, it will bear many more crops beside this. Here is the sombre, latent power that will go on producing, no matter what happens to the product. Here is the deep, black source from whence all these little contents of lives are drawn. And the contents of the small lives are spilled and wasted. There is savage satisfaction in it: for so much more remains to come, such a black, powerful fecundity is working there that what does it matter?

Three people die and are taken back into the Heath; they mingle their strong earth again with its powerful soil, having been broken off at their stem. It is very good. Not Egdon is futile, sending forth life on the powerful heave of passion. It cannot be futile, for it is eternal. What is futile is the purpose of man.

Man has a purpose which he has divorced from the passionate purpose that issued him out of the earth into being. The Heath threw forth its shaggy heather and furze and fern, clean into being. It threw forth Eustacia and Wildeve and Mistress Yeobright and Clym, but to what purpose? Eustacia thought she wanted the hats and bonnets of Paris. Perhaps she was right. The heavy, strong soil of Egdon, breeding original native beings, is under Paris as well as under Wessex, and Eustacia sought herself in the gay city. She thought life there, in Paris, would be tropical, and all her energy and passion out of Egdon would there come into handsome flower. And if Paris real had been Paris as she imagined it, no doubt she was right, and her instinct was soundly expressed. But Paris real was not Eustacia's imagined Paris. Where was her imagined Paris, the place where her powerful nature could come to blossom? Beside some strong-passioned, unconfined man, her mate.

Which mate Clym might have been. He was born out of passionate Egdon to live as a passionate being whose strong feelings moved him ever further into being. But quite early his life became narrowed down to a small purpose: he must of necessity go into business, and submit his whole being, body and soul as well as mind, to the business and to the greater system it represented. His feelings, that should have produced the man, were suppressed and contained, he worked according to a system imposed from without. The dark struggle of Egdon, a struggle into being as the furze struggles into flower, went on in him, but could not burst the enclosure of the idea, the system which contained him. Impotent to *be*, he must transform himself, and live in an abstraction, in a generalization, he must identify himself with the system. He must live as Man or Humanity, or as the Community, or as Society, or as Civilization. 'An inner strenuousness was preying on his outer symmetry, and they rated his look as singular. ... His countenance was overlaid with legible meanings. Without being thought-worn, he yet had certain marks derived from a perception of his surroundings, such as are not infrequently found on man at the end of the four or five years of endeavour which follow the close of placid pupilage. He already showed that thought is a disease of the flesh, and indirectly bore evidence that ideal physical beauty is incompatible with emotional development and a full recognition of the coil of things. Mental luminousness must be fed with the oil of life, even if there is already a physical seed for it; and the pitiful sight of two demands on one supply was just showing itself here.'*

But did the face of Clym show that thought is a disease of flesh, or merely that in his case a dis-ease, an un-ease, of flesh produced thought? One does not catch thought like a fever: one produces it. If it be in any way a disease of flesh, it is rather the rash that indicates the disease than the disease itself. The 'inner strenuousness' of Clym's nature was not fighting against his physical symmetry, but against the limits imposed on his physical movement. By nature, as a passionate, violent product of Egdon, he should have loved and suffered in flesh and in soul from love, long before this age. He should have lived and moved and had his being,* whereas he had only his business, and afterwards his inactivity. His years of pupilage were past, 'he was one of whom something original was expected,'* yet he continued in pupilage. For he produced nothing original in being or in act, and certainly no original thought. None of his ideas were original. Even he himself was not original. He was over-taught, had become an echo. His life had been arrested, and his activity turned into repetition. Far from being emotionally developed, he was emotionally undeveloped, almost entirely. Only his mental faculties were developed. And, hid, his emotions were obliged to work according to the label he put upon them: a ready-made label.

Yet he remained for all that an original, the force of life was in him, however much he frustrated and suppressed its natural movement. 'As is usual with bright natures, the deity that lies ignominiously chained within an ephemeral human carcass shone out of him like a ray.'* But was the deity chained within his ephemeral human carcass, or within his limited human consciousness? Was it his blood, which rose dark and potent out of Egdon, which hampered and confined the deity, or was it his mind, that house built of extraneous knowledge and guarded by his will, which formed the prison?

He came back to Egdon—what for? To re-unite himself with the strong, free flow of life that rose out of Egdon as from a source? No—'to preach to the Egdon eremites that they might rise to a serene comprehensiveness without going through the process of enriching themselves.'* As if the Egdon eremites had not already far more serene comprehensiveness than ever he had himself, rooted as they were in the soil of all things, and living from the root! What did it matter how they enriched themselves, so long as they kept this strong, deep root in the primal soil, so long as their instincts moved out to action and to expression? The system was big enough for them, and had no power over their instincts. They should have taught him rather than he them.

And Egdon made him marry Eustacia. Here was action and life, here was a move into being on his part. But as soon as he got her, she became an idea to him, she had to fit in his system of ideas. According to his way of living, he knew her already, she was labelled and classed and fixed down. He had got into this way of living, and he could not get out of it. He had identified himself with the system, and he could not extricate himself. He did not know that Eustacia had her being beyond his. He did not know that she existed untouched by his system and his mind, where no system had sway and where no consciousness had risen to the surface. He did not know that she was Egdon, the powerful, eternal origin seething with production. He thought he knew. Egdon to him was the tract of common land, producing familiar rough herbage, and having some few unenlightened inhabitants. So he skated over heaven and hell, and having made a map of the surface, thought he knew all. But underneath and among his mapped world, the eternal powerful fecundity worked on heedless of him and his arrogance. His preaching, his superficiality made no difference. What did it matter if he had calculated a moral chart from the surface of life? Could that affect life, any more than a chart of the heavens affects the stars, affects the whole stellar universe which exists beyond our knowledge? Could the sound of his words affect the working of the body of Egdon, where in the unfathomable womb was begot and conceived all that would ever come forth? Did not his own heart beat far removed and immune from his thinking and talking? Had he been able to put even his own heart's mysterious resonance upon his map, from which he charted the course of lives in his moral system? And how much more completely, then, had he left out, in utter ignorance, the dark, powerful source whence all things rise into being, whence they will always continue to rise, to struggle forward to further being? A little of the static surface he could see, and map out. Then he thought his map was the thing itself. How blind he was, how utterly blind to the tremendous movement carrying and producing the surface. He did not know that the greater part of every life is underground, like roots in the dark in contact with the beyond. He preached, thinking lives could be moved like hen-houses from here to there. His blindness indeed brought on the calamity. But what matter if Eustacia or Wildeve or Mrs Yeobright died: what matter if he himself became a mere rattle of repetitive words—what did it matter? It was regrettable; no more. Egdon, the primal impulsive body, would go on producing all that was to be produced, eternally, though the will of man should destroy the blossom yet in bud, over and over again. At last he must learn what it is to be at one, in his mind and will, with the primal impulses that rise in him. Till then, let him perish or preach. The great reality on which the little tragedies enact themselves cannot be detracted from. The will and words which militate against it are the only vanity.

This is a constant revelation in Hardy's novels: that there exists a great background, vital and vivid, which matters more than the people who move upon it. Against the background of dark, passionate Egdon, of the leafy, sappy passion and sentiment of the woodlands, of the unfathomed stars, is drawn the lesser scheme of lives: *The Return of the Native*, *The Woodlanders*, or *Two on a Tower*. Upon the vast, incomprehensible pattern of some primal morality greater than ever the human mind can grasp, is drawn the little, pathetic pattern of man's moral life and struggle, pathetic, almost ridiculous. The little fold of law and order, the little walled city within which man has to defend himself from the waste enormity of nature, becomes always too small, and the pioneers venturing out with the code of the walled city upon them, die in the bonds of that code, free and yet unfree, preaching the walled city and looking to the waste.

This is the wonder of Hardy's novels, and gives them their

beauty. The vast, unexplored morality of life itself, what we call the immorality of nature, surrounds us in its eternal incomprehensibility, and in its midst goes on the little human morality play, with its queer frame of morality and its mechanized movement; seriously, portentously, till some one of the protagonists chances to look out of the charmed circle, weary of the stage, to look into the wilderness raging round. Then he is lost, his little drama falls to pieces, or becomes mere repetition, but the stupendous theatre outside goes on enacting its own incomprehensible drama, untouched. There is this quality in almost all Hardy's work, and this is the magnificent irony it all contains, the challenge, the contempt. Not the deliberate ironies, little tales of widows or widowers, contain the irony of human life as we live it in our self-aggrandized gravity, but the big novels, *The Return of the Native*, and the others.

And this is the quality Hardy shares with the great writers, Shakespeare or Sophocles or Tolstoi, this setting behind the small action of his protagonists the terrific action of unfathomed nature; setting a smaller system of morality, the one grasped and formulated by the human consciousness within the vast, uncomprehended and incomprehensible morality of nature or of life itself, surpassing human consciousness. The difference is, that whereas in Shakespeare or Sophocles the greater, uncomprehended morality, or fate, is actively transgressed and gives active punishment, in Hardy and Tolstoi the lesser, human morality, the mechanical system is actively transgressed, and holds, and punishes the protagonist, whilst the greater morality is only passively, negatively transgressed, it is represented merely as being present in background, in scenery, not taking any active part, having no direct connexion with the protagonist. Oedipus,* Hamlet, Macbeth set themselves up against, or find themselves set up against, the unfathomed moral forces of nature, and out of this unfathomed force comes their death. Whereas Anna Karenina,* Eustacia, Tess, Sue and Jude find themselves up against the established system of human government and morality, they cannot detach themselves, and are brought down. Their real tragedy is that they are unfaithful to the greater unwritten morality, which would have bidden Anna Karenina be patient and wait until she, by virtue of greater right, could take what she needed from society; would have bidden Vronsky detach himself from the system, become an individual, creating a new colony of morality with Anna; would have bidden Eustacia fight Clym for his own soul, and Tess take and claim her Angel, since she had the greater light; would have bidden Jude and Sue endure for very honour's sake, since one must bide by the best that one has known, and not succumb to the lesser good.

Had Oedipus, Hamlet, Macbeth been weaker, less full of real, potent life, they would have made no tragedy; they would have comprehended and contrived some arrangement of their affairs, sheltering in the human morality from the great stress and attack of the unknown morality. But being, as they are, men to the fullest capacity, when they find themselves, daggers drawn, with the very forces of life itself, they can only fight till they themselves are killed, since the morality of life, the greater morality, is eternally unalterable and invincible. It can be dodged for some time, but not opposed. On the other hand, Anna, Eustacia, Tess or Sue—what was there in their position that was necessarily tragic? Necessarily painful it was, but they were not at war with God, only with Society. Yet they were all cowed by the mere judgment of man upon them, and all the while by their own souls they were right. And the judgment of men killed them, not the judgment of their own souls or the judgment of Eternal God.

Which is the weakness of modern tragedy, where transgression against the social code is made to bring destruction, as though the social code worked our irrevocable fate. Like Clym, the map appears to us more real than the land. Shortsighted almost to blindness, we pore over the chart, map our journeys, and confirm them: and we cannot see life itself giving us the lie the whole time. [...]

Looking over the Hardy novels, it is interesting to see which of the heroes one would call a distinct individuality, more or less achieved, which an unaccomplished potential individuality, and which an impure, unindividualized life embedded in the matrix, either achieving its own lower degree of distinction, or not achieving it.

In *Desperate Remedies* there are scarcely any people at all, particularly when the plot is working. The tiresome part about Hardy is that, so often, he will neither write a morality play nor a novel.

The people of the first book, as far as the plot is concerned, are not people: they are the heroine, faultless and white; the hero, with a small spot on his whiteness; the villainess, red and black, but more red than black; the villain, black and red; the Murderer, aided by the Adulteress, obtains power over the Virgin, who, rescued at the last moment by the Virgin Knight, evades the evil clutch. Then the Murderer, overtaken by vengeance, is put to death, whilst Divine justice descends upon the Adulteress. Then the Virgin unites with the Virgin Knight, and receives Divine Blessing.

That is a morality play, and if the morality were vigorous and original, all well and good. But, between-whiles, we see that the Virgin is being played by a nice, rather ordinary girl.

In *The Laodicean*, there is all the way through a *prédilection d'artiste** for the aristocrat, and all the way through a moral condemnation of him, a substituting the middle or lower-class personage with bourgeois virtues into his place. This was the root of Hardy's pessimism. Not until he comes to Tess and Jude does he ever sympathize with the aristocrat—unless it be in *The Mayor of Casterbridge*, and then he sympathizes only to slay. He always, always represents them the same, as having some vital weakness, some radical ineffectuality. From first to last it is the same.

Miss Aldclyffe and Manston, Elfride and the sickly lord she married, Troy and Farmer Boldwood, Eustacia Vye and Wildeve, de Stancy in *The Laodicean*, Lady Constantine in *Two on a Tower*, the Mayor of Casterbridge and Lucetta, Mrs Charmond and Dr Fitzpiers in *The Woodlanders*, Tess and Alec d'Urberville, and, though different, Jude. There is also the blond, passionate, yielding man: Sergeant Troy, Wildeve, and, in spirit, Jude.

These are all, in their way, the aristocrat-characters of Hardy. They must every one die, every single one.

Why has Hardy this *prédilection d'artiste* for the aristocrat, and why, at the same time, this moral antagonism to him?

It is fairly obvious in *The Laodicean*, a book where, the spirit being small, the complaint is narrow. The heroine, the daughter of a famous railway engineer, lives in the castle of the old de Stancys. She sighs, wishing she were of the de Stancy line: the tombs and portraits have a spell over her. 'But,' says the hero to her, 'have you forgotten your father's line of ancestry: Archimedes, Newcomen, Watt, Telford, Stephenson?'*—'But I have a *prédilection d'artiste* for ancestors of the other sort,' sighs Paula. And the hero despairs of impressing her with the list of his architect ancestors: Phidias, Ictinus and Callicrates, Chersiphron, Vitruvius, Wilars of Cambray, William of Wykeham.* He deplores her marked preference for an 'animal pedigree'.

But what is this 'animal pedigree'? If a family pedigree of her ancestors, working-men and burghers, had been kept, Paula would not have gloried in it, animal though it were. Hers was a *prédilection d'artiste.*

And this because the aristocrat alone has occupied a position where he could afford to *be*, to be himself, to create himself, to live as himself. That is his eternal fascination. This is why the preference for him is a *prédilection d'artiste.* The preference for the architect line would be a *prédilection de savant*, the preference for the engineer pedigree would be a *prédilection d'economiste.**

The prédilection d'artiste—Hardy has it strongly, and it is rooted deeply in every imaginative human being. The glory of mankind has been to produce lives, to produce vivid, independent, individual men, not buildings or engineering works or even art, not even the public good. The glory of mankind is not in a host of secure, comfortable, law-abiding citizens, but in the few more fine, clear lives, beings, individuals, distinct, detached, single as may be from the public.

And these the artist of all time has chosen. Why, then, must the aristocrat always be condemned to death, in Hardy? Has the community come to consciousness in him, as in the French Revolutionaries, determined to destroy all that is not the average? Certainly in the Wessex novels, all but the average people die. But why? Is there the germ of death in these more single, distinguished people, or has the artist himself a bourgeois taint, a jealous vindictiveness that will now take revenge, now that the community, the average, has gained power over the aristocrat, the exception?

It is evident that both is true. Starting with the bourgeois morality, Hardy makes every exceptional person a villain, all exceptional or strong individual traits he holds up as weaknesses or wicked faults. So in *Desperate Remedies, Under the Greenwood Tree, Far from the Madding Crowd, The Hand of Ethelberta, The Return of the Native* (but in *The Trumpet-Major* there is an ironical dig in the ribs to this civic communal morality), *The Laodicean, Two on a*

Tower, *The Mayor of Casterbridge*, and *Tess*, in steadily weakening degree. The blackest villain is Manston, the next, perhaps, Troy, the next Eustacia, and Wildeve, always becoming less villainous and more human. The first show of real sympathy, nearly conquering the bourgeois or commune morality, is for Eustacia, whilst the dark villain is becoming merely a weak, pitiable person in Dr Fitzpiers. In *The Mayor of Casterbridge* the dark villain is already almost the hero. There is a lapse in the maudlin, weak but not wicked Dr Fitzpiers, duly condemned, Alec d'Urberville is not unlikable, and Jude is a complete tragic hero, at once the old Virgin Knight and Dark Villain. The condemnation gradually shifts over from the dark villain to the blond bourgeois virgin hero, from Alec d'Urberville to Angel Clare, till in Jude they are united and loved, though the preponderance is of a dark villain, now dark, beloved, passionate hero. The condemnation shifts over at last from the dark villain to the white virgin, the bourgeois in soul: from Arabella to Sue. Infinitely more subtle and sad is the condemnation at the end, but there it is: the virgin knight is hated with intensity, yet still loved; the white virgin, the beloved, is the arch-sinner against life at last, and the last note of hatred is against her.

It is a complete and devastating shift-over, it is a complete *volte-face* of moralities. Black does not become white, but it takes white's place as good; white remains white, but it is found bad. The old, communal morality is like a leprosy, a white sickness: the old, anti-social, individualist morality is alone on the side of life and health.

But yet, the aristocrat must die, all the way through: even Jude. Was the germ of death in him at the start? Or was he merely at outs with his times, the times of the Average in triumph? Would Manston, Troy, Farmer Boldwood, Eustacia, de Stancy, Henchard, Alec d'Urberville, Jude have been real heroes in heroic times, without tragedy? It seems as if Manston, Boldwood, Eustacia, Henchard, Alec d'Urberville, and almost Jude, might have been. In an heroic age they might have lived and more or less triumphed. But Troy, Wildeve, de Stancy, Fitzpiers, and Jude have something fatal in them. There is a rottenness at the core of them. The failure, the misfortune, or the tragedy, whichever it may be, was inherent in them: as it was in Elfride, Lady Constantine, Marty

South in *The Woodlanders*, and Tess. They have all passionate natures, and in them all failure is inherent.

So that we have, of men, the noble Lord in *A Pair of Blue Eyes*, Sergeant Troy, Wildeve, de Stancy, Fitzpiers, and Jude, all passionate, aristocratic males, doomed by their very being, to tragedy, or to misfortune in the end.

Of the same class among women are Elfride, Lady Constantine, Marty South, and Tess, all aristocratic, passionate, yet necessarily unfortunate females.

We have also, of men, Manston, Farmer Boldwood, Henchard, Alec d'Urberville, and perhaps Jude, all passionate, aristocratic males, who fell before the weight of the average, the lawful crowd, but who, in more primitive times, would have formed romantic rather than tragic figures.

Of women in the same class are Miss Aldclyffe, Eustacia, Lucetta, Mrs Charmond.

The third class, of bourgeois or average hero, whose purpose is to live and have his being in the community, contains the successful hero of *Desperate Remedies*, the unsuccessful but not very much injured two heroes of *A Pair of Blue Eyes*, the successful Gabriel Oak, the unsuccessful, left-preaching Clym, the unsuccessful but not very much injured astronomer of *Two on a Tower*, the successful Scotchman of Casterbridge, the unsuccessful and expired Giles Winterborne of *The Woodlanders*, the arch-type, Angel Clare, and perhaps a little of Jude.

The companion women to these men are: the heroine of *Desperate Remedies*, Bathsheba, Thomasin, Paula, Henchard's daughter, Grace in *The Woodlanders*, and Sue.

This, then, is the moral conclusion drawn from the novels:

1. The physical individual is in the end an inferior thing which must fall before the community: Manston, Henchard, etc.

2. The physical and spiritual individualist is a fine thing which must fall because of its own isolation, because it is a sport, not in the true line of life: Jude, Tess, Lady Constantine.

3. The physical individualist and spiritual bourgeois or communist is a thing, finally, of ugly, undeveloped, non-distinguished or perverted physical instinct, and must fall physically. Sue, Angel Clare, Clym, Knight. It remains, however, fitted into the community.

4. The undistinguished, bourgeois or average being with average or civic virtues usually succeeds in the end. If he fails, he is left practically uninjured. If he expire during probation, he has flowers on his grave.

By individualist is meant, not a selfish or greedy person, anxious to satisfy appetites, but a man of distinct being, who must act in his own particular way to fulfil his own individual nature. He is a man who, being beyond the average, chooses to rule his own life to his own completion, and as such is an aristocrat.

The artist always has a predilection for him. But Hardy, like Tolstoi, is forced in the issue always to stand with the community in condemnation of the aristocrat. He cannot help himself, but must stand with the average against the exception, he must, in his ultimate judgment, represent the interests of humanity, or the community as a whole, and rule out the individual interest.

To do this, however, he must go against himself. His private sympathy is always with the individual against the community: as is the case with the artist. Therefore he will create a more or less blameless individual and, making him seek his own fulfilment, his highest aim, will show him destroyed by the community, or by that in himself which represents the community, or by some close embodiment of the civic idea. Hence the pessimism. To do this, however, he must select his individual with a definite weakness, a certain coldness of temper, inelastic, a certain inevitable and inconquerable adhesion to the community.

This is obvious in Troy, Clym, Tess, and Jude. They have naturally distinct individuality but, as it were, a weak life-flow, so that they cannot break away from the old adhesion, they cannot separate themselves from the mass which bore them, they cannot detach themselves from the common. Therefore they are pathetic rather than tragic figures. They have not the necessary strength: the question of their unfortunate end is begged in the beginning.

Whereas Oedipus or Agamemnon or Clytemnestra or Orestes, or Macbeth or Hamlet or Lear, these are destroyed by their own conflicting passions. Out of greed for adventure, a desire to be off, Agamemnon sacrifices Iphigenia: moreover he has his love-affairs outside Troy: and this brings on him death from the mother of his daughter, and from his pledged wife.* Which is the working of the natural law. Hamlet, a later Orestes, is commanded by the Erinyes of his father to kill his mother and his uncle: but his maternal filial feeling tears him. It is almost the same tragedy as Orestes, without any goddess or god to grant peace.

In these plays, conventional morality is transcended. The action is between the great, single, individual forces in the nature of Man, not between the dictates of the community and the original passion. The Commandment says: 'Thou shalt not kill.'* But doubtless Macbeth had killed many a man who was in his way. Certainly Hamlet suffered no qualms about killing the old man behind the curtain. Why should he? But when Macbeth killed Duncan, he divided himself in twain, into two hostile parts. It was all in his own soul and blood: it was nothing outside himself: as it was, really, with Clym, Troy, Tess, Jude. Troy would probably have been faithful to his little unfortunate person, had she been a lady, and had he not felt himself cut off from society in his very being, whilst all the time he cleaved to it. Tess allowed herself to be condemned, and asked for punishment from Angel Clare. Why? She had done nothing particularly, or at least irrevocably, unnatural, were her life young and strong. But she sided with the community's condemnation of her. And almost the bitterest, most pathetic, deepest part of Jude's misfortune was his failure to obtain admission to Oxford, his failure to gain his place and standing in the world's knowledge, in the world's work.

There is a lack of sternness, there is a hesitating betwixt life and public opinion, which diminishes the Wessex novels from the rank of pure tragedy. It is not so much the eternal, immutable laws of being which are transgressed, it is not that vital life-forces are set in conflict with each other, bringing almost inevitable tragedy— yet not necessarily death, as we see in the most splendid Aeschylus. It is, in Wessex, that the individual succumbs to what is in its shallowest, public opinion, in its deepest, the human compact by which we live together, to form a community. [...]

It is only when the Greek stimulus is received, with its addition of male influence, its addition of relative movement, its revelation of movement driving the object, the highest revelation which had yet been made, that mediaeval art became complete Renaissance art, that there was the union and fusion of the male and female spirits, creating a perfect expression for the time being.

During the mediaeval times, the God had been Christ on the

Cross, the Body Crucified, the flesh destroyed, the Virgin Chastity combating Desire. Such had been the God of the Aspiration. But the God of Knowledge, of that which they acknowledged as themselves, had been the Father, the God of the Ancient Jew.

But now, with the Renaissance, the God of Aspiration became in accord with the God of Knowledge, and there was a great outburst of joy, and the theme was not Christ Crucified, but Christ born of Woman, the Infant Saviour and the Virgin; or of the Annunciation, the Spirit embracing the flesh in pure embrace.

This was the perfect union of male and female, in this the hands met and clasped, and never was such a manifestation of Joy. This Joy reached its highest utterance perhaps in Botticelli, as in his *Nativity of the Saviour*,* in our National Gallery. Still there is the architectural composition, but what an outburst of movement from the source of motion. The Infant Christ is a centre, a radiating spark of movement, the Virgin is bowed in Absolute Movement, the earthly father, Joseph, is folded up, like a clod or a boulder, obliterated, whilst the Angels fly round in ecstasy, embracing and linking hands.

The bodily father is almost obliterated. As balance to the Virgin Mother he is there, presented, but silenced, only the movement of his loin conveyed. He is not the male. The male is the radiant infant, over which the mother leans. They two are the ecstatic centre, the complete origin, the force which is both centrifugal and centripetal.

This is the joyous utterance of the Renaissance, to which we listen for ever. Perhaps there is a melancholy in Botticelli, a pain of Woman mated to the Spirit, a nakedness of the Aphrodite* issued exposed to the clear elements, to the fleshlessness of the male. But still it is joy transparent over pain. It is the utterance of complete, perfect religious art, unwilling, perhaps, when the true male and the female meet. In the Song of Solomon,* the female was preponderant, the male was impure, not single. But here the heart is satisfied for the moment, there is a moment of perfect being.

And it seems to be so in other religions: the most perfect moment centres round the mother and the male child, whilst the physical male is deified separately, as a bull, perhaps.

After Botticelli came Correggio.* In him the development from gesture to articulate expression was continued, unconsciously, the movement from the symbolic to the representation went on in him, from the object to the animate creature. The Virgin and Child are no longer symbolic, in Correggio: they no longer belong to religious art, but are distinctly secular. The effort is to render the living person, the individual perceived, and not the great aspiration, or an idea. Art now passes from the naïve, intuitive stage to the state of knowledge. The female impulse, to feel and to live in feeling, is now embraced by the male impulse—to know, and almost carried off by knowledge. But not yet. Still Correggio is unconscious, in his art; he is in that state of elation which represents the marriage of male and female, with the pride of the male perhaps predominant. In the *Madonna with the Basket*, of the National Gallery, the Madonna is most thoroughly a wife, the child is most triumphantly a man's child. The Father is the origin. He is seen labouring in the distance, the true support of this mother and child. There is no Virgin worship, none of the mystery of woman. The artist has reached to a sufficiency of knowledge. He knows his woman. What he is now concerned with is not her great female mystery, but her individual character. The picture has become almost lyrical—it is the woman as known by the man, it is the woman as he has experienced her. But still she is also unknown, also she is the mystery. But Correggio's chief business is to portray the woman of his own experience and knowledge, rather than the woman of his aspiration and fear. The artist is now concerned with his own experience rather than with his own desire. The female is now more or less within the power and reach of the male. But still she is there, to centralize and control his movement, still the two react and are not resolved. But for the man, the woman is henceforth part of a stream of movement, she is herself a stream of movement, carried along with himself. He sees everything as motion, retarded perhaps by the flesh, or by the stable being of this life in the body. But still man is held and pivoted by the object, even if he tend to wear down the pivot to a nothingness.

Thus Correggio leads on to the whole of modern art, where the male still wrestles with the female, in unconscious struggle, but where he gains ever gradually over her, reducing her to nothing. Ever there is more and more vibration, movement, and less and less stability, centralization. Ever man is more and more occupied with his own experience, with his own overpowering of resistance, ever less and less aware of any resistance in the object, less and less aware of any stability, less and less aware of anything unknown, more and more preoccupied with that which he knows, till his knowledge tends to become an abstraction, because it is limited by no unknown.

It is the contradiction of Dürer, as the Parthenon Frieze* was the contradiction of Babylon and Egypt. To Dürer woman did not exist; even as to a child at the breast, woman does not exist separately. She is the overwhelming condition of life. She was to Dürer that which possessed him, and not that which he possessed. Her being overpowered him, he could only see in her terms, in terms of stability and of stable, incontrovertible being. He is overpowered by the vast assurance at whose breasts he is suckled, and, as if astounded, he grasps at the unknown. He knows that he rests within some great stability, and, marvelling at his own power for movement, touches the objects of this stability, becomes familiar with them. It is a question of the starting-point. Dürer starts with a sense of that which he does not know and would discover; Correggio with the sense of that which he has known, and would re-create.

And in the Renaissance, after Botticelli, the motion begins to divide in these two directions. The hands no longer clasp in perfect union, but one clasp overbears the other. Botticelli develops to Correggio and to Andrea del Sarto, develops forward to Rembrandt, and Rembrandt to the Impressionists, to the male extreme of motion. But Botticelli, on the other hand, becomes Raphael, Raphael and Michelangelo.*

In Raphael we see the stable, architectural developing out further, and becoming the geometric: the denial or refusal of all movement. In the *Madonna degli Ansidei** the child is drooping, the mother stereotyped, the picture geometric, static, abstract. When there is any union of male and female, there is no goal of abstraction: the abstract is used in place, as a means of a real union. The goal of the male impulse is the announcement of motion, endless motion, endless diversity, endless change. The goal of the female impulse is the announcement of infinite oneness, of infinite stability. When the two are working in combination, as they must in life, there is, as it were, a dual motion, centrifugal for the male, fleeing abroad, away from the centre, outward to infinite vibration, and centripetal for the female, fleeing in to the eternal centre of rest. A combination of the two movements produces a sum of motion and stability at once, satisfying. But in life there tends always to be more of one than the other. The Cathedrals, Fra Angelico,* frighten us or bore us with their final annunciation of centrality and stability. We want to escape. The influence is too female for us.

In Botticelli, the architecture remains, but there is the wonderful movement outwards, the joyous, if still clumsy, escape from the centre. His religious pictures tend to be stereotyped, resigned. The Primavera* herself is static, melancholy, a stability become almost a negation. It is as if the female, instead of being the great, unknown Positive, towards which all must flow, became the great Negative, the centre which denied all motion. And the Aphrodite stands there not as a force, to draw all things unto her, but as the naked, almost unwilling pivot, as the keystone which endured all thrust and remained static. But still there is the joy, the great motion around her, sky and sea, all the elements and living, joyful forces.

Raphael, however, seeks and finds nothing there. He goes to the centre to ask: 'What is this mystery we are all pivoted upon?' To Fra Angelico it was the unknown Omnipotent. It was a goal, to which man travelled inevitably. It was the desired, the end of the long horizontal journey. But to Raphael it was the negation. Still he is a seeker, an aspirant, still his art is religious art. But the Virgin, the essential female, was to him a negation, a neutrality. Such must have been his vivid experience. But still he seeks her. Still he desires the stability, the positive keystone which grasps the arch together, not the negative keystone neutralizing the thrust, itself a neutrality. And reacting upon his own desire, the male reacting upon itself, he creates the Abstraction, the geometric conception of life. The fundament of all is the geometry of all. Which is the Plato conception.* And the desire is to formulate the complete geometry.

So Raphael, knowing that his desire reaches out beyond the range of possible experience, sensible that he will not find satisfaction in any one woman, sensible that the female impulse does not, or cannot unite in him with the male impulse sufficiently to create a stability, an eternal moment of truth for him, of realization, closes his eyes and his mind upon experience, and abstracting himself, reacting upon himself, produces the geometric conception of the fundamental truth, departs from religion, from any God idea, and becomes philosophic.

Raphael is the real end of Renaissance in Italy; almost he is the real end of Italy, as Plato was the real end of Greece. When the God-idea passes into the philosophic or geometric idea, then there is a sign that the male impulse has thrown the female impulse, and has recoiled upon itself, has become abstract, asexual.

Michelangelo, however, too physically passionate, containing too much of the female in his body ever to reach the geometric abstraction, unable to abstract himself, and at the same time, like Raphael, unable to find any woman who in her being should resist him and reserve still some unknown from him, strives to obtain his own physical satisfaction in his art. He is obsessed by the desire of the body. And he must react upon himself to produce his own bodily satisfaction, aware that he can never obtain it through woman. He must seek the moment, the consummation, the key-stone, the pivot, in his own flesh. For his own body is both male and female.

Raphael and Michelangelo are men of different nature placed in the same position and resolving the same question in their several ways. Socrates and Plato are a parallel pair, and, in another degree, Tolstoi and Turgenev, and, perhaps, St Paul and St John the Evangelist, and, perhaps, Shakespeare and Shelley.

The body it is which attaches us directly to the female. Sex, as we call it, is only the point where the dual stream begins to divide, where it is nearly together, almost one. An infant is of no very determinate sex: that is, it is of both. Only at adolescence is there a real differentiation, the one is singled out to predominate. In what we call happy natures, in the lazy, contented people, there is a fairly equable balance of sex. There is sufficient of the female in the body of such a man as to leave him fairly free. He does not suffer the torture of desire of a more male being. It is obvious even from the physique of such a man that in him there is a proper proportion between male and female, so that he can be easy, balanced, and without excess. The Greek sculptors of the 'best' period, Phidias* and then Sophocles, Alcibiades, then Horace,* must have been fairly well-balanced men, not passionate to any excess, tending to voluptuousness rather than to passion. So also Victor Hugo and

Schiller* and Tennyson. The real voluptuary is a man who is female as well as male, and who lives according to the female side of his nature, like Lord Byron.

The pure male is himself almost an abstraction, almost bodiless, like Shelley or Edmund Spenser. But, as we know humanity, this condition comes of an omission of some vital part. In the ordinary sense, Shelley never lived. He transcended life. But we do not want to transcend life, since we are of life.

Why should Shelley say of the skylark:

'Hail to thee, blithe Spirit—bird thou never wert!—'?*

Why should he insist on the bodilessness of beauty, when we cannot know of any save embodied beauty? Who would wish that the skylark were not a bird, but a spirit? If the whistling skylark were a spirit, then we should all wish to be spirits. Which were impious and flippant.

I can think of no being in the world so transcendently male as Shelley. He is phenomenal. The rest of us have bodies which contain the male and the female. If we were so singled out as Shelley, we should not belong to life, as he did not belong to life. But it were impious to wish to be like the angels. So long as mankind exists it must exist in the body, and so long must each body pertain both to the male and the female.

In the degree of pure maleness below Shelley are Plato and Raphael and Wordsworth, then Goethe and Milton and Dante, then Michelangelo, then Shakespeare, then Tolstoi, then St Paul.

A man who is well balanced between male and female, in his own nature, is, as a rule, happy, easy to mate, easy to satisfy, and content to exist. It is only a disproportion, or a dissatisfaction, which makes the man struggle into articulation. And the articulation is of two sorts, the cry of desire or the cry of realization, the cry of satisfaction, the effort to prolong the sense of satisfaction, to prolong the moment of consummation.

A bird in spring sings with the dawn, ringing out from the moment of consummation in wider and wider circles. Dürer, Fra Angelico, Botticelli, all sing of the moment of consummation, some of them still marvelling and lost in the wonder at the other being, Botticelli poignant with distinct memory. Raphael too sings of the moment of consummation. But he was not lost in the moment, only sufficiently lost to know what it was. In the moment, he was not completely consummated. He must strive to complete his satisfaction from himself. So, whilst making his great acknowledgment to the Woman, he must add to her to make her whole, he must give her his completion. So he rings her round with pure geometry, till she becomes herself almost of the geometric figure, an abstraction. The picture becomes a great ellipse crossed by a dark column. This is the *Madonna degli Ansidei*. The Madonna herself is almost insignificant. She and the child are contained within the shaft thrust across the ellipse.

This column must always stand for the male aspiration, the arch or ellipse for the female completeness containing this aspiration. And the whole picture is a geometric symbol of the consummation of life.

What we call the Truth is, in actual experience, that momentary state when in living the union between the male and the female is consummated. This consummation may be also physical, between the male body and the female body. But it may be only spiritual, between the male and female spirit.

And the symbol by which Raphael expresses this moment of consummation is by a dark, strong shaft or column leaping up into, and almost transgressing a faint, radiant, inclusive ellipse.

To express the same moment Botticelli uses no symbol, but builds up a complicated system of circles, of movements wheeling in their horizontal plane about their fixed centres, the whole builded up dome-shape, and then the dome surpassed by another singing cycle in the open air above.

This is Botticelli always: different cycles of joy, different moments of embrace, different forms of dancing round, all contained in one picture, without solution. He has not solved it yet.

And Raphael, in reaching the pure symbolic solution, has surpassed art and become almost mathematics. Since the business of art is never to solve, but only to declare.

There is no such thing as solution. Nietzsche talks about the *Ewige Wiederkehr.** It is like Botticelli singing cycles. But each cycle is different. There is no real recurrence.

And to single out one cycle, one moment, and to exclude from this moment all context, and to make this moment timeless, this is what Raphael does, and what Plato does. So that their absolute Truth, their geometric Truth, is only true in timelessness.

Michelangelo, on the other hand, seeks for no absolute Truth. His desire is to realize in his body, in his feeling, the moment-consummation which is for Man the perfect truth-experience. But he knows of no embrace. For him, personally, woman does not exist. For Botticelli she existed as the Virgin-Mother, and as the Primavera, and as Aphrodite. She existed as the pure origin of life on the female side, as the bringer of light and, delight, and as the passionately Desired of every man, as the Known and Unknown in one: to Raphael she existed either as a minor part of his experience, having nothing to do with his aspiration, or else his aspiration merely used her as a statement included within the Great Abstraction.

To Michelangelo the female scarcely existed outside his own physique. There he knew of her and knew the desire of her. But Raphael, in his passion to be self-complete, roused his desire for consummation to a white-hot pitch, so that he became incandescent, reacting on himself, consuming his own flesh and his own bodily life, to reach the pitch of perfect abstraction, the resisting body holding back the raging stream of outward force, till the two formed a stable incandescence, a luminous geometric conception of permanence and inviolability. Meanwhile his body burned away, overpowered, in this state of incandescence.

Michelangelo's will was different. The body in him, that which knew of the female and therefore was the female, was stronger and more insistent. His desire for consummation was desire for the satisfying moment when the male and female spirits touch in closest embrace, vivifying each other, not one destroying the other, but still are two. He knew that for Man consummation is a temporal state. The pure male spirit must ever conceive of timelessness, the pure female of the moment. And Michelangelo, more mixed than Raphael, must always rage within the limits of time and of temporal forms. So he reacted upon himself, sought the female in himself, aggrandized it, and so reached a wonderful momentary stability of flesh exaggerated till it became tenuous, but filled and balanced by the outward-pressing force. And he reached his consummation in that way, reached the perfect moment, when he

realized and revealed his figures in all their marvellous equilibrium.
The Jewish tradition, with its great physical God, source of male
and female, attracted him. By turning towards the female goal, of
utter stability and permanence in Time, he arrived at his
consummation. But only by reacting on himself, by withdrawing
his own mobility. Thus he made his great figures, the Moses, static
and looming, announcing, like the Jewish God, the magnificence
and eternality of the physical law; the David, young, but with too
much body for a young figure, the physique exaggerated, the clear,
outward-leaping, essential spirit of the young man smothered over,
the real maleness cloaked, so that the statue is almost a falsity
Then the slaves, heaving in body, fastened in bondage that refuses
them movement; the motionless Madonna, no Virgin but Woman
in the flesh, not the pure female conception, but the spouse of
man, the mother of bodily children. The men are not male, nor the
women female, to any degree.

The Adam* can scarcely stir into life. That large body of almost
transparent, tenuous texture is not established enough for motion.
It is not that it is too ponderous: it is too unsubstantial, unreal. It is
not motion, life, he craves, but body. Give him but a firm, concentrated physique. That is the cry of all Michelangelo's pictures.

But, powerful male as he was, he satisfies his desire by insisting
upon and exaggerating the body in him, he reaches the point of
consummation in the most marvellous equilibrium which his
figures show. To attain this equilibrium he must exaggerate and
exaggerate and exaggerate the flesh, make it ever more tenuous,
keeping it really in true ratio. And then comes the moment, the
perfect stable poise, the perfect balance between object and movement, the perfect combination of male and female in one figure.

It is wonderful, and peaceful, this equilibrium, once reached.
But it is reached through anguish and self-battle and self-
repression, therefore it is sad. Always, Michelangelo's pictures are
full of joy, of self-acceptance and self-proclamation. Michelangelo
fought and arrested the mobile male in him; Raphael was proud in
the male he was, and gave himself utter liberty, at the female
expense.

And it seems as though Italy had ever since the Renaissance
been possessed by the Raphaelesque conception of the ultimate
geometric basis of life, the geometric essentiality of all things.

There is in the Italian, at the very bottom of all, the fundamental, geometric conception of absolute static combination. There is the shaft enclosed in the ellipse, as a permanent symbol. There exists no shaft, no ellipse separately, but only the whole complete thing; there is neither male nor female, but an absolute interlocking of the two in one, an absolute combination, so that each is gone in the complete identity. There is only the geometric abstraction of the moment of consummation, a moment made timeless. And this conception of a long, clinched, timeless embrace, this overwhelming conception of timeless consummation, of which there is no beginning nor end, from which there is no escape, has arrested the Italian race for three centuries. It is the source of its indifference and its fatalism and its positive abandon, and of its utter incapacity to be sceptical, in the Russian sense.

This conception contains also, naturally, as part of the same idea, Aphrodite-worship and Phallic-worship. But these are subordinate, and belong to a sort of initiatory period. The real conception, for the individual, is marriage, inviolable marriage, which always was and always has been, no matter what apparent aberrations there may or may not be. And the manifestation of divinity is the child. In marriage, in utter, interlocked marriage, man and woman cease to be two beings and become one, one and one only, not two in one as with us, but absolute One, a geometric absolute, timeless, the Absolute, the Divine. And the child, as issue of this divine and timeless state, is hailed with love and joy.

But the Italian is now beginning to withdraw from his clinched and timeless embrace, from his geometric abstraction, into the northern conception of himself and the woman as two separate identities, which meet, combine, but always must withdraw again.

So that the Futurist Boccioni now makes his sculpture, *Development of a Bottle through Space*,* try to express the withdrawal, and at the same time he must adhere to the conception of this same interlocked state of marriage between centripetal and centrifugal forces, the geometric abstraction of the bottle. But he can neither do one thing nor the other. He wants to re-state the real abstraction. And at the same time he has an unsatisfied desire to satisfy. He must insist on the centrifugal force, and so destroy at once his abstraction. He must insist on the male spirit of motion outwards, because, during three static centuries, there has necessarily come to pass a preponderance of the female in the race, so that the Italian is rather more female than male now, as is the whole Latin race rather voluptuous than passionate, too much aware of their utter lockedness male with female, and too hopeless, as males, to act, to be passionate. So that when I look at Boccioni's sculpture, and see him trying to state the timeless abstract being of a bottle, the pure geometric abstraction of the bottle, I am fascinated. But then, when I see him driven by his desire for the male complement into portraying motion, simple motion, trying to give expression to the bottle in terms of mechanics, I am confused. It is for science to explain the bottle in terms of force and motion. Geometry, pure mathematics, is very near to art, and the vivid attempt to render the bottle as a pure geometric abstraction might give rise to a work of art, because of the resistance of the medium, the stone. But a representation in stone of the lines of force which create that state of rest called a bottle, that is a model in mechanics.

And the two representations require two different states of mind in the appreciator, so that the result is almost nothingness, mere confusion. And the portraying of a state of mind is impossible. There can only be made scientific diagrams of states of mind. A state of mind is a resultant between an attack and a resistance. And how can one produce a resultant without first causing the collision of the originating forces?

The attitude of the Futurists is the scientific attitude, as the attitude of Italy is mainly scientific. It is the forgetting of the old, perfect Abstraction, it is the departure of the male from the female, it is the act of withdrawal: the denying of consummation and the starting afresh, the learning of the alphabet. [...]

Most fascinating in all artists is this antinomy between Law and Love, between the flesh and the Spirit, between the Father and the Son.

For the moralist it is easy. He can insist on that aspect of the Law or Love which is in the immediate line of development for his age, and he can sternly and severely exclude or suppress all the rest.

So that all morality is of temporary value, useful to its times. But Art must give a deeper satisfaction. It must give fair play all round.

Yet every work of art adheres to some system of morality. But if it be really a work of art, it must contain the essential criticism on the morality to which it adheres. And hence the antinomy, hence the conflict necessary to every tragic conception.

The degree to which the system of morality, or the metaphysic, of any work of art is submitted to criticism within the work of art makes the lasting value and satisfaction of that work. Aeschylus, having caught the oriental idea of Love, correcting the tremendous Greek conception of the Law with this new idea, produces the intoxicating satisfaction of the Orestean trilogy.* The Law, and Love, they are here the Two-in-One in all their magnificence. But Euripides,* with his aspiration towards Love, Love the supreme, and his almost hatred of the Law, Law the Triumphant but Base Closer of Doom, is less satisfactory, because of the very fact that he holds Love always Supreme, and yet must endure the chagrin of seeing Love perpetually transgressed and overthrown. So he makes his tragedy: the higher thing eternally pulled down by the lower. And this unfairness in the use of terms, higher and lower, but above all, the unfairness of showing Love always violated and suffering, never supreme and triumphant, makes us disbelieve Euripides in the end. For we have to bring in pity, we must admit that Love is at a fundamental disadvantage before the Law, and cannot therefore ever hold its own. Which is weak philosophy.

If Aeschylus has a metaphysic to his art, this metaphysic is that Love and Law are Two, eternally in conflict, and eternally being reconciled. This is the tragic significance of Aeschylus.

But the metaphysic of Euripides is that the Law and Love are two eternally in conflict, and unequally matched, so that Love must always be borne down. In Love a man shall only suffer. There is also a Reconciliation, otherwise Euripides were not so great. But there is always the unfair matching, this disposition insisted on, which at last leaves one cold and unbelieving.

The moments of pure satisfaction come in the choruses, in the pure lyrics, when Love is put into true relations with the Law, apart from knowledge, transcending knowledge, transcending the metaphysic, where the aspiration to Love meets the acknowledgment of the Law in a consummate marriage, for the moment.

Where Euripides adheres to his metaphysic, he is unsatisfactory. Where he transcends his metaphysic, he gives that supreme equilibrium wherein we know satisfaction.

The adherence to a metaphysic does not necessarily give artistic form. Indeed the over-strong adherence to a metaphysic usually destroys any possibility of artistic form. Artistic form is a revelation of the two principles of Love and the Law in a state of conflict and yet reconciled: pure motion struggling against and yet reconciled with the Spirit: active force meeting and overcoming and yet not overcoming inertia. It is the conjunction of the two which makes form. And since the two must always meet under fresh conditions, form must always be different. Each work of art has its own form, which has no relation to any other form. When a young painter studies an old master, he studies, not the form, that is an abstraction which does not exist: he studies maybe the method of the old great artist: but he studies chiefly to understand how the old great artist suffered in himself the conflict of Love and Law, and brought them to a reconciliation. Apart from artistic method, it is not Art that the young man is studying, but the State of Soul of the great old artist, so that he, the young artist, may understand his own soul and gain a reconciliation between the aspiration and the resistant.

It is most wonderful in poetry, this sense of conflict contained within a reconciliation:

> Hail to thee, blithe Spirit!
> Bird thou never wert,
> That from Heaven, or near it,
> Pourest thy full heart
> In profuse strains of unpremeditated art.*

Shelley wishes to say, the skylark is a pure, untrammelled spirit, a pure motion. But the very 'Bird thou never wert' admits that the skylark *is* in very fact a bird, a concrete, momentary thing. If the line ran, 'Bird thou never art', that would spoil it all. Shelley wishes to say, the song is poured out of heaven: but 'or near it', he admits. There is the perfect relation between heaven and earth. And the last line is the tumbling sound of a lark's singing, the real Two-in-One.

The very adherence to rhyme and regular rhythm is a concession to the Law, a concession to the body, to the being and requirements of the body. They are an admission of the living, positive inertia which is the other half of life, other than the pure will to motion. In this consummation, they are the resistance and response of the Bride in the arms of the Bridegroom. And according as the Bride and Bridegroom come closer together, so is the response and resistance more fine, indistinguishable, so much the more, in this act of consummation, is the movement that of Two-in-One, indistinguishable each from the other, and not the movement of two brought together clumsily.

So that in Swinburne, where almost all is concession to the body, so that the poetry becomes almost a sensation and not an experience or a consummation, justifying Spinoza's 'Amor est titillatio, concomitante idea causae externae',* we find continual adherence to the body, to the Rose, to the Flesh, the physical in everything, in the sea, in the marshes; there is an overbalance in the favour of Supreme Law; Love is not Love, but passion, part of the Law; there is no Love, there is only Supreme Law. And the poet sings the Supreme Law to gain rebalance in himself, for he hovers always on the edge of death, of Not-Being, he is always out of reach of the Law, bodiless, in the faintness of Love that has triumphed and denied the Law, in the dread of an over-developed, over-sensitive soul which exists always on the point of dissolution from the body.

But he is not divided against himself. It is the novelists and dramatists who have the hardest task in reconciling their metaphysic, their theory of being and knowing, with their living sense of being. Because a novel is a microcosm, and because man in viewing the universe must view it in the light of a theory, therefore every novel must have the background or the structural skeleton of some theory of being, some metaphysic. But the metaphysic must always subserve the artistic purpose beyond the artist's conscious aim. Otherwise the novel becomes a treatise.

And the danger is, that a man shall make himself a metaphysic to excuse or cover his own faults or failure. Indeed, a sense of fault or failure is the usual cause of a man's making himself a metaphysic, to justify himself.

Then, having made himself a metaphysic of self-justification, or a metaphysic of self-denial, the novelist proceeds to apply the world to this, instead of applying this to the world.

Tolstoi is a flagrant example of this. Probably because of profligacy in his youth, because he had disgusted himself in his own flesh, by excess or by prostitution, therefore Tolstoi, in his metaphysic, renounced the flesh altogether, later on, when he had tried and had failed to achieve complete marriage in the flesh. But above all things, Tolstoi was a child of the Law, he belonged to the Father. He had a marvellous sensuous understanding, and very little clarity of mind.

So that, in his metaphysic, he had to deny himself, his own being, in order to escape his own disgust of what he had done to himself, and to escape admission of his own failure.

Which made all the later part of his life a crying falsity and shame. Reading the reminiscences of Tolstoi, one can only feel shame at the way Tolstoi denied all that was great in him, with vehement cowardice. He degraded himself infinitely, he perjured himself far more than did Peter when he denied Christ. Peter repented.* But Tolstoi denied the Father, and propagated a great system of his recusancy, elaborating his own weakness, blaspheming his own strength. 'What difficulty is there in writing about how an officer fell in love with a married woman?' he used to say of his *Anna Karenina*; 'there's no difficulty in it, and, above all, no good in it.'*

Because he was mouthpiece to the Father in uttering the law of passion, he said there was no difficulty in it, because it came naturally to him. Christ might just as easily have said, there was no difficulty in the Parable of the Sower,* and no good in it, either, because it flowed out of him without effort.

And Thomas Hardy's metaphysic is something like Tolstoi's. 'There is no reconciliation between Love and the Law', says Hardy. 'The spirit of Love must always succumb before the blind, stupid, but overwhelming power of the Law.'

Already as early as *The Return of the Native* he has come to this theory, in order to explain his own sense of failure. But before that time, from the very start, he has had an overweening theoretic antagonism to the Law. 'That which is physical, of the body, is weak, despicable, bad', he said at the very start. He represented his fleshy heroes as villains, but very weak and maundering villains. At its worst, the Law is a weak, craven sensuality: at its best, it is a passive inertia. It is the gap in the armour, it is the hole in the foundation.

Such a metaphysic is almost silly. If it were not that man is much stronger in feeling than in thought, the Wessex novels would be sheer rubbish, as they are already in parts. *The Well-Beloved* is sheer rubbish, fatuity, as is a good deal of *The Dynasts* conception.

But it is not as a metaphysician that one must consider Hardy. He makes a poor show there. For nothing in his work is so pitiable as his clumsy efforts to push events into line with his theory of being, and to make calamity fall on those who represent the principle of Love. He does it exceedingly badly, and owing to this effort his form is execrable in the extreme.

His feeling, his instinct, his sensuous understanding is, however, apart from his metaphysic, very great and deep, deeper than that, perhaps, of any other English novelist. Putting aside his metaphysic, which must always obtrude when he thinks of people, and turning to the earth, to landscape, then he is true to himself.

Always he must start from the earth, from the great source of the Law, and his people move in his landscape almost insignificantly, somewhat like tame animals wandering in the wild. The earth is the manifestation of the Father, of the Creator, Who made us in the Law. God still speaks aloud in His Works, as to Job, so to Hardy, surpassing human conception and the human law. 'Dost thou know the balancings of the clouds, the wondrous works of him which is perfect in knowledge? How thy garments are warm, when he quieteth the earth by the south wind? Hast thou with him spread out the sky, which is strong?'

This is the true attitude of Hardy—'With God is terrible majesty.' The theory of knowledge, the metaphysic of the man, is much smaller than the man himself. So with Tolstoi.

'Knowest thou the time when the wild goats of the rock bring forth? Or canst thou mark when the hinds do calve? Canst thou number the months that they fulfil? Or knowest thou the time when they bring forth? They bow themselves, they bring forth their young ones, they cast out their sorrows. Their young ones are good in liking, they grow up with corn; they go forth, and return not unto them.'

There is a good deal of this in Hardy. But in Hardy there is more than the concept of Job, protesting his integrity. Job says in the end: 'Therefore have I uttered that I understood not; things too wonderful for me, which I knew not.

'I have heard of thee by hearing of the ear; but now mine eye seeth thee.

'Wherefore I abhor myself, and repent in dust and ashes.'*

But Jude ends where Job began, cursing the day and the services of his birth, and in so much cursing the act of the Lord, 'Who made him in the womb.'*

It is the same cry all through Hardy, this curse upon the birth in the flesh, and this unconscious adherence to the flesh. The instincts, the bodily passions are strong and sudden in all Hardy's men. They are too strong and sudden. They fling Jude into the arms of Arabella, years after he has known Sue, and against his own will.

For every man comprises male and female in his being, the male always struggling for predominance. A woman likewise consists in male and female, with female predominant.

And a man who is strongly male tends to deny, to refute the female in him. A real 'man' takes no heed for his body, which is the more female part of him. He considers himself only as an instrument, to be used in the service of some idea.

The true female, on the other hand, will eternally hold herself superior to any idea, will hold full life in the body to be the real happiness. The male exists in doing, the female in being. The male lives in the satisfaction of some purpose achieved, the female in the satisfaction of some purpose contained.

In Aeschylus, in the *Eumenides*, there is Apollo, Loxias,* the Sun God, the prophet, the male: there are the Erinyes, daughters of primeval Mother Night, representing here the female risen in retribution for some crime against the flesh; and there is Pallas, unbegotten daughter of Zeus, who is as the Holy Spirit in the Christian religion, the spirit of wisdom.

Orestes is bidden by the male god, Apollo, to avenge the murder of his father, Agamemnon, by his mother: that is, the male, murdered by the female, must be avenged by the male. But Orestes is child of his mother. He is in himself female. So that in himself the conscience, the madness, the violated part of his own self, his own body, drives him to the Furies. On the male side, he is right; on the female, wrong. But peace is given at last by Pallas, the Arbitrator, the spirit of wisdom.

And although Aeschylus in his consciousness makes the Furies hideous, and Apollo supreme, yet, in his own self and in very fact, he makes the Furies wonderful and noble, with their tremendous hymns, and makes Apollo a trivial, sixth-form braggart and ranter. Clytemnestra also, wherever she appears, is wonderful and noble. Her sin is the sin of pride: she was the first to be injured. Agamemnon is a feeble thing beside her.

So Aeschylus adheres still to the Law, to Right, to the Creator who created man in His Own Image,* and in His Law. What he has learned of Love, he does not yet quite believe.

Hardy has the same belief in the Law, but in conceipt of his own understanding, which cannot understand the Law, he says that the Law is nothing, a blind confusion.

And in conceipt of understanding, he deprecates and destroys both women and men who would represent the old primeval Law, the great Law of the Womb, the primeval Female principle. The Female shall not exist. Where it appears, it is a criminal tendency, to be stamped out.

This in Manston, Troy, Boldwood, Eustacia, Wildeve, Henchard, Tess, Jude, everybody. The women approved of are not Female in any real sense. They are passive subjects to the male, the re-echo from the male. As in the Christian religion, the Virgin worship is no real Female worship, but worship of the Female as she is passive and subjected to the male. Hence the sadness of Botticelli's Virgins.

Thus Tess sets out, not as any positive thing, containing all purpose, but as the acquiescent complement to the male. The female in her has become inert. Then Alec d'Urberville comes along, and possesses her. From the man who takes her Tess expects her own consummation, the singling out of herself, the addition of the male complement. She is of an old line, and has the aristocratic quality of respect for the other being. She does not see the other person as an extension of herself, existing in a universe of which she is the centre and pivot. She knows that other people are outside her. Therein she is an aristocrat. And out of this attitude to the other person came her passivity. It is not the same as the passive quality in the other little heroines, such as the girl in *The Woodlanders*, who is passive because she is small.

Tess is passive out of self-acceptance, a true aristocratic quality, amounting almost to self-indifference. She knows she is herself incontrovertibly, and she knows that other people are not herself. This is a very rare quality, even in a woman. And in a civilization so unequal, it is almost a weakness.

Tess never tries to alter or to change anybody, neither to alter nor to change nor to divert. What another person decides, that is his decision. She respects utterly the other's right to be. She is herself always.

But the others do not respect her right to be. Alec d'Urberville sees her as the embodied fulfilment of his own desire: something, that is, belonging to him. She cannot, in his conception, exist apart from him nor have any being apart from his being. For she is the embodiment of his desire.

This is very natural and common in men, this attitude to the world. But in Alec d'Urberville it applies only to the woman of his desire. He cares only for her. Such a man adheres to the female like a parasite.

It is a male quality to resolve a purpose to its fulfilment. It is the male quality, to seek the motive power in the female, and to convey this to a fulfilment; to receive some impulse into his senses, and to transmit it into expression.

Alec d'Urberville does not do this. He is male enough, in his way; but only physically male. He is constitutionally an enemy of the principle of self-subordination, which principle is inherent in every man. It is this principle which makes a man, a true male, see his job through, at no matter what cost. A man is strictly only himself when he is fulfilling some purpose he has conceived: so that the principle is not of self-subordination, but of continuity, of development. Only when insisted on, as in Christianity, does it become self-sacrifice. And this resistance to self-sacrifice on Alec d'Urberville's part does not make him an individualist, an egoist, but rather a non-individual, an incomplete, almost a fragmentary thing.

There seems to be in d'Urberville an inherent antagonism to any progression in himself. Yet he seeks with all his power for the source of stimulus in woman. He takes the deep impulse from the female. In this he is exceptional. No ordinary man could really have betrayed Tess. Even if she had had an illegitimate child to another man, to Angel Clare, for example, it would not have shattered her as did her connexion with Alec d'Urberville. For Alec d'Urberville could reach some of the real sources of the female in a woman, and draw from them. Troy could also do this. And, as a woman instinctively knows, such men are rare. Therefore they have a power over a woman. They draw from the depth of her being.

And what they draw, they betray. With a natural male, what he draws from the source of the female, the impulse he receives from the source he transmits through his own being into utterance, motion, action, expression. But Troy and Alec d'Urberville, what they received they knew only as gratification in the senses; some perverse will prevented them from submitting to it, from becoming instrumental to it.

Which was why Tess was shattered by Alec d'Urberville, and why she murdered him in the end. The murder is badly done, altogether the book is botched, owing to the way of thinking in the author, owing to the weak yet obstinate theory of being. Nevertheless, the murder is true, the whole book is true, in its conception.

Angel Clare has the very opposite qualities to those of Alec d'Urberville. To the latter, the female in himself is the only part of himself he will acknowledge: the body, the senses, that which he shares with the female, which the female shares with him. To Angel Clare, the female in himself is detestable, the body, the senses, that which he will share with a woman, is held degraded. What he wants really is to receive the female impulse other than through the body. But his thinking has made him criticize Christianity, his deeper instinct has forbidden him to deny his body any further, a deadlock in his own being, which denies him any purpose, so that he must take to hand, labour out of sheer impotence to resolve himself, drives him unwillingly to woman. But he must see her only as the Female Principle, he cannot bear to see her as the Woman in the Body. Her he thinks degraded. To marry her, to have a physical marriage with her, he must overcome all his ascetic revulsion, he must, in his own mind, put off his own divinity, his pure maleness, his singleness, his pure completeness, and descend to the heated welter of the flesh. It is objectionable to him. Yet his body, his life, is too strong for him.

Who is he, that he shall be pure male, and deny the existence of the female? This is the question the Creator asks of him. Is then the male the exclusive whole of life?—is he even the higher or supreme part of life? Angel Clare thinks so: as Christ thought.

Yet it is not so, as even Angel Clare must find out. Life, that is Two-in-One, Male and Female. Nor is either part greater than the other.

It is not Angel Clare's fault that he cannot come to Tess when he finds that she has, in his words, been defiled. It is the result of generations of ultra-Christian training, which had left in him an inherent aversion to the female, and to all in himself which pertained to the female. What he, in his Christian sense, conceived of as Woman, was only the servant and attendant and administering spirit to the male. He had no idea that there was such a thing as positive Woman, as the Female, another great living Principle counterbalancing his own male principle. He conceived of the world as consisting of the One, the Male Principle.

Which conception was already gendered in Botticelli, whence the melancholy of the Virgin. Which conception reached its fullest in Turner's* pictures, which were utterly bodiless; and also in the great scientists or thinkers of the last generation, even Darwin and Spencer and Huxley.* For these last conceived of evolution, of one spirit or principle starting at the far end of time, and lonelily traversing Time. But there is not one principle, there are two, travelling always to meet, each step of each one lessening the distance between the two of them. And Space, which so frightened Herbert Spencer, is as a Bride to us. And the cry of Man does not ring out into the Void. It rings out to Woman, whom we know not.

This Tess knew, unconsciously. An aristocrat she was, developed through generations to the belief in her own self-establishment. She could help, but she could not be helped. She could give, but she could not receive. She could attend to the wants of the other person, but no other person, save another aristocrat—and there is scarcely such a thing as another aristocrat—could attend to her wants, her deepest wants.

So it is the aristocrat alone who has any real and vital sense of 'the neighbour', of the other person; who has the habit of submerging himself, putting himself entirely away before the other person: because he expects to receive nothing from the other person. So that now he has lost much of his initiative force, and exists almost isolated, detached, and without the surging ego of the ordinary man, because he has controlled his nature according to the other man, to exclude him.

And Tess, despising herself in the flesh, despising the deep Female she was, because Alec d'Urberville had betrayed her very source, loved Angel Clare, who also despised and hated the flesh. She did not hate d'Urberville. What a man did, he did, and if he did it to her, it was her look-out. She did not conceive of him as having any human duty towards her.

The same with Angel Clare as with Alec d'Urberville. She was very grateful to him for saving her from her despair of contamination, and from her bewildered isolation. But when he accused her, she could not plead or answer. For she had no right to his goodness. She stood alone.

The female was strong in her. She was herself. But she was out of place, utterly out of her element and her times. Hence her utter bewilderment. This is the reason why she was so overcome. She was outwearied from the start, in her spirit. For it is only by receiving from all our fellows that we are kept fresh and vital. Tess was herself, female, intrinsically a woman.

The female in her was indomitable, unchangeable, she was utterly constant to herself. But she was, by long breeding, intact from mankind. Though Alec d'Urberville was of no kin to her, yet, in the book, he has always a quality of kinship. It was as if only a kinsman, an aristocrat, could approach her. And this to her undoing. Angel Clare would never have reached her. She would have abandoned herself to him, but he would never have reached her. It needed a physical aristocrat. She would have lived with her husband, Clare, in a state of abandon to him, like a coma. Alec d'Urberville forced her to realize him, and to realize herself. He came close to her, as Clare could never have done. So she murdered him. For she was herself.

And just as the aristocratic principle had isolated Tess, it had isolated Alec d'Urberville. For though Hardy consciously made the young betrayer a plebeian and an impostor, unconsciously, with the supreme justice of the artist, he made him the same as de Stancy, a true aristocrat, or as Fitzpiers, or Troy. He did not give him the tiredness, the touch of exhaustion necessary, in Hardy's mind, to an aristocrat. But he gave him the intrinsic qualities.

With the men as with the women of old descent: they have nothing to do with mankind in general, they are exceedingly personal. For many generations they have been accustomed to regard their own desires as their own supreme laws. They have not been bound by the conventional morality: this they have transcended, being a code unto themselves. The other person has been always present to their imagination, in the spectacular sense. He has always existed to them. But he has always existed as something other than themselves.

Hence the inevitable isolation, detachment of the aristocrat. His one aim, during centuries, has been to keep himself detached. At last he finds himself, by his very nature, cut off.

Then either he must go his own way, or he must struggle towards reunion with the mass of mankind. Either he must be an incomplete individualist, like de Stancy, or like the famous Russian nobles, he must become a wild humanitarian and reformer.

For as all the governing power has gradually been taken from the nobleman, and as, by tradition, by inherent inclination, he does not occupy himself with profession other than government, how shall he use that power which is in him and which comes into him?

He is, by virtue of breed and long training, a perfect instrument. He knows, as every pure-bred thing knows, that his root and source is in his female. He seeks the motive power in the woman. And, having taken it, has nothing to do with it, can find, in this democratic, plebeian age, no means by which to transfer it into action, expression, utterance. So there is a continual gnawing of unsatisfation, a constant seeking of another woman, still another woman. For each time the impulse comes fresh, everything seems all right.

It may be, also, that in the aristocrat a certain weariness makes him purposeless, vicious, like a form of death. But that is not necessary. One feels that in Manston, and Troy, and Fitzpiers, and Alec d'Urberville, there is good stuff gone wrong. Just as in Angel Clare, there is good stuff gone wrong in the other direction.

There can never be one extreme of wrong, without the other extreme. If there had never been the extravagant Puritan idea, that the Female Principle was to be denied, cast out by man from his soul, that only the Male Principle, of Abstraction, of Good, of Public Good, of the Community, embodied in 'Thou shalt love thy neighbour as thyself',* really existed, there would never have been produced the extreme Cavalier type, which says that only the Female Principle endures in man, that all the Abstraction, the Good, the Public Elevation, the Community, was a grovelling cowardice, and that man lived by enjoyment, through his senses, enjoyment which ended in his senses. Or perhaps better, if the extreme Cavalier type had never been produced, we should not have had the Puritan, the extreme correction.

The one extreme produces the other. It is inevitable for Angel Clare and for Alec d'Urberville mutually to destroy the woman they both loved. Each does her the extreme of wrong, so she is destroyed.

The book is handled with very uncertain skill, botched and bungled. But it contains the elements of the greatest tragedy: Alec d'Urberville, who has killed the male in himself, as Clytemnestra symbolically for Orestes killed Agamemnon; Angel Clare, who has killed the female in himself, as Orestes killed Clytemnestra: and Tess, the Woman, the Life, destroyed by a mechanical fate, in the communal law.

There is no reconciliation. Tess, Angel Clare, Alec d'Urberville, they are all as good as dead. For Angel Clare, though still apparently alive, is in reality no more than a mouth, a piece of paper, like Clym left preaching.

There is no reconciliation, only death. And so Hardy really states his case, which is not his consciously stated metaphysic, by any means, but a statement how man has gone wrong and brought death on himself: how man has violated the Law, how he has supererogated himself, gone so far in his male conceit as to supersede the Creator, and win death as a reward. Indeed, the works of supererogation of our male assiduity help us to a better salvation.

Jude is only Tess turned round about. Instead of the heroine containing the two principles, male and female, at strife within her one being, it is Jude who contains them both, whilst the two women with him take the place of the two men to Tess. Arabella is Alec d'Urberville, Sue is Angel Clare. These represent the same pair of principles.

But, first, let it be said again that Hardy is a bad artist. Because he must condemn Alec d'Urberville, according to his own personal creed, therefore he shows him a vulgar intriguer of coarse lasses, and as ridiculous convert to evangelism. But Alec d'Urberville, by the artist's account, is neither of these. It is, in actual life, a rare man who seeks and seeks among women for one of such character and intrinsic female being as Tess. The ordinary sensualist avoids such characters. They implicate him too deeply. An ordinary sensualist would have been much too common, much too afraid, to turn to Tess. In a way, d'Urberville was her mate. And his subsequent passion for her is in its way noble enough. But whatever his passion, as a male, he must be a betrayer, even if he had been the most faithful husband on earth. He betrayed the female in a woman, by taking her, and by responding with no male impulse from himself. He roused her, but never satisfied her. He could never satisfy her. It was like a soul-disease in him: he was, in the strict though not the technical sense, impotent. But he must have wanted, later on, not to be so. But he could not help himself. He was spiritually impotent in love.

Arabella was the same. She, like d'Urberville, was converted by an evangelical preacher. It is significant in both of them. They were not just shallow, as Hardy would have made them out.

He is, however, more contemptuous in his personal attitude to the woman than to the man. He insists that she is a pig killer's daughter; he insists that she drag Jude into pig-killing; he lays stress on her false tail of hair. That is not the point at all. This is only Hardy's bad art. He himself, as an artist, manages in the whole picture of Arabella almost to make insignificant in her these pig-sticking, false-hair crudities. But he must have his personal revenge on her for her coarseness, which offends him, because he is something of an Angel Clare.

The pig-sticking and so forth are not so important in the real picture. As for the false tail of hair, few women dared have been so open and natural about it. Few women, indeed, dared have made Jude marry them. It may have been a case with Arabella of 'fools rush in'.* But she was not such a fool. And her motives are explained in the book. Life is not, in the actual, such a simple affair of getting a fellow and getting married. It is, even for Arabella, an affair on which she places her all. No barmaid marries anybody, the first man she can lay hands on. She cannot. It must be a personal thing to her. And no ordinary woman would want Jude. Moreover, no ordinary woman could have laid her hands on Jude.

It is an absurd fallacy this, that a small man wants a woman bigger and finer than he is himself. A man is as big as his real desires. Let a man, seeing with his eyes a woman of force and being, want her for his own, then that man is intrinsically an equal of that woman. And the same with a woman.

A coarse, shallow woman does not want to marry a sensitive, deep-feeling man. She feels no desire for him, she is not drawn to him, but repelled, knowing he will contemn her. She wants a man to correspond to herself: that is, if she is a young woman looking for a mate, as Arabella was.

What an old, jaded, yet still unsatisfied woman or man wants is another matter. Yet not even one of these will take a young creature of real character, superior in force. Instinct and fear prevent it.

Arabella was, under all her disguise of pig-fat and false hair, and vulgar speech, in character somewhat an aristocrat. She was, like Eustacia, amazingly lawless, even splendidly so. She believed in herself and she was not altered by any outside opinion of herself. Her fault was pride. She thought herself the centre of life, that all which existed belonged to her in so far as she wanted it.

In this she was something like Job. His attitude was 'I am strong and rich, and, also, I am a good man.' He gave out of his own sense of bounty, and felt no indebtedness. Arabella was almost the same. She felt also strong and abundant, arrogant in her hold on life. She needed a complement; and the nearest thing to her satisfaction was Jude. For as she, intrinsically, was a strong female, by far overpowering her Annies and her friends, so was he a strong male.

The difference between them was not so much a difference of quality, or degree, as a difference of form. Jude, like Tess, wanted full consummation. Arabella, like Alec d'Urberville, had that in her which resisted full consummation, wanted only to enjoy herself in contact with the male. She would have no transmission.

There are two attitudes to love. A man in love with a woman says either: 'I, the man, the male, am the supreme, I am the one, and the woman is administered unto me, and this is her highest function, to be administered unto me.' This was the conscious attitude of the Greeks. But their unconscious attitude was the reverse: they were in truth afraid of the female principle, their vaunt was empty, they went in deep, inner dread of her. So did the Jews, so do the Italians. But after the Renaissance, there was a change. Then began conscious Woman-reverence, and a lack of instinctive reverence, rather only an instinctive pity. It is according to the balance between the Male and Female principles.

The other attitude of a man in love, besides this of 'she is administered unto my maleness', is, 'She is the unknown, the undiscovered, into which I plunge to discovery, losing myself.'

And what we call real love has always this latter attitude.

The first attitude, which belongs to passion, makes a man feel proud, splendid. It is a powerful stimulant to him, the female administered to him. He feels full of blood, he walks the earth like a Lord. And it is to this state Nietzsche aspires in his *Wille zur Macht*.* It is this the passionate nations crave.

And under all this there is, naturally, the sense of fear, transition, and the sadness of mortality. For, the female being herself an independent force, may she not withdraw, and leave a man empty, like ash, as one sees a Jew or an Italian so often?

This first attitude, too, of male pride receiving the female administration may, and often does, contain the corresponding intense fear and reverence of the female, as of the unknown. So that, starting from the male assertion, there came in the old days the full consummation; as often there comes the full consummation now.

But not always. The man may retain all the while the sense of himself, the primary male, receiving gratification. This constant reaction upon himself at length dulls his senses and his sensibility, and makes him mechanical, automatic. He grows gradually incapable of receiving any gratification from the female, and becomes a *roué*, only automatically alive, and frantic with the knowledge thereof.

It is the tendency of the Parisian—or has been—to take this attitude to love, and to intercourse. The woman knows herself all the while as the primary female receiving administration of the male. So she becomes hard and external, and inwardly jaded, tired out. It is the tendency of English women to take this attitude also. And it is this attitude of love, more than anything else, which devitalizes a race, and makes it barren.

It is an attitude natural enough to start with. Every young man must think that it is the highest honour he can do to a woman, to receive from her her female administration to his male being, whilst he meanwhile gives her the gratification of himself. But intimacy usually corrects this, love, or use, or marriage: a married man ceases to think of himself as the primary male: hence often his dullness. Unfortunately, he also fails in many cases to realize the gladness of a man in contact with the unknown in the female, which gives him a sense of richness and oneness with all life, as if, by being part of life, he were infinitely rich. Which is different from the sense of power, of dominating life. The *Wille zur Macht* is a spurious feeling.

For a man who dares to look upon, and to venture within the unknown of the female, losing himself, like a man who gives himself to the sea, or a man who enters a primeval, virgin forest, feels, when he returns, the utmost gladness of singing. This is certainly the gladness of a male bird in his singing, the amazing joy of return from the adventure into the unknown, rich with addition to his soul, rich with the knowledge of the utterly illimitable depth and breadth of the unknown; the ever-yielding extent of the unacquired, the unattained; the inexhaustible riches lain under unknown skies over unknown seas, all the magnificence that *is*, and yet which is unknown to any of us. And the knowledge of the reality with which it awaits me, the male, the knowledge of the calling and struggling of all the unknown, illimitable Female towards me, unembraced as yet, towards those men who will endlessly follow me, who will endlessly struggle after me, beyond me, further into this calling, unrealized vastness, nearer to the outstretched, eager, advancing unknown in the woman.

It is for this sense of All the magnificence that is unknown to me, of All that which stretches forth arms and breast to the Inexhaustible Embrace of all the ages, towards me, whose arms are outstretched, for this moment's embrace which gives me the inkling of the Inexhaustible Embrace that every man must and does yearn. And whether he be a *roué*, and vicious, or young and virgin, this is the bottom of every man's desire, for the embrace, for the advancing into the unknown, for the landing on the shore of the undiscovered half of the world, where the wealth of the female lies before us.

What is true of men is so of women. If we turn our faces west, towards nightfall and the unknown within the dark embrace of a wife, they turn their faces east, towards the sunrise and the brilliant, bewildering, active embrace of a husband. And as we are dazed with the unknown in her, so is she dazed with the unknown in us. It is so. And we throw up our joy to heaven like towers and spires and fountains and leaping flowers, so glad we are.

But always, we are divided within ourselves. Is it not that I am wonderful? Is it not a gratification for me when a stranger shall land on my shores and enjoy what he finds there? Shall I not also enjoy it? Shall I not enjoy the strange motion of the stranger, like a pleasant sensation of silk and warmth against me, stirring unknown fibres? Shall I not take this enjoyment without venturing out in dangerous waters, losing myself, perhaps destroying myself seeking the unknown? Shall I not stay at home, and by feeling the swift, soft airs blow out of the unknown upon my body, shall I not have rich pleasure of myself?

And, because they were afraid of the unknown, and because they wanted to retain the full-veined gratification of self-pleasure, men have kept their women tightly in bondage. But when the men were no longer afraid of the unknown, when they deemed it exhausted, they said, 'There are no women; there are only daughters of men'*—as we say now, as the Greeks tried to say. Hence the 'Virgin' conception of woman, the passionless, passive conception, progressing from Fielding's Amelia to Dickens's Agnes,* and on to Hardy's Sue.

Whereas Arabella in *Jude the Obscure* has what one might call the selfish instinct for love, Jude himself has the other, the unselfish. She sees in him a male who can gratify her. She takes him, and is gratified by him. Which makes a man of him. He becomes a grown, independent man in the arms of Arabella, conscious of having met, and satisfied, the female demand in him. This makes a man of any youth. He is proven unto himself as a male being, initiated into the freedom of life.

But Arabella refused his purpose. She refused to combine with him in one purpose. Just like Alec d'Urberville, she had from the outset an antagonism to the submission to any change in herself, to any development. She had the will to remain where she was, static, and to receive and exhaust all impulse she received from the male, in her senses. Whereas in a normal woman, impulse received from the male drives her on to a sense of joy and wonder and glad freedom in touch with the unknown of which she is made aware, so that she exists on the edge of the unknown half in rapture. Which is the state the writers wish to portray in 'Amelia' and 'Agnes', but particularly in the former; which Reynolds* wishes to portray in his pictures of women.

To all this Arabella was antagonistic. It seems like a perversion in her, as if she played havoc with the stuff she was made of, as Alec d'Urberville did. Nevertheless she remained always unswervable female, she never truckled to the male idea, but was self-responsible, without fear. It is easier to imagine such a woman, out of one's desires, than to find her in real life. For, where a half-criminal type, a reckless, dare-devil type resembling her, may be found on the outskirts of society, yet these are not Arabella. Which criminal type, or reckless, low woman, would want to marry Jude? Arabella wanted Jude. And it is evident she was not too coarse for him, since she made no show of refinement from the first. The female in her, reckless and unconstrained, was strong enough to draw him after her, as her male, right to the end. Which other woman could have done this? At least let acknowledgment be made to her great female force of character. Her coarseness seems to me exaggerated to make the moralist's case good against her.

Jude could never hate her. She did a great deal for the true making of him, for making him a grown man. She gave him to himself.

And there was danger at the outset that he should never become a man, but that he should remain incorporeal, smothered out under his idea of learning. He was somewhat in Angel Clare's position. Not that generations of particular training had made him almost rigid and paralysed to the female: but that his whole passion was concentrated away from woman to reinforce in him the male impulse towards extending the consciousness. His family was a difficult family to marry. And this because, whilst the men were physically vital, with a passion towards the female from which no moral training had restrained them, like a plant tied to a stick and diverted, they had at the same time an inherent complete contempt of the female, valuing only that which was male. So that they were strongly divided against themselves, with no external hold, such as a moral system, to grip to.

It would have been possible for Jude, monkish, passionate, medieval, belonging to woman yet striving away from her, refusing to know her, to have gone on denying one side of his nature, adhering to his idea of learning, till he had stultified the physical impulse of his being and perverted it entirely. Arabella brought him to himself, gave him himself, made him free, sound as a physical male.

That she would not, or could not, combine her life with him for the fulfilment of a purpose was their misfortune. But at any rate, his purpose of becoming an Oxford don was a cut-and-dried purpose which had no connexion with his living body, and for which probably no woman could have united with him.

No doubt Arabella hated his books, and hated his whole attitude to study. What had he, a passionate, emotional nature, to do with learning for learning's sake, with mere academics? Any woman must know it was ridiculous. But he persisted with the tenacity of all perverseness. And she, in this something of an aristocrat, like Tess, feeling that she had no right to him, no right to receive anything from him, except his sex, in which she felt she gave and did not receive, for she conceived of herself as the primary female, as that which, in taking the male, conferred on him his greatest boon, she left him alone. Her attitude was, that he would find all he desired in coming to her. She was occupied with herself. It was not that she wanted *him*. She wanted to have the sensation of herself in contact with him. His being she refused. She allowed only her own being.

Therefore she scarcely troubled him, when he earned little money and took no notice of her. He did not refuse to take notice of her because he hated her, or was deceived by her, or disappointed in her. He was not. He refused to consider her seriously because he adhered with all his pertinacity to the idea of study, from which he excluded her.

Which she saw and knew, and allowed. She would not force him to notice her, or to consider her seriously. She would compel him to nothing. She had had a certain satisfaction of him, which would be no more if she stayed for ever. For she was non-developing. When she knew him in her senses she knew the end of him, as far as she was concerned. That was all.

So she just went her way. He did not blame her. He scarcely missed her. He returned to his books.

Really, he had lost nothing by his marriage with Arabella: neither innocence nor belief nor hope. He had indeed gained his manhood. She left him the stronger and completer.

And now he would concentrate all on his male idea, of arresting himself, of becoming himself a non-developing quality, an academic mechanism. That was his obsession. That was his craving: to have nothing to do with his own life. This was the same as Tess when she turned to Angel Clare. She wanted life merely in the secondary, outside form, in the consciousness.

It was another form of the disease, or decay of old family, which possessed Alec d'Urberville; a different form, but closely related. D'Urberville wanted to arrest all his activity in his senses. Jude Fawley wanted to arrest all his activity in his mind. Each of them wanted to become an impersonal force working automatically. Each of them wanted to deny, or escape the responsibility and trouble of living as a complete person, a full individual.

And neither was able to bring it off. Jude's real desire was, not to live in the body. He wanted to exist only in his mentality. He was as if bored, or *blasé*, in the body, just like Tess. This seems to be the result of coming of an old family, that had been long conscious, long self-conscious, specialized, separate, exhausted.

This drove him to Sue. She was his kinswoman, as d'Urberville was kinsman to Tess. She was like himself in her being and her desire. Like Jude, she wanted to live partially, in the consciousness, in the mind only. She wanted no experience in the senses, she wished only to know.

She belonged, with Tess, to the old woman-type of witch or prophetess, which adhered to the male principle, and destroyed the female. But in the true prophetess, in Cassandra,* for example, the denial of the female cost a strong and almost maddening effect. But in Sue it was done before she was born.

She was born with the vital female atrophied in her: she was almost male. Her *will* was male. It was wrong for Jude to take her physically, it was a violation of her. She was not the virgin type, but the witch type, which has no sex. Why should she be forced into intercourse that was not natural to her?

It was not natural for her to have children. It is inevitable that her children die. It is not natural for Tess nor for Angel Clare to have children, nor for Arabella nor for Alec d'Urberville. Because none of these wished to give of themselves to the lover, none of them wished to mate: they only wanted their own experience. For Jude alone it was natural to have children, and this in spite of himself.

Sue wished to identify herself utterly with the male principle. That which was female in her she wanted to consume within the male force, to consume it in the fire of understanding, of giving utterance. Whereas an ordinary woman knows that she *contains* all understanding, that she is the unutterable which man must for ever continue to try to utter, Sue felt that all must be uttered, must be given to the male, that, in truth, only Male existed, that everything was the Word, and the Word was everything.

Sue is the production of the long selection by man of the woman in whom the female is subordinated to the male principle. A long line of Amelias and Agneses, those women who submitted to the man-idea, flattered the man, and bored him, the Gretchens and the Turgenev heroines,* those who have betrayed the female and who therefore only seem to exist to be betrayed by their men, these have produced at length a Sue, the pure thing. And as soon as she is produced she is execrated.

What Cassandra and Aspasia* became to the Greeks, Sue has become to the northern civilization. But the Greeks never pitied Woman. They did not show her that highest impertinence—not even Euripides.*

But Sue is scarcely a woman at all, though she is feminine enough. Cassandra submitted to Apollo, and gave him the Word of affiance, brought forth prophecy to him, not children. She received the embrace of the spirit, He breathed His Grace upon her: and she conceived and brought forth a prophecy. It was still a marriage. Not the marriage of the Virgin with the Spirit, but the marriage of the female spirit with the male spirit, bodiless.

With Sue, however, the marriage was no marriage, but a sub-mission, a service, a slavery. Her female spirit did not wed with the male spirit: she could not prophesy. Her spirit submitted to the male spirit, owned the priority of the male spirit, wished to become the male spirit. That which was female in her, resistant, gave her only her critical faculty. When she sought out the physical quality in the Greeks, that was her effort to make even the unknowable physique a part of knowledge, to contain the body within the mind.

One of the supremest products of our civilization is Sue, and a product that well frightens us. It is quite natural that, with all her mental alertness, she married Phillotson without ever considering the physical quality of marriage. Deep instinct made her avoid the consideration. And the duality of her nature made her extremely liable to self-destruction. The suppressed, atrophied female in her, like a potent fury, was always there, suggesting to her to make the fatal mistake. She contained always the rarest, most deadly anarchy in her own being.

It needed that she should have some place in society where the clarity of her mental being, which was in itself a form of death, could shine out without attracting any desire for her body. She needed a refinement on Angel Clare. For she herself was a more specialized, more highly civilized product on the female side, than Angel Clare on the male. Yet the atrophied female in her would still want the bodily male.

She attracted to herself Jude. His experience with Arabella had for the time being diverted his attention altogether from the female. His attitude was that of service to the pure male spirit. But the physical male in him, that which knew and belonged to the female, was potent, and roused the female in Sue as much as she wanted it roused, so much that it was a stimulant to her, making her mind the brighter.

It was a cruelly difficult position. She must, by the constitution of her nature, remain quite physically intact, for the female was atrophied in her, to the enlargement of the male activity. Yet she wanted some quickening for this atrophied female. She wanted even kisses. That the new rousing might give her a sense of life. But she could only *live* in the mind.

Then, where could she find a man who would be able to feed her with his male vitality, through kisses, proximity, without demanding the female return? For she was such that she could only receive quickening from a strong male, for she was herself no small thing. Could she then find a man, a strong, passionate male, who would devote himself entirely to the production of the mind in her, to the production of male activity, or of female activity critical to the male?

She could only receive the highest stimulus, which she must inevitably seek, from a man who put her in constant jeopardy. Her essentiality rested upon her remaining intact. Any suggestion of the physical was utter confusion to her. Her principle was the ultra-Christian principle—of living entirely according to the Spirit, to the One, male spirit, which knows, and utters, and shines, but exists beyond feeling, beyond joy or sorrow, or pain, exists only in Knowing. In tune with this, she was herself. Let her, however, be turned under the influence of the other dark, silent, strong principle, of the female, and she would break like a fine instrument under discord.

Yet, to live at all in tune with the male spirit, she must receive the male stimulus from a man. Otherwise she was as an instrument without a player. She must feel the hands of a man upon her, she must be infused with his male vitality, or she was not alive.

Here then was her difficulty: to find a man whose vitality could infuse her and make her live, and who would not, at the same time, demand of her a return, the return of the female impulse into him. What man could receive this drainage, receiving nothing back again? He must either die, or revolt.

One man had died. She knew it well enough. She knew her own fatality. She knew she drained the vital, male stimulus out of a man, producing in him only knowledge of the mind, only mental clarity: which man must always strive to attain, but which is not life in him, rather the product of life.

Just as Alec d'Urberville, on the other hand, drained the female vitality out of a woman, and gave her only sensation, only experience in the senses, a sense of herself, nothing to the soul or spirit, thereby exhausting her.

Now Jude, after Arabella, and following his own *idée fixe*, hunted this mental clarity, this knowing, above all. What he contained in himself, of male and female impulse, he wanted to bring forth, to draw into his mind, to resolve into understanding, as a plant resolves that which it contains into flower.

This Sue could do for him. By creating a vacuum, she could cause the vivid flow which clarified him. By rousing him, by drawing from him his turgid vitality, made thick and heavy and physical with Arabella, she could bring into consciousness that which he contained. For he was heavy and full of unrealized life, clogged with untransmuted knowledge, with accretion of his senses. His whole life had been till now an indrawing, ingestion. Arabella had been a vital experience for him, received into his blood. And how was he to bring out all this fulness into knowledge or utterance? For all the time he was being roused to new physical desire, new life-experience, new sense-enrichening, and he could not perform his male function of transmitting this into expression, or action. The particular form his flowering should take, he could not find. So he hunted and studied, to find the call, the appeal which should call out of him that which was in him.

And great was his transport when the appeal came from Sue. She wanted, at first, only his words. That of him which could come to her through speech, through his consciousness, her mind, like a bottomless gulf, cried out for. She wanted satisfaction through the mind, and cried out for him to satisfy her through the mind.

Great, then, was his joy at giving himself out to her. He gave, for it was more blessed to give than to receive.* He gave, and she received some satisfaction. But where she was not satisfied, there he must try still to satisfy her. He struggled to bring it all forth. She was, as himself, asking himself what he was. And he strove to answer, in a transport.

And he answered in a great measure. He singled himself out from the old matrix of the accepted idea, he produced an individual flower of his own.

It was for this he loved Sue. She did for him quickly what he would have done for himself slowly, through study. By patient, diligent study, he would have used up the surplus of that turgid energy in him, and would, by long contact with old truth, have arrived at the form of truth which was in him. What he indeed wanted to get from study was, not a store of learning, nor the vanity of education, a sort of superiority of educational wealth, though this also gave him pleasure. He wanted, through familiarity with the true thinkers and poets, particularly with the classic and theological thinkers, because of their comparative sensuousness, to find conscious expression for that which he held in his blood. And to do this, it was necessary for him to resolve and to reduce his blood, to overcome the female sensuousness in himself, to transmute his sensuous being into another state, a state of clarity, of consciousness. Slowly, laboriously, struggling with the Greek and the Latin, he would have burned down his thick blood as fuel, and have come to the true light of himself.

This Sue did for him. In marriage, each party fulfils a dual function with regard to the other: exhaustive and enrichening. The female at the same time exhausts and invigorates the male, the male at the same time exhausts and invigorates the female. The exhaustion and invigoration are both temporary and relative. The male, making the effort to penetrate into the female, exhausts himself and invigorates her. But that which, at the end, he discovers and carries off from her, some seed of being, enrichens him and exhausts her. Arabella, in taking Jude, accepted very little from him. She absorbed very little of his strength and vitality into herself. For she only wanted to be aware of herself in contact with him, she did not want him to penetrate into her very being, till he moved her to her very depths, till she loosened to him some of her very self for his enrichening. She was intrinsically impotent, as was Alec d'Urberville.

So that in her Jude went very little further in Knowledge, or in Self-Knowledge. He took only the first steps: of knowing himself sexually, as a sexual male. That is only the first, the first necessary, but rudimentary, step.

When he came to Sue, he found her physically impotent, but spiritually potent. That was what he wanted. Of Knowledge in the blood he had a rich enough store: more than he knew what to do with. He wished for the further step, of reduction, of essentializing into Knowledge. Which Sue gave to him.

So that his experience with Arabella, plus his first experience of trembling intimacy and incandescent realization with Sue made one complete marriage: that is, the two women added together made One Bride.

When Jude had exhausted his surplus self, in spiritual intimacy with Sue, when he had gained through her all the wonderful understanding she could evoke in him, when he was clarified to himself, then his marriage with Sue was over. Jude's marriage with Sue was over before he knew her physically. She had, physically, nothing to give him.

Which, in her deepest instinct, she knew. She made no mistake in marrying Phillotson. She acted according to the pure logic of her nature. Phillotson was a man who wanted no marriage whatsoever with the female. Sexually, he wanted her as an instrument through which he obtained relief, and some gratification: but, really, relief. Spiritually, he wanted her as a thing to be wondered over and delighted in, but quite separately from himself. He knew quite well he could never marry her. He was a human being as near to mechanical function as a human being can be. The whole process of digestion, masticating, swallowing, digesting, excretion, is a sort of super-mechanical process. And Phillotson was like this. He was an organ, a function-fulfilling organ, he had no separate existence. He could not create a single new movement or thought or expression. Everything he did was a repetition of what had been. All his study was a study of what had been. It was a mechanical, functional process. He was a true, if small, form of the *Savant*. He could understand only the functional laws of living, but these he understood honestly. He was true to himself, he was not overcome by any cant or sentimentalizing. So that in this he was splendid. But it is a cruel thing for a complete, or a spiritual, individuality to be submitted to a functional organism.

The Widow Edlin* said that there are some men no woman of any feeling could touch, and Phillotson was one of them. If the Widow knew this, why was Sue's instinct so short?

But Mrs Edlin was a full human being, creating life in a new form through her personality. She must have known Sue's deficiency. It was natural for Sue to read and to turn again to:

> Thou hast conquered, O pale Galilean!
> The world has grown grey from Thy breath.*

In her the pale Galilean had indeed triumphed. Her body was as insentient as hoar-frost. She knew well enough that she was not alive in the ordinary human sense. She did not, like an ordinary woman, receive all she knew through her senses, her instincts, but through her consciousness. The pale Galilean had a pure disciple in her: in her He was fulfilled. For the senses, the body, did not exist in her; she existed as a consciousness. And this is so much so, that she was almost an Apostate. She turned to look at Venus and Apollo. As if she could know either Venus or Apollo, save as ideas. Nor Venus nor Aphrodite had anything to do with her, but only Pallas* and Christ.

She was unhappy every moment of her life, poor Sue, with the knowledge of her own non-existence within life. She felt all the time the ghastly sickness of dissolution upon her, she was as a void unto herself.

So she married Phillotson, the only man she could, in reality, marry. To him she could be a wife: she could give him the sexual relief he wanted of her, and supply him with the transcendence which was a pleasure to him; it was hers to seal him with the seal which made an honourable human being of him. For he felt, deep within himself, something a reptile feels. And she was his guarantee, his crown.

Why does a snake horrify us, or even a newt? Why was Phillotson like a newt? What is it, in our life or in our feeling, to which a newt corresponds? Is it that life has the two sides, of growth and of decay, symbolized most acutely in our bodies by the semen and the excreta? Is it that the newt, the reptile, belong to the putrescent activity of life; the bird, the fish to the growth activity? Is it that the newt and the reptile are suggested to us through those sensations connected with excretion? And was Phillotson more or less connected with the decay activity of life? Was it his function to reorganize the life-excreta of the ages? At any rate, one can honour him, for he was true to himself.

Sue married Phillotson according to her true instinct. But being almost pure Christian, in the sense of having no physical life, she had turned to the Greeks, and with her mind was an Aphrodite-worshipper. In craving for the highest form of that which she lacked, she worshipped Aphrodite. There are two sets of Aphrodite-worshippers: daughters of Aphrodite and the almost neutral daughters of Mary of Bethany.* Sue was, oh, cruelly far from being a daughter of Aphrodite. She was the furthest alien from Aphrodite. She might excuse herself through her Venus Urania*—but it was hopeless.

Therefore, when she left Phillotson, in whose marriage she consummated her own crucifixion, to go to Jude, she was deserting the

God of her being for the God of her hopeless want. How much could she become a living, physical woman? But she would get away from Phillotson.

She went to Jude to continue the spiritual marriage, bodiless. That was all very well, if he had been satisfied. If he had been satisfied, they might have lived in this spiritual intimacy, without physical contact, for the rest of their lives, so strong was her true instinct for herself.

He, however, was not satisfied. He reached the point where he was clarified, where he had reduced from his blood into his consciousness all that was uncompounded before. He had become himself as far as he could, he had fulfilled himself. All that he had gathered in his youth, all that he had gathered from Arabella, was assimilated now, fused and transformed into one clear Jude.

Now he wants that which is necessary for him if he is to go on. He wants, at its lowest, the physical, sexual relief. For continually baulked sexual desire, or necessity, makes a man unable to live freely, scotches him, stultifies him. And where a man is roused to the fullest pitch, as Jude was roused by Sue, then the principal connexion becomes a necessity, if only for relief. Anything else is a violation.

Sue ran away to escape physical connexion with Phillotson, only to find herself in the arms of Jude. But Jude wanted of her more than Phillotson wanted. This was what terrified her to the bottom of her nature. Whereas Phillotson always only wanted sexual relief of her, Jude wanted the consummation of marriage. He wanted that deepest experience, that penetrating far into the unknown and undiscovered which lies in the body and blood of man and woman, during life. He wanted to receive from her the quickening, the primitive seed and impulse which should start him to a new birth. And for this he must go back deep into the primal, unshown, unknown life of the blood, the thick source-stream of life in her.

And she was terrified lest he should find her out, that it was wanting in her. This was her deepest dread, to see him inevitably disappointed in her. She could not bear to be put into the balance, wherein she knew she would be found wanting.

For she knew in herself that she was cut off from the source and origin of life. For her, the way back was lost irrevocably. And when Jude came to her, wanting to retrace with her the course right back to the springs and the welling-out, she was more afraid than of death. For she could not. She was like a flower broken off from the tree, that lives a while in water, and even puts forth. So Sue lived sustained and nourished by the rarefied life of books and art, and by the inflow from the man. But, owing to centuries and centuries of weaning away from the body of life, centuries of insisting upon the supremacy and bodilessness of Love, centuries of striving to escape the conditions of being and of striving to attain the condition of Knowledge, centuries of pure Christianity, she had gone too far. She had climbed and climbed to be near the stars. And now, at last, on the topmost pinnacle, exposed to all the horrors and the magnificence of space, she could not go back. Her strength had fallen from her. Up at that great height, with scarcely any foothold, but only space, space all round her, rising up to her from beneath, she was like a thing suspended, supported almost at the point of extinction by the density of the medium. Her body was lost to her, fallen away, gone. She existed there as a point of consciousness, no more, like one swooned at a great height, held up at the tip of a fine pinnacle that drove upwards into nothingness.

Jude rose to that height with her. But he did not die as she died. Beneath him the foothold was more, he did not swoon. There came a time when he wanted to go back, down to earth. But she was fastened like Andromeda.*

Perhaps, if Jude had not known Arabella, Sue might have persuaded him that he too was bodiless, only a point of consciousness. But she was too late; another had been before her and given her the lie.

Arabella was never so jealous of Sue as Sue of Arabella. How shall the saint that tips the pinnacle, Saint Simon Stylites* thrust on the highest needle that pricks the heavens, be envied by the man who walks the horizontal earth? But Sue was cruelly anguished with jealousy of Arabella. It was only this, this knowledge that Jude wanted Arabella, which made Sue give him access to her own body.

When she did that, she died. The Sue that had been till then, the glimmering, pale, star-like Sue, died and was revoked on the night when Arabella called at their house at Aldbrickham, and Jude went out in his slippers to look for her, and did not find her, but came back to Sue, who in her anguish gave him then the access to her body. Till that day, Sue had been, in her will and in her very self, true to one motion, to Love, to Knowledge, to the Light, to the upward motion. Phillotson had not altered this. When she had suffered him, she had said: 'He does not touch me; I am beyond him.'

But now she must give her body to Jude. At that moment her light began to go out, all she had lived for and by began to turn into a falseness, Sue began to nullify herself.

She could never become physical. She could never return down to earth. But there, lying bound at the pinnacle-tip, she had to pretend she was lying on the horizontal earth, prostrate with a man.

It was a profanation and a pollution, worse than the pollution of Cassandra or of the Vestals.* Sue had her own form: to break this form was to destroy her. Her destruction began only when she said to Jude, 'I give in.'

As for Jude, he dragged his body after his consciousness. His instinct could never have made him actually desire physical connexion with Sue. He was roused by an appeal made through his consciousness. This appeal automatically roused his senses. His consciousness desired Sue. So his senses were forced to follow his consciousness.

But he must have felt, in knowing her, the *frisson* of sacrilege, something like the Frenchman who lay with a corpse.* Her body, the body of a Vestal, was swooned into that state of bloodless ecstasy wherein it was dead to the senses. Or it was the body of an insane woman, whose senses are directed from the disordered mind, whose mind is not subjected to the senses.

But Jude was physically undeveloped. Altogether he was medieval. His senses were vigorous but not delicate. He never realized what it meant to *him*, his taking Sue. He thought he was satisfied.

But if it was death to her, or profanation, or pollution, or breaking, it was unnatural to him, blasphemy. How could he, a living, loving man, warm and productive, take with his body the moonlit cold body of a woman who did not live to him, and did not want him? It was monstrous, and it sent him mad.

She knew it was wrong, she knew it should never be. But what else could she do? Jude loved her now with his will. To have left him to Arabella would have been to destroy him. To have shared him with Arabella would have been possible to Sue, but impossible to him, for he had the strong, purist idea that a man's body should follow and be subordinate to his spirit, his senses should be sub-ordinate to and subsequent to his mind. Which idea is utterly false.

So Jude and Sue are damned, partly by their very being, but chiefly by their incapacity to accept the conditions of their own and each other's being. If Jude could have known that he did not want Sue physically, and then have made his choice, they might not have wasted their lives. But he could not know.

If he could have known, after a while, after he had taken her many times, that it was wrong, still they might have made a life. He must have known that, after taking Sue, he was depressed as she was depressed. He must have known worse than that. He must have felt the devastating sense of the unlivingness of life, things must have ceased to exist for him, when he rose from taking Sue, and he must have felt that he walked in a ghastly blank, confronted just by space, void.

But he would acknowledge nothing of what he felt. He must feel according to his idea and his will. Nevertheless, they were too truthful ever to marry. A man as real and personal as Jude cannot, from his deeper religious sense, marry a woman unless indeed he can marry her, unless with her he can find or approach the real consummation of marriage. And Sue and Jude could not lie to themselves, in their last and deepest feelings. They knew it was no marriage; they knew it was wrong, all along; they knew they were sinning against life, in forcing a physical marriage between them-selves.

How many people, man and woman, live together, in England, and have children, and are never, never asked whether they have been through the marriage ceremony together? Why then should Jude and Sue have been brought to task? Only because of their own uneasy sense of wrong, of sin, which they communicated to other people. And this wrong or sin was not against the community, but against their own being, against life. Which is why they were, the pair of them, instinctively disliked.

They never knew happiness, actual, sure-footed happiness, not for a moment. That was incompatible with Sue's nature. But what they knew was a very delightful but poignant and unhealthy con-dition of lightened consciousness. They reacted on each other to stimulate the consciousness. So that, when they went to the flower-show, her sense of the roses, and Jude's sense of the roses, would be most, most poignant. There is always this pathos, this poignancy, this trembling on the verge of pain and tears, in their happiness.

'Happy?' he murmured. She nodded.

The roses, how the roses glowed for them! The flowers had more being than either he or she. But as their ecstasy over things sank a little, they felt, the pair of them, as if they themselves were wanting in real body, as if they were too unsubstantial, too thin and evanescent in substance, as if the other solid people might jostle right through them, two wandering shades as they were.

This they felt themselves. Hence their uncertainty in contact with other people, hence their abnormal sensitiveness. But they had their own form of happiness, nevertheless, this trembling on the verge of ecstasy, when, the senses strongly roused to the service of the consciousness, the things they contemplated took flaming being, became flaming symbols of their own emotions to them.

So that the real marriage of Jude and Sue was in the roses. Then, in the third state, in the spirit, these two beings met upon the roses and in the roses were symbolized in consummation. The rose is the symbol of marriage-consummation in its beauty. To them it is more than a symbol, it is a fact, a flaming experience.

They went home tremblingly glad. And then the horror when, because of Jude's unsatisfaction, he must take Sue sexually. The flaming experience became a falsity, or an *ignis fatuus* leading them on.

They exhausted their lives, he in the consciousness, she in the body. She was glad to have children, to prove she was a woman. But in her it was a perversity to wish to prove she was a woman. She was no woman. And her children, the proof thereof, vanished like hoar-frost from her.

It was not the stone-masonry that exhausted him and weakened him and made him ill. It was this continuous feeding of his consciousness from his senses, this continuous state of incandescence of the consciousness, when his body, his vital tissues, the very protoplasm in him, was being slowly consumed away. For he had no life in the body. Every time he went to Sue, physically, his inner experience must have been a shock back from life and from the form of outgoing, like that of a man who lies with a corpse. He had no life in the senses: he had no inflow from the source to make up for the enormous wastage. So he gradually became exhausted, burned more and more away, till he was frail as an ember.

And she, her body also suffered. But it was in the mind that she had had her being, and it was in the mind she paid her price. She tried and tried to receive and to satisfy Jude physically. She bore him children, she gave herself to the life of the body.

But as she was formed she was formed, and there was no altering it. She needed all the life that belonged to her, and more, for the supplying of her mind, since such a mind as hers is found only, healthily, in a person of powerful vitality. For the mind, in a common person, is created out of the surplus vitality, or out of the remainder after all the sensuous life has been fulfilled.

She needed all the life that belonged to her, for her mind. It was her form. To disturb that arrangement was to make her into somebody else, not herself. Therefore, when she became a physical wife and a mother, she forswore her own being. She abjured her own mind, she denied it, took her faith, her belief, her very living away from it.

It is most probable she lived chiefly in her children. They were her guarantee as a physical woman, the being to which she now laid claim. She had forsaken the ideal of an independent mind.

She would love her children with anguish, afraid always for their safety, never certain of their stable existence, never assured of their real reality. When they were out of her sight, she would be uneasy, uneasy almost as if they did not exist. There would be a gnawing at her till they came back. She would not be satisfied till she had them crushed on her breast. And even then, she would not be sure, she would not be sure. She could not be sure, in life, of anything. She could only be sure, in the old days, of what she saw with her mind. Of that she was absolutely sure.

Meanwhile Jude became exhausted in vitality, bewildered, aimless, lost, pathetically nonproductive.

Again one can see what instinct, what feeling it was which made Arabella's boy bring about the death of the children and of himself. He, sensitive, so bodiless, so selfless as to be a sort of automaton, is very badly suggested, exaggerated, but one can see what is meant. And he feels, as any child will feel, as many children feel today, that they are really anachronisms, accidents, fatal accidents, unreal, false notes in their mothers' lives, that, according to her, they have no being: that, if they have being, then she has not. So he takes away all the children.

And then Sue ceases to be: she strikes the line through her own existence, cancels herself. There exists no more Sue Fawley. She cancels herself. She wishes to cease to exist, as a person, she wishes to be absorbed away, so that she is no longer self-responsible.

For she denied and forsook and broke her own real form, her own independent, cool-lighted mind-life. And now her children are not only dead, but self-slain, those pledges of the physical life for which she abandoned the other.

She has a passion to expiate, to expiate, to expiate. Her children should never have been born: her instinct always knew this. Now their dead bodies drive her mad with a sense of blasphemy. And she blasphemed the Holy Spirit, which told her she is guilty of their birth and their death, of the horrible nothing which they are. She is even guilty of their little, palpitating sufferings and joys of mortal life, now made nothing. She cannot bear it—who could? And she wants to expiate, doubly expiate. Her mind, which she set up in her conceit, and then forswore, she must stamp it out of existence, as one stamps out fire. She would never again think or decide for herself. The world, the past, should have written every decision for her. The last act of her intellect was the utter renunciation of her mind and the embracing of utter orthodoxy, where every belief, every thought, every decision was made ready for her, so that she did not exist self-responsible. And then her loathed body, which had committed the crime of bearing dead children, which had come to life only to spread nihilism like a pestilence, that too should be scourged out of existence. She chose the bitterest penalty in going back to Phillotson.

There was no more Sue. Body, soul, and spirit, she annihilated herself. All that remained of her was the will by which she annihilated herself. That remained fixed, a locked centre of self-hatred, life-hatred so utter that it had no hope of death. It knew that life is life, and there is no death for life.

Jude was too exhausted himself to save her. He says of her she was not worth a man's love. But that was not the point. It was not a question of her worth. It was a question of her being. If he had said she was not capable of receiving a man's love as he wished to bestow it, he might have spoken nearer the truth. But she practically told him this. She made it plain to him what she wanted, what she could take. But he overrode her. She tried hard to abide by her own form. But he forced her. He had no case against her, unless she made the great appeal for him, that he should flow to her, whilst at the same time she could not take him completely, body and spirit both.

She asked for what he could not give—what perhaps no man can give: passionate love without physical desire. She had no blame for him: she had no love for him. Self-love triumphed in her when she first knew him. She almost deliberately asked for more, far more, than she intended to give. Self-hatred triumphed in the end. So it had to be.

As for Jude, he had been dying slowly, but much quicker than she, since the first night she took him. It was best to get it done quickly in the end.

And this tragedy is the result of over-development of one principle of human life at the expense of the other; an over-balancing; a laying of all the stress on the Male, the Love, the Spirit, the Mind, the Consciousness; a denying, a blaspheming against the Female, the Law, the Soul, the Senses, the Feelings. But she is developed to the very extreme, she scarcely lives in the body at all. Being of the feminine gender, she is yet no woman at all, nor male; she is almost neuter. He is nearer the balance, nearer the centre, nearer the wholeness. But the whole human effort, towards pure life in the spirit, towards becoming pure Sue, drags him along; he identifies himself with this effort, destroys himself and her in his adherence to this identification.

But why, in casting off one or another form of religion, has man ceased to be religious altogether? Why will he not recognize Sue and Jude, as Cassandra was recognized long ago, and Achilles,* and the Vestals, and the nuns, and the monks? Why must being be denied altogether?

Sue had a being, special and beautiful. Why must not Jude recognize it in all its speciality? Why must man be so utterly irreverent, that he approaches each being as if it were no-being? Why must it be assumed that Sue is an 'ordinary' woman—as if such a thing existed? Why must she feel ashamed if she is specialized? And why must Jude, owing to the conception he is brought up in, force her to act as if she were his 'ordinary' abstraction, a woman?

She was not a woman. She was Sue Bridehead, something very particular. Why was there no place for her? Cassandra had the Temple of Apollo. Why are we so foul that we have no reverence for that which we are and for that which is amongst us? If we had reverence for our life, our life would take at once religious form. But as it is, in our filthy irreverence, it remains a disgusting slough, where each one of us goes so thoroughly disguised in dirt that we are all alike and indistinguishable.

If we had reverence for what we are, our life would take real form, and Sue would have a place, as Cassandra had a place; she would have a place which does not yet exist, because we are all so vulgar, we have nothing.

Poetry of the Present

IT seems when we hear a skylark singing as if sound were running into the future, running so fast and utterly without consideration, straight on into futurity. And when we hear a nightingale, we hear the pause and the rich, piercing rhythm of recollection, the perfected past. The lark may sound sad, but with the lovely lapsing sadness that is almost a swoon of hope. The nightingale's triumph is a paean, but a death-paean.

So it is with poetry. Poetry is, as a rule, either the voice of the far future, exquisite and ethereal, or it is the voice of the past, rich, magnificent. When the Greeks heard the *Iliad* and the *Odyssey*, they heard their own past calling in their hearts, as men far inland sometimes hear the sea and fall weak with powerful, wonderful regret, nostalgia; or else their own future rippled its time-beats through their blood, as they followed the painful, glamorous progress of the Ithacan. This was Homer to the Greeks: their Past, splendid with battles won and death achieved, and their Future, the magic wandering of Ulysses through the unknown.

With us it is the same. Our birds sing on the horizons. They sing out of the blue, beyond us, or out of the quenched night. They sing at dawn and sunset. Only the poor, shrill, tame canaries whistle while we talk. The wild birds begin before we are awake, or as we drop into dimness, out of waking. Our poets sit by the gateways, some by the east, some by the west. As we arrive and as we go out our hearts surge with response. But whilst we are in the midst of life, we do not hear them.

The poetry of the beginning and the poetry of the end must have that exquisite finality, perfection which belongs to all that is far off. It is in the realm of all that is perfect. It is of the nature of all that is complete and consummate. This completeness, this consummateness, the finality and the perfection are conveyed in exquisite form: the perfect symmetry, the rhythm which returns upon itself like a dance where the hands link and loosen and link for the supreme moment of the end. Perfected bygone moments, perfected moments in the glimmering futurity, these are the treasured gem-like lyrics of Shelley and Keats.

But there is another kind of poetry: the poetry of that which is at hand: the immediate present. In the immediate present there is no perfection, no consummation, nothing finished. The strands are all flying, quivering, intermingling into the web, the waters are shaking the moon. There is no round, consummate moon on the face of running water, nor on the face of the unfinished tide. There are no gems of the living plasm. The living plasm vibrates unspeakably, it inhales the future, it exhales the past, it is the quick of both, and yet it is neither. There is no plasmic finality, nothing crystal, permanent. If we try to fix the living tissue, as the biologists fix it with formation, we have only a hardened bit of the past, the bygone life under our observation.

Life, the ever-present, knows no finality, no finished crystallization. The perfect rose is only a running flame, emerging and flowing off, and never in any sense at rest, static, finished. Herein lies its transcendent loveliness. The whole tide of all life and all time suddenly heaves, and appears before us as an apparition, a revelation. We look at the very white quick of nascent creation. A water-lily heaves herself from the flood, looks around, gleams, and is gone. We have seen the incarnation, the quick of the ever-swirling flood. We have seen the invisible. We have seen, we have touched, we have partaken of the very substance of creative change, creative mutation. If you tell me about the lotus, tell me of nothing changeless or eternal. Tell me of the mystery of the inexhaustible, forever-unfolding creative spark. Tell me of the incarnate disclosure of the flux, mutation in blossom, laughter and decay perfectly open in their transit, nude in their movement before us.

Let me feel the mud and the heavens in my lotus. Let me feel the heavy, silting, sucking mud, the spinning of sky winds. Let me feel them both in purest contact, the nakedness of sucking weight, nakedly passing radiance. Give me nothing fixed, set, static. Don't give me the infinite or the eternal: nothing of infinity, nothing of eternity. Give me the still, white seething, the incandescence and the coldness of the incarnate moment: the moment, the quick of all change and haste and opposition: the moment, the immediate present, the Now. The immediate moment is not a drop of water running downstream. It is the source and issue, the bubbling up of the stream. Here, in this very instant moment, up bubbles the stream of time, out of the wells of futurity, flowing on to the oceans of the past. The source, the issue, the creative quick.

There is poetry of this immediate present, instant poetry, as well as poetry of the infinite past and the infinite future. The seething poetry of the incarnate Now is supreme, beyond even the everlasting gems of the before and after. In its quivering momentaneity it surpasses the crystalline, pearl-hard jewels, the poems of the eternities. Do not ask for the qualities of the unfading timeless gems. Ask for the whiteness which is the seethe of mud, ask for that incipient putrescence which is the skies falling, ask for the never-pausing, never-ceasing life itself. There must be mutation, swifter than iridescence, haste, not rest, come-and-go, not fixity, inconclusiveness, immediacy, the quality of life itself, without denouement or close. There must be the rapid momentaneous association of things which meet and pass on the for ever incalculable journey of creation: everything left in its own rapid, fluid relationship with the rest of things.

This is the unrestful, ungraspable poetry of the sheer present, poetry whose very permanency lies in its wind-like transit. Whitman's* is the best poetry of this kind. Without beginning and without end, without any base and pediment, it sweeps past for ever, like a wind that is for ever in passage, and unchainable. Whitman truly looked before and after. But he did not sigh for what is not. The clue to all his utterance lies in the sheer appreciation of the instant moment, life surging itself into utterance at its very well-head. Eternity is only an abstraction from the actual present. Infinity is only a great reservoir of recollection, or a reservoir of aspiration: man-made. The quivering nimble hour of the present, this is the quick of Time. This is the immanence. The quick of the universe is the *pulsating*, *carnal self*, mysterious and palpable. So it is always.

Because Whitman put this into his poetry, we fear him and respect him so profoundly. We should not fear him if he sang only of the 'old unhappy far-off things', or of the 'wings of the morning'.* It is because his heart beats with the urgent, insurgent Now, which is even upon us all, that we dread him. He is so near the quick.

From the foregoing it is obvious that the poetry of the instant present cannot have the same body or the same motion as the poetry of the before and after. It can never submit to the same conditions. It is never finished. There is no rhythm which returns upon itself, no serpent of eternity with its tail in its own mouth.* There is no static perfection, none of that finality which we find so satisfying because we are so frightened.

Much has been written about free verse. But all that can be said, first and last, is that free verse is, or should be direct utterance from the instant, whole man. It is the soul and the mind and body surging at once, nothing left out. They speak all together. There is some confusion, some discord. But the confusion and the discord only belong to the reality, as noise belongs to the plunge of water. It is no use inventing fancy laws for free verse, no use drawing a melodic line which all the feet must toe. Free verse toes no melodic line, no matter what drill-sergeant. Whitman pruned away his clichés—perhaps his clichés of rhythm as well as of phrase. And this is about all we can do, deliberately, with free verse. We can get rid of the stereotyped movements and the old hackneyed associations of sound or sense. We can break down those artificial conduits and canals through which we do so love to force our utterance. We can break the stiff neck of habit. We can be in ourselves spontaneous and flexible as flame, we can see that utterance rushes out without artificial form or artificial smoothness. But we cannot positively prescribe any motion, any rhythm. All the laws we invent or discover—it amounts to pretty much the same—will fail to apply to free verse. They will only apply to some form of restricted, limited unfree verse.

All we can say is that free verse does *not* have the same nature as restricted verse. It is not of the nature of reminiscence. It is not the past which we treasure in its perfection between our hands. Neither is it the crystal of the perfect future, into which we gaze. Its tide is neither the full, yearning flow of aspiration, nor the sweet, poignant ebb of remembrance and regret. The past and the future are the two great bournes of human emotion, the two great homes of the human days, the two eternities. They are both conclusive, final. Their beauty is the beauty of the goal, finished, perfected. Finished beauty and measured symmetry belong to the stable, unchanging eternities.

But in free verse we look for the insurgent naked throb of the instant moment. To break the lovely form of metrical verse, and to dish up the fragments as a new substance, called *vers libre*,* this is what most of the free-versifiers accomplish. They do not know that free verse has its own *nature*, that it is neither star nor pearl, but instantaneous like plasm. It has no goal in either eternity. It has no finish. It has no satisfying stability, satisfying to those who like the immutable. None of this. It is the instant; the quick; the very jetting source of all will-be and has-been. The utterance is like a spasm, naked contact with all influences at once. It does not want to get anywhere. It just takes place.

For such utterance any externally applied law would be mere shackles and death. The law must come new each time from within. The bird is on the wing in the winds, flexible to every breath, a living spark in the storm, its very flickering depending upon its supreme mutability and power of change. Whence such a bird came: whither it goes: from what solid earth it rose up, and upon what solid earth it will close its wings and settle, this is not the question. This is a question of before and after. Now, *now*, the bird is on the wing in the winds.

Such is the rare new poetry. One realm we have never conquered: the pure present. One great mystery of time is terra incognita to us: the instant. The most superb mystery we have hardly recognized: the immediate, instant self. The quick of all time is the instant. The quick of all the universe, of all creation, is the incarnate, carnal self. Poetry gave us the clue: free verse: Whitman. Now we know.

The ideal—what is the ideal? A figment. An abstraction. A static abstraction, abstracted from life. It is a fragment of the before or the after. It is a crystallized aspiration, or a crystallized remembrance: crystallized, set, finished. It is a thing set apart, in the great storehouse of eternity, the storehouse of finished things.

We do not speak of things crystallized and set apart. We speak of the instant, the immediate self, the very plasm of the self. We speak also of free verse.

All this should have come as a preface to *Look! We Have Come Through!* But is it not better to publish a preface long after the book it belongs to has appeared? For then the reader will have had his fair chance with the book, alone.

Whitman

WHITMAN is the greatest of the Americans. One of the greatest poets of the world, in him an element of falsity troubles us still. Something is wrong: we cannot be quite at ease in his greatness.

This may be our own fault. But we sincerely feel that something is overdone in Whitman; there is something that is too much. Let us get over our quarrel with him first.

All the Americans, when they have trodden new ground, seem to have been conscious of making a breach in the established order. They have been self-conscious about it. They have felt that they were trespassing, transgressing, or going very far, and this has given a certain stridency, or portentousness, or luridness to their manner. Perhaps that is because the steps were taken so rapidly. From Franklin* to Whitman is a hundred years. It might be a thousand.

The Americans have finished in haste, with a certain violence and violation, that which Europe began two thousand years ago or more. Rapidly they have returned to lay open the secrets which the Christian epoch has taken two thousand years to close up.

With the Greeks started the great passion for the ideal, the passion for translating all consciousness into terms of spirit and ideal or idea. They did this in reaction from the vast old world which was dying in Egypt. But the Greeks, though they set out to conquer the animal or sensual being in man, did not set out to annihilate it. This was left for the Christians.

The Christians, phase by phase, set out actually to *annihilate* the sensual being in man. They insisted that man was in his reality *pure spirit*, and that he was perfectible as such. And this was their business, to achieve such a perfection.

They worked from a profound inward impulse, the Christian religious impulse. But their proceeding was the same, in living extension, as that of the Greek esoterics, such as John the Evangel or Socrates. They proceeded, by will and by exaltation, to overcome *all* the passions and all the appetites and prides.

Now, so far, in Europe, the conquest of the lower self has been objective. That is, man has moved from a great impulse within himself, unconscious. But once the conquest has been effected, there is a temptation for the conscious mind to return and finger and explore, just as tourists now explore battlefields. This self-conscious *mental* provoking of sensation and reaction in the great affective centres is what we call sentimentalism or sensationalism. The mind returns upon the affective centres, and sets up in them a deliberate reaction.

And this is what all the Americans do, beginning with Crèvecoeur, Hawthorne, Poe, all the transcendentalists, Melville, Prescott, Wendell Holmes,* Whitman, they are all guilty of this provoking of mental reactions in the physical self, passions exploited by the mind. In Europe, men like Balzac and Dickens, Tolstoi and Hardy, still act direct from the passional motive, and not inversely, from mental provocation. But the aesthetes and symbolists, from Baudelaire and Maeterlinck and Oscar Wilde* onwards, and nearly all later Russian, French, and English novelists set up their reactions in the mind and reflect them by a secondary process down into the body. This makes a vicious living and a spurious art. It is one of the last and most fatal effects of idealism. Everything becomes self-conscious and spurious, to the pitch of madness. It is the madness of the world of to-day. Europe and America are all alike; all the nations self-consciously provoking their own passional reactions from the mind, and *nothing* spontaneous.

And this is our accusation against Whitman, as against the others. Too often he deliberately, self-consciously *affects* himself. It puts us off, it makes us dislike him. But since such self-conscious secondariness is a concomitant of all American art, and yet not sufficiently so to prevent that art from being of rare quality, we must get over it. The excuse is that the Americans have had to perform in a century a curve which it will take Europe much longer to finish, if ever she finishes it.

Whitman has gone further, in actual living expression, than any man, it seems to me. Dostoevsky has burrowed underground* into the decomposing psyche. But Whitman has gone forward in life-knowledge. It is he who surmounts the grand climacteric of our civilization.

Whitman enters on the last phase of spiritual triumph. He really arrives at that stage of infinity which the seers sought. By subjecting the *deepest centres* of the lower self, he attains the maximum consciousness in the higher self: a degree of extensive consciousness greater, perhaps, than any man in the modern world.

We have seen Dana* and Melville, the two adventurers, setting out to conquer the last vast *element*, with the spirit. We have seen Melville touching at last the far end of the immemorial, prehistoric Pacific civilization, in *Typee*. We have seen his terrific cruise into universality.

Now we must remember that the way, even towards a state of infinite comprehension, is through the externals towards the quick. And the vast elements, the cosmos, the big things, the universals, these are always the externals. These are met first and conquered first. That is why science is so much easier than art. The quick is the living being, the quick of quicks is the individual soul. And it is here, at the quick, that Whitman proceeds to find the experience of infinitude, his vast extension, or concentrated intensification into Allness. He carries the conquest to its end.

If we read his paeans, his chants of praise and deliverance and accession, what do we find? All-embracing, indiscriminate, passional acceptance; surges of chaotic vehemence of invitation and embrace, catalogues, lists, enumerations. 'Whoever you are, to endless announcements ...' 'And of these one and all I weave the song of myself.' 'Lovers, endless lovers.'

Continually the one cry: I am everything and everything is me. I accept everything in my consciousness; nothing is rejected:—

> 'I am he that aches with amorous love;.
> Does the earth gravitate? does not all matter,
>   aching, attract all matter?
> So the body of me to all I meet or know.'*

At last everything is conquered. At last the lower centres are conquered. At last the lowest plane is submitted to the highest. At last there is nothing more to conquer. At last all is one, all is love, even hate is love, even flesh is spirit. The great oneness, the experience of infinity, the triumph of the living spirit, which at last includes everything, is here accomplished.

It is man's accession into wholeness, his knowledge in full. Now he is united with everything. Now he embraces everything into himself in a oneness. Whitman is drunk with the new wine of this new great experience, really drunk with the strange wine of infinitude. So he pours forth his words, his chants of praise and acclamation. It is man's maximum state of consciousness, his highest state of spiritual being. Supreme spiritual consciousness, and the divine drunkenness of supreme consciousness. It is reached through embracing love. 'And whoever walks a furlong without sympathy walks to his own funeral dressed in his own shroud.' And this supreme state, once reached, shows us the One Identity in everything, Whitman's cryptic *One Identity*.*

Thus Whitman becomes in his own person the whole world, the whole universe, the whole eternity of time. Nothing is rejected. Because nothing opposes him. All adds up to one in him. Item by item he identifies himself with the universe, and this accumulative identity he calls Democracy, En Masse, One Identity, and so on.

But this is the last and final truth, the last truth is at the quick. And the quick is the single individual soul, which is never more than itself, though it embrace eternity and infinity, and never *other* than itself, though it include all men. Each vivid soul is unique, and though one soul embrace another, and include it, still it cannot *become* that other soul, or livingly dispossess that other soul. In extending himself, Whitman still remains himself; he does not become the other man, or the other woman, or the tree, or the universe: in spite of Plato.*

Which is the maximum truth, though it appears so small in contrast to all these infinites, and En Masses, and Democracies, and Almightynesses. The essential truth is that a man is himself, and only himself, throughout all his greatnesses and extensions and intensifications.

The second truth which we must bring as a charge against Whitman is the one we brought before, namely, that his Allness, his One Identity, his En Masse, his Democracy, is only a half-truth— an enormous half-truth. The other half is Jehovah, and Egypt, and Sennacherib:* the other form of Allness, terrible and grand, even as in the Psalms.

Now Whitman's way to Allness, he tells us, is through endless sympathy, merging. But in merging you must merge away from something, as well as towards something, and in sympathy you must depart from one point to arrive at another. Whitman lays down this law of sympathy as the one law, the direction of merging as the one direction. Which is obviously wrong. Why not a right-about-turn? Why not turn slap back to the point from which you started to merge? Why not *that* direction, the reverse of merging, back to the single and overweening self? Why not, instead of endless dilation of sympathy, the retraction into isolation and pride?

Why not? The heart has its systole diastole, the shuttle comes and goes, even the sun rises and sets. We know, as a matter of fact, that all life lies between two poles. The direction is twofold. Whitman's *one direction* becomes a hideous tyranny once he has attained his goal of Allness. His One Identity is a prison of horror, once realized. For identities are manifold and each jewel-like, different as a sapphire from an opal. And the motion of merging becomes at last a vice, a nasty degeneration, as when tissue breaks down into a mucous slime. There must be the sharp retraction from isolation, following the expansion into unification, otherwise the integral being is overstrained and will break, break down like disintegrating tissue into slime, imbecility, epilepsy, vice, like Dostoevsky.

And one word more. Even if you reach the state of infinity, you can't sit down there. You just physically can't. You either have to strain still further into universality and become vaporish, or slimy: or you have to hold your toes and sit tight and practise Nirvana;* or you have to come back to common dimensions, eat your pudding and blow your nose and be just yourself; or die and have done with it. A grand experience is a grand experience. It brings a man to his maximum. But even at his maximum a man is not more than himself. When he is infinite he is still himself. He still has a nose to wipe. The state of infinity is *only* a state, even if it be the supreme one.

But in achieving this state Whitman opened a new field of living. He drives on to the very centre of life and sublimates even this into consciousness. Melville hunts the remote white whale of the deepest passional body, tracks it down. But it is Whitman who captures the whale. The pure sensual body of man, at its deepest remoteness and intensity, this is the White Whale. And this is what Whitman captures.

He seeks his consummation through one continual ecstasy: the ecstasy of *giving himself*, and of being taken. The ecstasy of his own reaping and merging with another, with others; the sword-cut of sensual death. Whitman's motion is always the motion of *giving himself*: This is my body—take, and eat.* It is the great sacrament. He knows nothing of the other sacrament, the sacrament in pride, where the communicant envelops the victim and host in a flame of ecstatic consuming, sensual gratification, and triumph.

But he is concerned with others beside himself: with woman, for example. But what is woman to Whitman? Not much: she is a great function—no more. Whitman's 'athletic mothers of these States'* are depressing. Muscles and wombs: functional creatures—no more.

> 'As I see myself reflected in Nature,
> As I see through a mist, One with inexpressible completeness,
>   sanity, beauty,
> See the bent head, and arms folded over the breast, the
>   Female I see.'

That is all. The woman is reduced, really, to a submissive function. She is no longer an individual being with a living soul. She must fold her arms and bend her head and submit to her functioning capacity. Function of sex, function of birth.

> 'This the nucleus—after the child is born of woman, man is
>   born of woman,
> This is the bath of birth, the merge of small and large,
>   and the outlet again—'*

Acting from the last and profoundest centres, man acts womanless. It is no longer a question of race continuance. It is a question of sheer, ultimate being, the perfection of life, nearest to death. Acting from these centres, man is an extreme being, the unthinkable warrior, creator, mover, and maker.

And the polarity is between man and man. Whitman alone of all moderns has known this positively. Others have known it negatively, *pour épater les bourgeois*.* Whitman knew it positively, in its tremendous knowledge, knew the extremity, the perfectness, and the fatality.

Even Whitman becomes grave, tremulous, before the last dynamic truth of life. In 'Calamus' he does not shout. He hesitates: he is reluctant, wistful. But none the less he goes on. And he tells the mystery of manly love, the love of comrades. Continually he tells us the same truth: the new world will be built upon the love of comrades, the new great dynamic of life will be manly love. Out of this inspiration the creation of the future.

The strange Calamus has its pink-tinged root by the pond, and it sends up its leaves of comradeship, comrades at one root, without the intervention of woman, the female. This comradeship is to be the final cohering principle of the new world, the new Democracy. It is the cohering principle of perfect soldiery, as he tells in 'Drum Taps'. It is the cohering principle of final *unison* in creative activity. And it is extreme and alone, touching the confines of death. It is something terrible to bear, terrible to be responsible for. It is the soul's last and most vivid responsibility, the responsibility for the circuit of final friendship, comradeship, manly love.

> 'Yet, you are beautiful to me you faint-tinged roots,
>   you make me think of death;
> Death is beautiful from you (what, indeed, is finally beautiful
>   except death and love?).
> I think it is not for life I am chanting here my chant of lovers,
>   I think it must be for death.
> For how calm, how solemn it grows to ascend to the
>   atmosphere of lovers;
> Death of life, I am then indifferent, my soul declines to
>   prefer, (I am not sure but the high soul of lovers welcomes
>   death most),
> Indeed, O death, I think now these leaves mean precisely
>   the same as you mean—'*

Here we have the deepest, finest Whitman, the Whitman who knows the extremity of life, and of the soul's responsibility. He has come near now to death, in his creative life. But creative life must come near to death, to link up the mystic circuit. The pure warriors must stand on the brink of death. So must the men of a pure creative nation. We shall have no beauty, no dignity, no essential freedom otherwise. And so it is from 'Sea Drift', where the male bird sings the lost female: not that she is lost, but lost to him who has had to go beyond her, to sing on the edge of the great sea, in the night. It is the last voice on the shore.

'Whereto answering, the sea
Delaying not, hurrying not,
Whispered me through the night, and very plainly before
    daybreak,
Lisp'd to me the low and delicious word death,
And again death, death, death, death,
Hissing melodious, neither like the bird nor like my
    aroused child's heart,
But edging near as privately for me rustling at my feet,
Creeping thence steadily up to my ears and laving me
    softly all over,
Death, death, death, death, death—'*

What a great poet Whitman is: great like a great Greek. For him the last enclosures have fallen, he finds himself on the shore of the last sea. The extreme of life: so near to death. It is a hushed, deep responsibility. And what is the responsibility? It is for the new great era of mankind. And upon what is this new era established? On the perfect circuits of vital flow between human beings. Irst, the great sexless normal relation between individuals, simple sexless friendships, unison of family, and clan, and nation, and group. Next, the powerful sex relation between man and woman, culminating in the eternal orbit of marriage. And, finally, the sheer friendship, the love between comrades, the manly love which alone can create a new era of life.

The one state, however, does not annul the other: it fulfils the other. Marriage is the great step beyond friendship, and family, and nationality, but it does not supersede these. Marriage should only give repose and perfection to the great previous bonds and relationships. A wife or husband who sets about to annul the old, pre-marriage affections and connections ruins the foundations of marriage. And so with the last, extremest love, the love of comrades. The ultimate comradeship which sets about to destroy marriage destroys its own *raison d'être.* The ultimate comradeship is the final progression from marriage; it is the last seedless flower of pure beauty, beyond purpose. But if it destroys marriage it makes itself purely deathly. In its beauty, the ultimate comradeship flowers on the brink of death. But it flowers from the root of all life upon the blossoming tree of life.

The life-circuit now depends entirely upon the sex-unison of marriage. This circuit must never be broken. But it must be still surpassed. We cannot help the laws of life.

If marriage is sacred, the ultimate comradeship is utterly sacred, since it has no ulterior motive whatever, like procreation. If marriage is eternal, the great bond of life, how much more is this bond eternal, being the great life-circuit which borders on death in all its round. The new, extreme, the sacred relationship of comrades awaits us, and the future of mankind depends on the way in which this relation is entered upon by us. It is a relation between fearless, honorable, self-responsible men, a balance in perfect polarity.

The last phase is entered upon, shakily, by Whitman. It will take us an epoch to establish the new, perfect circuit of our being. It will take an epoch to establish the love of comrades, as marriage is really established now. For fear of going on, forwards, we turn round and destroy, or try to destroy, what lies behind. We are trying to destroy marriage, because we have not the courage to go forward from marriage to the new issue. Marriage must never be wantonly attacked. *True* marriage is eternal; in it we have our consummation and being. But the final consummation lies in that which is beyond marriage.

And when the bond, or circuit of perfect comrades is established, what then, when we are on the brink of death, fulfilled in the vastness of life? Then, at last, we shall know a starry maturity.

Whitman put us on the track years ago. Why has no one gone on from him? The great poet, why does no one accept his greatest word? The Americans are not worthy of their Whitman. They take him like a cocktail, for fun. Miracle that they have not annihilated every word of him. But these miracles happen.

The greatest modern poet! Whitman, at his best, is purely himself. His verse springs sheer from the spontaneous sources of his being. Hence its lovely, lovely form and rhythm: at the best. It is sheer, perfect *human* spontaneity, spontaneous as a nightingale throbbing, but still controlled, the highest loveliness of human spontaneity, undecorated, unclothed. The whole being is there, sensually throbbing, spiritually quivering, mentally, ideally speaking. It is not, like Swinburne, an exaggeration of the one part of being. It is perfect and whole. The whole soul speaks at once, and is too pure for mechanical assistance of rhyme and measure. The perfect utterance of a concentrated spontaneous soul. The unforgettable loveliness of Whitman's lines!

'Out of the cradle endlessly rocking.'

*Ave America!**

The Spirit of Place

WE like to think of the old fashioned American classics as children's books. Just childishness, on our part. The old American art-speech contains an alien quality, which belongs to the American continent and to nowhere else. But, of course, so long as we insist on reading the books as children's tales, we miss all that.

One wonders what the proper highbrow Romans of the third and fourth or later centuries read into the strange utterances of Lucretius or Apuleius or Tertullian, Augustine or Athanasius. The uncanny voice of Iberian Spain, weirdness of old Carthage, the passion of Libya and North Africa;* you may bet the proper old Romans never heard these at all. They read old Latin inference over the top of it, as we read old European inference over the top of Poe or Hawthorne.

It is hard to hear a new voice, as hard as it is to listen to an unknown language. We just don't listen. There is a new voice in the old American classics. The world has declined to hear it, and has babbled about children's stories.

Why?—Out of fear. The world fears a new experience more than it fears anything. Because a new experience displaces so many old experiences. And it is like trying to use muscles that have perhaps never been used, or that have been going stiff for ages. It hurts horribly.

The world doesn't fear a new idea. It can pigeon-hole any idea. But it can't pigeon-hole a real new experience. It can only dodge. The world is a great dodger, and the Americans the greatest. Because they dodge their own very selves.

There is a new feeling in the old American books, far more than there is in the modern American books, which are pretty empty of any feeling, and proud of it. There is a 'different' feeling in the old American classics. It is the shifting over from the old psyche to something new, a displacement. And displacements hurt. This hurts. So we try to tie it up, like a cut finger. Put a rag round it.

It is a cut too. Cutting away the old emotions and consciousness. Don't ask what is left.

Art-speech is the only truth. An artist is usually a damned liar, but his art, if it be art, will tell you the truth of his day. And that is all that matters. Away with eternal truth. Truth lives from day to day, and the marvellous Plato of yesterday is chiefly bosh today.

The old American artists were hopeless liars. But they were artists, in spite of themselves. Which is more than you can say of most living practitioners.

And you can please yourself, when you read *The Scarlet Letter*,* whether you accept what that sugary, blue-eyed little darling of a Hawthorne has to say for himself, false as all darlings are, or whether you read the impeccable truth of his art-speech.

The curious thing about art-speech is that it prevaricates so terribly, I mean it tells such lies. I suppose because we always all the time tell ourselves lies. And out of a pattern of lies art weaves the truth. Like Dostoevsky posing as a sort of Jesus, but most truthfully revealing himself all the while as a little horror.

Truly art is a sort of subterfuge. But thank God for it, we can see through the subterfuge if we choose. Art has two great functions. First, it provides an emotional experience. And then, if we have the courage of our own feelings, it becomes a mine of practical truth. We have had the feelings *ad nauseam*. But we've never dared dig the actual truth out of them, the truth that concerns us, whether it concerns our grandchildren or not.

The artist usually sets out—or used to— to point a moral and adorn a tale.* The tale, however, points the other way, as a rule. Two blankly opposing morals, the artist's and the tale's. Never trust the artist. Trust the tale. The proper function of a critic is to save the tale from the artist who created it.

Now we know our business in these studies; saving the American tale from the American artist.

Let us look at this American artist first. How did he ever get to America, to start with? Why isn't he a European still, like his father before him?

Now listen to me, don't listen to him. He'll tell you the lie you expect. Which is partly your fault for expecting it.

He didn't come in search of freedom of worship. England had more freedom of worship in the year 1700 than America had. Won by Englishmen who wanted freedom, and so stopped at home and fought for it. And got it. Freedom of worship? Read the history of New England during the first century of its existence.

Freedom anyhow? The land of the free! This the land of the free! Why, if I say anything that displeases them, the free mob will lynch me, and that's my freedom. Free? Why I have never been in any country where the individual has such an abject fear of his fellow-countrymen. Because, as I say, they are free to lynch him the moment he shows he is not one of them.

No, no, if you're so fond of the truth about Queen Victoria, try a little about yourself.

Those Pilgrim Fathers* and their successors never came here for freedom of worship. What did they set up when they got here? Freedom, would you call it?

They didn't come for freedom. Or if they did, they sadly went back on themselves.

All right then, what did they come for? For lots of reasons. Perhaps least of all in search of freedom of any sort: positive freedom, that is.

They came largely to get *away*—that most simple of motives. To get away. Away from what? In the long run, away from themselves. Away from everything. That's why most people have come to America, and still do come. To get away from everything they are and have been.

'Henceforth be masterless.'

Which is all very well, but it isn't freedom. Rather the reverse. A hopeless sort of constraint. It is never freedom till you find something you really *positively want to be*. And people in America have always been shouting about the things they are *not*. Unless, of course, they are millionaires, made or in the making.

And after all there is a positive side to the movement. All that vast flood of human life that has flowed over the Atlantic in ships from Europe to America has not flowed over simply on a tide of revulsion from Europe and from the confinements of the European ways of life. This revulsion was, and still is, I believe, the prime motive in emigration. But there was some cause, even for the revulsion.

It seems as if at times man had a frenzy for getting away from any control of any sort. In Europe the old Christianity was the real master. The Church and the true aristocracy bore the responsibility for the working out of the Christian ideals: a little irregularly, maybe, but responsible nevertheless.

Mastery, kingship, fatherhood had their power destroyed at the time of the Renaissance.

And it was precisely at this moment that the great drift over the Atlantic started. What were men drifting away from? The old authority of Europe? Were they breaking the bonds of authority, and escaping to a new more absolute unrestrainedness? Maybe. But there was more to it.

Liberty is all very well, but men cannot live without masters. There is always a master. And men either live in glad obedience to the master they believe in, or they live in a frictional opposition to the master they wish to undermine. In America this frictional opposition has been the vital factor. It has given the Yankee his kick. Only the continual influx of more servile Europeans has provided America with an obedient labouring class. The true obedience never outlasting the first generation.

But there sits the old master, over in Europe. Like a parent. Somewhere deep in every American heart lies a rebellion against the old parenthood of Europe. Yet no American feels he has completely escaped its mastery. Hence the slow, smouldering patience of American opposition. The slow, smouldering, corrosive obedience to the old master Europe, the unwilling subject, the unremitting oposition.

Whatever else you are, be masterless.

> Ca Ca Caliban
> Get a new master, be a new man.*

Escaped slaves, we might say, people the republics of Liberia or Haiti. Liberia enough! Are we to look at America in the same way? A vast republic of escaped slaves. When you consider the hordes from eastern Europe, you might well say it: a vast republic of escaped slaves. But one dare not say this of the Pilgrim Fathers, and the great old body of idealist Americans, the modern Americans tortured with thought. A vast republic of escaped slaves. Look out, America! And a minority of earnest, self-tortured people.

The masterless.

> Ca Ca Caliban
> Get a new master, be a new man.

What did the Pilgrim Fathers come for, then, when they came

so gruesomely over the black sea? Oh, it was in a black spirit. A
black revulsion from Europe, from the old authority of Europe,
from kings and bishops and popes. And more. When you look into
it, more. They were black, masterful men, they wanted something
else. No kings, no bishops maybe. Even no God Almighty. But also,
no more of this new 'humanity' which followed the Renaissance.
None of this new liberty which was to be so pretty in Europe.
Something grimmer, by no means free-and-easy.

America has never been easy, and is not easy to-day. Americans
have always been at a certain tension. Their liberty is a thing of
sheer will, sheer tension: a liberty of THOU SHALT NOT. And it has
been so from the first. The land of THOU SHALT NOT. Only the
first commandment is: THOU SHALT NOT PRESUME TO BE A
MASTER. Hence democracy.

'We are the masterless.' That is what the American Eagle
shrieks. It's a Hen-Eagle.

The Spaniards refused the post-Renaissance liberty of Europe.
And the Spaniards filled most of America. The Yankees, too, refused, refused the post-Renaissance humanism of Europe. First
and foremost, they hated masters. But under that, they hated the
flowing ease of humour in Europe. At the bottom of the American
soul was always a dark suspense, at the bottom of the Spanish-
American soul the same. And this dark suspense hated and hates
the old European spontaneity, watches it collapse with satisfaction.

Every continent has its own great spirit of place. Every people is
polarised in some particular locality, which is home, the homeland.
Different places on the face of the earth have different vital ef-
fluence, different vibration, different chemical exhalation, different
polarity with different stars: call it what you like. But the spirit of
place is a great reality. The Nile valley produced not only the corn,
but the terrific religions of Egypt. China produces the Chinese,
and will go on doing so. The Chinese in San Francisco will in time
cease to be Chinese, for America is a great melting-pot.

There was a tremendous polarity in Italy, in the city of Rome.
And this seems to have died. For even places die. The Island of
Great Britain had a wonderful terrestrial magnetism or polarity of
its own, which made the British people. For the moment, this
polarity seems to be breaking. Can England die? And what if
England dies?

Men are less free than they imagine; ah, far less free. The freest are perhaps least free.

Men are free when they are in a living homeland, not when they are straying and breaking away. Men are free when they are obeying some deep, inward voice of religious belief. Obeying from within. Men are free when they belong to a living, organic, *believing* community, active in fulfilling some unfulfilled, perhaps unrealised purpose. Not when they are escaping to some wild west. The most unfree souls go west, and shout of freedom. Men are freest when they are most unconscious of freedom. The shout is a rattling of chains, always was.

Men are not free when they are doing just what they like. The moment you can do just what you like, there is nothing you care about doing. Men are only free when they are doing what the deepest self likes.

And there is getting down to the deepest self! It takes some diving.

Because the deepest self is way down, and the conscious self is an obstinate monkey. But of one thing we may be sure. If one wants to be free, one has to give up the illusion of doing what one likes, and seek what IT wishes done.

But before you can do what IT likes, you must first break the spell of the old mastery, the old IT.

Perhaps at the Renaissance, when kingship and fatherhood fell, Europe drifted into a very dangerous half-truth: of liberty and equality. Perhaps the men who went to America felt this, and so repudiated the old world altogether. Went one better than Europe. Liberty in America has meant so far the breaking away from *all* dominion. The true liberty will only begin when Americans discover IT, and proceed possibly to fulfil IT. IT being the deepest *whole* self of man, the self in its wholeness, not idealistic halfness.

That's why the Pilgrim Fathers came to America, then; and that's why we come. Driven by IT. We cannot see that invisible winds carry us, as they carry swarms of locusts, that invisible magnetism brings us as it brings the migrating birds to their unforeknown goal. But it is so. We are not the marvellous choosers and deciders we think we are. IT chooses for us, and decides for us. Unless, of course, we are just escaped slaves, vulgarly cocksure of our ready-made destiny. But if we are living people, in touch with the source, IT drives us and decides us. We are free only so long as we obey. When we run counter, and think we will do as we like, we just flee around like Orestes pursued by the Eumenides.

And still, when the great day begins, when Americans have at last discovered America and their own wholeness, still there will be the vast number of escaped slaves to reckon with, those who have no cocksure, ready-made destinies.

Which will win in America, the escaped slaves, or the new whole men?

The real American day hasn't begun yet. Or at least, not yet sunrise. So far it has been the false dawn. That is, in the progressive American consciousness there has been the one dominant desire, to do away with the old thing. Do away with masters, exalt the will of the people. The will of the people being nothing but a figment, the exalting doesn't count for much. So, in the name of the will of the people, get rid of masters. When you have got rid of masters, you are left with this mere phrase of the will of the people. Then you pause and bethink yourself, and try to recover your own wholeness.

So much for the conscious American motive, and for democracy over here. Democracy in America is just the tool with which the old master of Europe, the European spirit, is undermined. Europe destroyed, potentially, American democracy will evaporate. America will begin.

American consciousness has so far been a false dawn. The negative ideal of democracy. But underneath, and contrary to this open ideal, the first hints and revelations of IT. IT, the American whole soul.

You have got to pull the democratic and idealistic clothes off American utterance, and see what you can of the dusky body of IT underneath.

'Henceforth be masterless.'

Henceforth be mastered.

Fenimore Cooper's Leatherstocking Novels

IN his Leatherstocking books, Fenimore is off on another track. He is no longer concerned with social white Americans* that buzz with pins through them, buzz loudly against every mortal thing except the pin itself. The pin of the Great Ideal.

One gets irritated with Cooper because he never for once snarls at the Great Ideal Pin which transfixes him. No, indeed. Rather he tries to push it through the very heart of the Continent.

But I have loved the Leatherstocking books so dearly. Wish-fulfilment!

Anyhow, one is not supposed to take LOVE seriously, in these books. Eve Effingham,* impaled on the social pin, conscious all the time of her own ego and of nothing else, suddenly fluttering in throes of love: no, it makes me sick. LOVE is never LOVE until it has a pin pushed through it and becomes an IDEAL. The ego, turning on a pin, is wildly IN LOVE, always. Because that's the thing to be.

Cooper was a GENTLEMAN, in the worst sense of the word. In the Nineteenth Century sense of the word. A correct, clockwork man.

Not altogether, of course.

The great national Grouch was grinding inside him. Probably he called it COSMIC URGE. Americans usually do: in capital letters.

Best stick to National Grouch. The great American grouch. Cooper had it, gentleman that he was. That is why he flitted round Europe so uneasily. Of course, in Europe he could be, and was, a gentleman to his heart's content.

'In short', he says in one of his letters, 'we were at table two counts, one monsignore, an English Lord, an Ambassador, and my humble self.'

Were we really!

How nice it must have been to know that one self, at least, was humble.

And he felt the democratic American tomahawk wheeling over his uncomfortable scalp all the time.

The great American grouch.

Two monsters loomed in Cooper's horizon.

MRS COOPER   MY WORK
MY WORK   MY WIFE
MY WIFE   MY WORK
THE DEAR CHILDREN
MY WORK ! ! !

There you have the essential keyboard of Cooper's soul.

If there is one thing that annoys me more than a business man and his BUSINESS, it is an artist, a writer, painter, musician, and MY WORK. When an artist says MY WORK, the flesh goes tired on my bones. When he says MY WIFE, I want to hit him.

Cooper grizzled about his work. Oh, heaven, he cared so much whether it was good or bad, and what the French thought, and what Mr Snippy Knowall said, and how Mrs Cooper took it. The pin, the pin!

But he was truly an artist: then an American: then a gentleman. And the grouch grouched inside him, through all.

They seem to have been specially fertile in imagining themselves 'under the wigwam', do these Americans, just when their knees were comfortably under the mahogany, in Paris, along with the knees of

4	Counts
2	Cardinals
1	Milord
5	Cocottes
1	Humble self

You bet, though, that when the cocottes were being raffled off, Fenimore went home to his WIFE.

Wish Fulfilment		*Actuality*
THE WIGWAM	*vs.*	MY HOTEL
CHINGACHGOOK*	*vs.*	MY WIFE
NATTY BUMPPO	*vs.*	MY HUMBLE SELF

Fenimore, lying in his Louis-Quatorze hotel in Paris, passionately musing about Natty Bumppo and the pathless forest, and mixing his imagination with the Cupids and Butterflies on the painted ceiling, while Mrs Cooper was struggling with her latest gown in the next room, and the *déjeuner* was with the Countess at eleven. ...

Men live by lies.

In actuality, Fenimore loved the genteel continent of Europe, and waited gasping for the newspapers to praise his WORK.

In another actuality he loved the tomahawking continent of America, and imagined himself Natty Bumppo.

His actual desire was to be: *Monsieur Fenimore Cooper, le grand écrivain américain.**

His innermost wish was to be: Natty Bumppo.

Now Natty and Fenimore, arm-in-arm, are an odd couple.

You can see Fenimore: blue coat, silver buttons, silver-and-diamond buckle shoes, ruffles.

You see Natty Bumppo: a grizzled, uncouth old renegade, with gaps in his old teeth and a drop on the end of his nose.

But Natty was Fenimore's great wish: his wish-fulfilment.

'It was a matter of course,' says Mrs Cooper, 'that he should dwell on the better traits of the picture rather than on the coarser and more revolting, though more common points. Like West, he could see Apollo in the young Mohawk.'*

The coarser and more revolting, though more common points.

You see now why he depended so absolutely on MY WIFE. She had to look things in the face for him. The coarser and more revolting, and certainly more common points, she had to see.

He himself did so love seeing pretty-pretty, with the thrill of a red scalp now and then.

Fenimore, in his imagination, wanted to be Natty Bumppo, who, I am sure, belched after he had eaten his dinner. At the same time Mr Cooper was nothing if not a gentleman. So he decided to stay in France and have it all his own way.

In France, Natty would not belch after eating, and Chingachgook could be all the Apollo he liked.

As if ever any Indian was like Apollo. The Indians, with their curious female quality, their archaic figures, with high shoulders and deep, archaic waists, like a sort of woman! And their natural devilishness, their natural insidiousness.

But men see what they want to see: especially if they look from a long distance, across the ocean, for example.

Yet the Leatherstocking books are lovely. Lovely half-lies.

They form a sort of American Odyssey, with Natty Bumppo for Odysseus.

Only, in the original Odyssey, there is plenty of devil, Circes and swine and all. And Ithacus* is devil enough to outwit the devils. But Natty is a saint with a gun, and the Indians are gentlemen through and through, though they may take an occasional scalp.

There are five Leatherstocking novels: a *decrescendo* of reality, and a crescendo of beauty.

1. *Pioneers:* A raw frontier-village on Lake Champlain,* at the end of the eighteenth century. Must be a picture of Cooper's home, as he knew it when a boy. A very lovely book. Natty Bumppo an old man, an old hunter half civilised.

2. *The Last of the Mohicans:* A historical fight between the British and the French, with Indians on both sides, at a Fort by Lake Champlain. Romantic flight of the British general's two daughters, conducted by the scout, Natty, who is in the prime of life; romantic death of the last of the Delawares.

3. *The Prairie:* A wagon of some huge, sinister Kentuckians trekking west into the unbroken prairie. Prairie Indians, and Natty, an old, old man; he dies seated on a chair on the Rocky Mountains, looking east.

4. *The Pathfinder:* The Great Lakes. Natty, a man of about thirty-five, makes an abortive proposal to a bouncing damsel, daughter of the Sergeant at the Fort.

5. *Deerslayer:* Natty and Hurry Harry, both quite young, are hunting in the virgin wild. They meet two white women. Lake Champlain again.

These are the five Leatherstocking books: Natty Bumppo being Leatherstocking, Pathfinder, Deerslayer, according to his ages.

Now let me put aside my impatience at the unreality of this vision, and accept it as a wish-fulfilment vision, a kind of yearning myth. Because it seems to me that the things in Cooper that make one so savage, when one compares them with actuality, are perhaps, when one considers them as presentations of a deep subjective desire, real in their way, and almost prophetic.

The passionate love for America, for the soil of America, for example. As I say, it is perhaps easier to love America passionately, when you look at it through the wrong end of the telescope, across all the Atlantic water, as Cooper did so often, than when you are right there. When you are actually *in* America, America hurts, because it has a powerful disintegrative influence upon the white psyche. It is full of grinning, unappeased aboriginal demons, too, ghosts, and it persecutes the white men, like some Eumenides, until the white men give up their absolute whiteness. America is tense with latent violence and resistance. The very common sense of white Americans has a tinge of helplessness in it, and deep fear of what might be if they were not common-sensical.

Yet one day the demons of America must be placated, the ghosts must be appeased, the Spirit of Place atoned for. Then the true passionate love for American Soil will appear. As yet, there is too much menace in the landscape.

But probably, one day America will be as beautiful in actuality as it is in Cooper. Not yet, however. When the factories have fallen down again.

And again, this perpetual blood-brother theme of the Leatherstocking novels, Natty and Chingachgook, the Great Serpent. At present it is a sheer myth. The Red Man and the White Man are not blood-brothers: even when they are most friendly. When they are most friendly, it is as a rule the one betraying his race-spirit to the other. In the white man—rather highbrow—who 'loves' the Indian, one feels the white man betraying his own race. There is something unproud, underhand in it. Renegade. The same with the Americanised Indian who believes absolutely in the white mode. It is a betrayal. Renegade again.

In the actual flesh, it seems to me the white man and the red man cause a feeling of oppression, the one to the other, no matter what the good will. The red life flows in a different direction from the white life. You can't make two streams that flow in opposite directions meet and mingle soothingly.

Certainly, if Cooper had had to spend his whole life in the backwoods, side by side with a Noble Red Brother, he would have screamed with the oppression of suffocation. He had to have Mrs Cooper, a straight strong pillar of society, to hang on to. And he had to have the culture of France to turn back to, or he would just have been stifled. The Noble Red Brother would have smothered him and driven him mad.

So that the Natty and Chingachgook myth must remain a myth. It is a wish-fulfilment, an evasion of actuality. As we have said before, the folds of the Great Serpent would have been heavy, very heavy, too heavy, on any white man. Unless the white man were a true renegade, hating himself and his own race spirit, as sometimes happens.

It seems there can be no fusion in the flesh. But the spirit can change. The white man's spirit can never become as the red man's spirit. It doesn't want to. But it can cease to be the opposite and the negative of the red man's spirit. It can open out a new great area of consciousness, in which there is room for the red spirit too.

To open out a new wide area of consciousness means to slough the old consciousness. The old consciousness has become a tight-fitting prison to us, in which we are going rotten.

You can't have a new, easy skin before you have sloughed the old, tight skin.

You can't.

And you just can't, so you may as well leave off pretending.

Now the essential history of the people of the United States seems to me just this: At the Renaissance the old consciousness was becoming a little tight. Europe sloughed her last skin, and started a new, final phase.

But some Europeans recoiled from the last final phase. They wouldn't enter the *cul-de-sac* of post-Renaissance, 'liberal' Europe. They came to America.

They came to America for two reasons:

1. To slough the old European consciousness completely.

2. To grow a new skin underneath, a new form. This second is a hidden process.

The two processes go on, of course, simultaneously. The slow forming of the new skin underneath is the slow sloughing of the old skin. And sometimes this immortal serpent feels very happy, feeling a new golden glow of a strangely-patterned skin envelop him: and sometimes he feels very sick, as if his very entrails were being torn out of him, as he wrenches once more at his old skin, to get out of it.

Out! Out! he cries, in all kinds of euphemisms.

He's got to have his new skin on him before ever he can get out.

And he's got to get out before his new skin can ever be his own skin.

So there he is, a torn, divided monster.

The true American, who writhes and writhes like a snake that is long in sloughing.

Sometimes snakes can't slough. They can't burst their old skin. Then they go sick and die inside the old skin, and nobody ever sees the new pattern.

It needs a real desperate recklessness to burst your old skin at last. You simply don't care what happens to you, if you rip yourself in two, so long as you do get out.

It also needs a real belief in the new skin. Otherwise you are likely never to make the effort. Then you gradually sicken and go rotten and die in the old skin.

Now Fenimore stayed very safe inside the old skin: a gentleman, almost a European, as proper as proper can be. And, safe inside the old skin, he *imagined* the gorgeous American pattern of a new skin.

He hated democracy. So he evaded it, and had a nice dream of something beyond democracy. But he belonged to democracy all the while.

Evasion!—Yet even that doesn't make the dream worthless.

Democracy in America was never the same as Liberty in Europe. In Europe Liberty was a great life-throb. But in America Democracy was always something anti-life. The greatest democrats, like Abraham Lincoln, had always a sacrificial, self-murdering note in their voices. American Democracy was a form of self-murder, always. Or of murdering somebody else.

Necessarily. It was a *pis aller*. It was the *pis aller* to European Liberty. It was a cruel form of sloughing. Men murdered themselves into this democracy. Democracy is the utter hardening of the old skin, the old form, the old psyche. It hardens till it is tight and fixed and inorganic. Then it *must* burst, like a chrysalis shell. And out must come the soft grub, or the soft damp butterfly of the American-at-last.

America has gone the *pis aller* of her democracy. Now she must slough even that, chiefly that, indeed.

What did Cooper dream beyond democracy? Why, in his immortal friendship of Chingachgook and Natty Bumppo he dreamed the nucleus of a new society. That is, he dreamed a new human relationship. A stark, stripped human relationship of two men, deeper than the deeps of sex. Deeper than property, deeper than fatherhood, deeper than marriage, deeper than love. So deep that it is loveless. The stark, loveless, wordless unison of two men who have come to the bottom of themselves. This is the new nucleus of a new society, the clue to a new world-epoch. It asks for a great and cruel sloughing first of all. Then it finds a great release into a new world, a new moral, a new landscape.

Natty and the Great Serpent are neither equals nor unequals. Each obeys the other when the moment arrives. And each is stark and dumb in the other's presence, starkly himself, without illusion created. Each is just the crude pillar of a man, the crude living column of his own manhood. And each knows the godhead of this crude column of manhood. A new relationship.

The Leatherstocking novels create the myth of this new relation. And they go backwards, from old age to golden youth. That is the true myth of America. She starts old, old, wrinkled and writhing in an old skin. And there is a gradual sloughing of the old skin, towards a new youth. It is the myth of America.

You start with actuality. *Pioneers* is no doubt Cooperstown* when Cooperstown was in the stage of inception: a village of one wild street of log cabins under the forest hills by Lake Champlain: a village of crude, wild frontiersmen, reacting against civilisation.

Towards this frontier-village in the winter time, a negro slave drives a sledge through the mountains, over deep snow. In the sledge sits a fair damsel, Miss Temple, with her handsome pioneer father, Judge Temple. They hear a shot in the trees. It is the old hunter and backwoodsman, Natty Bumppo, long and lean and uncouth, with a long rifle and gaps in his teeth.

Judge Temple is 'squire' of the village, and he has a ridiculous, commodious 'hall' for his residence. It is still the old English form. Miss Temple is a pattern young lady, like Eve Effingham: in fact, she gets a young and very genteel but impoverished Effingham for a husband. The old world holding its own on the edge of the wild. A bit tiresomely too, with rather more prunes and prisms than one can digest. Too romantic.

Against the 'hall' and the gentry, the real frontiers-folk, the rebels. The two groups meet at the village inn, and at the frozen church, and at the Christmas sports, and on the ice of the lake, and at the great pigeon shoot. It is a beautiful, resplendent picture of life. Fenimore puts in only the glamour.

Perhaps my taste is childish, but these scenes in *Pioneers* seem to me marvellously beautiful. The raw village street, with wood fires blinking through the unglazed window-chinks, on a winter's night. The inn, with the rough woodsman and the drunken Indian John; the church, with the snowy congregation crowding to the fire. Then the lavish abundance of Christmas cheer, and turkey shooting in the snow. Spring coming, forests all green, maple-sugar taken from the trees: and clouds of pigeons flying from the south, myriads of pigeons, shot in heaps; and night-fishing on the teeming, virgin lake; and deer-hunting.

Pictures! Some of the loveliest, most glamorous pictures in all literature.

Alas, without the cruel iron of reality. It is all real enough. Except that one realises that Fenimore was writing from a safe distance, where he would idealise and have his wish-fulfilment.

Because, when one comes to America, one finds that there is always a certain slightly devilish resistance in the American landscape, and a certain slightly bitter resistance in the white man's heart. Hawthorne gives this. But Cooper glosses it over.

The American landscape has never been at one with the white man. Never. And white men have probably never felt so bitter anywhere, as here in America, where the very landscape, in its very beauty, seems a bit devilish and grinning, opposed to us.

Cooper, however, glosses over this resistance, which in actuality can never quite be glossed over. He *wants* the landscape to be at one with him. So he goes away to Europe and sees it as such. It is a sort of vision.

And, nevertheless, the oneing will surely take place—some day.

The myth is the story of Natty. The old, lean hunter and backwoodsman lives with his friend, the grey-haired Indian John, an old Delaware chief, in a hut within reach of the village. The Delaware is christianised and bears the Christian name of John. He is tribeless and lost. He humiliates his grey hairs in drunkenness, and dies, thankful to be dead, in a forest fire, passing back to the fire whence he derived.

And this is Chingachgook, the splendid Great Serpent of the later novels.

No doubt Cooper, as a boy, knew both Natty and the Indian John. No doubt they fired his imagination even then. When he is a man, crystallised in society and sheltering behind the safe pillar of Mrs Cooper, these two old fellows become a myth to his soul. He traces himself to a new youth in them.

As for the story: Judge Temple has just been instrumental in passing the wise game laws. But Natty has lived by his gun all his life in the wild woods, and simply childishly cannot understand how he can be poaching on the Judge's land among the pine trees. He shoots a deer in the close season. The Judge is all sympathy, but the law *must* be enforced. Bewildered Natty, an old man of seventy, is put in stocks and in prison. They release him as soon as possible. But the thing was done.

The letter killeth.*

Natty's last connexion with his own race is broken. John, the Indian, is dead. The old hunter disappears, lonely and severed, into the forest, away, away from his race.

In the new epoch that is coming, there will be no letter of the Law.

Chronologically, *The Last of the Mohicans* follows *Pioneers.* But in the myth, *The Prairie* comes next.

Cooper of course knew his own America. He travelled west and saw the prairies, and camped with the Indians of the prairie.

The Prairie, like *Pioneers,* bears a good deal the stamp of actuality. It is a strange, splendid book, full of sense of doom. The figures of the great Kentuckian men, with their wolf-women, loom colossal on the vast prairie, as they camp with their wagons. These are different pioneers from Judge Temple. Lurid, brutal, tinged with the sinisterness of crime; these are the gaunt white men who push west, push on and on against the natural opposition of the continent. On towards a doom. Great wings of vengeful doom seem spread over the west, grim against the intruder. You feel them again in Frank Norris's novel, *The Octopus.* While in the West of Bret Harte* there is a very devil in the air, and beneath him are sentimental self-conscious people being wicked and goody by evasion.

In *The Prairie* there is a shadow of violence and dark cruelty flickering in the air. It is the aboriginal demon hovering over the core of the continent. It hovers still, and the dread is still there.

Into such a prairie enters the huge figure of Ishmael, ponderous, pariah-like Ishmael and his huge sons and his were-wolf wife. With their wagons they roll on from the frontiers of Kentucky, like Cyclops* into the savage wilderness. Day after day they seem to force their way into oblivion. But their force of penetration ebbs. They are brought to a stop. They recoil in the throes of murder and entrench themselves in isolation on a hillock in the midst of the prairie. There they hold out like demi-gods against the elements and the subtle Indian.

The pioneering brute invasion of the West, crime-tinged!

And into this setting, as a sort of minister of peace, enters the old, old hunter Natty, and his suave, horse-riding Sioux Indians. But he seems like a shadow.

The hills rise softly west, to the Rockies. There seems a new peace: or is it only suspense, abstraction, waiting? Is it only a sort of beyond?

Natty lives in these hills, in a village of the suave, horse-riding Sioux. They revere him as an old wise father.

In these hills he dies, sitting in his chair and looking far east, to the forest and great sweet waters, whence he came. He dies gently, in physical peace with the land and the Indians. He is an old, old man.

Cooper could see no further than the foothills where Natty died, beyond the prairie.

The other novels bring us back east.

The Last of the Mohicans is divided between real historical narrative and true 'romance'. For myself, I prefer the romance. It has a myth meaning, whereas the narrative is chiefly record.

For the first time we get actual women: the dark, handsome Cora and her frail sister, the White Lily.* The good old division, the dark sensual woman and the clinging, submissive little blonde, who is so 'pure'.

These sisters are fugitives through the forest, under the protection of a Major Heyward, a young American officer and Englishman. He is just a 'white' man, very good and brave and generous, etc., but limited, most definitely *borné*. He would probably love Cora, if he dared, but he finds it safer to adore the clinging White Lily of a younger sister.

This trio is escorted by Natty, now Leatherstocking, a hunter and scout in the prime of life, accompanied by his inseparable friend Chingachgook, and the Delaware's beautiful son—Adonis rather than Apollo—Uncas, The Last of the Mohicans.

There is also a 'wicked' Indian, Magua, handsome and injured incarnation of evil.

Cora is the scarlet flower of womanhood, fierce, passionate offspring of some mysterious union between the British officer and a Creole woman in the West Indies. Cora loves Uncas, Uncas loves Cora. But Magua also desires Cora, violently desires her. A lurid little circle of sensual fire. So Fenimore kills them all off, Cora, Uncas, and Magua, and leaves the White Lily to carry on the race. She will breed plenty of white children to Major Heyward. These tiresome 'lilies that fester',* of our day.

Evidently Cooper—or the artist in him—has decided that there can be no blood-mixing of the two races, white and red. He kills 'em off.

Beyond all this heart-beating stand the figures of Natty and Chingachgook: the two childless, womanless men, of opposite races. They are the abiding thing. Each of them is alone, and final in his race. And they stand side by side, stark, abstract, beyond emotion, yet eternally together. All the other loves seem frivolous. This is the new great thing, the clue, the inception of a new humanity.

And Natty, what sort of a white man is he? Why, he is a man with a gun. He is a killer, a slayer. Patient and gentle as he is, he is a slayer. Self-effacing, self-forgetting, still he is a killer.

Twice, in the book, he brings an enemy down hurtling in death through the air, downwards. Once it is the beautiful, wicked Magua—shot from a height, and hurtling down ghastly through space, into death.

This is Natty, the white forerunner. A killer. As in *Deerslayer,* he shoots the bird that flies in the high, high sky, so that the bird falls out of the invisible into the visible, dead, he symbolises himself. He will bring the bird of the spirit out of the high air. He is the stoic

American killer of the old great life. But he kills, as he says, only to live.

Pathfinder takes us to the Great Lakes, and the glamour and beauty of sailing the great sweet waters. Natty is now called Pathfinder. He is about thirty-five years old, and he falls in love. The damsel is Mabel Dunham, daughter of Sergeant Dunham of the Fort garrison. She is blonde and in all things admirable. No doubt Mrs Cooper was very much like Mabel.

And Pathfinder doesn't marry her. She won't have him. She wisely prefers a more comfortable Jasper. So Natty goes off to grouch, and to end by thanking his stars. When he had got right clear, and sat by the campfire with Chingachgook, in the forest, didn't he just thank his stars! A lucky escape!

Men of an uncertain age are liable to these infatuations. They aren't always lucky enough to be rejected.

Whatever would poor Mabel have done, had she been Mrs Bumppo?

Natty had no business marrying. His mission was elsewhere.

The most fascinating Leatherstocking book is the last, *Deerslayer*. Natty is now a fresh youth, called Deerslayer. But the kind of silent prim youth who is never quite young, but reserves himself for different things.

It is a gem of a book. Or a bit of perfect paste. And myself, I like a bit of perfect paste in a perfect setting, so long as I am not fooled by pretence of reality. And the setting of Deerslayer *could* not be more exquisite. Lake Champlain again.

Of course it never rains: it is never cold and muddy and dreary: no one has wet feet or toothache: no one ever feels filthy, when they can't wash for a week. God knows what the women would really have looked like, for they fled through the wilds without soap, comb, or towel. They breakfasted off a chunk of meat, or nothing, lunched the same, and supped the same.

Yet at every moment they are elegant, perfect ladies, in correct toilet.

Which isn't quite fair. You need only go camping for a week, and you'll see.

But it is a myth, not a realistic tale. Read it as a lovely myth. Lake Glimmerglass.

Deerslayer, the youth with the long rifle, is found in the woods with a big, handsome, blond-bearded backwoodsman called Hurry Harry. Deerslayer seems to have been born under a hemlock tree out of a pine-cone: a young man of the woods. He is silent, simple, philosophic, moralistic, and an unerring shot. His simplicity is the simplicity of age rather than of youth. He is race-old. All his reactions and impulses are fixed, static. Almost he is sexless, so race-old. Yet intelligent, hardy, dauntless.

Hurry Harry is a big blusterer, just the opposite of Deerslayer. Deerslayer keeps the centre of his own consciousness steady and unperturbed. Hurry Harry is one of those floundering people who bluster from one emotion to another, very self-conscious, without any centre to them.

These two young men are making their way to a lovely, smallish lake, Lake Glimmerglass. On this water the Hutter family has established itself. Old Hutter, it is suggested, has a criminal, coarse, buccaneering past, and is a sort of fugitive from justice. But he is a good enough father to his two grown-up girls. The family lives in a log hut 'castle', built on piles in the water, and the old man has also constructed an 'ark', a sort of house-boat, in which he can take his daughters when he goes on his rounds to trap the beaver.

The two girls are the inevitable dark and light Judith, dark, fearless, passionate, a little lurid with sin, is the scarlet-and-black blossom. Hetty, the younger, blonde, frail and innocent, is the white lily again. But alas, the lily has begun to fester. She is slightly imbecile.

The two hunters arrive at the lake among the woods just as war has been declared. The Hutters are unaware of the fact. And hostile Indians are on the lake already. So, the story of thrills and perils.

Thomas Hardy's inevitable division of women into dark and fair, sinful and innocent, sensual and pure, is Cooper's division too. It is indicative of the desire in the man. He wants sensuality and sin, and he wants purity and 'innocence'. If the innocence goes a little rotten, slightly imbecile, bad luck!

Hurry Harry, of course, like a handsome impetuous meat-fly, at once wants Judith, the lurid poppy-blossom. Judith rejects him with scorn.

Judith, the sensual woman, at once wants the quiet, reserved, unmastered Deerslayer. She wants to master him. And Deerslayer is half tempted, but never more than half. He is not going to be mastered. A philosophic old soul, he does not give much for the temptations of sex. Probably he dies virgin.

And he is right of it. Rather than be dragged into a false heat of deliberate sensuality, he will remain alone. His soul is alone, for ever alone. So he will preserve his integrity, and remain alone in the flesh. It is a stoicism which is honest and fearless, and from which Deerslayer never lapses, except when, approaching middle age, he proposes to the buxom Mabel.

He lets his consciousness penetrate in loneliness into the new continent. His contacts are not human. He wrestles with the spirits of the forest and the American wild, as a hermit wrestles with God and Satan. His one meeting is with Chingachgook, and this meeting is silent, reserved, across an unpassable distance.

Hetty, the White Lily, being imbecile, although full of vaporous religion and the dear, good God, 'who governs all things by his providence', is hopelessly infatuated with Hurry Harry. Being innocence gone imbecile, like Dostoevsky's Idiot,* she longs to give herself to the handsome meat-fly. Of course he doesn't want her.

And so nothing happens: in that direction. Deerslayer goes off to meet Chingachgook, and help him woo an Indian maid. Vicarious.

It is the miserable story of the collapse of the white psyche. The white man's mind and soul are divided between these two things: innocence and lust, the Spirit and Sensuality. Sensuality always carries a stigma, and is therefore more deeply desired, or lusted after. But spirituality alone gives the sense of uplift, exaltation, and 'winged life', with the inevitable reaction into sin and spite. So the white man is divided against himself. He plays off one side of himself against the other side, till it is really a tale told by an idiot,* and nauseating.

Against this, one is forced to admire the stark, enduring figure of Deerslayer. He is neither spiritual nor sensual. He is a moraliser, but he always tries to moralise from actual experience, not from theory. He says: 'Hurt nothing unless you're forced to.' Yet he gets his deepest thrill of gratification, perhaps, when he puts a bullet through the heart of a beautiful buck, as its stoops to drink at the lake. Or when he brings the invisible bird fluttering down in death, out of the high blue. 'Hurt nothing unless you're forced to.' And yet he lives by death, by killing the wild things of the air and earth.

It's not good enough.

But you have there the myth of the essential white America. All the other stuff, the love, the democracy, the floundering into lust, is a sort of by-play. The essential American soul is hard, isolate, stoic, and a killer. It has never yet melted.

Of course, the soul often breaks down into disintegration, and you have lurid sin and Judith, imbecile innocence lusting, in Hetty, and bluster, bragging, and self-conscious strength, in Harry. But these are the disintegration products.

What true myth concerns itself with is not the disintegration product. True myth concerns itself centrally with the onward adventure of the integral soul. And this, for America, is Deerslayer. A man who turns his back on white society. A man who keeps his moral integrity hard and intact. An isolate, almost selfless, stoic, enduring man, who lives by death, by killing, but who is pure white.

This is the very intrinsic-most American. He is at the core of all the other flux and fluff. And when *this* man breaks from his static isolation, and makes a new move, then look out, something will be happening.

Herman Melville's *Typee* and *Omoo**

THE greatest seer and poet of the sea for me is Melville. His vision is more real than Swinburne's, because he doesn't personify the sea,* and far sounder than Joseph Conrad's, because Melville doesn't sentimentalise the ocean and the sea's unfortunates. Snivel in a wet hanky like Lord Jim.*

Melville has the strange, uncanny magic of sea-creatures, and some of their repulsiveness. He isn't quite a land animal. There is something slithery about him. Something always half-seas-over. In his life they said he was mad—or crazy. He was neither mad nor crazy. But he was over the border. He was half a water animal, like those terrible yellow-bearded Vikings who broke out of the waves in beaked ships.

He was a modern Viking. There is something curious about real blue-eyed people. They are never quite human, in the good classic sense, human as brown-eyed people are human: the human of the living humus. About a real blue-eyed person there is usually something abstract, elemental. Brown-eyed people are, as it were, like the earth, which is tissue of bygone life, organic, compound. In blue eyes there is sun and rain and abstract, uncreate element, water, ice, air, space, but not humanity. Brown-eyed people are people of the old, old world: *Allzu menschlich.** Blue-eyed people tend to be too keen and abstract.

Melville is like a Viking going home to the sea, encumbered with age and memories, and a sort of accomplished despair, almost madness. For he cannot accept humanity. He can't belong to humanity. Cannot.

The great Northern cycle of which he is the returning unit has almost completed its round, accomplished itself. Balder the beautiful is mystically dead, and by this time he stinketh.* Forget-me-nots and sea-poppies fall into water. The man who came from the sea to live among men can stand it no longer. He hears the horror of the cracked church bell, and goes back down the shore, back into the ocean again, home, into the salt water. Human life won't do. He turns back to the elements. And all the vast sun-and-wheat consciousness of his day he plunges back into the deeps, burying the flame in the deep, self-conscious and deliberate. As blue flax and sea-poppies fall into the waters and give back their created sun-stuff to the dissolution of the flood.

The sea-born people, who can meet and mingle no longer: who turn away from life, to the abstract, to the elements: the sea receives her own.

Let life come asunder, they say. Let water conceive no more with fire. Let mating finish. Let the elements leave off kissing, and turn their backs on one another. Let the merman turn away from his human wife and children, let the seal-woman* forget the world of men, remembering only the waters.

So they go down to the sea, the sea-born people. The Vikings are wandering again. Homes are broken up. Cross the seas, cross the seas, urges the heart. Leave love and home. Leave love and home. Love and home are a deadly illusion. Woman, what have I to do with thee? It is finished. *Consummatum est.** The crucifixion into humanity is over. Let us go back to the fierce, uncanny elements: the corrosive vast sea. Or Fire.

Basta!* It is enough. It is enough of life. Let us have the vast elements. Let us get out of this loathsome complication of living humanly with humans. Let the sea wash us clean of the leprosy of our humanity and humanness.

Melville was a northerner, sea-born. So the sea claimed him. We are most of us, who use the English language, water-people, sea-derived.

Melville went back to the oldest of all the oceans, to the Pacific. *Der Grosse oder Stille Ozean.**

Without doubt the Pacific Ocean is aeons older than the Atlantic or the Indian Oceans. When we say older, we mean it has not come to any modern consciousness. Strange convulsions have convulsed the Atlantic and Mediterranean peoples into phase after phase of consciousness, while the Pacific and the Pacific peoples have slept. To sleep is to dream: you can't stay unconscious. And, oh heaven, for how many thousands of years has the true Pacific been dreaming, turning over in its sleep and dreaming again: idylls: nightmares?

The Maoris, the Tongans, the Marquesans, the Fijians, the Polynesians: holy God, how long have they been turning over in the same sleep, with varying dreams? Perhaps, to a sensitive imagination, those islands in the middle of the Pacific are the most unbearable places on earth. It simply stops the heart, to be translated there, unknown ages back, back into that life, that pulse, that rhythm. The scientists say the South Sea Islanders belong to the Stone Age. It seems absurd to class people according to their implements. And yet there is something in it. The heart of the Pacific is still the Stone Age; in spite of steamers. The heart of the Pacific seems like a vast vacuum, in which, mirage-like, continues the life of myriads of ages back. It is a phantom-persistence of human beings who should have died, by our chronology, in the Stone Age. It is a phantom, illusion-like trick of reality: the glamorous South Seas.

Even Japan and China have been turning over in their sleep for countless centuries. Their blood is the old blood, their tissue the old soft tissue. Their busy day was myriads of years ago, when the world was a softer place, more moisture in the air, more warm mud on the face of the earth, and the lotus was always in flower. The great bygone world, before Egypt. And Japan and China have been turning over in their sleep, while we have 'advanced'. And now they are starting up into nightmare.

The world isn't what it seems.

The Pacific Ocean holds the dream of immemorial centuries. It is the great blue twilight of the vastest of all evenings: perhaps of the most wonderful of all dawns. Who knows?

It must once have been a vast basin of soft, lotus-warm civilisation, the Pacific. Never was such a huge man-day swung down into slow disintegration, as here. And now the waters are blue and ghostly with the end of immemorial peoples. And phantom-like the islands rise out of it, illusions of the glamorous Stone Age.

To this phantom Melville returned. Back, back, away from life. Never man instinctively hated human life, our human life, as we have it, more than Melville did. And never was a man so passionately filled with the sense of vastness and mystery of life which is non-human. He was mad to look over our horizons. Anywhere, anywhere out of *our* world. To get away. To get away, out!

To get away, out of our life. To cross a horizon into another life. No matter what life, so long as it is another life.

Away, away from humanity. To the sea. The naked, salt, elemental sea. To go to sea, to escape humanity.

The human heart gets into a frenzy at last, in its desire to dehumanise itself.

So he finds himself in the middle of the Pacific. Truly over a horizon. In another world. In another epoch. Back, far back, in the days of palm trees and lizards and stone implements. The sunny Stone Age.

Samoa, Tahiti, Raratonga, Nukuheva: the very names are a sleep and a forgetting. The sleep-forgotten past magnificence of human history. 'Trailing clouds of glory.'*

Melville hated the world: was born hating it. But he was looking for heaven. That is, choosingly. Choosingly, he was looking for paradise. Unchoosingly, he was mad with hatred of the world.

Well, the world is hateful. It is as hateful as Melville found it. He was not wrong in hating the world. *Delenda est Chicago.** He hated it to a pitch of madness, and not without reason.

But it's no good *persisting* in looking for paradise 'regained'.

Melville at his best invariably wrote from a sort of dream-self, so that events which he relates as actual fact have indeed a far deeper reference to his own soul, his own inner life.

So in *Typee* when he tells of his entry into the valley of the dread cannibals of Nukuheva. Down this narrow, steep, horrible dark gorge he slides and struggles as we struggle in a dream, or in the act of birth, to emerge in the green Eden of the Golden Age, the valley of the cannibal savages. This is a bit of birth-myth, or rebirth-myth, on Melville's part—unconscious, no doubt, because his running underconsciousness was always mystical and symbolical. He wasn't aware that he was being mystical.

There he is then, in Typee, among the dreaded cannibal savages. And they are gentle and generous with him, and he is truly in a sort of Eden.

Here at last is Rousseau's Child of Nature and Chateaubriand's Noble Savage* called upon and found at home. Yes, Melville loves his savage hosts. He finds them gentle, laughing lambs compared to the ravening wolves of his white brothers, left behind in America and on an American whale-ship.

The ugliest beast on earth is the white man, says Melville.

In short, Herman found in Typee the paradise he was looking

for. It is true, the Marquesans were 'immoral', but he rather liked that. Morality was too white a trick to take him in. Then again, they were cannibals. And it filled him with horror even to think of this. But the savages were very private and even fiercely reserved in their cannibalism, and he might have spared himself his shudder. No doubt he had partaken of the Christian Sacraments many a time. 'This is my body, take and eat. This is my blood. Drink it in remembrance of me.' And if the savages liked to partake of their sacrament without raising the transubstantiation quibble,* and if they liked to say, directly: 'This is thy body, which I take from thee and eat. This is thy blood, which I sip in annihilation of thee', why surely their sacred ceremony was as awe-inspiring as the one Jesus substituted. But Herman chose to be horrified. I confess, I am not horrified; though, of course, I am not on the spot. But the savage sacrament seems to me more valid than the Christian: less side-tracking about it. Thirdly, he was shocked by their wild methods of warfare. He died before the great European war, so his shock was comfortable.

Three little quibbles: morality, cannibal sacrament, and stone axes. You must have a fly even in Paradisal ointment. And the first was a ladybird.

But Paradise. He insists on it. Paradise. He could even go stark naked, as before the Apple episode. And his Fayaway, a laughing little Eve, naked with him, and hankering after no apple of knowledge,* so long as he would just love her when he felt like it. Plenty to eat, needing no clothes to wear, sunny, happy people, sweet water to swim in: everything a man can want. Then why wasn't he happy along with the savages?

Because he wasn't.

He grizzled in secret, and wanted to escape.

He even pined for Home and Mother, the two things he had run away from as far as ships would carry him. HOME and MOTHER. The two things that were his damnation.

There on the island, where the golden-green great palm-trees chinked in the sun, and the elegant reed houses let the sea-breeze through, and people went naked and laughed a great deal, and Fayaway put flowers in his hair for him—great red hibiscus flowers, and frangipani—O God, why wasn't he happy? Why wasn't he?

Because he wasn't.

Well, it's hard to make a man happy.

But I should not have been happy either. One's soul seems under a vacuum, in the South Seas.

The truth of the matter is, one cannot go back. Some men can: renegade. But Melville couldn't go back: and Gauguin* couldn't really go back: and I know now that I could never go back. Back towards the past, savage life. One cannot go back. It is one's destiny inside one.

There are these peoples, these 'savages'. One does not despise them. One does not feel superior. But there is a gulf. There is a gulf in time and being. I cannot commingle my being with theirs.

There they are, these South Sea Islanders, beautiful big men with their golden limbs and their laughing, graceful laziness. And they will call you brother, choose you as a brother. But why cannot one truly be brother?

There is an invisible hand grasps my heart and prevents it opening too much to these strangers. They are beautiful, they are like children, they are generous: but they are more than this. They are far off, and in their eyes is an easy darkness of the soft, uncreate past. In a way, they are uncreate. Far be it from me to assume any 'white' superiority. But they are savages. They are gentle and laughing and physically very handsome. But it seems to me, that in living so far, through all our bitter centuries of civilisation, we have still been living onwards, forwards. God knows it looks like a *cul-de-sac* now. But turn to the first negro, and then listen to your own soul. And your own soul will tell you that however false and foul our forms and systems are now, still, through the many centuries since Egypt, we have been living and struggling forwards along some road that is no road, and yet is a great life-development. We have struggled on, and on we must still go. We may have to smash things. Then let us smash. And our road may have to take a great swerve, that seems a retrogression.

But we can't go back. Whatever else the South Sea Islander is, he is centuries and centuries behind us in the life-struggle, the consciousness-struggle, the struggle of the soul into fulness. There is his woman, with her knotted hair and her dark, inchoate, slightly sardonic eyes. I like her, she is nice. But I would never want to touch her. I could not go back on myself so far. Back to their uncreate condition.

She has soft warm flesh, like warm mud. Nearer the reptile, the Saurian age. *Noli me tangere.**

We can't go back. We can't go back to the savages: not a stride. We can be in sympathy with them. We can take a great curve in their direction, onwards. But we cannot turn the current of our life backwards, back towards their soft warm twilight and uncreate mud. Not for a moment. If we do it for a moment, it makes us sick.

We can only do it when we are renegade. The renegade hates life itself. He wants the death of life. So these many 'reformers' and 'idealists' who glorify the savages in America. They are death-birds, life-haters. Renegades.

We can't go back, and Melville couldn't. Much as he hated the civilised humanity he knew. He couldn't go back to the savages; he wanted to, he tried to, and he couldn't.

Because, in the first place, it made him sick; it made him physically ill. He had something wrong with his leg, and this would not heal. It got worse and worse, during his four months on the island. When he escaped, he was in a deplorable condition—sick and miserable, ill, very ill.

Paradise!

But there you are. Try to go back to the savages, and you feel as if your very soul was decomposing inside you. That is what you feel in the South Seas, anyhow: as if your soul was decomposing inside you. And with any savages the same, if you try to go their way, take their current of sympathy.

Yet, as I say, we must make a great swerve in our onward-going life-course now, to gather up again the savage mysteries. But this does not mean going back on ourselves.

Going back to the savages made Melville sicker than anything. It made him feel as if he were decomposing. Worse even than Home and Mother.

And that is what really happens. If you prostitute your psyche by returning to the savages, you gradually go to pieces. Before you can go back, you *have* to decompose. And a white man decomposing is a ghastly sight. Even Melville in Typee.

We have to go on, on, on, even if we must smash a way ahead.

So Melville escaped, and threw a boat-hook full in the throat of one of his dearest savage friends, and sank him, because that savage was swimming in pursuit. That's how he felt about the savages when they wanted to detain him. He'd have murdered them one and all, vividly, rather than be kept from escaping. Away from them—he must get away from them—at any price.

And once he has escaped, immediately he begins to sigh and pine for the 'Paradise'—Home and Mother being at the other end even of a whaling voyage.

When he really was Home with Mother, he found it Purgatory. But Typee must have been even worse than Purgatory, a soft hell judging from the murderous frenzy which possessed him to escape.

But once aboard the whaler that carried him off from Nukuheva, he looked back and sighed for the Paradise he had just escaped from in such a fever.

Poor Melville! He was determined Paradise existed. So he was always in Purgatory.

He was born for Purgatory. Some souls are purgatorial by destiny.

The very freedom of this Typee was a torture to him. Its ease was slowly horrible to him. This time *he* was the fly in the odorous tropical ointment.

He needed to fight. It was no good to him, the relaxation of the non-moral tropics. He didn't really want Eden. He wanted to fight. Like every American. To fight. But with weapons of the spirit, not the flesh.

That was the top and bottom of it. His soul was in revolt, writhing for ever in revolt. When he had something definite to rebel against—like the bad conditions on a whaling ship—then he was much happier in his miseries. The mills of God were grinding inside him, and they needed something to grind on.

When they could grind on the injustice and folly of missionaries, or of brutal sea-captains, or of governments, he was easier. The mills of God were grinding inside him.

They are grinding inside every American. And they grind exceeding small.*

Why? Heaven knows. But we've got to grind down our old forms, our old selves, grind them very very small, to nothingness. Whether a new somethingness will ever start, who knows? Meanwhile the mills of God grind on, in American Melville, and it was himself he ground small: himself and his wife, when he was married. For the present, the South Seas.

He escapes on to the craziest, most impossible of whaling ships. Lucky for us Melville makes it fantastic. It must have been pretty sordid.

And anyhow, on the crazy *Julia*, his leg, that would never heal in the paradise of Typee, began quickly to get well. His life was falling into its normal pulse. The drain back into past centuries was over.

Yet, oh, as he sails away from Nukuheva, on the voyage that will ultimately take him to America, oh, the acute and intolerable nostalgia he feels for the island he has left.

The past, the Golden Age of the past—what a nostalgia we all feel for it. Yet we don't want it when we get it. Try the South Seas.

Melville had to fight, fight against the existing world, against his own very self. Only he would never quite put the knife in the heart of his paradisal ideal. Somehow, somewhere, somewhen, love should be a fulfilment, and life should be a thing of bliss. That was his fixed ideal. *Fata Morgana.**

That was the pin he tortured himself on, liked a pinned-down butterfly.

Love is never a fulfilment. Life is never a thing of continuous bliss. There is no paradise. Fight and laugh and feel bitter and feel bliss: and fight again. Fight, fight. That is life.

Why pin ourselves down on a paradisal ideal? It is only ourselves we torture.

Melville did have one great experience, getting away from humanity: the experience of the sea.

The South Sea Islands were not his great experience. They were a glamorous world outside New England. Outside. But it was the sea that was both outside and inside: the universal experience.

The book that follows on from *Typee* is *Omoo*.

Omoo is a fascinating book; picaresque, rascally, roving. Melville, as a bit of a beachcomber. The crazy ship *Julia* sails to Tahiti, and the mutinous crew are put ashore. Put in the Tahitian prison. It is good reading.

Perhaps Melville is at his best, his happiest, in *Omoo*. For once he is really reckless. For once he takes life as it comes. For once he is the gallant rascally epicurean, eating the world like a snipe, dirt and all baked into one *bonne bouche*.

For once he is really careless, roving with that scamp, Doctor

Long Ghost. For once he is careless of his actions, careless of his morals, careless of his ideals: ironic, as the epicurean must be. The deep irony of your real scamp: your real epicurean of the moment.

But it was under the influence of the Long Doctor. This long and bony Scotsman was not a mere ne'er-do-well. He was a man of humorous desperation, throwing his life ironically away. Not a mere loose-kneed loafer, such as the South Seas seem to attract.

That is good about Melville: he never repents. Whatever he did, in Typee or in Doctor Long Ghost's wicked society, he never repented. If he ate his snipe, dirt and all, and enjoyed it at the time, he didn't have bilious bouts afterwards, which is good.

But it wasn't enough. The Long Doctor was really knocking about in a sort of despair. He let his ship drift rudderless.

Melville couldn't do this. For a time, yes. For a time, in this Long Doctor's company, he was rudderless and reckless. Good as an experience. But a man who will not abandon himself to despair or indifference cannot keep it up.

Melville would never abandon himself either to despair or indifference. He always cared. He always cared enough to hate missionaries, and to be touched by a real act of kindness. He always cared.

When he saw a white man really 'gone savage', a white man with a blue shark tattooed over his brow, gone over to the savages, then Herman's whole being revolted. He couldn't bear it. He could not bear a renegade.

He enlisted at last on an American man-of-war. You have the record in *White Jacket*.* He was back in civilisation, but still at sea. He was in America, yet loose in the seas. Good regular days, after Doctor Long Ghost and the *Julia*.

As a matter of fact, a long thin chain was round Melville's ankle all the time, binding him to America, to civilisation, to democracy, to the ideal world. It was a long chain, and it never broke. It pulled him back.

By the time he was twenty-five his wild oats were sown; his reckless wanderings were over. At the age of twenty-five he came back to Home and Mother, to fight it out at close quarters. For you can't fight it out by running away. When you have run a long way from Home and Mother, then you realise that the earth is round, and if you keep on running you'll be back on the same old doorstep—like a fatality.

Melville came home to face out the long rest of his life. He married and had an ecstasy of a courtship and fifty years of disillusion.

He had just furnished his home with disillusions. No more Typees. No more paradises. No more Fayaways. A mother: a gorgon. A home: a torture box. A wife: a thing with clay feet. Life: a sort of disgrace. Fame: another disgrace, being patronised by common snobs who just know how to read.

The whole shameful business just making a man writhe.

Melville writhed for eighty years.

In his soul he was proud and savage.

But in his mind and will he wanted the perfect fulfilment of love; he wanted the lovey-doveyness of perfect mutual understanding.

A proud savage-souled man doesn't really want any perfect lovey-dovey fulfilment in love: no such nonsense. A mountain lion doesn't mate with a Persian cat; and when a grizzly bear roars after a mate, it is a she-grizzly he roars after—not after a silky sheep.

But Melville stuck to his ideal. He wrote *Pierre** to show that the more you try to be good the more you make a mess of things: that following righteousness is just disastrous. The better you are, the worse things turn out with you. The better you try to be, the bigger mess you make. Your very striving after righteousness only causes your own slow degeneration.

Well, it is true. No men are so evil today as the idealists, and no women half so evil as your earnest woman, who feels herself a power for good. It is inevitable. After a certain point, the ideal goes dead and rotten. The old pure ideal becomes in itself an impure thing of evil. Charity becomes pernicious, the spirit itself becomes foul. The meek are evil. The pure in heart have base, subtle revisions: like Dostoevsky's Idiot.* The whole Sermon on the Mount becomes a litany of white vice.

What then?

It's our own fault. It was *we* who set up the ideals. And if we are such fools, that we aren't able to kick over our ideals in time, the worse for us.

Look at Melville's eighty long years of writhing. And to the end he writhed on the ideal pin.

From the 'perfect woman lover' he passed on to the 'perfect friend'. He looked and looked for the perfect man friend.

Couldn't find him.

Marriage was a ghastly disillusion to him, because he looked for perfect marriage.

Friendship never even made a real start in him—save perhaps his half-sentimental love for Jack Chase,* in *White Jacket*.

Yet to the end he pined for this: a perfect relationship; perfect mating; perfect mutual understanding. A perfect friend.

Right to the end he could never accept the fact that *perfect* relationships cannot be. Each soul is alone, and the aloneness of each soul is a double barrier to perfect relationship between two beings.

Each soul *should* be alone. And in the end the desire for a 'perfect relationship' is just a vicious, unmanly craving. '*Tous nos malheurs viennent de ne pouvoir être seuls.*' *

Melville, however, refused to draw his conclusion. *Life* was wrong, he said. He refused Life. But he stuck to his ideal of perfect relationship, possible perfect love. The world *ought* to be a harmonious loving place. And it *can't* be. So life itself is wrong.

It is silly arguing. Because after all, only temporary man sets up the 'oughts'.

The world ought *not* to be a harmonious loving place. It ought to be a place of fierce discord and intermittent harmonies; which it is.

Love ought *not* to be perfect. It ought to have perfect moments, and wildernesses of thorn bushes—which it has.

A 'perfect' relationship ought *not* to be possible. Every relationship should have its absolute limits, its absolute reserves, essential to the singleness of the soul in each person. A truly perfect relationship is one in which each party leaves great tracts unknown in the other party.

No two persons can meet at more than a few points, consciously. If two people can just be together fairly often, so that the presence of each is a sort of balance to the other, that is the basis of perfect relationship. There must be true separatenesses as well.

Melville was, at the core, a mystic and an idealist.

Perhaps, so am I.

And he stuck to his ideal guns.

I abandon mine.

He was a mystic who raved because the old ideal guns shot havoc. The guns of the 'noble spirit'. Of 'ideal love'.

I say, let the guns rot.

Get new ones, and shoot straight.

Herman Melville's *Moby Dick*

MOBY DICK, *or the Whale Whale.**

A hunt. The last great hunt.

For what?

For Moby Dick, the huge white sperm whale: who is old, hoary, monstrous, and swims alone; who is unspeakably terrible in his wrath, having so often been attacked; and snow-white.

Of course he is a symbol.

Of what?

I doubt if even Melville knew exactly. That's the best of it.

He is warm-blooded, he is lovable. He is lonely Leviathan, not a Hobbes* sort. Or is he?

But he is warm-blooded and lovable. The South Sea Islanders, and Polynesians, and Malays, who worship shark, or crocodile, or weave endless frigate-bird distortions, why did they never worship the whale? So big!

Because the whale is not wicked. He doesn't bite. And their gods had to bite.

He's not a dragon. He is Leviathan. He never coils like the Chinese dragon of the sun. He's not a serpent of the waters. He is warm-blooded, a mammal. And hunted, hunted down.

It is a great book.

At first you are put off by the style. It reads like journalism. It seems spurious. You feel Melville is trying to put something over you. It won't do.

And Melville really is a bit sententious: aware of himself, self-conscious, putting something over even himself. But then it's not easy to get into the swing of a piece of deep mysticism when you just set out with a story.

Nobody can be more clownish, more clumsy and sententiously in bad taste, than Herman Melville, even in a great book like *Moby Dick*. He preaches and holds forth because he's not sure of himself And he holds forth, often, so amateurishly.

The artist was so *much* greater than the man. The man is rather a tiresome New Englander of the ethical mystical-transcendentalist sort: Emerson, Longfellow, Hawthorne* etc. So unrelieved, the solemn ass even in humour. So hopelessly *au grand sérieux*,* you feel like saying: Good God, what does it matter? If life is a tragedy, or a farce, or a disaster, or anything else, what do I care! Let life be what it likes. Give me a drink, that's what I want just now.

For my part, life is so many things I don't care what it is. It's not my affair to sum it up. Just now it's a cup of tea. This morning it was wormwood and gall. Hand me the sugar.

One wearies of the *grand sérieux*. There's something false about it. And that's Melville. Oh dear, when the solemn ass brays! brays! brays!

But he was a deep, great artist, even if he was rather a sententious man. He was a real American in that he always felt his audience in front of him. But when he ceases to be American, when he forgets all audience, and gives us his sheer apprehension of the world, then he is wonderful, his book commands a stillness in the soul, an awe.

In his 'human' self, Melville is almost dead. That is, he hardly reacts to human contacts any more; or only ideally: or just for a moment. His human-emotional self is almost played out. He is abstract, self-analytical and abstracted. And he is more spell-bound by the strange slidings and collidings of Matter than by the things men do. In this he is like Dana.* It is the material elements he really has to do with. His drama is with them. He was a futurist long before futurism found paint. The sheer naked slidings of the elements. And the human soul experiencing it all. So often, it is almost over the border: psychiatry. Almost spurious. Yet so great.

It is the same old thing as in all Americans. They keep their old-fashioned ideal frock-coat on, and an old-fashioned silk hat, while they do the most impossible things. There you are: you see Melville hugged in bed by a huge tattooed South Sea Islander, and solemnly offering burnt offering to this savage's little idol,* and his ideal frock-coat just hides his shirt-tails and prevents us from seeing his bare posterior as he salaams, while his ethical silk hat sits correctly over his brow the while. That is so typically American: doing the most impossible things without taking off their spiritual get-up. Their ideals are like armour which has rusted in, and will never more come off. And meanwhile in Melville his bodily knowledge moves naked, a living quick among the stark elements. For with sheer physical vibrational sensitiveness, like a marvellous wireless-station, he registers the effects of the outer world. And he records also, almost beyond pain or pleasure, the extreme transitions of the isolated, far-driven soul, the soul which is now alone, without any real human contact.

The first days in New Bedford introduce the only human being who really enters into the book, namely, Ishmael,* the 'I' of the book. And then the moment's heart's-brother, Queequeg, the tattooed, powerful South Sea harpooner, whom Melville loves as Dana loves 'Hope'.* The advent of Ishmael's bedmate is amusing and unforgettable. But later the two swear 'marriage', in the language of the savages. For Queequeg has opened again the floodgates of love and human connection in Ishmael.

As I sat there in that now lonely room, the fire burning low, in that mild stage when, after its first intensity has warmed the air, it then only glows to be looked at; the evening shades and phantoms gathering round the casements, and peering in upon us silent, solitary twain: I began to be sensible of strange feelings. I felt a melting in me. No more my splintered heart and maddened hand were turned against the wolfish world. This soothing savage had redeemed it. There he sat, his very indifference speaking a nature in which there lurked no civilized hypocrisies and bland deceits. Wild he was; a very sight of sights to see; yet I began to feel myself mysteriously drawn towards him.

So they smoked together, and are clasped in each other's arms. The friendship is finally sealed when Ishmael offers sacrifice to Queequeg's little idol, Gogo.

I was a good Christian, born and bred in the bosom of the infallible Presbyterian Church. How then could I unite with the idolater in worshipping his piece of wood? But what is worship?—to do the will of God—*that* is worship. And what is the will of God?—to do to my fellow man what I would have my fellow man do to me—*that* is the will of God.

—Which sounds like Benjamin Franklin,* and is hopelessly bad theology. But it is real American logic.

Now Queequeg is my fellow man. And what do I wish that this Queequeg would do to me? Why, unite with me in my particular Presbyterian form of worship. Consequently, I must unite with him; ergo I must turn idolater. So I kindled the shavings; helped prop up the innocent little idol; offered him burnt biscuit with Queequeg; salaamed before him twice or thrice; kissed his nose; and that done, we undressed and went to bed, at peace with our own consciences and all the world. But we did not go to sleep without some little chat. How it is I know not; but there is no place like bed for confidential disclosures between friends. Man and wife, they say, open the very bottom of their souls to each other; and some old couples often lie and chat over old times till nearly morning. Thus, then, lay I and Queequeg—a cosy, loving pair—*

You would think this relation with Queequeg meant something to Ishmael. But no. Queequeg is forgotten like yesterday's newspaper. Human things are only momentary excitements or amusements to the American Ishmael. Ishmael, the hunted. But much more Ishmael the hunter. What's a Queequeg? What's a wife? The white whale must be hunted down. Queequeg must be just 'KNOWN', then dropped into oblivion.

And what in the name of fortune is the white whale?

Elsewhere Ishmael says he loved Queequeg's eyes: 'large, deep eyes, fiery black and bold'. No doubt like Poe, he wanted to get the 'clue* to them. That was all.

The two men go over from New Bedford to Nantucket, and there sign on to the Quaker whaling ship, the *Pequod*. It is all strangely fantastic, phantasmagoric. The voyage of the soul. Yet curiously a real whaling voyage, too. We pass on into the midst of the sea with this strange ship and its incredible crew. The Argonauts were mild lambs in comparison. And Ulysses went *defeating* the Circes and overcoming the wicked hussies of the isles.* But the *Pequod*'s crew is a collection of maniacs fanatically hunting down a lonely, harmless white whale.

As a soul history, it makes one angry. As a sea yarn, it is marvellous: there is always something a bit over the mark, in sea yarns. Should be. Then again the masking up of actual seaman's experience with sonorous mysticism sometimes gets on one's nerves. And again, as a revelation of destiny the book is too deep even for sorrow. Profound beyond feeling.

You are some time before you are allowed to see the captain, Ahab: the mysterious Quaker. Oh, it is a God-fearing Quaker ship.

Ahab, the captain. The captain of the soul.

> I am the master of my fate,
> I am the captain of my soul!

Ahab!

'Oh, captain, my captain, our fearful trip is done.'*

The gaunt Ahab, Quaker, mysterious person, only shows himself after some days at sea. There's a secret about him! What?

Oh, he's a portentous person. He stumps about on an ivory stump, made from sea-ivory. Moby Dick, the great white whale, tore off Ahab's leg at the knee, when Ahab was attacking him.

Quite right, too. Should have torn off both his legs, and a bit more besides.

But Ahab doesn't think so. Ahab is now a monomaniac. Moby Dick is his monomania. Moby Dick Must DIE, or Ahab can't live any longer. Ahab is atheist by this.

All right.

This *Pequod*, ship of the American soul, has three mates.

1. Starbuck: Quaker, Nantucketer, a good responsible man of reason, forethought, intrepidity, what is called a dependable man. At the bottom, *afraid*.

2. Stubb: 'Fearless as fire, and as mechanical.'* Insists on being reckless and jolly on every occasion. Must be afraid too, really.

3. Flask: Stubborn, obstinate, without imagination. To him 'the wondrous whale was but a species of magnified mouse or water-rat—'*

There you have them: a maniac captain and his three mates, three splendid seamen, admirable whalemen, first-class men at their job.

America!

It is rather like Mr Wilson and his admirable, 'efficient' crew, at the Peace Conference.* Except that none of the Pequodders took their wives along.

A maniac captain of the soul, and three eminently practical mates.

America!

Then such a crew. Renegades, castaways, cannibals: Ishmael, Quakers.

America!

Three giant harpooners to spear the great white whale.

1. Queequeg, the South Sea Islander, all tattooed, big and powerful.

2. Tashtego, the Red Indian of the sea-coast, where the Indian meets the sea.

3. Daggoo, the huge black negro.

There you have them, three savage races, under the American flag, the maniac captain, with their great keen harpoons, ready to spear the white whale.

And only after many days at sea does Ahab's own boat-crew appear on deck. Strange, silent, secret, black-garbed Malays, fire worshipping Parsees. These are to man Ahab's boat, when it leaps in pursuit of that whale.

What do you think of the ship *Pequod,* the ship of the soul of an American?

Many races, many peoples, many nations, under the Stars and Stripes. Beaten with many stripes.

Seeing stars sometimes.

And in a mad ship, under a mad captain, in a mad, fanatic's hunt.

For what?

For Moby Dick, the great white whale.

But splendidly handled. Three splendid mates. The whole thing practical, eminently practical in its working. American industry!

And all this practicality in the service of a mad, mad chase.

Melville manages to keep it a real whaling ship, on a real cruise, in spite of all fanatics. A wonderful, wonderful voyage. And a beauty that is so surpassing only because of the author's awful flounderings in mystical waters. He wanted to get metaphysically deep. And he got deeper than metaphysics. It is a surpassingly beautiful book, with an awful meaning, and bad jolts.

It is interesting to compare Melville with Dana, about the albatross—Melville a bit sententious.

I remember the first albatross I ever saw. It was during a prolonged gale in waters hard upon the Antarctic seas. From my forenoon watch below I ascended to the overcrowded deck, and there, lashed upon the main hatches, I saw a regal feathered thing of unspotted whiteness, and with a booked Roman bill sublime. At intervals it arched forth its vast, archangel wings—wondrous throbbings and flutterings shook it. Though bodily unharmed, it uttered cries, as some King's ghost in supernatural distress. Through its inexpressible strange eyes methought I peeped to secrets not below the heavens—the white thing was so white, its wings so wide, and in those for ever exiled waters, I had lost the miserable warping memories of traditions and of towns. I assert then, that in the wondrous bodily whiteness of the bird chiefly lurks the secret of the spell—*

Melville's albatross is a prisoner, caught by a bait on a hook.

Well, I have seen an albatross, too: following us in waters hard upon the Antarctic, too, south of Australia. And in the Southern winter. And the ship, a P. and O. boat, nearly empty. And the lascar crew shivering.

The bird with its long, long wings following, then leaving us. No one knows till they have tried, how lost, how lonely those Southern waters are. And glimpses of the Australian coast.

It makes one feel that our day is only a day. That in the dark of the night ahead other days stir fecund, when we have lapsed from existence.

Who knows how utterly we shall lapse.

But Melville keeps up his disquisition about 'whiteness'. The great abstract fascinated him. The abstract where we end, and cease to be. White or black. Our white, abstract end!

Then again it is lovely to be at sea on the *Pequod*, with never a grain of earth to us.

It was a cloudy, sultry afternoon; the seamen were lazily lounging about the decks, or vacantly gazing over into the lead-coloured waters. Queequeg and I were mildly employed weaving what is called a sword-mat, for an additional lashing to our boat. So still and subdued, and yet somehow preluding was all the scene, and such an incantation of reverie lurked in the air that each silent sailor seemed resolved into his own invisible self—

In the midst of this preluding silence came the first cry: 'There she blows! there! there! there! She blows!'* And then comes the first chase, a marvellous piece of true sea-writing, the sea, and sheer sea-beings on the chase, sea-creatures chased. There is scarcely a taint of earth—pure sea-motion.

'Give way, men,' whispered Starbuck, drawing still further aft the sheet of his sail; 'there is time to kill a fish yet before the squall comes. There's white water again!—Close to!—Spring!' Soon after, two cries in quick succession on each side of us denoted that the other boats had got fast; but hardly were they overheard, when with a lightning-like hurtling whisper Starbuck said: 'Stand up!' and Queequeg, harpoon in hand, sprang to his feet.—Though not one of the oarsmen was then facing the life and death peril so close to them ahead, yet, their eyes on the intense countenance of the mate in the stern of the boat, they knew that the imminent instant had come; they heard, too, an enormous wallowing sound, as of fifty elephants stirring in their litter. Meanwhile the boat was still booming through the mist, the waves curbing and hissing around us like the erected crests of enraged serpents.

'That's his hump. *There! There*, give it to him!' whispered Starbuck.—A short rushing sound leapt out of the boat; it was the darted iron of Queequeg. Then all in one welded motion came a push from astern, while forward the boat seemed striking on a ledge; the sail collapsed and exploded; a gush of scalding vapour shot up near by; something rolled and tumbled like an earthquake beneath us. The whole crew were half suffocated as they were tossed helter-skelter into the white curling cream of the squall. Squall, whale, and harpoon had all blended together; and the whale, merely grazed by the iron, escaped—*

Melville is a master of violent, chaotic physical motion; he can keep up a whole wild chase without a flaw. He is as perfect at creating stillness. The ship is cruising on the Carrol Ground, south of St Helena.—

It was while gliding through these latter waters that one serene and moonlight night, when all the waves rolled by like scrolls of silver; and by their soft, suffusing seethings, made what seemed a silvery silence, not a solitude; on such a silent night a silvery jet was seen far in advance of the white bubbles at the bow—*

Then there is the description of brit.

Steering north-eastward from the Crozetts we fell in with vast meadows of brit, the minute, yellow substance upon which the Right Whale largely feeds. For leagues and leagues it undulated round us, so that we seemed to be sailing through boundless fields of ripe and golden wheat. On the second day, numbers of Right Whales were seen, who, secure from the attack of a Sperm Whaler like the *Pequod*, with open jaws sluggishly swam through the brit, which, adhering to the fringing fibres of that wondrous Venetian blind in their mouths, was in that manner separated from the water that escaped at the lip. As moving mowers who, side by side, slowly and seethingly advance their scythes through the long wet grass of the marshy meads; even so these monsters swam, making a strange grassy, cutting sound; and leaving behind them endless swaths of blue on the yellow sea. But it was only the sound they made as they parted the brit which at all reminded one of mowers. Seen from the mast-heads, especially when they paused and were stationary for a while, their vast black forms looked more like lifeless masses of rock than anything else—*

This beautiful passage brings us to the apparition of the squid.

Slowly wading through the meadows of brit, the *Pequod* still held her way northeastward towards the island of Java; a gentle air impelling her keel, so that in the surrounding serenity her three tall, tapering masts mildly waved to that languid breeze, as three mild palms on a plain. And still, at wide intervals, in the silvery night, that lonely alluring jet would be seen.

But one transparent-blue morning, when a stillness almost preternatural spread over the sea, however unattended with any stagnant calm; when the long burnished sunglade on the waters seemed a golden finger laid across them, enjoining secrecy; when all the slippered waves whispered together as they softly ran on; in this profound hush of the visible sphere a strange spectre was seen by Daggoo from the main-mast head.

In the distance, a great white mass lazily rose, and rising higher and higher, and disentangling itself from the azure, at last gleamed before our prow like a snow-slide, new slid from the hills. Thus glistening for a moment, as slowly it subsided, and sank. Then once more arose, and silently gleamed. It seemed not a whale; and yet, is this Moby Dick? thought Daggoo—

The boats were lowered and pulled to the scene.

In the same spot where it sank, once more it slowly rose. Almost forgetting for the moment all thoughts of Moby Dick, we now gazed at the most wondrous phenomenon which the secret seas have hitherto revealed to mankind. A vast pulpy mass, furlongs in length and breadth, of a glancing cream-colour, lay floating on the water, innumerable long arms radiating from its centre, and curling and twisting like a nest of anacondas, as if blindly to clutch at any hapless object within reach. No perceptible face or front did it have; no conceivable token of either sensation or instinct; but undulated there on the billows, an unearthly, formless, chance-like apparition of life. And with a low sucking it slowly disappeared again.*

The following chapters, with their account of whale hunts, the killing, the stripping, the cutting up, are magnificent records of actual happening. Then comes the queer tale of the meeting of the

Jeroboam, a whaler met at sea, all of whose men were under the domination of a religious maniac, one of the ship's hands. There are detailed descriptions of the actual taking of the sperm oil from a whale's head. Dilating on the smallness of the brain of a sperm whale, Melville significantly remarks—'for I believe that much of man's character will be found betokened in his backbone. I would rather feel your spine than your skull, whoever you are—' And of the whale, he adds:

'For, viewed in this light, the wonderful comparative smallness of his brain proper is more than compensated by the wonderful comparative magnitude of his spinal cord.'*

In among the rush of terrible awful hunts, come touches of pure beauty.

As the three boats lay there on that gently rolling sea, gazing down into its eternal blue noon; and as not a single groan or cry of any sort, nay not so much as a ripple or a thought, came up from its depths; what landsman would have thought that beneath all that silence and placidity the utmost monster of the seas was writhing and wrenching in agony!*

Perhaps the most stupendous chapter is the one called *The Grand Armada,* at the beginning of Volume III. The *Pequod* was drawing through the Sunda Straits towards Java when she came upon a vast host of sperm whales.

Broad on both bows, at a distance of two or three miles, and forming a great semicircle embracing one-half of the level horizon, a continuous chain of whale-jets were up-playing and sparkling in the noonday air.

Chasing this great herd, past the Straits of Sunda, themselves chased by Javan pirates, the whalers race on. Then the boats are lowered. At last that curious state of inert irresolution came over the whales, when they were, as the seamen say, gallied. Instead of forging ahead in huge martial array they swam violently hither and thither, a surging sea of whales, no longer moving on. Starbuck's boat, made fast to a whale, is towed in amongst this howling Leviathan chaos. In mad career it cockles through the boiling surge of monsters, till it is brought into a clear lagoon in the very centre of the vast, mad, terrified herd. There a sleek, pure calm reigns. There the females swam in peace, and the young whales came snuffing tamely at the boat, like dogs. And there the astonished seamen watched the love-making of these amazing monsters, mammals, now in rut far down in the sea—

But far beneath this wondrous world upon the surface, another and still stranger world met our eyes, as we gazed over the side. For, suspended in these watery vaults, floated the forms of the nursing mothers of the whales, and those that by their enormous girth seemed shortly to become mothers. The lake, as I have hinted, was to a considerable depth exceedingly transparent; and as human infants while sucking will calmly and fixedly gaze away from the breast, as if leading two different lives at a time; and while yet drawing moral nourishment, be still spiritually feasting upon some unearthly reminiscence, even so did the young of these whales seem looking up towards us, but not at us, as if we were but a bit of gulf-weed in their newborn sight. Floating on their sides, the mothers also seemed quietly eyeing us. – Some of the subtlest secrets of the seas seemed divulged to us in this enchanted pond. We saw young Leviathan amours in the deep. And thus, though surrounded by circle upon circle of consternation and affrights, did these inscrutable creatures at the centre freely and fearlessly indulge in all peaceful concernments; yea, serenely revelled in dalliance and delight—*

There is something really overwhelming in these whale-hunts, almost superhuman or inhuman, bigger than life, more terrific than human activity. The same with the chapter on ambergris: it is so curious, so real, yet so unearthly. And again in the chapter called *The Cassock*—surely the oldest piece of phallicism in all the world's literature.

After this comes the amazing account of the Try-works, when the ship is turned into the sooty, oily factory in mid-ocean, and the oil is extracted from the blubber. In the night of the red furnace burning on deck, at sea, Melville has his startling experience of reversion. He is at the helm, but has turned to watch the fire: when suddenly he feels the ship rushing backward from him, in mystic reversion—

Uppermost was the impression, that whatever swift, rushing thing I stood on was not so much bound to any haven ahead, as rushing from all havens astern. A stark bewildering feeling, as of death, came over me. Convulsively my hands grasped the tiller, but with the crazy conceit that the tiller was, somehow, in some enchanted way, inverted. My God! What is the matter with me, I thought!*

This dream-experience is a real soul-experience. He ends with an injunction to all men, not to gaze on the red fire when its redness makes all things look ghastly. It seems to him that his gazing on fire has evoked this horror of reversion, undoing.

Perhaps it had. He was water-born.

After some unhealthy work on the ship, Queequeg caught a fever and was like to die.

How he wasted and wasted in those few, long-lingering days, till there seemed but little left of him but his frame and tattooing. But as all else in him thinned, and his cheek-bones grew sharper, his eyes, nevertheless, seemed growing fuller and fuller; they took on a strangeness of lustre; and mildly but deeply looked out at you there from his sickness, a wondrous testimony to that immortal health in him which could not die, or be weakened. And like circles on the water, which as they grow fainter, expand; so his eyes seemed rounding and rounding, like the circles of Eternity. An awe that cannot be named would steal over you as you sat by the side of this waning savage—*

But Queequeg did not die—and the *Pequod* emerges from the Eastern Straits, into the full Pacific. 'To any meditative Magian rover, this serene Pacific once beheld, must ever after be the sea of his adoption. It rolls the midmost waters of the world—'*

In this Pacific the fights go on:

It was far down the afternoon, and when all the spearings of the crimson fight were done, and floating in the lovely sunset sea and sky, sun and whale both stilly died together; then such a sweetness and such a plaintiveness, such inwreathing orisons curled up in that rosy air, that it almost seemed as if far over from the deep green convent valleys of the Manila isles, the Spanish land-breeze had gone to sea, freighted with these vesper hymns. Soothed again, but only soothed to deeper gloom, Ahab, who had sterned off from the whale, sat intently watching his final wanings from the now tranquil boat. For that strange spectacle, observable in all sperm whales dying—the turning of the head sunwards, and so expiring—that strange spectacle, beheld of such a placid evening, somehow to Ahab conveyed wondrousness unknown before. 'He turns and turns him to it; how slowly, but how steadfastly, his homage-rendering and invoking brow, with his last dying motions. He too worships fire ...'*

So Ahab soliloquizes: and so the warm-blooded whale turns for the last time to the sun, which begot him in the waters.

But as we see in the next chapter, it is the Thunder-fire which Ahab really worships: that living sundering fire of which he bears the brand, from head to foot; it is storm, the electric storm of the *Pequod*, when the corposants burn in high, tapering flames of supernatural pallor upon the masthead, and when the compass is reversed. After this all is fatality. Life itself seems mystically reversed. In these hunters of Moby Dick there is nothing but madness and possession. The captain, Ahab, moves hand in hand with the poor imbecile negro boy, Pip, who has been so cruelly demented, left swimming alone in the vast sea. It is the imbecile child of the sun hand in hand with the northern monomaniac, captain and master.

The voyage surges on. They meet one ship, then another. It is all ordinary day-routine, and yet all is a tension of pure madness and horror, the approaching horror of the last fight.

Hither and thither, on high, glided the snow-white wings of small unspecked birds; these were the gentle thoughts of the feminine air; but to and fro in the deeps, far down in the bottomless blue, rushed mighty leviathans, sword-fish and sharks; and these were the strong, troubled, murderous thinkings of the masculine sea—

On this day Ahab confesses his weariness, the weariness of his burden. 'But do I look very old, so very, very old, Starbuck? I feel deadly faint, and bowed, and humped, as though I were Adam staggering beneath the piled centuries since Paradise—'* It is the Gethsemane* of Ahab, before the last fight: the Gethsemane of the human soul seeking the last self-conquest, the last attainment of extended consciousness—infinite consciousness.

At last they sight the whale. Ahab sees him from his hoisted perch at the masthead—'From this height the whale was now seen some mile or so ahead, at every roll of the sea revealing his high, sparkling hump, and regularly jetting his silent spout into the air.' The boats are lowered, to draw near the white whale.

At length the breathless hunter came so nigh his seemingly unsuspectful prey that his entire dazzling hump was distinctly visible, sliding along the sea as if an isolated thing, and continually set in a revolving ring of finest, fleecy, greenish foam. He saw the vast involved wrinkles of the slightly projecting head, beyond. Before it, far out on the soft, Turkish rugged waters, went the glistening white shadow from his broad milky forehead, a musical rippling playfully accompanying the shade; and behind, the blue waters interchangeably flowed over the moving valley of his steady wake; and on either side bright bubbles arose and danced by his side. But these were broken again by the light toes of hundreds of gay fowl softly feathering the sea, alternate with their fitful flight; and like to some flagstaff rising from the pointed hull of an argosy, the tall but shattered pole of a recent lance projected from the white whale's back; and at intervals one of the clouds of soft-toed fowls hovering, and to and fro shimmering like a canopy over the fish, silently perched and rocked on this pole, the long tail-feathers streaming like pennons.

A gentle joyousness—a mighty mildness of repose in swiftness, invested the gliding whale—*

The fight with the whale is too wonderful and too awful, to be quoted apart from the book. It lasted three days. The fearful sight, on the third day, of the torn body of the Parsee harpooner, lost on the previous day, now seen lashed on to the flanks of the white whale by the tangle of harpoon lines, has a mystic dream-horror. The awful and infuriated whale turns upon the ship, symbol of this civilized world of ours. He smites her with a fearful shock. And a few minutes later, from the last of the fighting whale-boats comes the cry:

'The ship! Great God, where is the ship?' Soon they, through dim bewildering mediums, saw her sidelong fading phantom, as in the gaseous Fata Morgana; only the uppermost masts out of the water; while fixed by infatuation, or fidelity, or fate, to their once lofty perches, the pagan harpooners still maintained their sinking lookouts on the sea. And now concentric circles seized the lone boat itself, and all its crew, and each floating oar, and every lance-pole, and spinning, animate and inanimate, all round and round in one vortex, carried the smallest chip of the *Pequod* out of sight—

The bird of heaven, the eagle, St John's bird, the Red Indian bird, the American, goes down with the ship, nailed by Tashtego's hammer, the hammer of the American Indian. The eagle of the spirit. Sunk!

Now small fowls flew screaming over the yet yawning gulf; a sullen white surf beat against its steep sides; then all collapsed; and the great shroud of the sea rolled on as it rolled five thousand years ago.*

So ends one of the strangest and most wonderful books in the world, closing up its mystery and its tortured symbolism. It is an epic of the sea such as no man has equalled; and it is a book of esoteric symbolism of profound significance, and of considerable tiresomeness.

But it is a great book, a very great book, the greatest book of the sea ever written. It moves awe in the soul.

The terrible fatality.

Fatality.

Doom.

Doom! Doom! Doom! Something seems to whisper it in the very dark trees of America. Doom!

Doom of what?

Doom of our white day. We are doomed, doomed. And the doom is in America. The doom of our white day.

Ah, well, if my day is doomed, and I am doomed with my day, it is something greater than I which dooms me, so I accept my doom as a sign of the greatness which is more than I am.

Melville knew. He knew his race was doomed. His white soul, doomed. His great white epoch, doomed. Himself, doomed. The idealist, doomed. The spirit, doomed.

The reversion. 'Not so much bound to any haven ahead, as rushing from all havens astern.'*

That great horror of ours! It is our civilization rushing from all havens astern.

The last ghastly hunt. The White Whale.

What then is Moby Dick? He is the deepest blood-being of the white race; he is our deepest blood-nature.

And he is hunted, hunted, hunted by the maniacal fanaticism of our white mental consciousness. We want to hunt him down. To subject him to our will. And in this maniacal conscious hunt of ourselves we get dark races and pale to help us, red, yellow, and black, east and west, Quaker and fire-worshipper, we get them all to help us in this ghastly maniacal hunt which is our doom and our suicide.

The last phallic being of the white man. Hunted into the death of upper consciousness and the ideal will. Our blood-self subjected to our will. Our blood-consciousness sapped by a parasitic mental or ideal consciousness.

Hot blooded sea-born Moby Dick. Hunted by monomaniacs of the idea.

Oh God, oh God, what next, when the *Pequod* has sunk?

She sank in the war, and we are all flotsam.

Now what next?

Who knows? *Quien sabe? Quien sabe, senor?**

Neither Spanish nor Saxon America has any answer.

The *Pequod* went down. And the *Pequod* was the ship of the white American soul. She sank, taking with her negro and Indian and Polynesian, Asiatic and Quaker and good, businesslike Yankees and Ishmael: she sank all the lot of them.

Boom! as Vachel Lindsay* would say.

To use the words of Jesus, IT IS FINISHED.

Consummatum est!*

But *Moby Dick* was first published in 1851. If the Great White Whale sank the ship of the Great White Soul in 1851, what's been happening ever since?

Post-mortem effects, presumably.

Because, in the first centuries, Jesus was Cetus, the Whale.* And the Christians were the little fishes. Jesus, the Redeemer, was Cetus, Leviathan. And all the Christians all his little fishes.

The Future of the Novel

YOU talk about the future of the baby, little cherub, when he's in the cradle cooing; and it's a romantic, glamorous subject. You also talk, with the parson, about the future of the wicked old grandfather who is at last lying on his death-bed. And there again you have a subject for much vague emotion, chiefly of fear this time.

How do we feel about the novel? Do we bounce with joy thinking of the wonderful novelistic days ahead? Or do we grimly shake our heads and hope the wicked creature will be spared a little longer? Is the novel on his death-bed, old sinner? Or is he just toddling round his cradle, sweet little thing? Let us have another look at him before we decide this rather serious case.

There he is, the monster with many faces, many branches to him, like a tree: the modern novel. And he is almost dual, like Siamese twins. On the one hand, the pale-faced, high-browed, earnest novel, which you have to take seriously; on the other, that smirking, rather plausible hussy, the popular novel.

Let us just for the moment feel the pulses of *Ulysses* and of Miss Dorothy Richardson and M. Marcel Proust, on the earnest side of Briareus; on the other, the throb of *The Sheik* and Mr Zane Grey, and, if you will, Mr Robert Chambers* and the rest. Is *Ulysses* in his cradle? Oh, dear! What a grey face! And *Pointed Roofs*, are they a gay little toy for nice little girls? And M. Proust? Alas! You can hear the death-rattle in their throats. They can hear it themselves. They are listening to it with acute interest, trying to discover whether the intervals are minor thirds or major fourths. Which is rather infantile, really.

So there you have the 'serious' novel, dying in a very long-drawn-out fourteen-volume death-agony, and absorbedly, childishly interested in the phenomenon. 'Did I feel a twinge in my little toe, or didn't I?' asks every character of Mr Joyce or of Miss Richardson or M. Proust. Is my aura a blend of frankincense and orange pekoe and boot-blacking, or is it myrrh and bacon-fat and Shetland tweed? The audience round the death-bed gapes for the answer. And when, in a sepulchral tone, the answer comes at length, after hundreds of pages: 'It is none of these, it is abysmal chloro-coryambasis',* the audience quivers all over, and murmurs: 'That's just how I feel myself.'

Which is the dismal, long-drawn-out comedy of the death-bed of the serious novel. It is self-consciousness picked into such fine bits that the bits are most of them invisible, and you have to go by smell. Through thousands and thousands of pages Mr Joyce and Miss Richardson tear themselves to pieces, strip their smallest emotions to the finest threads, till you feel you are sewed inside a wool mattress that is being slowly shaken up, and you are turning to wool along with the rest of the woolliness.

It's awful. And it's childish. It really is childish, after a certain age, to be absorbedly self-conscious. One has to be self-conscious at seventeen: still a little self-conscious at twenty-seven; but if we are going it strong at thirty-seven, then it is a sign of arrested development, nothing else. And if it is still continuing at forty-seven, it is obvious senile precocity.

And there's the serious novel: senile-precocious. Absorbedly, childishly concerned with *what I am*. 'I am this, I am that, I am the other. My reactions are such, and such, and such. And, oh, Lord, if I liked to watch myself closely enough, if I liked to analyse my feelings minutely, as I unbutton my gloves, instead of saying crudely I unbuttoned them, then I could go on to a million pages instead of a thousand. In fact, the more I come to think of it, it is gross, it is uncivilized bluntly to say: I unbuttoned my gloves. After all, the absorbing adventure of it! Which button did I begin with?' etc.

The people in the serious novels are so absorbedly concerned with themselves and what they feel and don't feel, and how they react to every mortal button; and their audience as frenziedly absorbed in the application of the author's discoveries to their own reactions: 'That's me! That's exactly it! I'm just finding myself in this book!' Why, this is more than death-bed, it is almost post-mortem behaviour.

Some convulsion or cataclysm will have to get this serious novel out of its self-consciousness. The last great war made it worse. What's to be done? Because, poor thing, it's really young yet. The novel has never become fully adult. It has never quite grown to years of discretion. It has always youthfully hoped for the best, and felt rather sorry for itself on the last page. Which is just childish.

The childishness has become very long-drawn-out. So very many adolescents who drag their adolescence on into their forties and their fifties and their sixties! There needs some sort of surgical operation, somewhere.

Then the popular novels—the *Sheiks* and *Babbitts** and Zane Grey novels. They are just as self-conscious, only they do have more illusions about themselves. The heroines do think they are lovelier, and more fascinating, and purer. The heroes do see themselves more heroic, braver, more chivalrous, more fetching. The mass of the populace 'find themselves' in the popular novels. But nowadays it's a funny sort of self they find. A Sheik with a whip up his sleeve, and a heroine with weals on her back, but adored in the end, adored, the whip out of sight, but the weals still faintly visible.

It's a funny sort of self they discover in the popular novels. And the essential moral of *If Winter Comes,** for example, is so shaky. 'The gooder you are, the worse it is for you, poor you, oh, poor you. Don't you be so blimey good, it's not good enough.' Or *Babbitt:* 'Go on, you make your pile, and then pretend you're too good for it. Put it over the rest of the grabbers that way. They're only pleased with themselves when they've made their pile. You go one better.'

Always the same sort of baking-powder gas to make you rise: the soda counteracting the cream of tartar, and the tartar counteracted by the soda. Sheik heroines, duly whipped, wildly adored. Babbitts with solid fortunes, weeping from self-pity. Winter-Comes heroes as good as pie, hauled off to jail. *Moral:* Don't be too good, because you'll go to jail for it. *Moral:* Don't feel sorry for yourself till you've made your pile and don't need to feel sorry for yourself. *Moral:* Don't let him adore you till he's whipped you into it. Then you'll be partners in mild crime as well as in holy matrimony.

Which again is childish. Adolescence which *can't* grow up. Got into the self-conscious rut and going crazy, quite crazy in it. Carrying on their adolescence into middle age and old age, like the loony Cleopatra in *Dombey and Son*, murmuring 'Rose-coloured curtains'* with her dying breath.

The future of the novel? Poor old novel, it's in a rather dirty, messy tight corner. And it's either got to get over the wall or knock a hole through it. In other words, it's got to grow up. Put away childish things* like: Do I love the girl, or don't I?'—'Am I pure and sweet, or am I not?'—'Do I unbutton my right glove first, or my left?'—'Did my mother ruin my life by refusing to drink the cocoa which my bride had boiled for her? These questions and their answers don't really interest me any more, though the world still goes sawing them over. I simply don't care for any of these things now, though I used to. The purely emotional and self-analytical stunts are played out in me. I'm finished. I'm deaf to the whole band. But I'm neither *blasé* nor cynical, for all that. I'm just interested in something else.

Supposing a bomb were put under the whole scheme of things, what would we be after? What feelings do we want to carry through into the next epoch? What feelings will carry us through? What is the underlying impulse in us that will provide the motive power for a new state of things, when this democratic-industrial-lovey-dovey-darling-take-me-to-mamma state of things is bust?

What next? That's what interests me. 'What now?' is no fun any more.

If you wish to look into the past for what-next books, you can go back to the Greek philosophers. Plato's Dialogues* are queer little novels. It seems to me it was the greatest pity in the world, when philosophy and fiction got split. They used to be one, right from the days of myth. Then they went and parted, like a nagging married couple, with Aristotle and Thomas Aquinas and that beastly Kant.* So the novel went sloppy, and philosophy went abstract-dry. The two should come together again—in the novel.

You've got to find a new impulse for new things in mankind, and it's really fatal to find it through abstraction. No, no; philosophy and religion, they've both gone too far on the algebraical tack: Let X stand for sheep and Y for goats: then X minus Y equals Heaven, and X plus Y equals Earth, and Y minus X equals Hell. Thank you! But what coloured shirt does X have on?

The novel has a future. It's got to have the courage to tackle new propositions without using abstractions; it's got to present us with new, really new feelings, a whole line of new emotion, which will get us out of the emotional rut. Instead of snivelling about what is and has been, or inventing new sensations in the old line, it's got to break a way through, like a hole in the wall. And the public will scream and say it is sacrilege: because, of course, when you've been jammed for a long time in a tight corner, and you get really used to its stuffiness and its tightness, till you find it suffocatingly cozy; then, of course, you're horrified when you see a new glaring hole in what was your cosy wall. You're horrified. You back away from the cold stream of fresh air as if it were killing you. But gradually, first one and then another of the sheep filters through the gap, and finds a new world outside.

Review of
A Second Contemporary Verse Anthology

'IT is not merely an assembly of verse, but the spiritual record of an entire people.'—This from the wrapper of *A Second Contemporary Verse Anthology*.* The spiritual record of an entire people sounds rather impressive. The book as a matter of fact is a collection of pleasant verse, neat and nice and easy as eating candy.

Naturally, any collection of contemporary verse in any country at any time is bound to be more or less a box of candy. Days of Horace, days of Milton, days of Whitman, it would be pretty much the same, more or less a box of candy. Would it be at the same time the spiritual record of an entire people? Why not? If we had a good representative anthology of the poetry of Whitman's day, and if it contained two poems by Whitman, then it would be a fairly true spiritual record of the American people of that day. As if the whole nation had whispered or chanted its inner experience into the horn of a gramophone.

And the bulk of the whisperings and murmurings would be candy: sweet nothings, tender trifles, and amusing things. For of such is the bulk of the spiritual experience of any entire people.

The Americans have always been good at 'occasional' verse. Sixty years ago they were very good indeed: making their little joke against themselves and their century. Today there are fewer jokes. There are also fewer footprints on the sands of time. Life is still earnest, but a little less real. And the soul has left off asserting that dust it isn't nor to dust returneth.* The spirit of verse prefers now a 'composition salad' of fruits of sensation, in a cooked mayonnaise of sympathy. Odds and ends of feelings smoothed into unison by some prevailing sentiment:

> My face is wet with the rain
> But my heart is warm to the core ...

Or you can call it a box of chocolate candies. Let me offer you a sweet! Candy! Isn't everything candy?

> There be none of beauty's daughters
>   With a magic like thee—
> And like music on the waters
>   Is thy sweet voice to me.*

Is that candy? Then what about this?

> But you are a girl and run
>   Fresh bathed and warm and sweet,
> After the flying ball
>   On little, sandalled feet.

One of those two fragments is a classic. And one is a scrap from the contemporary spiritual record.

> The river boat had loitered down its way,
> The ropes were coiled, and business for the day
> Was done—
>
> Now fades the glimmering landscape on the sight,
> And all the air a solemn stillness holds;
> Save where—*

Two more bits. Do you see any intrinsic difference between them? After all, the one *means* as much as the other. And what is there in the mere stringing together of words?

For some mysterious reason, there is everything.

> When lilacs last in the dooryard bloomed—*

It is a string of words, but it makes me prick my innermost ear. So do I prick my ear to: 'Fly low, vermilion dragon'. But the next line: 'With the moon horns', makes me lower that same inward ear once more, in indifference.

There is an element of danger in all new utterance. We prick our ears like an animal in a wood at a strange sound.

Alas! though there is a modicum of 'strange sound' in this contemporary spiritual record, we are not the animal to prick our ears at it. Sounds sweetly familiar, linked in a new crochet pattern. 'Christ, what are patterns for?' But why invoke Deity? Ask the *Ladies' Home Journal.* You may know a new utterance by the element of danger in it. 'My heart aches', says Keats,* and you bet it's no joke.

Why do I think of stairways
With a rush of hurt surprise?

Heaven knows, my dear, unless you once fell down.

The element of danger. Man is always, all the time and for ever on the brink of the unknown. The minute you realize this, you prick your ears in alarm. And the minute any man steps alone, with his whole naked self, emotional and mental, into the everlasting hinterland of consciousness, you hate him and you wonder over him. Why can't he stay cozily playing word-games around the camp fire?

Now it is time to invoke the Deity, who made man an adventurer into the everlasting unknown of consciousness.

The spiritual record of any people is 99 per cent a record of games around a camp fire: word-games and picture-games. But the one per cent is a step into the grisly dark, which is for ever dangerous and wonderful. Nothing is wonderful unless it is dangerous. Dangerous to the *status quo* of the soul. And therefore to some degree detestable.

When the contemporary spiritual record warbles away about the wonder of the blue sky and the changing seas, etc., etc., etc., it is all candy. The sky is a blue hand-mirror to the modern poet and he goes on smirking before it. The blue sky of our particular heavens is painfully well known to us all. In fact, it is like the glass bowl to the goldfish, a *ne plus ultra* in which he sees himself as he goes round and round.

The actual heavens can suddenly roll up like the heavens of Ezekiel.* That's what happened at the Renaissance. The old heavens shrivelled and men found a new empyrean above them. But they didn't get at it by playing word-games around the camp fire. Somebody has to jump like a desperate clown through the vast blue hoop of the upper air. Or hack a slow way through the dome of crystal.

Play! Play! Play! All the little playboys and playgirls of the western world,* playing at goodness, playing at badness, playing at sadness, and playing deafeningly at gladness. Playboys and playgirls of the western world, harmlessly fulfilling their higher destinies and registering the spiritual record of an entire people. Even playing at death, and playing with death. Oh, poetry, you child in a bathing dress, playing at ball!

You say nature is always nature, the sky is always the sky. But sit still and consider for one moment what sort of nature it was the Romans saw on the face of the earth, and what sort of heavens the medievals knew above them, and your sky will begin to crack like glass. The world is what it is, and the chimerical universe of the ancients was always child's play. The camera cannot lie. And the eye of man is nothing but a camera photographing the outer world in colour-process.

This sounds very well. But the eye of man photographs the chimera of nature, as well as the so-called scientific vision. The eye of man photographs gorgons and chimeras, as the eye of the spider photographs images unrecognizable to us and the eye of the horse photographs flat ghosts and looming motions. We are at the phase of scientific vision. This phase will pass and this vision will seem as chimerical to our descendants as the medieval vision seems to us.

The upshot of it all is that we are pot-bound in our consciousness. We are like a fish in a glass bowl, swimming round and round and gaping at our own image reflected on the walls of the infinite: the infinite being the glass bowl of our conception of life and the universe. We are prisoners inside our own conception of life and being. We have exhausted the possibilities of the universe, as we know it. All that remains is to telephone to Mars for a new word of advice.

Our consciousness is pot-bound. Our ideas, our emotions, our experiences are all pot-bound. For us there is nothing new under the sun.* What there is to know, we know it already, and experience adds little. The girl who is going to fall in love knows all about it beforehand from books and the movies. She knows what she wants and she wants what she knows. Like candy. It is still nice to eat candy, though one has eaten it every day for years. It is still nice to eat candy. But the spiritual record of eating candy is a rather thin noise.

There is nothing new under the sun, once the consciousness becomes pot-bound. And this is what ails all art today. But particularly American art. The American consciousness is peculiarly pot-bound. It doesn't even have that little hole in the bottom of the pot through which desperate roots straggle. No, the American consciousness is not only potted in a solid and everlasting pot, it is placed moreover in an immovable ornamental vase. A double hide to bind it and a double bond to hide it.

European consciousness still has cracks in its vessel and a hole in the bottom of its absoluteness. It still has strange roots of memory groping down to the heart of the world.

But American consciousness is absolutely free of such danglers. It is free from all loop-holes and crevices of escape. It is absolutely safe inside a solid and ornamental concept of life. There it is Free! Life is good, and all men are meant to have a good time. Life is good! that is the flower-pot. The ornamental vase is: Having a good time.

So they proceed to have it, even with their woes. The young maiden knows exactly when she falls in love: she knows exactly how she feels when her lover or husband betrays her or when she betrays him: she knows precisely what it is to be a forsaken wife, an adoring mother, an erratic grandmother. All at the age of eighteen. *Vive la vie!**

There is nothing new under the sun, but you can have a jolly good old time all the same with the old things. A nut sundae or a new beau, a baby or an automobile, a divorce or a troublesome appendix: my dear, that's Life! You've got to get a good time out of it, anyhow, so here goes!

In which attitude there is a certain piquant stoicism. The stoicism of having a good time. The heroism of enjoying yourself. But, as I say, it makes rather thin hearing in a spiritual record. *Rechauffés* of *rechauffés*. Old soup of old bones of life, heated up again for a new consommé. Nearly always called *printanière.**

> I know a forest, stilly-deep ...

Mark the poetic novelty of stilly-deep, and then say there is nothing new under the sun.

> My soul-harp never thrills to peaceful tunes;

I should say so.

> For after all, the thing to do
> Is just to put your heart in song—

Or in pickle.

I sometimes wish that God were back
  In this dark world and wide;
For though some virtues he might lack,
  He had his pleasant side.

'Getting on the pleasant side of God, and how to stay there.'—
Hints by a Student of Life.

Oh, ho! Now I am masterful!
Now I am filled with power.
Now I am brutally myself again
And my own man.

For I have been among my hills today,
On the scarred dumb rocks standing;

And it made a man of him…
Open confession is good for the soul.
The spiritual record of an entire … what?

The Proper Study

IF no man lives for ever, neither does any precept. And if even the weariest river winds somewhere safe to sea,* so also does the weariest wisdom. And there it is lost. Also incorporated.

> Know then thyself, presume not God to scan;
> The proper study of mankind is man.

It was Alexander Pope* who absolutely struck the note of our particular epoch: not Shakespeare or Luther or Milton. A man of first magnitude never fits his age perfectly.

> Know then thyself, presume not God to scan;
> The proper study of mankind is Man—with a capital M.

This stream of wisdom is very weary now: weary to death. It started such a gay little trickle, and is such a spent muddy ebb by now. It will take a big sea to swallow all its alluvia.

'Know then thyself.' All right! I'll do my best. Honestly I'll do my best, sincerely to know myself. Since it is the great commandment to consciousness of our long era, let us be men, and try to obey it. Jesus gave the emotional commandment, 'Love thy neighbour.'* But the Greeks set the even more absolute motto, in its way, a more deeply religious motto: 'Know thyself.'*

Very well! Being man, and the son of man, I find it only honorable to obey. To do my best. To do my best to know myself. And particularly that part, or those parts of myself that have not yet been admitted into consciousness. Man is nothing, less than a tick stuck in a sheep's back, unless he adventures. Either into the unknown of the world, of his environment. Or into the unknown of himself.

Allons! * the road is before us. Know thyself! Which means, *really*, know thine own *unknown* self. It's no good knowing something you know already. The thing is to discover the tracts as yet unknown. And as the only unknown now lies deep in the passional soul, *allons!* the road is before us. We write a novel or two, we are called erotic or depraved or idiotic or boring. What does it matter, we go the road just the same. If you see the point of the great old commandment, *Know thyself,* then you see the point of all art.

But knowing oneself, like knowing anything else, is not a process that can continue to infinity, in the same direction. The fact that I myself *am* only myself makes me very specifically finite. True, I may argue that my Self is a mystery that impinges on the infinite. Admitted. But the moment my Self impinges on the infinite, it ceases to be just myself.

The same is true of all knowing. You start to find out the chemical composition of a drop of water, and before you know where you are, your river of knowledge is winding very unsatisfactorily into a very vague sea, called the ether. You start to study electricity, you track the wretch down till you get some mysterious and misbehaving atom of energy or unit of force that goes pop under your nose and leaves you with the dead body of a mere word.

You sail down your stream of knowledge, and you find yourself absolutely at sea. Which may be safety for the weary river, but is a sad look-out for you, who are a land animal.

Now all science starts gaily from the inland source of *I Don't Know.* Gaily it says: I don't know, but I'm going to know. It's like a little river bubbling up cheerfully in the determination to dissolve the whole world in its waves. And science, like the little river, winds wonderingly out again into the final *I Don't Know* of the ocean.

All this is platitudinous as regards science. Science has learned an uncanny lot, *by the way.*

Apply the same to the Know Thyself motto. We have learned something by the way. But as far as I'm concerned, I see land receding, and the great ocean of the last *I Don't Know* enveloping me.

But the human consciousness is never allowed finally to say: 'I Don't Know.' It has *got* to know, even if it must metamorphose to do so.

> Know then thyself, presume not God to scan.

Now as soon as you come across a Thou Shalt Not commandment, you may be absolutely sure that sometime or other, you'll have to break this commandment. You needn't make a practice of breaking it. But the day will come when you'll have to break it. When you'll have to take the name of the Lord Your God in vain, and have other gods, and worship idols, and steal, and kill, and commit adultery,* and all the rest. A day will come. Because, as Oscar Wilde says, what's a temptation for, except to be succumbed to!*

There comes a time to every man when he has to break one or other of the Thou Shalt Not commandments. And then is the time to Know Yourself just a bit different from what you thought you were.

So that in the end, this Know Thyself commandment brings me up against the Presume-Not-God-to-Scan fence. Trespassers will be prosecuted. Know then thyself, presume not God to scan.

It's a dilemma. Because this business of knowing myself has led me slap up against the forbidden enclosure where, presumably, this God mystery is kept in corral. It isn't my fault. I followed the road. And it leads over the edge of a precipice on which stands up a signboard: Danger! Don't go over the edge!

But I've *got* to go over the edge. The way lies that way.

Flop! Over we go, and into the endless sea. There drown.

No! Out of the drowning something else gurgles awake. And that's the best of the human consciousness. When you fall into the final sea of *I Don't Know*, then, if you can but gasp *Teach Me*, you turn into a fish, and twiddle your fins and twist your tail and gorp in amazement, in a new element.

That's why they called Jesus: The Fish. Pisces.* Because he fell, like the weariest river, into the great Ocean that is outside the shore, and there took on a new way of knowledge.

The Proper Study is Man, sure enough. But the proper study of man, like the proper study of anything else, will in the end leave you no option. You'll have to presume to study God. Even the most hard-boiled scientist, if he is a brave and honest man, is landed in this unscientific dilemma. Or rather, he is all at sea in it.

The river of human consciousness, like ancient Ocean, goes in a circle. It starts gaily, bubblingly, fiercely from an inland source which it invariably calls God. A bubbling, mysterious inland pool, where it surges up in obvious mystery and Godliness, the human consciousness. And here is the God of the Beginning, call him Jehovah or Ra or Ammon or Jupiter* or what you like. One bubbles up in Greece, one in India, one in Jerusalem. From their various

God-sources the streams of human consciousness rush variously
down. Then begin to meander and to doubt. Then fall slow. Then
start to silt up. Then pass into the great Ocean, which is the God
of the End.

In the great ocean of the End, most men are lost. But Jesus
turned into a fish, he had the other consciousness of the Ocean
which is the divine End of us all. And then like a salmon he beat
his way up stream again, to speak from the source.

And this is the greater history of man, as distinguished from the
lesser history, in which figure Mr Lloyd George and Monsieur
Poincaré.*

We are in the deep, muddy estuary of our era, and terrified of
the emptiness of the sea beyond. Or we are at the end of the great
road, that Jesus and Francis and Whitman walked. We are on the
brink of a precipice, and terrified at the great void below.

No help for it. We are men, and for men there is no retreat.
Over we go.

Over we must and shall go, so we may as well do it voluntarily,
keeping our soul alive; and as we drown in our terrestrial nature,
transmogrify into fishes. Pisces. That which knows the Oceanic
Godliness of the End.

The proper study of mankind is man. Agreed entirely! But in
the long run, it becomes again as it was before, man in his relation
to the deity. The proper study of mankind is man in his relation to
the deity.

And yet not as it was before. Not the specific deity of the inland
source. The vast deity of the End, Oceanus* whom you can only
know by becoming a Fish. Let us become Fishes, and try.

They talk about the sixth sense. They talk as if it were an
extension of the other senses. A mere *dimensional* sense. It's
nothing of the sort. There is a sixth sense right enough. Jesus had
it. The sense of the God that is the End and the Beginning. And
the proper study of mankind is man in his relation to this Oceanic
God.

We have come to the end, for the time being, of the study of
man in his relation to man. Or man in his relation to himself. Or
man in his relation to woman. There is nothing more of
importance to be said, by us or for us, on this subject. Indeed, we
have no more to say.

Of course, there is the literature of perversity. And there is the literature of little playboys* and playgirls, not only of the western world. But the literature of perversity is a brief weed. And the playboy playgirl stuff, like the movies, though a very monstrous weed, won't live long.

As the weariest river winds by no means safely to sea, all the muddy little individuals begin to chirrup: Let's play! Let's play at something! We're so godlike when we *play*.

But it won't do, my dears. The sea will swallow you up, and all your play and perversions and personalities.

You can't get any more literature out of man in his relation to man. Which of course should be writ large, to mean man in his relation to woman, to other men, and to the whole environment of men: or woman in her relation to man, or other women, or the whole environment of women. You can't get any more literature out of that. Because any new book must needs be a new stride. And the next stride lands you over the sand-bar in the open ocean, where the first and greatest relation of every man and woman is to the Ocean itself, the great God of the End, who is the All-Father of all sources, as the sea is father of inland lakes and springs of water.

But get a glimpse of this new relation of men and women to the great God of the End, who is the Father, not the Son, of all our beginnings: and you get a glimpse of the new literature. Think of the true novel of St Paul, for example. Not the sentimental looking-backward Christian novel, but the novel looking out to sea, to the great Source, and End, of all beginnings. Not the St Paul with his human feelings repudiated, to give play to the new divine feelings. Not the St Paul violent in reaction against worldliness and sensuality,* and therefore a dogmatist with his sheaf of Shalt-Nots ready. But a St Paul two thousand years older, having his own epoch behind him, and having again the great knowledge of the deity, the deity which Jesus knew, the vast Ocean God which is at the end of all our consciousness.

Because, after all, if chemistry winds wearily to sea in the ether, or some such universal, don't we also, not as chemists but as conscious men, also wind wearily to sea in a divine ether, which means nothing to us but space and words and emptiness? We wind wearily to sea in words and emptiness.

But man is a mutable animal. Turn into the Fish, the Pisces of man's final consciousness, and you'll start to swim again in the great life which is so frighteningly godly that you realise your previous presumption.

And then you realise the new relation of man. Men like fishes lifted on a great wave of the God of the End, swimming together, and apart, in a new medium. A new relation, in a new whole.

Review of *The Book of Revelation* by Dr John Oman

THE Apocalypse is a strange and mysterious book. One therefore welcomes any serious work upon it. Now Dr John Oman (*The Book of Revelation*, Cambridge University Press, 7s. 6d. net) has undertaken the rearrangement of the sections into an intelligible order. The clue to the order lies in the idea that the theme is the conflict between true and false religion, false religion being established upon the Beast of world empire. Behind the great outward happenings of the world lie the greater, but more mysterious happenings of the divine ordination. The Apocalypse unfolds in symbols the dual event of the crashing-down of world-empire and world-civilization, and the triumph of men in the way of God.

Doctor Oman's rearrangement and his exposition give one a good deal of satisfaction. The main drift we can surely accept. John's* passionate and mystic hatred of the civilization of his day, a hatred so intense only because he knew that the living realities of men's being were displaced by it, is something to which the soul answers now again. His fierce, new usage of the symbols of the four Prophets* of the Old Testament gives one a feeling of relief, of release into passionate actuality, after the tight pettiness of modern intellect.

Yet we cannot agree that Dr Oman's explanation of the Apocalypse is exhaustive. No explanation of symbols is final. Symbols are not intellectual quantities, they are not to be exhausted by the intellect.

And an Apocalypse has, must have, is intended to have various levels or layers or strata of meaning. The fall of World Rule and World Empire before the Word of God is certainly one stratum. And perhaps it would be easier to leave it at that. Only it is not satisfying.

Why should Doctor Oman oppose the view that, besides the drama of the fall of World Rule and the triumph of the Word, there is another drama, or rather several other concurrent dramas? We gladly accept Dr Oman's interpretation of the two Women* and the Beasts. But why should he appear so unwilling to accept any astrological reference? Why should not the symbols have an astrological meaning, and the drama be also a drama of cosmic man, in terms of the stars?

As a matter of fact, old symbols have many meanings, and we only define one meaning in order to leave another undefined. So with the meaning of the Book of Revelation. Hence the inexhaustibility of its attraction.

Climbing Down Pisgah*

SOMETIMES one pulls oneself up short, and asks: 'What am I doing this for?' One writes novels, stories, essays: and then suddenly: 'What on earth am I doing it for?'

What indeed?

For the sake of humanity?

Pfui! The very words *human, humanity, humanism* make one sick. For the sake of humanity as such, I wouldn't lift a little finger, much less write a story.

For the sake of the Spirit?

Tampoco!—But what do we mean by the Spirit? Let us be careful. Do we mean that One Universal Intelligence of which every man has his modicum? Or further, that one Cosmic Soul, or Spirit, of which every individual is a broken fragment, and towards which every individual strives back, to escape the raw edges of his own fragmentariness, and to experience once more the sense of wholeness?

The sense of wholeness! Does one write books in order to give one's fellow-men a sense of wholeness: first, a oneness with all men, then a oneness with all things, then a oneness with our cosmos, and finally a oneness with the vast invisible universe? Is that it? Is that our achievement and our peace?

Anyhow, it would be a great achievement. And this has been the aim of the great ones. It was the aim of Whitman, for example.

Now it is the aim of the little ones, since the big ones are all gone. Thomas Hardy, a last big one, rings the knell of our Oneness. Virtually, he says: Once you achieve the great identification with the One, whether it be the One Spirit, or the Oversoul,* or God, or whatever name you like to give it, you find that this God, this One, this Cosmic Spirit isn't human at all, hasn't any human feelings, doesn't concern itself for a second with the individual, and is, all told, a gigantic cold monster. It is a machine. The moment you attain that sense of Oneness and Wholeness, you become cold, de-humanised, mechanical, and monstrous. The greatest of all illusions is the Infinite of the Spirit.

Whitman really rang the same knell. (I don't expect anyone to agree with me.)

The sense of wholeness is a most terrible let-down. The big ones have already decided it. But the little ones, sneakingly too selfish to care, go on sentimentally tinkling away at it.

This we may be sure of: all talk of brotherhood, universal love, sacrifice, and so on, is a sentimental pose for us. We reached the top of Pisgah, and looking down, saw the graveyard of humanity. Those meagre spirits who could never get to the top, and are careful never to try, because it costs too much sweat and a bleeding at the nose, they sit below and still snivellingly invent Pisgah-sights. But strictly, it is all over. The game is up.

The little ones, of course, are writing at so many cents a word— or a line, according to their success. They may say I do the same. Yes, I demand my cents, a Shylock. Nevertheless, if I wrote for cents I should write differently, and with far more 'success'.

What, then, does one write for? There must be some imperative.

Probably it is the sense of adventure, to start with. Life is no fun for a man, without an adventure.

The Pisgah-top of spiritual oneness looks down upon a hopeless squalor of industrialism, the huge cemetery of human hopes. This is our Promised Land. 'There's a good time coming, boys, a good time coming.'* Well, we've rung the bell, and here it is.

Shall we climb hurriedly down from Pisgah, and keep the secret? Mum's the word!

This is what our pioneers are boldly doing. We used, as boys, to sing parodies of most of the Sunday-school hymns.

> They climbed the steep ascent of heaven
> Through peril, toil, and pain.
> O God to us may grace be given
> To scramble down again.*

This is the grand hymn of the little ones. But it's harder getting down from a height, very often, than getting up. It's a predicament. Here we are, cowering on the brinks of precipices half-way up, or down, Pisgah. The Pisgah of Oneness, the Oneness of Mankind, the Oneness of Spirit.

Hie, boys, over we go! Pisgah's a fraud, and the Promised Land is Pittsburgh,* the Chosen Few, there are billions of 'em, and

Canaan smells of kerosene. Let's break our necks if we must, but let's get down, and look over the brink of some other horizon. We're like the girl who took the wrong turning: thought it was the right one.*

It's an adventure. And there's only one left, the venture in consciousness. Curse these ancients, they have said everything for us. Curse these moderns, they have done everything for us. The aeroplane descends and lays her egg-shells of empty tin cans on the top of Everest, in the Ultimate Thule,* and all over the North Pole; not to speak of tractors waddling across the inviolate Sahara* and over the jags of Arabia Petraea, laying the same addled eggs of our civilisation, tin cans, in every camp-nest.

Well then, they can have the round earth. They've got it anyhow. And they can have the firmament: they've got that too. The moon is a cold egg in the astronomical nest. *Heigho! for the world well lost!*

That's the Known World, the world of the One Intelligence. That's the Human World! I'm getting out of it. *Homo sum. Omnis a me humanum alienum puto.*

Of the thing we call human, I've had enough. And enough is as good as a feast.

Inside of me, there's a little demon—maybe he's a big demon—that says *Basta! Basta!* to all my oneness. 'Farewell, a long farewell to all my greatness.'* In short, come off the perch, Polly, and look what a mountain of droppings you've crouched upon.

Are you human, and do you want me to sympathise with you for that? Let me hand you a roll of toilet paper.

After looking down from the Pisgah-top onto the oneness of all mankind safely settled these several years in Canaan, I admit myself dehumanised.

> Fair waved the golden corn
> In Canaan's pleasant land.*

The factory smoke waves much higher. And in the sweet smoke of industry I don't care a button who loves whom, nor what babies are born. The sight of all of it *en masse* was a little too much for my human spirit, it dehumanised me. Here I am, without a human sympathy left. Looking down on Human Oneness was too much for my human stomach, so I vomited it away.

Remains a demon which says *Ha-ha! So you've conquered the earth, have you, oh man! Now swallow the pill.*

For if the proof of the pudding is in the eating, the proof of a conquest is in digesting it. Humanity is an ostrich. But even the ostrich thinks twice before it bolts a rolled-up hedgehog. The earth is conquered as the hedgehog is conquered when he rolls himself up into a ball, and the dog spins him with his paw.

But that is not the point, at least for anyone except the Great Dog of Humanity. The point for us is, *What then?*

'Whither, oh splendid ship, thy white sails crowding—?'*

To have her white sail dismantled and a gasoline engine fitted into her guts. That is whither, oh Poet!

When you've got to the bottom of Pisgah once more, where are you? Sitting on a sore posterior, murmuring: *Oneness is all bunk. There is no Oneness, till you've invented it and killed your goose to get it out of her belly. It takes millions of little people to lay the egg of the Universal Spirit, and then it's an addled omelette, and stinks in our nostrils. And all the millions of little people have over-reached themselves, trying to lay the mundane egg* of oneness. They're all damaged inside, and they can't face the addled omelette they've laid. What a mess!*

What then?

Heigho! Whither, oh patched canoe, your kinked keel thrusting!

We've been over the rapids, and the creature that crawls out of the whirlpool feels that most things human are foreign to him. *Homo sum!* means a vastly different thing to him, from what it meant to his father.

Homo sum! a demon who knows nothing of oneness or of perfection. *Homo sum!* a demon who knows nothing of any First Creator who created the universe from His own perfection. *Homo sum!* a man who knows that all creation lives like some great demon inhabiting space, and pulsing with a dual desire, a desire to give himself forth into creation, and a desire to take himself back, in death.

Child of the great inscrutable demon, *Homo sum!* Adventurer from the first Adventurer, *Homo sum!* Son of the blazing-hearted father who wishes beauty and harmony and perfection, *Homo sum!*

Child of the raging-hearted demon-father who fights that nothing shall surpass his crude and demonish range, *Homo sum*!

Whirling in the midst of Chaos, the demon of the beginning who is forever willing and unwilling to surpass the *status quo*. Like a bird he spreads wings to surpass himself. Then like a serpent he coils to strike at that which would surpass him. And the bird of the first desire must either soar quickly, or strike back with his talons at the snake, if there is to be any surpassing of the thing that was, the *status quo*.

It is the joy forever, the agony forever, and above all, the fight forever. For all the universe is alive, and whirling in the same fight, the same joy and anguish. The vast demon of life has made himself habits which, except in the whitest heat of desire and rage, he will never break. And these habits are the laws of our scientific universe. But all the laws of physics, dynamic, kinetic, static, all are but the settled habits of a vast living incomprehensibility, and they can all be broken, superseded, in a moment of great extremity.

Homo sum! child of the demon. *Homo sum*! willing and unwilling. *Homo sum*! giving and taking. *Homo sum*! hot and cold. *Homo sum*! loving and loveless. *Homo sum*! the adventurer.

This we see, this we know as we crawl down the dark side of Pisgah, or slip down on a sore posterior. *Homo sum*! has changed its meaning for us.

That is, if we are young men. Old men and elderly will sit tight on heavy posteriors in some crevice upon Pisgah, babbling about 'all for love, and the world well saved'. Young men with hearts still for the life adventure will rise up with their trouser-seats scraped away, after the long slither from the heights down the well-nigh bottomless pit, having changed their minds. They will change their minds and change their pants. Wisdom is sometimes in a sore bottom, and the new pants will no longer be neutral.

Young men will change their minds and their pants, having done with Oneness and neutrality. Even the stork meditates on an orange leg, and the bold drake pushes the water behind him with a red foot. Young men are the adventurers.

Let us scramble out of this ash-hole at the foot of Pisgah. The universe isn't a machine after all. It's alive and kicking. And in spite of the fact that man with his cleverness has discovered some of the habits of our old earth, and so lured him into a trap; in spite of the fact that man has trapped the great forces, and they go round and round at his bidding like a donkey in a gin; the old demon isn't quite nabbed. We didn't quite catch him napping. He'll turn round on us with bare fangs, before long. He'll turn into a python, coiling, coiling, coiling till we're nicely mashed. Then he'll bolt us.

Let's get out of the vicious circle. Put on new bright pants to show that we're meditative fowl who have thought the thing out and decided to migrate. To assert that our legs are not grey machine-sections, but live and limber members who know what it is to have their rear well scraped and punished, in the slither down Pisgah, and are not going to be diddled any more into mechanical service of mountain-climbing up to the great summit of Wholeness and Bunk.

Art and Morality

IT is a part of the common claptrap that 'art is immoral'. Behold, everywhere, artists running to put on jazz underwear, to demoralize themselves; or, at least, to *débourgeoiser* themselves.

For the bourgeois is supposed to be the fount of morality. Myself, I have found artists far more morally finicky.

Anyhow, what has a water-pitcher and six insecure apples on a crumpled tablecloth got to do with bourgeois morality? Yet I notice that most people, who have not learnt the trick of being arty, feel a real moral repugnance for a Cézanne* still-life. They think it is not *right*.

For them, it isn't.

Yet how can they feel, as they do, that it is subtly *immoral*?

The very same design, if it was humanized, and the tablecloth was a draped nude and the water-pitcher a nude semi-draped, weeping over the draped one, would instantly become highly moral. Why?

Perhaps from painting better than from any other art we can realize the subtlety of the distinction between what is dumbly *felt* to be moral, and what is felt to be immoral. The moral instinct in the man in the street.

But instinct is largely habit. The moral instinct of the man in the street is largely an emotional defence of an old habit.

Yet what can there be in a Cézanne still-life to rouse the aggressive moral instinct of the man in the street? What ancient habit in man do these six apples and a water-pitcher succeed in hindering?

A water-pitcher that isn't so very much like a water-pitcher, apples that aren't very appley, and a tablecloth that's not particularly much of a tablecloth. I could do better myself!

Probably! But then, why not dismiss the picture as a poor attempt? Whence this anger, this hostility? The derisive resentment?

Six apples, a pitcher, and a tablecloth can't suggest improper *behaviour*. They don't—not even to a Freudian. If they did, the man in the street would feel much more at home with them.

Where, then, does the immorality come in? Because come in it does.

Because of a very curious habit that civilized man has been forming down the whole course of civilization, and in which he is now hard-boiled. The slowly formed habit of seeing just as the photographic camera sees.

You may say, the object reflected on the retina is *always* photographic. It may be. I doubt it. But whatever the image on the retina may be, it is rarely, even now, the photographic image of the object which is actually *taken in* by the man who sees the object. He does not, even now, see for himself. He sees what the Kodak has taught him to see. And man, try as he may, is not a Kodak.

When a child sees a man, what does the child *take in*, as an impression? Two eyes, a nose, a mouth of teeth, two straight legs, two straight arms: a sort of hieroglyph which the human child has used through all the ages to represent man. At least, the old hieroglyph was still in use when I was a child.

Is this what the child actually *sees*?

If you mean by seeing, consciously registering, then this is what the child actually sees. The photographic image may be there all right, upon the retina. But there the child leaves it: outside the door, as it were.

Through many ages, mankind has been striving to register the image on the retina *as it is:* no more glyphs and hieroglyphs. We'll have the real objective reality.

And we have succeeded. As soon as we succeed, the Kodak is invented, to prove our success. Could lies come out of a black box, into which nothing but light had entered? Impossible! It takes life to tell a lie.

Colour also, which primitive man cannot really *see*, is now seen by us, and fitted to the spectrum.

Eureka! We have seen it, with our own eyes.

When we see a red cow, we see a red cow. We are quite sure of it, because the unimpeachable Kodak sees exactly the same.

But supposing we had all of us been born blind, and had to get our image of a red cow by touching her, and smelling her, hearing her moo, and 'feeling' her? Whatever should we think of her? Whatever sort of image should we have of her, in our dark minds? Something very different, surely!

As vision developed towards the Kodak, man's idea of himself developed towards the snapshot. Primitive man simply didn't know *what* he was: he was always half in the dark. But we have learned to see, and each of us has a complete Kodak idea of himself.

You take a snap of your sweetheart, in the field among the buttercups, smiling tenderly at the red cow with a calf, and dauntlessly offering a cabbage-leaf.

Awfully nice, and absolutely 'real'. There is your sweetheart, complete in herself, enjoying a sort of absolute objective reality: complete, perfect, all her surroundings contributing to her, incontestable. She is really a 'picture'.

This is the habit we have formed: of visualizing *everything*. Each man to himself is a picture. That is, he is a complete little objective reality, complete in himself, existing by himself, absolutely, in the middle of the picture. All the rest is just setting, background. To every man, to every woman, the universe is just a setting to the absolute little picture of himself, herself.

This has been the development of the conscious ego in man, through several thousand years: since Greece first broke the spell of 'darkness'. Man has learnt to *see* himself. So now, he *is* what he sees. He makes himself in his own image.

Previously, even in Egypt, men had not learnt to *see straight*. They fumbled in the dark, and didn't quite know where they were, or what they were. Like men in a dark room, they only *felt* their own existence surging in the darkness of other creatures.

We, however, have learned to see ourselves for what we are, as the sun sees us. The Kodak bears witness. We see as the All-Seeing Eye sees, with the universal vision. And we *are* what is seen: each man to himself an identity, an isolated absolute, corresponding with a universe of isolated absolutes. A picture! A Kodak snap, in a universal film of snaps.

We have achieved universal vision. Even God could not see *differently* from what we see: only more extensively, like a telescope, or more intensively, like a microscope. But the same vision. A vision of images which are real, and each one limited to itself.

We behave as if we had got to the bottom of the sack, and seen the Platonic Idea*' with our own eyes, in all its photographically developed perfection, lying in the bottom of the sack of the universe. Our own ego!

The identifying of ourselves with the visual image of ourselves has become an instinct; the habit is already old. The picture of me, the me that is *seen*, is me.

As soon as we are supremely satisfied about it, somebody starts to upset us. Comes Cézanne with his pitcher and his apples, which not only are not life-like, but are a living lie. The Kodak will prove it.

The Kodak will take all sorts of snaps, misty, atmospheric, sun-dazed, dancing—all quite different. Yet the image is *the* image. There is only more or less sun, more or less vapour, more or less light and shade.

The All-Seeing Eye sees with every degree of intensity and in every possible kind of mood: Giotto, Titian, El Greco,* Turner, all so different, yet all the true image in the All-Seeing Eye.

This Cézanne still-life, however, is *contrary* to the All-Seeing Eye. Apples, to the eye of God, could not look like that, nor could a tablecloth, nor could a pitcher. So, it is *wrong*.

Because man, since he grew out of a personal God, has taken over to himself all the attributes of the Personal Godhead. It is the all-seeing human eye which is now the Eternal Eye.

And if apples don't *look* like that, in any light or circumstance, or under any mood, then they shouldn't be painted like that.

Oh, *là-là-là!* The apples *are* just like that, to me! cries Cézanne. They *are* like that, no matter what they look like.

Apples are always apples! says Vox Populi, Vox Dei.*

Sometimes they're a sin, sometimes they're a knock on the head,* sometimes they're a bellyache, sometimes they're part of a pie, sometimes they're sauce for the goose.

And you can't see a bellyache, neither can you see a sin, neither can you see a knock on the head. So paint the apple in these aspects, and you get—probably, or approximately—a Cézanne still-life.

What an apple looks like to an urchin, to a thrush, to a browsing cow, to Sir Isaac Newton, to a caterpillar, to a hornet, to a mackerel who finds one bobbing on the sea, I leave you to conjecture. But the All-Seeing must have mackerel's eyes, as well as man's.

And this is the immorality in Cézanne: he begins to see more than the All-Seeing Eye of humanity can possibly see, Kodak-wise. If you can see in the apple a bellyache and a knock on the head, and paint these in the image, among the prettiness, then it is the death of the Kodak and the movies, and must be immoral.

It's all very well talking about decoration and illustration, significant form, or tactile values, or plastique, or movement, or space-composition, or colour-mass relations,* afterwards. You might as well force your guest to eat the menu card, at the end of the dinner.

What art has got to do, and will go on doing, is to reveal things in their different relationships. That is to say, you've got to see in the apple the bellyache, Sir Isaac's knock on the cranium, the vast, moist wall through which the insect bores to lay her eggs in the middle, and the untasted, unknown quality which Eve saw hanging on a tree. Add to this the glaucous glimpse that the mackerel gets as he comes to the surface, and Fantin-Latour's* apples are no more to you than enamelled rissoles.

The true artist doesn't substitute immorality for morality. On the contrary, he *always* substitutes a finer morality for a grosser. And as soon as you see a finer morality, the grosser becomes relatively immoral.

The universe is like Father Ocean, a stream of all things slowly moving. We move, and the rock of ages* moves. And since we move and move for ever, in no discernible direction, there is no centre to the movement, to us. To us, the centre shifts at every moment. Even the pole-star ceases to sit on the pole. *Allons!** there is no road before us!

There is nothing to do but to maintain a true relationship to the things we move with and amongst and against. The apple, like the moon, has still an unseen side. The movement of Ocean will turn it round to us, or us to it.

There is nothing man can do but maintain himself in true relationship to his contiguous universe. An ancient Rameses* can sit in stone absolute, absolved from visual contact, deep in the silent ocean of sensual contact. Michelangelo's Adam can open his eyes for the first time, and see the old man in the skies, objectively. Turner can tumble into the open mouth of the objective universe of light, till we see nothing but his disappearing heels. As the stream carries him, each in his own relatedness, each one differently, so a man must go through life.

Each thing, living or unliving, streams in its own odd, intertwin-

ing flux, and nothing, not even man nor the God of man, nor anything that man has thought or felt or known, is fixed or abiding. All
moves. And nothing is true, or good, or right, except in its own
living relatedness to its own circumambient universe; to the things
that are in the stream with it.

Design, in art, is a recognition of the relation between various
things, various elements in the creative flux. You can't *invent* a design. You recognize it, in the fourth dimension.* That is, with your
blood and your bones, as well as with your eyes.

Egypt had a wonderful relation to a vast living universe, only
dimly visual in its reality. The dim eye-vision and the powerful
blood-feeling of the Negro African, even today, gives us strange
images, which our eyes can hardly see, but which we know are surpassing. The big silent statue of Rameses is like a drop of water,
hanging through the centuries in dark suspense, and never static.
The African fetish-statues have no movement, visually represented. Yet one little motionless wooden figure stirs more than
all the Parthenon frieze. It sits in the place where no Kodak can
snap it.

As for us, we have our Kodak-vision, all in bits that group or jig.
Like the movies, that jerk but never move. An endless shifting and
rattling together of isolated images, 'snaps', miles of them, all of
them jigging, but each one utterly incapable of movement or
change, in itself. A kaleidoscope of inert images, mechanically
shaken.

And this is our vaunted 'consciousness', made up, really, of inert
visual images and little else: like the cinematograph.

Let Cézanne's apples go rolling off the table for ever. They live
by their own laws, in their own *ambiente*,* and not by the laws of
the Kodak—or of man. They are casually related to man. But to
those apples, man is by no means the absolute.

A new relationship between ourselves and the universe means a
new morality. Taste the unsteady apples of Cézanne, and the
nailed-down apples of Fantin-Latour are apples of Sodom.* If the
status quo were paradise, it would indeed be a sin to taste the new
apples; but since the *status quo* is much more prison than paradise,
we can go ahead.

Morality and the Novel

THE business of art is to reveal the relation between man and his circumambient universe, at the living moment. As mankind is always struggling in the toils of old relationships, art is always ahead of the 'times', which themselves are always far in the rear of the living moment.

When Van Gogh paints sunflowers,* he reveals, or achieves, the vivid relation between himself, as man, and the sunflower, as sunflower, at that quick moment of time. His painting does not represent the sunflower itself. We shall never know what the sunflower itself is. And the camera will *visualize* the sunflower far more perfectly than Van Gogh can.

The vision on the canvas is a third thing, utterly intangible and inexplicable, the offspring of the sunflower itself and Van Gogh himself. The vision on the canvas is for ever incommensurable with the canvas, or the paint, or Van Gogh as a human organism, or the sunflower as a botanical organism. You cannot weigh nor measure nor even describe the vision on the canvas. It exists, to tell the truth, only in the much-debated fourth dimension.* In dimensional space it has no existence.

It is a revelation of the perfected relation, at a certain moment, between a man and a sunflower. It is neither man-in-the-mirror nor flower-in-the-mirror, neither is it above or below or across anything. It is in between everything, in the fourth dimension.

And this perfected relation between man and his circumambient universe is life itself, for mankind. It has the fourth-dimensional quality of eternity and perfection. Yet it is momentaneous.

Man and the sunflower both pass away from the moment, in the process of forming a new relationship. The relation between all things changes from day to day, in a subtle stealth of change. Hence art, which reveals or attains to another perfect relationship, will be for ever new.

At the same time, that which exists in the non-dimensional space of pure relationship is deathless, lifeless, and eternal. That is, it gives us the *feeling* of being beyond life or death. We say an Assyrian lion or an Egyptian hawk's head 'lives'. What we really mean is that it is beyond life, and therefore beyond death. It gives us that feeling. And there is something inside us which must also be beyond life and beyond death, since that 'feeling' which we get from an Assyrian lion or an Egyptian hawk's head is so infinitely precious to us. As the evening star, that spark of pure relation between night and day, has been precious to man since time began.

If we think about it, we find that our life *consists in* this achieving of a pure relationship between ourselves and the living universe about us. This is how I 'save my soul' by accomplishing a pure relationship between me and another person, me and other people, me and a nation, me and a race of men, me and the animals, me and the trees or flowers, me and the earth, me and the skies and sun and stars, me and the moon: an infinity of pure relations, big and little, like the stars of the sky: that makes our eternity, for each one of us. Me and the timber I am sawing, the lines of force I follow, me and the dough I knead for bread, me and the very motion with which I write, me and the bit of gold I have got. This, if we knew it, is our life and our eternity: the subtle, perfected relation between me and my whole circumambient universe.

And morality is that delicate, for ever trembling and changing *balance* between me and my circumambient universe, which precedes and accompanies a true relatedness.

Now here we see the beauty and the great value of the novel. Philosophy, religion, science, they are all of them busy nailing things down, to get a stable equilibrium. Religion, with its naileddown One God, who says *Thou shalt, Thou shan't*, and hammers home every time; philosophy, with its fixed ideas; science with its 'laws': they, all of them, all the time, want to nail us on to some tree or other.

But the novel, no. The novel is the highest example of subtle inter-relatedness that man has discovered. Everything is true in its own time, place, circumstance, and untrue outside of its own place, time, circumstance. If you try to nail anything down, in the novel, either it kills the novel, or the novel gets up and walks away with the nail.

Morality in the novel is the trembling instability of the balance. When the novelist puts his thumb in the scale, to pull down the balance to his own predilection, that is immorality.

The modern novel tends to become more and more immoral, as the novelist tends to press his thumb heavier and heavier in the pan: either on the side of love, pure love: or on the side of licentious 'freedom'.

The novel is not, as a rule, immoral because the novelist has any dominant *idea*, or *purpose*. The immorality lies in the novelist's helpless, unconscious predilection. Love is a great emotion. But if you set out to write a novel, and you yourself are in the throes of the great predilection for love, love as the supreme, the only emotion worth living for, then you will write an immoral novel.

Because *no* emotion is supreme, or exclusively worth living for. *All* emotions go to the achieving of a living relationship between a human being and the other human being or creature or thing he becomes purely related to. All emotions, including love and hate, and rage and tenderness, go to the adjusting of the oscillating, unestablished balance between two people who amount to anything. If the novelist puts his thumb in the pan, for love, tenderness, sweetness, peace, then he commits an immoral act: he *prevents* the possibility of a pure relationship, a pure relatedness, the only thing that matters: and he makes inevitable the horrible reaction, when he lets his thumb go, towards hate and brutality, cruelty and destruction.

Life is so made that opposites sway about a trembling centre of balance. The sins of the fathers are visited on the children.* If the fathers drag down the balance on the side of love, peace, and production, then in the third or fourth generation the balance will swing back violently to hate, rage, and destruction. We must balance as we go.

And of all the art forms, the novel most of all demands the trembling and oscillating of the balance. The 'sweet' novel is more falsified, and therefore more immoral, than the blood-and-thunder novel.

The same with the smart and smudgily cynical novel, which says it doesn't matter what you do, because one thing is as good as another, anyhow, and prostitution is just as much 'life' as anything else.

This misses the point entirely. A thing isn't life just because somebody does it. This the artist ought to know perfectly well. The ordinary bank clerk buying himself a new straw hat isn't 'life' at all:

it is just existence, quite all right, like everyday dinners: but not 'life'.

By life, we mean something that gleams, that has the fourth-dimensional quality. If the bank clerk feels really piquant about his hat, if he establishes a lively relation with it, and goes out of the shop with the new straw on his head, a changed man, be-aureoled, then that is life.

The same with the prostitute. If a man establishes a living relation to her, if only for one moment, then it is life. But if it *doesn't*: if it is just money and function, then it is not life, but sordidness, and a betrayal of living.

If a novel reveals true and vivid relationships, it is a moral work, no matter what the relationships may consist in. If the novelist *honours* the relationship in itself, it will be a great novel.

But there are so many relationships which are not real. When the man in *Crime and Punishment* murders the old woman* for sixpence, although it is *actual* enough, it is never quite real. The balance between the murderer and the old woman is gone entirely; it is only a mess. It is actuality, but it is not 'life', in the living sense.

The popular novel, on the other hand, dishes up a réchauffé of old relationships: *If Winter Comes.** And old relationships dished up are likewise immoral. Even a magnificent painter like Raphael does nothing more than dress up in gorgeous new dresses relationships which have already been experienced. And this gives a gluttonous kind of pleasure to the mass: a voluptuousness, a wallowing. For centuries, men say of their voluptuously ideal woman: 'She is a Raphael Madonna.' And women are only just learning to take it as an insult.

A new relation, a new relatedness hurts somewhat in the attaining; and will always hurt. So life will always hurt. Because real voluptuousness lies in re-acting old relationships, and at the best, getting an alcoholic sort of pleasure out of it, slightly depraving.

Each time we strive to a new relation, with anyone or anything, it is bound to hurt somewhat. Because it means the struggle with and the displacing of old connexions, and this is never pleasant. And moreover, between living things at least, an adjustment means also a fight, for each party, inevitably, must 'seek its own' in the other, and be denied. When, in the two parties, each of them seeks his own, her own, absolutely, then it is a fight to the death. And this is true of the thing called 'passion'. On the other hand, when, of the two parties, one yields utterly to the other, this is called sacrifice, and it also means death. So the Constant Nymph died* of her eighteen months of constancy.

It isn't the nature of nymphs to be constant. She should have been constant in her nymph-hood. And it is unmanly to accept sacrifices. He should have abided by his own manhood.

There is, however, the third thing, which is neither sacrifice nor fight to the death: when each seeks only the true relatedness to the other. Each must be true to himself, herself, his own manhood, her own womanhood, and let the relationship work out of itself. This means courage above all things: and then discipline. Courage to accept the life-thrust from within oneself, and from the other person. Discipline, not to exceed oneself any more than one can help. Courage, when one has exceeded oneself, to accept the fact and not whine about it.

Obviously, to read a really new novel will *always* hurt, to some extent. There will always be resistance. The same with new pictures, new music. You may judge of their reality by the fact that they do arouse a certain resistance, and compel, at length, a certain acquiescence.

The great relationship, for humanity, will always be the relation between man and woman. The relation between man and man, woman and woman, parent and child, will always be subsidiary.

And the relation between man and woman will change for ever, and will for ever be the new central clue to human life. It is the *relation itself* which is the quick and the central clue to life, not the man, nor the woman, nor the children that result from the relationship, as a contingency.

It is no use thinking you can put a stamp on the relation between man and woman, to keep it in the *status quo*. You can't. You might as well try to put a stamp on the rainbow or the rain.

As for the bond of love, better put it off when it galls. It is an absurdity, to say that men and women *must love*. Men and women will be for ever subtly and changingly related to one another; no need to yoke them with any 'bond' at all. The only morality is to have man true to his manhood, woman to her womanhood, and let the relationship form of itself, in all honour. For it is, to each, *life itself.*

If we are going to be moral, let us refrain from driving pegs through anything, either through each other or through the third thing, the relationship, which is for ever the ghost of both of us. Every sacrificial crucifixion needs five pegs, four short ones and a long one, each one an abomination. But when you try to nail down the relationship itself, and write over it *Love* instead of *This is the King of the Jews*, then you can go on putting in nails for ever. Even Jesus called it the Holy Ghost,* to show you that you can't lay salt on its tail.

The novel is a perfect medium for revealing to us the changing rainbow of our living relationships. The novel can help us to live, as nothing else can: no didactic Scripture, anyhow. If the novelist keeps his thumb out of the pan.

But when the novelist *has* his thumb in the pan, the novel becomes an unparalleled perverter of men and women. To be compared only, perhaps, to that great mischief of sentimental hymns, like 'Lead, Kindly Light',* which have helped to rot the marrow in the bones of the present generation.

The Novel

SOMEBODY says the novel is doomed. Somebody else says it is the green bay tree getting greener. Everybody says something, so why shouldn't I!

Mr Santayana* sees the modern novel expiring because it is getting so thin; which means, Mr Santayana is bored.

I am rather bored myself. It becomes harder and harder to read the *whole* of any modern novel. One reads a bit, and knows the rest; or else one doesn't want to know any more.

This is sad. But again, I don't think it's the novel's fault. Rather the novelists'.

You can put anything you like in a novel. So why do people *always* go on putting the same thing? Why is the *vol au vent* always chicken! Chicken *vol au vents* may be the rage. But who sickens first shouts first for something else.

The novel is a great discovery: far greater than Galileo's telescope or somebody else's* wireless. The novel is the highest form of human expression so far attained. Why? Because it is so incapable of the absolute.

In a novel, everything is relative to everything else, if that novel is art at all. There may be didactic bits, but they aren't the novel. And the author may have a didactic 'purpose' up his sleeve. Indeed most great novelists have, as Tolstoi had his Christian-Socialism, and Hardy his pessimism, and Flaubert his intellectual desperation. But even a didactic purpose so wicked as Tolstoi's or Flaubert's cannot put to death the novel.

You can tell me, Flaubert had a 'philosophy', not a 'purpose'. But what is a novelist's philosophy but a purpose on a rather higher level? And since every novelist who amounts to anything has a philosophy—even Balzac—any novel of importance has a purpose. If only the 'purpose' be large enough, and not at outs with the passional inspiration.

Vronsky sinned, did he? But also the sinning was a consummation devoutly to be wished.* The novel makes that obvious: in spite of old Leo Tolstoi. And the would-be-pious

Prince in *Resurrection* is a muff,* with his piety that nobody wants
or believes in.

There you have the greatness of the novel itself. It won't *let* you
tell didactic lies, and put them over. Nobody in the world is
anything but delighted when Vronsky gets Anna Karenina. Then
what about the sin?—Why, when you look at it, all the tragedy
comes from Vronsky's and Anna's fear of *society*. The monster was
social, not phallic at all. They couldn't live in the pride of their
sincere passion, and spit in Mother Grundy's* eye. And that, that
cowardice, was the real 'sin'. The novel makes it obvious, and
knocks all old Leo's teeth out. 'As an officer I am still useful. But as
a man, I am a ruin,' says Vronsky*—or words to that effect. Well
what a skunk, collapsing as a man and a male, and remaining
merely as a social instrument; an 'officer', God love us!—merely
because people at the opera turn backs on him!* As if people's
backs weren't preferable to their faces, anyhow!

And old Leo tries to make out, it was all because of the phallic
sin. Old liar! Because where would any of Leo's books be, without
the phallic splendour? And then to blame the column of blood,
which really gave him all his life riches! The Judas! Cringe to a
mangy, bloodless Society, and try to dress up that dirty old Mother
Grundy in a new bonnet and face-powder of Christian-Socialism.
Brothers indeed! Sons of a castrated Father!

The novel itself gives Vronsky a kick in the behind, and knocks
old Leo's teeth out, and leaves us to learn.

It is such a bore that nearly all great novelists have a didactic
purpose, otherwise a philosophy, directly opposite to their
passional inspiration. In their passional inspiration, they are all
phallic worshippers. From Balzac to Hardy, it is so. Nay, from
Apuleius to E. M. Forster.* Yet all of them, when it comes to their
philosophy, or what they think-they-are, they are all crucified
Jesuses. What a bore! And what a burden for the novel to carry!

But the novel has carried it. Several thousands of thousands of
lamentable crucifixions of self-heroes and self-heroines. Even the
silly duplicity of *Resurrection*, and the wickeder duplicity of
Salammbô,* with that flayed phallic Matho, tortured upon the
Cross of a gilt Princess.

You can't fool the novel. Even with man crucified upon a
woman: his 'dear cross'. The novel will show you how dear she

was: dear at any price. And it will leave you with a bad taste of disgust against these heroes who *turn* their women into a 'dear cross', and *ask* for their own crucifixion.

You can fool pretty nearly every other medium. You can make a poem pietistic, and still it will be a poem. You can write *Hamlet* in drama: if you wrote him in a novel, he'd be half comic, or a trifle suspicious: a suspicious character, like Dostoevsky's Idiot.* Somehow, you sweep the ground a bit too clear in the poem or the drama, and you let the human Word fly a bit too freely. Now in a novel there's always a tom-cat, a black tom-cat that pounces on the white dove of the Word, if the dove doesn't watch it; and there is a banana-skin to trip on; and you know there is a water-closet on the premises. All these things help to keep the balance.

If, in Plato's *Dialogues*, somebody had suddenly stood on his head and given smooth Plato a kick in the wind, and set the whole school in an uproar, then Plato would have been put into a much truer relation to the universe. Or if, in the midst of the Timaeus,* Plato had only paused to say: 'And now, my dear Cleon—(or whoever it was)—I have a belly-ache, and must retreat to the privy: this too is part of the Eternal Idea of man', then we never need have fallen so low as Freud.

And if, when Jesus told the rich man to take all he had and give it to the poor,* the rich man had replied: '*All right, old sport! You are poor, aren't you? Come on, I'll give you a fortune. Come on!*' Then a great deal of snivelling and mistakenness would have been spared us all, and we might never have produced a Marx and a Lenin. If only Jesus had *accepted the* fortune!

Yes, it's a pity of pities that Matthew, Mark, Luke, and John didn't write straight novels. They did write novels; but a bit crooked. The Evangels are wonderful novels, by authors 'with a purpose'. Pity there's so much Sermon-on-the-Mounting.

> 'Matthew, Mark, Luke, and John
> Went to bed with their breeches on!'—*

as every child knows. Ah, if only they'd taken them off!

Greater novels, to my mind, are the books of the Old Testament, Genesis, Exodus, Samuel, Kings, by authors whose purpose was so big, it didn't quarrel with their passionate inspiration. The purpose and the inspiration were almost one.

Why, in the name of everything bad, the two ever should have got separated, is a mystery! But in the modern novel they are hopelessly divorced. When there *is* any inspiration there, to be divorced from.

This, then, is what is the matter with the modern novel. The modern novelist is possessed, hag-ridden, by such a stale old 'purpose', or idea-of-himself, that his inspiration succumbs. Of course he denies having any didactic purpose at all: because a purpose is supposed to be like catarrh, something to be ashamed of. But he's got it. They've all got it: the same snivelling purpose.

They're all little Jesuses in their own eyes, and their 'purpose' is to prove it. Oh Lord!—*Lord Jim! Sylvestre Bonnard! If Winter Comes! Main Street! Ulysses! Pan!** They are all pathetic or sympathetic or antipathetic little Jesuses *accomplis* or *manqués.** And there is a heroine who is always 'pure', usually, nowadays, on the muck-heap! Like the Green Hatted Woman.* She is all the time at the feet of Jesus, though her behaviour there may be misleading. Heaven knows what the Saviour really makes of it: whether she's a Green Hat or a Constant Nymph* (eighteen months of constancy, and her heart failed), or any of the rest of 'em. They are all, heroes and heroines, novelists and she-novelists, little Jesuses or Jesusesses. They may be wallowing in the mire: but then didn't Jesus harrow Hell! *A la bonne heure!**

Oh, they are all novelists with an idea of themselves! Which is a 'purpose', with a vengeance! For what a weary, false, sickening idea it is nowadays! The novel gives them away. They can't fool the novel.

Now really, it's time we left *off* insulting the novel any further. If your purpose is to prove your own Jesus qualifications, and the thin stream of your inspiration is 'sin', then dry up, for the interest is dead. *Life as it is!* What's the good of pretending that the lives of a set of tuppenny Green Hats and Constant Nymphs is Life-as-it-is, when the novel itself proves that all it amounts to is life as it is isn't life, but a sort of everlasting and intricate and boring habit: of Jesus peccant and *Jesusa peccante.**

These wearisome sickening little personal novels! After all, they aren't novels at all. In every great novel, who is the hero all the time? Not any of the characters, but some unnamed and nameless flame behind them all. Just as God is the pivotal interest in the books of the Old Testament. But just a trifle too intimate, too *frère* *et cochon*,* there. In the great novel, the felt but unknown flame stands behind all the characters, and in their words and gestures there is a flicker of the presence. If you are *too personal, too human*, the flicker fades out, leaving you with something awfully lifelike, and as lifeless as most people are.

We have to choose between the quick and the dead. The quick is God-flame, in everything. And the dead is dead. In this room where I write, there is a little table that is dead: it doesn't even weakly exist. And there is a ridiculous little iron stove, which for some unknown reason is quick. And there is an iron wardrobe trunk, which for some still more mysterious reason is quick. And there are several books, whose mere corpus is dead, utterly dead and non-existent. And there is a sleeping cat, very quick. And a glass lamp, that, alas, is dead.

What makes the difference? *Quien sabe!** But difference there is. And I *know* it.

And the sum and source of all quickness, we will call God. And the sum and total of all deadness we may call human.

And if one tries to find out, wherein the quickness of the quick lies, it is in a certain weird relationship between that which is quick and—I don't know; perhaps all the rest of things. It seems to consist in an odd sort of fluid, changing, grotesque or beautiful relatedness. That silly iron stove somehow *belongs*. Whereas this thin-shanked table doesn't belong. It is a mere disconnected lump, like a cut-off finger.

And now we see the great, great merits of the novel. It can't exist without being 'quick'. The ordinary unquick novel, even if it be a best seller, disappears into absolute nothingness, the dead burying their dead with surprising speed. For even the dead like to be tickled. But the next minute, they've forgotten both the tickling and the tickler.

Secondly, the novel contains no didactive absolute. All that is quick, and all that is said and done by the quick, is, in some way, godly. So that Vronsky's taking Anna Karenina we must count godly, since it is quick. And that Prince in *Resurrection*, following the convict girl,* we must count dead. The convict train is quick and alive. But that would-be-expiatory Prince is as dead as lumber.

The novel itself lays down these laws for us, and we spend our time evading them. The man in the novel must be 'quick'. And this means one thing, among a host of unknown meaning: it means he must have a quick relatedness to all the other things in the novel: snow, bed-bugs, sunshine, the phallus, trains, silk-hats, cats, sorrow, people, food, diphtheria, fuchsias, stars, ideas, God, tooth-paste, lightning, and toilet-paper. He must be in quick relation to all these things. What he says and does must be relative to them all.

And this is why Pierre, for example, in *War and Peace*,* is more dull and less quick than Prince André. Pierre is quite nicely related to ideas, tooth-paste, God, people, foods, trains, silk-hats, sorrow, diphtheria, stars. But his relation to snow and sunshine, cats, lightning and the phallus, fuchsias and toilet-paper, is sluggish and mussy. He's not quick enough.

The really quick, Tolstoi loved to kill them or muss them over. Like a true Bolshevist. One can't help feeling Natasha is rather mussy and unfresh, married to that Pierre.

Pierre was what we call, 'so human'. Which means, 'so limited'. Men clotting together into social masses in order to limit their individual liabilities: this is humanity. And this is Pierre. And this is Tolstoi, the philosopher with a very nauseating Christian-brotherhood idea of himself. Why limit man to a Christian-brotherhood? I myself, I could belong to the sweetest Christian-brotherhood one day, and ride after Attila with a raw beefsteak for my saddle-cloth,* to see the red cock crow in flame over all Christendom, next day.

And that is man! That, really, was Tolstoi. That, even, was Lenin, God in the machine of Christian-brotherhood, that hashes men up into social sausage-meat.*

Damn all absolutes. Oh damn, damn, damn all absolutes! I tell you, no absolute is going to make the lion lie down with the lamb: unless, like the limerick,* the lamb is inside.

> 'They returned from the ride
> With lamb Leo inside
> And a smile on the face of the tiger!
> Sing fol-di-lol-lol!
> Fol-di-lol-lol!
> Fol-di-lol-ol-di-lol-olly!'

For man, there is neither absolute nor absolution. Such things should be left to monsters like the right-angled triangle, which does only exist in the ideal consciousness. A man can't have a square on his hypotenuse, let him try as he may.

Ay! Ay! Ay!—Man handing out absolutes to man, as if we were all books of geometry with axioms, postulates and definitions in front. God with a pair of compasses! Moses with a set square! Man a geometric bifurcation, not even a radish!*

Holy Moses!

'Honour thy father and thy mother!' That's awfully cute! But supposing they are not honorable? How then, Moses?

Voice of thunder from Sinai: *'Pretend to honour them!'*

'Love thy neighbour as thyself.'*

Alas, my neighbour happens to be mean and detestable.

Voice of the lambent Dove, cooing: *'Put it over him, that you love him.'*

Talk about the cunning of serpents!* I never saw even a serpent kissing his instinctive enemy.

Pfui! I wouldn't blacken my mouth, kissing my neighbour, who, I repeat, to me is mean and detestable.

Dove, go home!

The Goat and Compasses,* indeed!

Everything is relative. Every Commandment that ever issued out of the mouth of God or man, is strictly relative: adhering to the particular time, place and circumstance.

And this is the beauty of the novel; everything is true in its own relationship, and no further.

For the relatedness and interrelatedness of all things flows and changes and trembles like a stream, and like a fish in the stream the characters in the novel swim and drift and float and turn belly-up when they're dead.

So, if a character in a novel wants two wives—or three—or thirty: well, that is true of that man, at that time, in that circumstance. It may be true of other men, elsewhere and elsewhen. But to infer that all men at all times want two, three, or thirty wives; or that the novelist himself is advocating furious polygamy; is just imbecility.

It has been just as imbecile to infer that, because Dante worshipped a remote Beatrice,* every man, all men, should go worshipping remote Beatrices.

And that wouldn't have been so bad, if Dante had put the thing in its true light. Why do we slur over the actual fact that Dante had a cosy bifurcated wife in his bed, and a family of lusty little Dantinos? Petrarch, with his Laura* in the distance, had *twelve* little legitimate Petrarchs of his own, between his knees. Yet all we hear is *Laura! Laura! Beatrice! Beatrice! Distance! Distance!*

What bunk! Why didn't Dante and Petrarch chant in chorus:

> Oh be my spiritual concubine
>   Beatrice! ⎱
>   Laura! ⎰
> My old girl's got several babies that are mine,
> But *thou* be my spiritual concubine,
>   Beatrice! ⎱
>   Laura! ⎰

Then there would have been an honest relation between all the bunch. Nobody grudges the gents their spiritual concubines. But keeping a wife and family—twelve children—up one's sleeve, has always been recognised as a dirty trick.

Which reveals how *immoral* the absolute is! Invariably keeping some vital fact dark! Dishonorable!

Here we come upon the third essential quality of the novel. Unlike the essay, the poem, the drama, the book of philosophy, or the scientific treatise: all of which may beg the question, when they don't downright filch it; the novel inherently is and must be:

1. Quick.
2. Interrelated in all its parts, vitally, organically.
3. Honorable.

I call Dante's *Commedia** slightly dishonorable, with never a mention of the cosy bifurcated wife, and the kids. And *War and Peace* I call downright dishonorable, with that fat, diluted Pierre for a hero, stuck up as preferable and desirable, when everybody knows that he *wasn't* attractive, even to Tolstoi.

Of course Tolstoi, being a great creative artist, was true to his characters. But being a man with a philosophy, he wasn't true to his *own character*.

Character is a curious thing. It is the flame of a man, which burns brighter or dimmer, bluer or yellower or redder, rising or sinking or flaring according to the draughts of circumstance and the changing air of life, changing itself continually, yet remaining one single, separate flame, flickering in a strange world: unless it be blown out at last by too much adversity.

If Tolstoi had looked into the flame of his own belly, he would have seen that he didn't really like the fat, fuzzy Pierre, who was a poor tool, after all. But Tolstoi was a personality even more than a character. And a personality is a self-conscious *I am:* being all that is left in us of a once-almighty Personal God. So being a personality and an almighty *I am,* Leo proceeded deliberately to lionise that Pierre, who was a domestic sort of house-dog.

Doesn't anybody call that dishonorable on Leo's part? He might just as well have been true to *himself!* But no! His self-conscious personality was superior to his own belly and knees, so he thought he'd improve on himself, by creeping inside the skin of a lamb; the doddering old lion that he was! Leo! Léon!

Secretly, Leo worshipped the human male, man as a column of rapacious and living blood. He could hardly meet three lusty, roisterous young guardsmen in the street, without crying with envy: and ten minutes later, fulminating on them black oblivion and annihilation, utmost moral thunder-bolts.*

How boring, in a great man! And how boring, in a great nation like Russia, to let its old Adam manhood* be so improved upon by these reformers, who all feel themselves short of something, and therefore live by spite, that at last there's nothing left but a lot of shells of men, improving themselves steadily emptier and emptier, till they rattle with words and formulae, as if they'd swallowed the whole encyclopaedia of socialism.

But wait! There is life in the Russians. Something new and strange will emerge out of their weird transmogrification into Bolshevists.

When the lion swallows the lamb, fluff and all, he usually gets a pain, and there's a rumpus. But when the lion tries to force himself down the throat of the huge and popular lamb—a nasty old sheep, really—then it's a phenomenon. Old Leo did it: wedged himself bit by bit down the throat of woolly Russia. And now out of the mouth of the bolshevist lambkin still waves an angry, mistaken, tufted leonine tail, like an agitated exclamation mark.

Meanwhile it's a deadlock.

But what a dishonorable thing for that claw-biting little Leo to do! And in his novels you see him at it. So that the papery lips of *Resurrection* whisper: *'Alas! I would have been a novel. But Leo spoiled me.'*

Count Tolstoi had that last weakness of a great man: he wanted the absolute: the absolute of love, if you like to call it that. Talk about the 'last infirmity of noble minds'!* It's a perfect epidemic of senility. He wanted to *be* absolute: a universal brother. Leo was too tight for Tolstoi. He wanted to puff, and puff, and puff, till he became Universal Brotherhood itself, the great gooseberry of our globe.

Then pop went Leo! And from the bits sprang up bolshevists.

It's all bunk. No man can be absolute. No man can be absolutely good or absolutely right, nor absolutely lovable, nor absolutely beloved, nor absolutely loving. Even Jesus, the paragon, was only relatively good and relatively right. Judas could take him by nose.

No god, that men can conceive of, could possibly be absolute or absolutely right. All the gods that men ever discovered are still God: and they contradict one another and fly down one another's throats, marvellously. Yet they are *all* God: the incalculable Pan.*

It is rather nice, to know what a lot of gods there are, and have been, and will be, and that they are all of them God all the while. Each of them utters an absolute: which, in the ears of all the rest of them, falls flat. This makes even eternity lively.

But man, poor man, bobbing like a cork in the stream of time, must hitch himself to some absolute star of righteousness overhead. So he throws out his line, and hooks on. Only to find, after a while, that his star is slowly falling: till it drops into the stream of time with a fizzle, and there's *another* absolute star gone out.

Then we scan the heavens afresh.

As for the babe of love, we're simply tired of changing its napkins. Put the brat down, and let it learn to run about, and manage its own little breeches.

But it's nice to think that all the gods are God all the while. And if a god only genuinely feels to you like God, then it *is* God. But if it doesn't feel quite, quite altogether like God to you, then wait awhile, and you'll hear him fizzle.

The novel knows all this, irrevocably. 'My dear,' it kindly says, 'one God is relative to another god, until he gets into a machine; and then it's a case for the traffic cop!'

'But what am I to do!' cries the despairing novelist. 'From Amon and Ra to Mrs Eddy, from Ashtaroth and Jupiter to Annie Besant,* I don't know where I am.'

'Oh yes you do, my dear!' replies the novel. 'You are where you are, so you needn't hitch yourself on to the skirts either of Ashtaroth or Eddy. If you meet them, say *how-do-you-do!* to them quite courteously. But don't hook on, or I shall turn you down.'

'Refrain from hooking on!' says the novel.

'But be honorable among the host!' he adds.

Honour! Why, the gods are like the rainbow, all colours and shades. Since light itself is invisible, a manifestation has got to be pink or black or blue or white or yellow or vermilion, or 'tinted'.

You may be a theosophist, and then you will cry: *Avaunt! Thou dark-red aura! Away!!!—Oh come! Thou pale-blue or thou primrose aura, come!*

This you may cry if you are a theosophist. And if you put a theosophist in a novel, he or she may cry *avaunt!* to the heart's content.

But a theosophist cannot be a novelist, as a trumpet cannot be a regimental band. A theosophist, or a Christian, or a Holy Roller,* may be *contained* in a novelist. But a novelist may not put up a fence. The wind bloweth where it listeth,* and auras will be red when they want to.

As a matter of fact, only the Holy Ghost knows truly what righteousness is. And heaven only knows what the Holy Ghost is! But it sounds all right. So the Holy Ghost hovers among the flames, from the red to the blue and the black to the yellow, putting brand to brand and flame to flame, as the wind changes, and life travels in flame from the unseen to the unseen, men will never know how or why. Only travel it must, and not die down in nasty fumes.

And the honour, which the novel demands of you, is only that you shall be true to the flame that leaps in you. When that Prince in *Resurrection* so cruelly betrayed and abandoned the girl,* at the beginning of her life, he betrayed and wetted on the flame of his own manhood. When, later, he bullied her with his repentant bene-volence, he again betrayed and slobbered upon the flame of his waning manhood, till in the end his manhood is extinct, and he's just a lump of half-alive elderly meat.

It's the oldest Pan-mystery. God is the flame-life in all the universe; multifarious, multifarious flames, all colours and beauties and pains and sombrenesses. Whichever flame flames in your manhood, that is you, for the time being. It is your manhood, don't make water on it, says the novel. A man's manhood is to honour the flames in him, and to know that none of them is absolute: even a flame is only relative.

But see old Leo Tolstoi wetting on the flame. As if even his wet were absolute!

Sex is flame, too, the novel announces. Flame burning against every absolute, even against the phallic. For sex is so much more than phallic, and so much deeper than functional desire. The flame of sex singes your absolute, and cruelly scorches your ego. What, will you assert your ego in the universe? Wait till the flames of sex leap at you like striped tigers.

> 'They returned from the ride
> With the lady inside,
> And a smile on the face of the tiger.'

You will play with sex, will you! You will tickle yourself with sex as with an ice-cold drink from a soda-fountain! You will pet your best girl, will you, and spoon with her, and titillate yourself and her, and do as you like with your sex?

Wait! Only wait till the flame you have dribbled on flies back at you, later! Only wait!

Sex is a life-flame, a dark one, reserved and mostly invisible. It is a deep reserve in a man, one of the core-flames of his manhood.

What, would you play with it? Would you make it cheap and nasty!

Buy a king-cobra, and try playing with that.

Sex is even a majestic reserve in the sun.

Oh, give me the novel! Let me hear what the novel says.

As for the novelist, he is usually a dribbling liar.

Him With His Tail in His Mouth*

ANSWER a fool according to his folly,* philosophy ditto.

Solemnity is a sign of fraud.

Religion and philosophy both have the same dual purpose: to get at the beginning of things, and at the goal of things. They have both decided that the serpent has got his tail in his mouth, and that the end is one with the beginning.

It seems to me time somebody gave that serpent of eternity another dummy to suck.

They've all decided that the beginning of all things is the life-stream itself, energy, ether, libido, not to mention the Sanskrit joys of Purusha, Pradhana, Kala.*

Having postulated the serpent of the beginning, now see all the heroes, from Moses and Plato to Bergson,* wrestling with him might and main, to push his tail into his mouth.

Jehovah creates man in His Own Image,* according to His Own Will. If man behaves according to the ready-made Will of God, formulated in a bunch of somewhat unsavoury commandments, then lucky man will be received into the bosom of Jehovah.

Man isn't very keen. And that is Sin, original and perpetual.

Then Plato discovers how lovely the intellectual idea is: in fact, the only perfection is ideal.*

But the old dragon of creation, who fathered us all, didn't have an idea in his head.

Plato was prepared. He popped the Logos* into the mouth of the dragon, and the serpent of eternity was rounded off. The old dragon, ugly and venomous, wore yet the precious jewel of the Platonic idea in his head.* Unable to find the dragon wholesale, modern philosophy sets up a retail shop. You can't lay salt on the old scoundrel's tail, because, of course, he's got it in his mouth, according to postulate. He doesn't seem to be sprawling in his old lair, across the heavens. In fact, he appears to have vamoosed. Perhaps, instead of being one big old boy, he is really an infinite number of little tiny boys: atoms, electrons, units of force or energy, tiny little birds all spinning with their tails in their beaks. Just the same in detail as in the gross. Nothing will come out of the egg that isn't in it. Evolution sings away at the same old song. Out of the amoeba, or some such old-fashioned entity, the dragon of evolved life stretches himself enormous and more enormous, only, at last, to return each time, and put his tail into his own mouth, and be an amoeba once more. The amoeba, or the electron, or whatever it may lately be—the rose would be just as scentless*—is the constant, from which all manifest living creation starts out, and to which it all returns.

There was a time when man was not, nor monkey, nor cow, nor catfish. But the amoeba (or the electron, or the atom, or whatever it is) always was and always will be.

Boom! tiddy-ra-ta! Boom!

Boom! tiddy-ra-ta! Boom!

How do you know? How does anybody know, what always was or wasn't? Bunk of geology, and strata, and all that, biology or evolution.

> 'One, two, three four five,
> Catch a little fish alive.
> Six, seven, eight nine ten,
> I have let him go again ...'*

Bunk of beginnings and of ends, and heads and tails. Why does man always want to know so damned much? Or rather, so damned little. If he can't draw a ring round creation, and fasten the serpent's tail into its mouth with the padlock of one final clinching idea, then creation can go to hell, as far as man is concerned.

There is such a thing as life, or life-energy. We know, because we've got it, or had it. It isn't a constant. It comes and it goes. But we *want* it.

This I think is incontestable.

More than anything else in the world, we want to have life, and life-energy abundant in us. We think if we eat yeast, vitamines and proteids,* we're sure of it. We're had. We diddle ourselves for the million millionth time.

What we want is life, and life-energy inside us. Where it comes from, or what it is, we don't know, and never shall. It is the capital X of all our knowledge.*

But we want it, we must have it. It is the all in all.*

This we know, now, for good and all: that which is good, and moral, is that which brings into us a stronger, deeper flow of life and life-energy: evil is that which impairs the life-flow.

But man's difficulty is, that he can't have life for the asking. 'He asked life of Thee, and Thou gavest it him: even length of days for ever and ever.'* There's a pretty motto for the tomb!

It isn't length of days for ever and ever that a man wants. It is strong life within himself, while he lives.

But how to get it? You may be as healthy as a cow, and yet have fear inside you, because your life is not enough.

We know, really, that we can't have life for the asking, nor find it, by seeking, nor get it by striving. The river flows into us from behind and below. We must turn our backs to it, and go ahead. The faster we go ahead, the stronger the river rushes into us. The moment we turn round to embrace the river of life, it ebbs away, and we see nothing but a stony fiumara.*

We must go ahead.

But which way is ahead?

We don't know.

We only know that, continuing in the way we are going, the river of life flows feebler and feebler in us, and we lose all sense of vital direction. We begin to talk about vitamines. We become idiotic. We cunningly prepare our own suicide.

This is the philosophic problem: to find the way ahead.

Allons!—there is no road before us.

Plato said that ahead, ahead was the perfect Idea, gleaming in the brow of the dragon.

We have pretty well caught up with the perfect Idea, and we find it a sort of vast, white, polished tomb-stone.

If the mouth of the serpent is the open grave, into which the tail disappears, then three cheers for the Logos, and down she goes.

We children of a later Pa, know that Life is real, Life is earnest, and the Grave is not its Goal.*

Let us side-step.

All goals become graves.

Every goal is a grave, when you get there.

Well, I came out of an egg-cell, like an amoeba, and I go into the grave. I can't help it. It's not my fault, and it's not my business.

I don't want eternal life, nor length of days for ever and ever. Nothing so long drawn out.

I give up all that sort of stuff.

Yet while I live, I want to live. Death, no doubt, solves its own problems. Let Life solve the problem of living.

> 'Teach me to live that so I may
> Rise glorious at the Judgment Day.'*

I have no desire to rise glorious at any Judgment Day, when the serpent finally chokes himself with his own tail.

> 'Teach me to live that so I may
> Go gaily on from day to day.'

Nay, in all the world, I feel the life-urge weakening. It may be, there are too many people alive. I feel it is, because there is too much automatic consciousness and self-consciousness in the world.

We can't live by loving life, alone.* Life is like a capricious mistress: the more you woo her the more she despises you. You have to get up and go to something more interesting. Then she'll pelt after you.

Life is the river, darkly sparkling, that enters into us from behind, when we set our faces towards the unknown. Towards some goal!!!

But there is no eternal goal. Every attempt to find an eternal goal puts the tail of the serpent into his mouth again, whereby he chokes himself in one more last gasp.

What is there then, if there is no eternal goal?

By itself, the river of life just gets nowhere. It sinks into the sand.

The river of life follows the living. If the living don't get anywhere, the river of life doesn't. The old serpent lays him down and goes into a torpor, instead of dancing at our heels and sending the life-sparks up our legs and spine, as we travel.

So we've got to get somewhere.

Is there no goal?

'Oh man! on your four legs, your two, and your three, where are you going?'—says the Sphinx.*

'I'm just going to say *How-do-you-do?* to Susan,'* replies the man. And he passes without a scratch.

When the cock crows, he says *How-do-you-do?*
How-do-you-do, Peter? How-do-you-do? old liar!

How-do-you-do, Oh Sun!

A challenge and a greeting.

We live in a multiple universe. I am a chick that absolutely refuses to chirp inside the monistic* egg. See me walk forth, with a bit of the egg-shell sticking to my tail!

When the cuckoo, the cow, and the coffee-plant chipped the Mundane Egg, at various points, they stepped out, and immediately set off in different directions. Not different directions of space and time, but different directions in creation: within the fourth dimension.* The cuckoo went cuckoo-wards, the cow went cow-wise, and the coffee-plant started coffing. Three very distinct roads across the fourth dimension.

> The cow was dumb, and the cuckoo too.
> They went their ways, as creatures do,
> Till they chanced to meet, in the Lord's green
>   Zoo.

> The bird gave a cluck, the cow gave a coo,
> At the sight of each other the pair of them flew
> Into tantrums, and started their hullabaloo.

> They startled creation; and when they were
>   through
> Each said to the other: Till I came across you
> I wasn't aware of the things I could do!
>   Cuckoo!
>   Moo!
>   Cuckoo!

And this, I hold, is the true history of evolution.

The Greeks made equilibrium their goal.* Equilibrium is hardly a goal you travel towards. Yet it's something to attain. You travel in the fourth dimension, not in yards and miles, like the eternal serpent.

Equilibrium argues either a dualistic or a pluralistic universe. The Greeks, being sane, were pantheists and pluralists, and so am I.

Creation is a fourth dimension, and in it there are all sorts of things, gods and what-not. That brown hen, scratching with her hind leg in such a common fashion, is a sort of goddess in the creative dimension. Of course, if you stay outside the fourth dimension, and try to measure creation in length, breadth and height, you've set yourself the difficult task of measuring up the Monad, the Mundane Egg. Which is a game, like any other. The solution is, of course (let me whisper): *Put his tail in his mouth*!

Once you realise that, willy nilly, you're *inside* the Monad, you give it up. You're inside it, you always will be. Therefore, Jonah, sit still in the whale's belly,* and have a look round. For you'll *never* measure the whale, since you're inside him.

And then you see it's a fourth dimension, with all sorts of gods and goddesses in it. That brown hen, who, being a Rhode Island Red, is big and stuffy like plush-upholstery, is of course, a goddess in her own rights. If I myself had to make a poem to her, I should begin:

> 'Oh my flat-footed plush arm-chair
> So commonly scratching in the yard—!'

But this poem would only reveal my own limitations.

Because Flatfoot is the favourite of the white leghorn cock, and he shakes the tit-bit for her with a most wooing noise, and when she lays an egg, he bristles like a double white poppy, and rushes to meet her, as she flounders down from the chicken-house, and his echo of her *I've-laid-an-egg* cackle is rich and resonant. Every pine-tree on the mountains hears him: $\left.{She's \atop I've}\right\}$ *laid an egg!*

And his poem to her would be:

Oh you who make me feel so good, when you sit next me on the
    perch,
At night! (temporarily, of course!)
Oh you who make my feathers bristle with the vanity of life!
Oh you whose cackle makes my throat go off like a rocket!
Oh you who walk so slowly, and make me feel swifter
Than the boss!
Oh you who bend your head down, and move in the under
Circle, while I prance in the upper!
Oh you, come! come! come! for here is a bit of fat from
The roast veal, I am shaking it for you.

In the fourth dimension, in the creative world, we live in a pluralistic universe, full of gods and strange gods and unknown gods; a universe where that Rhode Island Red hen is a goddess in her own rights, and the white cock is a god indisputable, with a little red ring on his leg: which the boss put there.

Why? Why, I mean, is he a god?

Because he is something that nothing else is. Certainly he is something that I am not.

And she is something that neither he is nor I am.

When she scratches and finds a bug in the earth, she seems fairly to gobble down the monad of all monads; and when she lays, she certainly thinks she's put the mundane egg in the nest.

Just part of her naïve nature!

As for the goal, which doesn't exist, but which we are always coming back to: well, it doesn't spatially, or temporally, or eternally exist: but in the fourth dimension, it does.

What the Greeks called equilibrium: what I call relationship. Equilibrium is just a bit mechanical. It became very mechanical, with the Greeks: an intellectual nail put through it.

I don't *want* to be 'good', or 'righteous'—and I won't even be 'virtuous', unless 'vir' means a man, and 'vis'* means the life-river.

But I *do* want to be alive. And to be alive, I must have a goal: in the *creative*, not in the spatial universe.

I want, in the Greek sense, an equilibrium between me and the rest of the universe. That is, I want a relationship between me and the brown hen.

The Greek equilibrium took too much for granted. The Greek never asked the brown hen, nor the horse, nor the swan, if it would kindly be equilibrated with him. He took it for granted that hen and horse would only be too delighted.

You can't take it for granted. That brown hen is extraordinarily callous to my god-like presence. She doesn't even choose to know me to nod to. If I've got to strike a balance between us, I've got to work at it.

But that is what I want: that she shall nod to me, with a *Howdy*!—and I shall nod to her, more politely: *How-do-you-do, Flatfoot?* And between us there shall exist the third thing, the *connaissance.** That is the goal.

I shall not betray myself nor my own life-passion for her. When she walks into my bedroom and makes droppings in my shoes, I shall chase her with disgust, and she will flutter and squawk. And I shall not ask her to be human for my sake.

That is the mistake the Greeks made. They talked about equilibrium, and then, when they wanted to equilibrate themselves with a horse, or an ox, or an acanthus, then horse, ox, and acanthus had to become nine-tenths human, to accommodate them. Call that equilibrium? The same with woman. When the Greek wanted to equilibrate with a woman, she had to become more and more a man, approximate to the man. Call that equilibrium?

As a matter of fact, we don't call it equilibrium, we call it anthropomorphism. And anthropomorphism is a bore. Too much anthropos* makes the world a dull hole.

So Greek sculpture tends to become a bore. If it's a horse, it's an anthropomorphised horse. If it's a Praxiteles *Hermes,** it's a Hermes so Praxitelised, that it begins sugarily to bore us.

Equilibrium, in its very best sense—in the sense the Greeks *originally* meant it—stands for the strange spark that flies between two creatures, two things that are equilibrated, or in living relationship. It is a goal: to come to that state when the spark will fly from me to Flatfoot, the brown hen, and from her to me.

I shall leave off addressing her: *Oh my flat-footed plush arm-chair!* I realise that is only impertinent anthropomorphism on my part. She might as well address me: *Oh my skin-flappy split pole!* Which would be like her impudence.—Skin-flappy, of course, would refer to my blue shirt and baggy cord trousers. How would *she* know I don't grow them like a loose skin!

In the early Greeks, the spark between man and man, stranger and stranger, man and woman, stranger and strangeress, was alive and vivid. Even those Doric Apollos.

In the Egyptians, the spark between man and the living universe remains alight for ever in those early, silent, motionless statues of Pharaohs. They say, it is the statue of the soul of the man.* But what is the soul of a man, except that in him which is himself alone, suspended in immediate relation to the sum of things? Not isolated or cut off. The Greeks began the cutting apart business. And Rodin's re-merging* was only an intellectual tacking on again.

The serpent hasn't got his tail in his mouth. He is on the alert, with lifted head like a listening, sparky* flower. The Egyptians knew.

But when the oldest Egyptians carve a hawk or a Sekhet-cat,* or paint birds or oxen or people: and when the Assyrians carve a she-lion: and when the cave-men drew the charging bison, or the reindeer, in the caves of Altamira: or when the Hindoo paints geese or elephants or lotus, in the great caves of India whose name I forget—Ajanta!*—then how marvellous it is! How marvellous is the living relation between man and his object! be it man or woman, bird, beast, flower or rock or rain: the exquisite frail moment of pure conjunction, which, in the fourth dimension, is timeless. An Egyptian hawk, a Chinese painting of a camel, an Assyrian sculpture of a lion, an African fetish-idol of a woman pregnant, an Aztec rattlesnake, an early Greek Apollo, a cave-man's painting of a prehistoric mammoth, on and on, how perfect the timeless moments between man and the other Pan-creatures of this earth of ours!

And by the way, speaking of cave-men, how did those prognathous semi-apes of Altamira come to depict so delicately, so beautifully, a female bison charging, with swinging udder, or deer stooping feeding, or an antediluvian mammoth deep in contemplation. It is art on a pure, high level, beautiful as Plato, far, far more 'civilised' than Burne Jones.*—Hadn't somebody better write Mr Wells' History* backwards, to prove how we've degenerated, in our stupid visionlessness, since the cave-men?

The pictures in the cave represent moments of purity which are the quick of civilisation. The pure relation between the cave-man and the deer: fifty per-cent man, and fifty per-cent bison, or mammoth, or deer. It is not ninety-nine per-cent man, and one per-cent horse: as in a Raphael horse. Or hundred per-cent fool, as when G. F. Watts sculpts a bronze horse and calls it Physical Energy.*

If it is to be life, then it is fifty per-cent me, fifty per-cent thee: and the third thing, the spark, which springs from out of the balance, is timeless. Jesus, who saw it a bit vaguely, called it The Holy Ghost.

Between man and woman, fifty per-cent man, fifty per-cent woman: then the pure spark. Either this, or less than nothing.

As for ideal relationships, and pure love, you might as well start to water tin pansies with carbolic acid (which is pure enough, in the antiseptic sense) in order to get the Garden of Paradise.

Review of *Hadrian the Seventh* by Baron Corvo

IN *Hadrian the Seventh*, Frederick Baron Corvo* falls in, head over heels, in deadly earnest. A man must keep his earnestness nimble, to escape ridicule. The so-called Baron Corvo by no means escapes. He reaches heights, or depths, of sublime ridiculousness.

It doesn't kill the book, however. Neither ridicule nor dead earnest kills it. It is extraordinarily alive, even though it has been buried for twenty years. Up it rises to confront us. And, great test, it does not 'date' as do Huysmans's* books, or Wilde's or the rest of them. Only a first-rate book escapes its date.

Frederick Rolfe was a fantastic figure of the nineties, the nineties of the *Yellow Book*, Oscar Wilde, Aubrey Beardsley, Simeon Solomon,* and all the host of the godly. The whole decade is now a little ridiculous, ridiculous decadence as well as ridiculous pietism. They said of Rolfe that he was certainly possessed of a devil. At least his devil is still alive, it hasn't turned into a sort of gollywog, like the bulk of the nineties' devils.

Rolfe was one of the Catholic converts of the period, very intense. But if ever a man was a Protestant in all his being, this one was. The acuteness of his protest drove him, like a crazy serpent, into the bosom of the Roman Catholic Church.

He seems to have been a serpent of serpents in the bosom of all the nineties. That in itself endears him to one. The way everyone dropped him with a shudder is almost fascinating.

He died about 1912, when he was already forgotten: an outcast and in a sense a wastrel.

We can well afford to remember him again: he was not nothing, as so many of the estimables were. He was a gentleman of education and culture, pining, for the show's sake, to be a priest. The Church shook him out of her bosom before he could take orders. So he wrote himself Fr. Rolfe. It would do for Frederick, and if you thought it meant Father Rolfe, good old you!

But then his other passion, for medieval royalism, overcame him, and he was Baron Corvo when he signed his name. Lord Rook, Lord Raven, the bird was the same as Fr. Rolfe.

Hadrian the Seventh is, as far as his connection with the Church was concerned, largely an autobiography of Frederick Rolfe. It is the story of a young English convert, George Arthur Rose (Rose for Rolfe), who has had bitter experience with the priests and clergy, and years of frustration and disappointment, till he arrives at about the age of forty, a highly-bred, highly-sensitive, super-aesthetic man, ascetic out of aestheticism, athletic the same, religious the same. He is to himself beautiful, with a slim, clean-muscled grace, much given to cold baths, white-faced with a healthy pallor, and pure, that is sexually chaste, because of his almost morbid repugnance for women. He had no desires to conquer or to purify. Women were physically repulsive to him, and therefore chastity cost him nothing, the Church would be a kind of asylum.

The priests and clergy, however, turned him down, or dropped him like the proverbial snake in the bosom, and inflamed him against them, so that he was burned through and through with white, ceaseless anger. His anger had become so complete as to be pure: it really was demonish. But it was all nervous and imaginative, an imaginative, sublimated hate, of a creature born crippled in its affective organism.

The first part of the book, describing the lonely man in a London lodging, alone save for his little cat, whose feline qualities of aloofness and self-sufficiency he so much admires, fixes the tone at once. And in the whole of literature I know nothing that resembles those amazing chapters, when the bishop and the archbishop come to him, and when he is ordained and makes his confession. Then the description* of the election of the new pope, the cardinals shut up in the Vatican, the failure of the Way of Scrutiny and the Way of Access, the fantastic choice, by the Way of Compromise, of George Arthur Rose, is too extraordinary and daring ever to be forgotten.

From being a rejected aspirant to the priesthood, George Arthur Rose, the man in the London lodging, finds himself suddenly not only consecrated, but elected head of all the Catholic Church. He becomes Pope Hadrian the Seventh.

Then the real fantasy and failure begins. George Arthur Rose, triple-crowned and in the chair of Peter, is still very much Frederick Rolfe, and perfectly consistent. He is the same man, but now he has it all his own way: a White Pope, pure, scrupulous, chaste, living on two dollars a day, an aesthetic idealist, and really, a super-Protestant. He has the British instinct of authority, which is now gloriously gratified. But he has no inward *power*, power to make true change in the world. Once he is on the throne of high power, we realize his futility.

He is, like most modern men, especially reformers and idealists, through and through a Protestant. Which means, his life is a changeless fervour of protest. He can't help it. Everything he comes into contact with he must criticize, with all his nerves, and react from. Fine, subtle, sensitive, and almost egomaniac, he can accept nothing but the momentary thrill of aesthetic appreciation. His life-flow is like a stream washing against a false world, and ebbing itself out in a marsh and a hopeless bog.

So it is with George Arthur Rose, become Pope Hadrian the Seventh, while he is still in a state of pure protest, he is vivid and extraordinary. But once he is given full opportunity to do as he wishes, and his *raison d'être* as a Protestant is thereby taken away, he becomes futile, and lapses into the ridiculous.

He can criticize men, exceedingly well: hence his knack of authority. But the moment he has to build men into a new form, construct something out of men by making a new unity among them, swarming them upon himself as bees upon a queen, he is ridiculous and powerless, a fraud.

It is extraordinary how *blind* he is, with all his keen insight. He no more 'gets' his cardinals than we get the men on Mars. He can criticize them, and analyse them, and reject or condone them. But the real old Adam* that is in them, the old male instinct for *power*, this, to him, does not exist.

In actual life, of course, the cardinals would drop a Hadrian down the oubliette, in ten minutes, and without any difficulty at all, once he was inside the Vatican. And Hadrian would be utterly flabbergasted, and call it villainy.

And what's the good of being Pope, if you've nothing but protest and aesthetics up your sleeve? Just like the reformers who are excellent, while fighting authority. But once authority disappears, they fall into nothingness. So with Hadrian the Seventh. As Pope, he is a fraud. His critical insight makes him a politician of the League of Nations sort, on a vast and curious scale. His medievalism makes him a truly comical royalist. But as a *man*, a real power in the world, he does not exist.

Hadrian unwinding the antimacassar is a sentimental farce. Hadrian persecuted to the point of suicide by a blowsy lodging-house keeper is a bathetic farce. Hadrian and the Socialist 'with gorgonzola teeth'* is puerile beyond words. It is all amazing, that a man with so much insight and fineness, on the one hand, should be so helpless and just purely ridiculous, when it comes to actualities.

He simply has no conception of what it is to be a natural or honestly animal man, with the repose and the power that goes with the honest animal in man. His attempt to appreciate his Cardinal Ragna—probably meant for Rampolla*—is funny. It is as funny as would be an attempt on the part of the late President Wilson to appreciate Hernán Cortés, or even Theodore Roosevelt,* supposing they were put face to face.

*The time has come for stripping:** cries Hadrian. Strip then, if there are falsities to throw away. But if you go on and on and on peeling the onion down, you'll be left with blank nothing between your hands, at last. And this is Hadrian's plight. He is assassinated in the streets of Rome by a Socialist, and dies supported by three Majesties, sublimely absurd. And there is nothing to it. Hadrian has stripped himself and everything else till nothing is left but absurd conceit, expiring in the arms of the Majesties.

*Lord! be to me a Saviour, not a judge!** is Hadrian's prayer: when he is not affectedly praying in Greek. But why should such a white streak of blamelessness as Hadrian need saving so badly? Saved from what? If he has done his best, why mind being judged—at least by Jesus, who in this sense is any man's peer?

The brave man asks for justice: the rabble cries for favours! says some old writer.* Why does Hadrian, in spite of all his protest, go in with the rabble?

It is a problem. The book remains a clear and definite book of our epoch, not to be swept aside. If it is the book of a demon, as the contemporaries said, it is the book of a man-demon, not of a mere poseur. And if some of it is caviare, at least it came out of the belly of a live fish.

Why the Novel Matters

WE have curious ideas of ourselves. We think of ourselves as a body with a spirit in it, or a body with a soul in it, or a body with a mind in it. *Mens sana in corpore sano.** The years drink up the wine, and at last throw the bottle away, the body, of course, being the bottle.

It is a funny sort of superstition. Why should I look at my hand, as it so cleverly writes these words, and decide that it is a mere nothing compared to the mind that directs it? Is there really any huge difference between my hand and my brain? Or my mind? My hand is alive, it flickers with a life of its own. It meets all the strange universe in touch, and learns a vast number of things, and knows a vast number of things. My hand, as it writes these words, slips gaily along, jumps like a grasshopper to dot an *i*, feels the table rather cold, gets a little bored if I write too long, has its own rudiments of thought, and is just as much *me* as is my brain, my mind, or my soul. Why should I imagine that there is a *me* which is more *me* than my hand is? Since my hand is absolutely alive, me alive.

Whereas, of course, as far as I am concerned, my pen isn't alive at all. My pen *isn't me* alive. Me alive ends at my finger-tips.

Whatever is me alive is me. Every tiny bit of my hands is alive, every little freckle and hair and fold of skin. And whatever is me alive is me. Only my finger-nails, those ten little weapons between me and an inanimate universe, they cross the mysterious Rubicon between me alive and things like my pen, which are not alive, in my own sense.

So, seeing my hand is all alive, and me alive, wherein is it just a bottle, or a jug, or a tin can, or a vessel of clay, or any of the rest of that nonsense? True, if I cut it it will bleed, like a can of cherries. But then the skin that is cut, and the veins that bleed, and the bones that should never be seen, they are all just as alive as the blood that flows. So the tin can business, or vessel of clay, is just bunk.

And that's what you learn, when you're a novelist. And that's what you are very liable *not* to know, if you're a parson, or a philosopher, or a scientist, or a stupid person. If you're a parson, you talk about souls in heaven. If you're a novelist, you know that paradise is in the palm of your hand, and on the end of your nose, because both are alive; and alive, and man alive, which is more than you can say, for certain, of paradise. Paradise is after life, and I for one am not keen on anything that is *after* life. If you are a philosopher, you talk about infinity, and the pure spirit which knows all things. But if you pick up a novel, you realize immediately that infinity is just a handle to this self-same jug of a body of mine; while as for knowing, if I find my finger in the fire, I know that fire burns, with a knowledge so emphatic and vital, it leaves Nirvana merely a conjecture. Oh, yes, my body, me alive, *knows*, and knows intensely. And as for the sum of all knowledge, it can't be anything more than an accumulation of all the things I know in the body, and you, dear reader, know in the body.

These damned philosophers, they talk as if they suddenly went off in steam, and were then much more important than they are when they're in their shirts. It is nonsense. Every man, philosopher included, ends in his own finger-tips. That's the end of his man alive. As for the words and thoughts and sighs and aspirations that fly from him, they are so many tremulations in the ether, and not alive at all. But if the tremulations reach another man alive, he may receive them into his life, and his life may take on a new colour, like a chameleon creeping from a brown rock on to a green leaf. All very well and good. It still doesn't alter the fact that the so-called spirit, the message or teaching of the philosopher or the saint, isn't alive at all, but just a tremulation upon the ether, like a radio message. All this spirit stuff is just tremulations upon the ether. If you, as man alive, quiver from the tremulation of the ether into new life, that is because you are man alive, and you take sustenance and stimulation into your alive man in a myriad ways. But to say that the message, or the spirit which is communicated to you, is more important than your living body, is nonsense. You might as well say that the potato at dinner was more important.

Nothing is important but life. And for myself, I can absolutely see life nowhere but in the living. Life with a capital L is only man alive. Even a cabbage in the rain is cabbage alive. All things that are alive are amazing. And all things that are dead are subsidiary to the living. Better a live dog than a dead lion. But better a live lion than a live dog. *C'est la vie!**

It seems impossible to get a saint, or a philosopher, or a scientist, to stick to this simple truth. They are all, in a sense, renegades. The saint wishes to offer himself up as spiritual food for the multitude. Even Francis of Assisi turns himself into a sort of angel-cake, of which anyone may take a slice. But an angel-cake is rather less than man alive. And poor St Francis might well apologize to his body, when he is dying: 'Oh, pardon me, my body, the wrong I did you through the years!'* It was no wafer, for others to eat.*

The philosopher, on the other hand, because he can think, decides that nothing but thoughts matter. It is as if a rabbit, because he can make little pills, should decide that nothing but little pills matter. As for the scientist, he has absolutely no use for me so long as I am man alive. To the scientist, I am dead. He puts under the microscope a bit of dead me, and calls it me. He takes me to pieces, and says first one piece, and then another piece, is me. My heart, my liver, my stomach have all been scientifically me, according to the scientist; and nowadays I am either a brain, or nerves, or glands, or something more up-to-date in the tissue line.

Now I absolutely flatly deny that I am a soul, or a body, or a mind, or an intelligence, or a brain, or a nervous system, or a bunch of glands, or any of the rest of these bits of me. The whole is greater than the part. And therefore, I, who am man alive, am greater than my soul, or spirit, or body, or mind, or consciousness, or anything else that is merely a part of me. I am a man, and alive. I am man alive, and as long as I can, I intend to go on being man alive.

For this reason I am a novelist. And being a novelist, I consider myself superior to the saint, the scientist, the philosopher, and the poet, who are all great masters of different bits of man alive, but never get the whole hog.

The novel is the one bright book of life. Books are not life. They are only tremulations on the ether. But the novel as a tremulation can make the whole man alive tremble. Which is more than poetry, philosophy, science, or any other book-tremulation can do.

The novel is the book of life. In this sense, the Bible is a great confused novel. You may say, it is about God. But it is really about man alive. Adam, Eve, Sarai, Abraham, Isaac, Jacob, Samuel, David, Bath-Sheba, Ruth, Esther, Solomon, Job, Isaiah, Jesus, Mark, Judas, Paul, Peter: what is it but man alive, from start to finish? Man alive, not mere bits. Even the Lord is another man alive, in a burning bush, throwing the tablets of stone* at Moses's head.

I do hope you begin to get my idea, why the novel is supremely important, as a tremulation on the ether. Plato makes the perfect ideal being tremble in me. But that's only a bit of me. Perfection is only a bit, in the strange make-up of man alive. The Sermon on the Mount makes the selfless spirit of me quiver. But that, too, is only a bit of me. The Ten Commandments set the old Adam* shivering in me, warning me that I am a thief and a murderer, unless I watch it. But even the old Adam is only a bit of me.

I very much like all these bits of me to be set trembling with life and the wisdom of life. But I do ask that the whole of me shall tremble in its wholeness, some time or other.

And this, of course, must happen in me, living.

But as far as it can happen from a communication, it can only happen when a whole novel communicates itself to me. The Bible—but *all* the Bible—and Homer, and Shakespeare: these are the supreme old novels. These are all things to all men. Which means that in their wholeness they affect the whole man alive, which is the man himself, beyond any part of him. They set the whole tree trembling with a new access of life, they do not just stimulate growth in one direction.

I don't want to grow in any one direction any more. And, if I can help it, I don't want to stimulate anybody else into some particular direction. A particular direction ends in a *cul-de-sac.* We're in a *cul-de-sac* at present.

I don't believe in any dazzling revelation, or in any supreme Word. 'The grass withereth, the flower fadeth, but the Word of the Lord shall stand for ever.'* That's the kind of stuff we've drugged ourselves with. As a matter of fact, the grass withereth, but comes up all the greener for that reason, after the rains. The flower fadeth, and therefore the bud opens. But the Word of the Lord, being man-uttered and a mere vibration on the ether, becomes staler and staler, more and more boring, till at last we turn a deaf ear and it ceases to exist, far more finally than any withered grass. It is grass that renews its youth like the eagle,* not any Word.

We should ask for no absolutes, or absolute. Once and for all and for ever, let us have done with the ugly imperialism of any absolute.

There is no absolute good, there is nothing absolutely right. All things flow and change, and even change is not absolute. The whole is a strange assembly of apparently incongruous parts, slipping past one another.

Me, man alive, I am a very curious assembly of incongruous parts. My yea! of today is oddly different from my yea! of yesterday. My tears of tomorrow will have nothing to do with my tears of a year ago. If the one I love remains unchanged and unchanging, I shall cease to love her. It is only because she changes and startles me into change and defies my inertia, and is herself staggered in her inertia by my changing, that I can continue to love her. If she stayed put, I might as well love the pepper-pot.

In all this change, I maintain a certain integrity. But woe betide me if I try to put my finger on it. If I say of myself, I am this, I am that!—then, if I stick to it, I turn into a stupid fixed thing like a lamp-post. I shall never know wherein lies my integrity, my individuality, my me. I *can* never know it. It is useless to talk about my ego. That only means that I have made up an *idea* of myself, and that I am trying to cut myself out to pattern. Which is no good. You can cut your cloth to fit your coat, but you can't clip bits off your living body, to trim it down to your idea. True, you can put yourself into ideal corsets. But even in ideal corsets, fashions change.

Let us learn from the novel. In the novel, the characters can do nothing but *live*. If they keep on being good, according to pattern, or bad, according to pattern, or even volatile, according to pattern, they cease to live, and the novel falls dead. A character in a novel has got to live, or it is nothing.

We, likewise, in life have got to live, or we are nothing.

What we mean by living is, of course, just as indescribable as what we mean by *being*. Men get ideas into their heads, of what they mean by Life, and they proceed to cut life out to pattern. Sometimes they go into the desert to seek God, sometimes they go into the desert to seek cash, sometimes it is wine, woman, and song,* and again it is water, political reform, and votes. You never know what it will be next: from killing your neighbour with hideous bombs and gas that tears the lungs, to supporting a Foundlings Home and preaching infinite Love, and being co-respondent in a divorce.

In all this wild welter, we need some sort of guide. It's no good inventing Thou Shalt Nots!

What then? Turn truly, honorably to the novel, and see wherein you are man alive, and wherein you are dead man in life. You may love a woman as man alive, and you may be making love to a woman as sheer dead man in life. You may eat your dinner as man alive, or as a mere masticating corpse. As man alive you may have a shot at your enemy. But as a ghastly simulacrum of life you may be firing bombs into men who are neither your enemies nor your friends, but just things you are dead to. Which is criminal, when the things happen to be alive.

To be alive, to be man alive, to be whole man alive: that is the point. And at its best, the novel, and the novel supremely, can help you. It can help you not to be dead man in life. So much of a man walks about dead and a carcass in the street and house, today: so much of women is merely dead. Like a pianoforte with half the notes mute.

But in the novel you can see, plainly, when the man goes dead, the woman goes inert. You can develop an instinct for life, if you will, instead of a theory of right and wrong, good and bad.

In life, there is right and wrong, good and bad, all the time. But what is right in one case is wrong in another. And in the novel you see one man becoming a corpse, because of his so-called goodness, another going dead because of his so-called wickedness. Right and wrong is an instinct: but an instinct of the whole consciousness in a man, bodily, mental, spiritual at once. And only in the novel are *all* things given full play, or at least, they may be given full play, when we realize that life itself, and not inert safety, is the reason for living. For out of the full play of all things emerges the only thing that is anything, the wholeness of a man, the wholeness of a woman, man alive, and live woman.

John Galsworthy*

LITERARY criticism can be no more than a reasoned account of the feeling produced upon the critic by the book he is criticising. Criticism can never be a science: it is, in the first place, much too personal, and in the second, it is concerned with values that science ignores. The touchstone is emotion, not reason. We judge a work of art by its effect on our sincere and vital emotion, and nothing else. All the critical twiddle-twaddle about style and form, all this pseudo-scientific classifying and analysing of books in an imitation-botanical fashion, is mere impertinence and mostly dull jargon.

A critic must be able to *feel* the impact of a work of art in all its complexity and its force. To do so, he must be a man of force and complexity himself, which few critics are. A man with a paltry, impudent nature will never write anything but paltry, impudent criticism. And a man who is *emotionally* educated is rare as a phoenix. The more scholastically educated a man is generally, the more he is an emotional boor.

More than this, even an artistically and emotionally educated man must be a man of good faith. He must have the courage to admit what he feels, as well as the flexibility to *know* what he feels. So Sainte Beuve remains, to me, a great critic. And a man like Macaulay,* brilliant as he is, is unsatisfactory, because he is not honest. He is emotionally very alive, but he juggles his feelings. He prefers a fine effect to the sincere statement of his aesthetic and emotional reaction. He is quite intellectually capable of giving us a true account of what he feels. But not morally. A critic must be emotionally alive in every fibre, intellectually capable and skilful in essential logic, and then morally very honest.

Then it seems to me a good critic should give his reader a few standards to go by. He can change the standards for every new critical attempt, so long as he keeps good faith. But it is just as well to say: This and this is the standard we judge by.

Sainte Beuve, on the whole, set up the standard of the 'good man'. He sincerely believed that the great man was essentially the good man in the widest range of human sympathy. This remained his universal standard. Pater's standard was the lonely philosopher of pure thought and pure aesthetic truth. Macaulay's standard was tainted by a political or democratic bias, he must be on the side of the weak. Gibbon* tried a purely moral standard, individual morality.

Reading Galsworthy again—or most of him, for all is too much—one feels oneself in need of a standard, some conception of a real man and a real woman, by which to judge all these Forsytes* and their contemporaries. One cannot judge them by the standard of the good man, nor of the man of pure thought, nor of the treasured humble nor the moral individual. One would like to judge them by the standard of the human being, but what, after all, is that? This is the trouble with the Forsytes. They are human enough, since anything in humanity is human, just as anything in nature is natural. Yet not one of them seems to be a really vivid human being. They are social beings. And what do we mean by that?

It remains to define, just for the purpose of this criticism, what we mean by a social being as distinct from a human being. The necessity arises from the sense of dissatisfaction which these Forsytes give us. Why can't we admit them as human beings? Why can't we have them in the same category as Sairey Gamp for example, who is satirically conceived, or of Jane Austen's people, who are social enough? We can accept Mrs Gamp or Jane Austen's characters or even George Meredith's Egoist* as human beings in the same category as ourselves. Whence arises this repulsion from the Forsytes, this refusal, this emotional refusal, to have them identified with our common humanity? Why do we feel so instinctively that they are inferiors?

It is because they seem to us to have lost caste as human beings, and to have sunk to the level of the social being, that peculiar creature that takes the place in our civilisation of the slave in the old civilisations. The human individual is a queer animal, always changing. But the fatal change today is the collapse from the psychology of the free human individual into the psychology of the social being, just as the fatal change in the past was a collapse from the freeman's psyche to the psyche of the slave. The free moral and the slave moral,* the human moral and the social moral: these are the abiding antitheses.

While a man remains a man, a true human individual, there is at the core of him a certain innocence or naïveté which defies all analysis, and which you cannot bargain with, you can only deal with it in good faith from your own corresponding innocence or naïveté. This does not mean that the human being is nothing but naïve or innocent. He is Mr Worldly Wiseman* also to his own degree. But in his essential core he is naïve, and money does not touch him. Money, of course, with every man living goes a long way. With the alive human being it may go as far as his penultimate feeling. But in the last naked him it does not enter.

With the social being it goes right through the centre and is the controlling principle no matter how much he may pretend, nor how much bluff he may put up. He may give away all he has to the poor* and still reveal himself as a social being swayed finally and helplessly by the money-sway, and by the social moral, which is inhuman.

It seems to me that when the human being becomes too much divided between his subjective and objective consciousness, at last something splits in him and he becomes a social being. When he becomes too much aware of objective reality, and of his own isolation in the face of a universe of objective reality, the core of his identity splits, his nucleus collapses, his innocence or his naïveté perishes, and he becomes only a subjective-objective reality, a divided thing hinged together but not strictly individual.

While a man remains a man, before he falls and becomes a social individual, he innocently feels himself altogether within the great continuum of the universe. He is not divided nor cut off. Men may be against him, the tide of affairs may be rising to sweep him away. But he is one with the living continuum of the universe. From this he cannot be swept away. Hamlet and Lear feel it, as does Oedipus or Phaedra.* It is the last and deepest feeling that is in a man while he remains a man. It is there the same in a deist like Voltaire or a scientist like Darwin: it is there, imperishable, in every great man: in Napoleon the same, till material things piled too much on him and he lost it and was doomed. It is the essential innocence and naïveté of the human being, the sense of being at one with the great universe-continuum of space-time-life, which is vivid in a great man, and a pure nuclear spark in every man who is still free.

But if man loses his mysterious naïve assurance, which is his innocence; if he gives *too* much importance to the external objective reality and so collapses in his natural innocent pride, then he becomes obsessed with the idea of objectives or material assurance; he wants to *insure* himself, and perhaps everybody else: universal insurance. The impulse rests on fear. Once the individual loses his naïve at-oneness with the living universe he falls into a state of fear and tries to insure himself with wealth. If he is an altruist he wants to insure everybody, and feels it is the tragedy of tragedies if this can't be done. But the whole necessity for thus materially insuring oneself with wealth, money, arises from the state of fear into which a man falls who has lost his at-oneness with the living universe, lost his peculiar nuclear innocence and fallen into fragmentariness. Money, material salvation is the only salvation. What is salvation is God. Hence money is God. The social being may rebel even against this god, as do many of Galsworthy's characters. But that does not give them back their innocence. They are only anti-materialists instead of positive materialists. And the anti-materialist is a social being just the same as the materialist, neither more nor less. He is castrated just the same, made a neuter by having lost his innocence, the bright little individual spark of his at-oneness.

When one reads Mr Galsworthy's books it seems as if there were not on earth one single human individual. They are all these social beings, positive and negative. There is not a free soul among them, not even Pendyce,* or June Forsyte. If money does not actively determine their being, it does negatively. Money, or property, which is the same thing. Mrs Pendyce, lovable as she is, is utterly circumscribed by property. Ultimately, she is not lovable at all, she is part of the fraud, she is prostituted to property. And there is nobody else. Old Jolyon is merely a sentimental materialist. Only for one moment do we see a man, and that is the road-sweeper in *Fraternity* after he comes out of prison and covers his face. But even *his* manhood has to be explained away by a wound in the head:* an abnormality.

Now it looks as if Mr Galsworthy set out to make that very point: to show that the Forsytes were not full human individuals, but social beings fallen to a lower level of life. They have lost that bit of free manhood and free womanhood which makes men and women. *The Man of Property* has the elements of a very great novel, a very great satire. It sets out to reveal the social being in all his strength and inferiority. But the author has not the courage to carry it through. The greatness of the book rests in its new and sincere and amazingly profound satire. It is the ultimate satire on modern humanity, and done from the inside, with really consummate skill and sincere creative passion, something quite new. It seems to be a real effort to show up the social being in all his weirdness. And then it fizzles out.

Then, in the love affair of Irene and Bosinney, and in the sentimentalising of old Jolyon Forsyte, the thing is fatally blemished. Galsworthy had not quite enough of the superb courage of his satire. He faltered, and gave in to the Forsytes. It is a thousand pities. He might have been the surgeon the modern soul needs so badly, to cut away the proud flesh of our Forsytes from the living body of men who are fully alive. Instead, he put down the knife and laid on a soft, sentimental poultice, and helped to make the corruption worse.

Satire exists for the very purpose of killing the social being, showing him what an inferior he is and, with all his parade of social honesty, how subtly and corruptly debased. Dishonest to life, dishonest to the living universe on which he is parasitic as a louse. By ridiculing the social being, the satirist helps the true individual, the real human being, to rise to his feet again and go on with the battle. For it is always a battle, and always will be.

Not that the majority are necessarily social beings. But the majority is only *conscious* socially: humanly, mankind is helpless and unconscious, unaware even of the thing most precious to any human being, that core of manhood or womanhood, naïve, innocent at-oneness with the living universe-continuum, which alone makes a man individual and, as an individual, essentially happy, even if he be driven mad like Lear. Lear was *essentially* happy, even in his greatest misery. A happiness from which Goneril and Regan* were excluded as lice and bugs are excluded from happiness, being social beings, and, as such, parasites, fallen from true freedom and independence.

But the tragedy today is that men are only materially and socially conscious. They are unconscious of their own manhood, and so they let it be destroyed. Out of free men we produce social beings by the thousand every week.

The Forsytes are all parasites, and Mr Galsworthy set out, in a really magnificent attempt, to let us see it. They are parasites upon the thought, the feelings, the whole body of life of really living individuals who have gone before them and who exist alongside with them. All they can do, having no individual life of their own, is out of fear to rake together property, and to feed upon the life that has been given by living men to mankind. They have no life, and so they live forever, in perpetual fear of death, accumulating property to ward off death. They can keep up conventions, but they cannot carry on a tradition. There is a tremendous difference between the two things. To carry on a tradition you must add something to the tradition. But to keep up a convention needs only the monotonous persistency of a parasite, the endless endurance of the craven, those who fear life because they are not alive, and who cannot die because they cannot live—the social beings.

As far as I can see, there is nothing but Forsyte in Galsworthy's books: Forsyte positive or Forsyte negative, Forsyte successful or Forsyte *manqué*.* That is, every single character is determined by money: either the getting it, or the having it, or the wanting it, or the utter lacking it. Getting it are the Forsytes as such; having it are the Pendyces and patricians and Hilarys and Biancas* and all that lot; wanting it are the Irenes and Bosinneys and young Jolyons; and utterly lacking it are all the charwomen and squalid poor who form the background—the shadows of the 'having' ones, as old Mr Stone says.* This is the whole Galsworthy gamut, all absolutely determined by money, and not an individual soul among them. They are all fallen, all social beings, a castrated lot.

Perhaps the overwhelming numerousness of the Forsytes frightened Mr Galsworthy from utterly damning them. Or perhaps it was something else, something more serious in him. Perhaps it was his utter failure to see what you were when you *weren't* a Forsyte. What was there *besides* Forsytes in all the wide human world? Mr Galsworthy looked, and found nothing. Strictly and truly, after his frightened search, he had found nothing. But he came back with Irene and Bosinney, and offered us that. Here! he seems to say. Here is the anti-Forsyte! Here! Here you have it! Love! Pa-assion! PASSION.

We look at this love, this PASSION, and we see nothing but a doggish amorousness and a sort of anti-Forsytism. They are the *anti* half of the show. Runaway dogs of these Forsytes, running in the back garden and furtively and ignominiously copulating—this is the effect, on me, of Mr Galsworthy's grand love affairs, Dark Flowers or Bosinneys, or Apple Trees or George Pendyce*— whatever they be. About every one of them something ignominious and doggish, like dogs copulating in the street, and looking round to see if the Forsytes are watching.

Alas! this is the Forsyte trying to be freely sensual. He can't do it; he's lost it. He can only be doggishly messy. Bosinney is not only a Forsyte, but an anti-Forsyte, with a vast grudge against property. And the thing a man has a vast grudge against is the man's determinant. Bosinney is a property hound, but he has run away from the kennels, or been born outside the kennels, so he is a rebel. So he goes sniffing round the property bitches, to get even with the successful property hounds that way. One cannot help preferring Soames Forsyte, in a choice of evils.

Just as one prefers June or any of the old aunts to Irene. Irene seems to me a sneaking, creeping, spiteful sort of bitch, an anti-Forsyte, absolutely living off the Forsytes—yes, to the very end; absolutely living off their money and trying to do them dirt. She is like Bosinney, a property mongrel doing dirt in the property kennels. But she is a real property prostitute, like the little model in *Fraternity*. Only she is *anti*! It is a type recurring again and again in Galsworthy: the parasite upon the parasites, 'Big fleas have little fleas, etc.' And Bosinney and Irene, as well as the vagabond in *Island Pharisees*,* are among the little fleas. And as a tramp loves his own vermin, so the Forsytes and the Hilarys love these, their own particular body parasites, their *antis*.

It is when he comes to sex that Mr Galsworthy collapses finally. He becomes nastily sentimental. He wants to make sex important, and he only makes it repulsive. Sentimentalism is the working off on yourself of feelings you haven't really got. We all *want* to have certain feelings: feelings of love, of passionate sex, of kindliness, and so forth. Very few people really feel love, or sex passion, or kindliness, or anything else that goes at all deep. So the mass just fake these feelings inside themselves. Faked feelings! The world is all gummy with them. They are better than real feelings, because you can spit them out when you brush your teeth; and then to-morrow you can fake them afresh.

Shelton, in *The Island Pharisees*, is the first of Mr Galsworthy's lovers, and he might as well be the last. He is almost comical. All we know of his passion for Antonia is that he feels at the beginning a 'hunger' for her,* as if she were a beefsteak. And towards the end he once kisses her, and expects her, no doubt, to fall instantly at his feet overwhelmed. He never for a second feels a moment of gentle sympathy with her. She is class-bound, but she doesn't seem to have been inhuman. The inhuman one was the lover. He can gloat over her in the distance, as if she were a dish of pig's trotters, *pieds truffés:** she can be an angelic *vision* to him a little way off, but when the poor thing has to be just a rather ordinary middle-class girl to him, quite near, he hates her with a comical, rancorous hate. It is most queer. He is helplessly *anti*. He hates her for even existing as a woman of her own class, for even having her own existence. Apparently she should just be a floating female sex-organ, hovering round to satisfy his little 'hungers', and then *basta*.* Anything of the real meaning of sex, which involves the whole of a human being, never occurs to him. It is a function, and the female is a sort of sexual appliance, no more.

And so we have it again and again, on this low and bastard level, all the human correspondence lacking. The sexual level is extraordinarily low, like dogs. The Galsworthy heroes are all weirdly in love with themselves, when we know them better, afflicted with chronic narcissism. They know just three types of women: the Pendyce mother, prostitute to property; the Irene, the essential *anti* prostitute, the floating, flaunting female organ; and the social woman, the mere lady. All three are loved and hated in turn by the recurrent heroes. But it is all on the debased level of property, positive or *anti*. It is all a doggy form of prostitution. Be quick and have done.

One of the funniest stories is *The Apple Tree*. The young man finds, at a lonely Devon farm, a little Welsh farm-girl who, being a Celt and not a Saxon, at once falls for the Galsworthian hero.* This young gentleman, in the throes of narcissistic love for his marvellous self, falls for the maid because she has fallen so utterly and abjectly for him. She doesn't call him 'My King', not being Wellsian;* she only says: 'I can't live away from you. Do what you like with me. Only let me come with you!' The proper prostitutional announcement!

For this, of course, a narcissistic young gentleman just down from Oxford falls at once. Ensues a grand pa-assion. He goes to buy her a proper frock to be carried away in, meets a college friend with a young lady sister, has jam for tea and stays the night, and the grand pa-assion has died a natural death by the time he spreads the marmalade on his bread. He has returned to his own class, and nothing else exists. He marries the young lady, true to his class. But to fill the cup of his vanity, the maid drowns herself. It is funny that maids only seem to do it for these narcissistic young gentlemen who, looking in the pool for their own image, desire the added satisfaction of seeing the face of drowned Ophelia* there as well; saving them the necessity of taking the narcissus plunge in person. We have gone one better than the myth. Narcissus in Mr Galsworthy doesn't drown himself. He asks Ophelia, or Megan, kindly to drown herself instead. And in this fiction she actually does. And he feels so *wonderful* about it!

Mr Galsworthy's treatment of passion is really rather shameful. The whole thing is doggy to a degree. The man has a temporary 'hunger'; he is 'on the heat' as they say of dogs. The heat passes. It's done. Trot away, if you're not tangled. Trot off, looking shamefacedly over your shoulder. People have been watching! Damn them! But never mind, it'll blow over. Thank God, the bitch is trotting in the other direction. She'll soon have another trail of dogs after her. That'll wipe out my traces. Good for that! Next time I'll get properly married and do my doggishness in my own house.

With the fall of the individual, sex falls into a dog's heat. Oh, if only Mr Galsworthy had had the strength to satirise this too, instead of pouring a sauce of sentimental savouriness over it. Of course, if he had done so he would never have been a popular writer, but he would have been a great one.

However, he chose to sentimentalise and glorify the most doggy sort of sex. Setting out to satirise the Forsytes, he glorifies the *anti*, who is one worse. While the individual remains real and unfallen, sex remains a vital and supremely important thing. But once you have the fall into social beings, sex becomes disgusting, like dogs on the heat. Dogs are social beings, with no true canine individuality. Wolves and foxes don't copulate on the pavement. Their sex is wild and in act utterly private. Howls you may hear, but you will never see anything. But the dog is tame—and he makes excrement and he copulates on the pavement, as if to spite you. He is the Forsyte *anti*.

The same with human beings. Once they become tame they become, in a measure, exhibitionists, as if to spite everything. They have no real feelings of their own. Unless somebody 'catches them at it' they don't really feel they've felt anything at all. And this is how the mob is today. It is Forsyte *anti*. It is the social being spiting society.

Oh, if only Mr Galsworthy had satirised *this* side of Forsytism, the anti-Forsyte posturing of the 'rebel', the narcissus and the exhibitionist, the dogs copulating on the pavement! Instead of that, he glorified it, to the eternal shame of English literature.

The satire, which in *The Man of Property* really had a certain noble touch, soon fizzles out, and we get that series of Galsworthian 'rebels' who are, like all the rest of the modern middle-class rebels, not in rebellion at all. They are merely social beings behaving in an anti-social manner. They worship their own class, but they pretend to go one better and sneer at it. They are Forsyte *antis*, feeling snobbish about snobbery. Nevertheless, they want to attract attention and make money. That's why they are *anti*. It is the vicious circle of Forsytism. Money means more to them than it does to a Soames Forsyte, so they pretend to go one better, and despise it, but they will do anything to have it—things which Soames Forsyte would not have done.

If there is one thing more repulsive than the social being positive, it is the social being negative, the mere *anti*. In the great debacle of decency this gentleman is the most indecent. In a subtle way Bosinney and Irene are more dishonest and more indecent than Soames and Winifred, but they are *anti*, so they are glorified. It is pretty sickening.

The introduction to *Island Pharisees* explains the whole show: 'Each man born into the world is born to go a journey, and for the most part he is born on the high road. ... As soon as he can toddle, he moves, by the queer instinct we call the love of life, along this road: ... his fathers went this way before him, they made this road for him to tread, and, when they bred him, passed into his fibre the love of doing things as they themselves had done them. So he walks on and on. ... Suddenly, one day, without intending to, he notices a path or opening in the hedge, leading to right or left, and he stands looking at the undiscovered. After that he stops at all the openings in the hedge; one day, with a beating heart, he tries one. And this is where the fun begins.' … Nine out of ten get back to the broad road again, and side-track no more. They snuggle down comfortably in the next inn, and think where they might have been. 'But the poor silly tenth is faring on. Nine times out of ten he goes down in a bog; the undiscovered has engulfed him.' But the tenth time he gets across, and a new road is opened to mankind.

It is a class-bound consciousness, or at least a hopeless social consciousness which sees life as a high road between two hedges. And the only way out is gaps in the hedge and excursions into naughtiness! These little *anti* excursions, from which the wayfarer slinks back to solid comfort nine times out of ten; an odd one goes down in a bog; and a very rare one finds a way across and opens out a new road.

In Mr Galsworthy's novels we see the nine, the ninety-nine, the nine hundred and ninety-nine slinking back to solid comfort; we see an odd Bosinney go under a bus, because he hadn't guts enough to do something else, the poor *anti*! but that rare figure side-tracking into the unknown we do *not* see. Because, as a matter of fact, the whole figure is faulty at that point. If life is a great highway, then it must forge on ahead into the unknown. Side-tracking gets nowhere. That is mere *anti*. The tip of the road is always unfinished, in the wilderness. If it comes to a precipice and a canyon—well, then, there is need for some exploring. But we see Mr Galsworthy, after *The Country House*, very safe on the old highway, very secure in comfort, wealth, and renown. He at least has gone down in no bog, nor lost himself striking new paths. The hedges nowadays are ragged with gaps, anybody who likes strays out on the little trips of 'unconventions'. But the Forsyte road has not moved on at all. It has only become dishevelled and sordid with excursionists doing the *anti* tricks and being 'unconventional', and leaving tin cans behind.

In the three early novels, *Island Pharisees*, *The Man of Property*, *Fraternity*, it looked as if Mr Galsworthy might break through the blind end of the highway with the dynamite of satire, and help us out on to a new lap. But the sex ingredient of his dynamite was damp and muzzy, the explosion gradually fizzled off in sentimentality, and we are left in a worse state than before.

The later novels are purely commercial, and, if it had not been for the early novels, of no importance. They are popular, they sell well, and there's the end of them. They contain the explosive powder of the first books in minute quantities, fizzling as silly squibs. When you arrive at *To Let*, and the end, at least the *promised* end, of the Forsytes,* what have you? Just money! Money, money, money and a certain snobbish silliness, and many more *anti* tricks and poses. Nothing else. The story is feeble, the characters have no blood and bones, the emotions are faked, faked, faked. It is one great fake. Not necessarily of Mr Galsworthy. The characters fake their own emotions. But that doesn't help us. And if you look closely at the characters, the meanness and low-level vulgarity are very distasteful. You have all the Forsyte meanness, with none of the energy. Jolyon and Irene are meaner and more treacherous to their son than the older Forsytes were to theirs. The young ones are of a limited, mechanical, vulgar egoism far surpassing that of Swithin or James, their ancestors. There is in it all a vulgar sense of being rich, and therefore we do as we like: an utter incapacity for anything like *true* feeling, especially in the women, Fleur, Irene, Annette, June: a glib crassness, a youthful spontaneity which is just impertinence and lack of feeling; and all the time, a creeping, 'having' sort of vulgarity of money and self-will, money and self-will, so that we wonder sometimes if Mr Galsworthy is not treating his public in real bad faith, and being cynical and rancorous under his rainbow sentimentalism.

Fleur he destroys in one word: she is 'having'.* It is perfectly true. We don't blame the young Jon for clearing out. Irene he destroys in a phrase put of Fleur's mouth to June: 'Didn't she spoil your life too?'—and it is precisely what she did. Sneaking and mean, Irene prevented June from getting her lover. Sneaking and mean, she prevents Fleur. She is the bitch in the manger. She is the sneaking *anti*. Irene, the most beautiful woman on earth! And Mr Galsworthy, with the cynicism of a successful old sentimentalist, turns it off by making June say: 'Nobody can spoil a life, my dear. That's nonsense. Things happen, but we bob up.'*

This is the final philosophy of it all. 'Things happen, but we bob up.' Very well, then, write the book in that key, the keynote of a frank old cynic. There's no point in sentimentalising it and being a sneaking old cynic. Why pour out masses of feelings that pretend to be genuine and then turn it all off with: 'Things happen, but we bob up'?

It is quite true, things happen, and we bob up. If we are vulgar sentimentalists, we bob up just the same, so nothing has happened and nothing can happen. All is vulgarity. But it pays. There is money in it.

Vulgarity pays, and cheap cynicism smothered in sentimentalism pays better than anything else. Because nothing *can* happen to the degraded social being. So let's pretend it does, and then bob up!

It is time somebody began to spit out the jam of sentimentalism, at least, which smothers the 'bobbing-up' philosophy. It is time we turned a straight light on this horde of rats, these younger Forsyte sentimentalists whose name is legion.* It is sentimentalism which is stifling us. Let the social beings keep on bobbing up while ever they can. But it is time an effort was made to turn a hosepipe on the sentimentalism they ooze over everything. The world is one sticky mess, in which the little Forsytes indeed may keep on bobbing still, but in which an honest feeling can't breathe.

But if the sticky mess gets much deeper, even the little Forsytes won't be able to bob up any more. They'll be smothered in their own slime along with everything else. Which is a comfort.

Introduction to *Mastro-don Gesualdo**
by Giovanni Verga

GIOVANNI VERGA was born in the year 1840, and he died at the beginning of 1922, so that he is almost as much of a contemporary as Thomas Hardy. He seems more remote, because he left off writing many years before he died. He was a Sicilian from one of the lonely little townships in the south of the island, where his family were provincial gentlefolk. But he spent a good deal of his youth in Catania, the city on the sea, under Etna, and then he went to Naples, the metropolis; for Sicily was still part of the Bourbon kingdom of Naples.

As a young man he lived for a time in Milan and Florence, the intellectual centres, leading a more or less fashionable life and also practising journalism. A real provincial, he felt that the great world must be conquered, that it must hold some vital secret. He was apparently a great beau, and had a series of more or less distinguished love affairs, like an Alfred de Vigny or a Maupassant.* In his early novels we see him in this phase. *Tigre Reale*,* one of his most popular novels, is the story of a young Italian's love for a fascinating but very enigmatical (no longer so enigmatical) Russian countess of great wealth, married, but living in distinguished isolation alone in Florence. The enigmatical lady is, however, consumptive, and the end, in Sicily, is truly horrible, in the morbid and deathly tone of some of Matilde Serao's novels.* The southerners seem to go that way, macabre. Yet in Verga the savage, manly tone comes through the morbidity, and we feel how he must have loathed the humiliation of fashionable life and fashionable love affairs. He kept it up, however, till after forty, then he retired back to his own Sicily, and shut himself up away from the world. He lived in aristocratic isolation for almost another forty years, and died in Catania, almost forgotten. He was a rather short, broad-shouldered man with a big red moustache.

It was after he had left the fashionable world that he wrote his best work. And this is no longer Italian, but Sicilian. In his Italian style, he manages to get the rhythm of colloquial Sicilian, and Italy no longer exists. Now Verga turns to the peasants of his boyhood, and it is they who fill his soul. It is their lives that matter.

There are three books of Sicilian sketches and short stories, very brilliant, and drenched with the atmosphere of Sicily. They are *Cavalleria Rusticana*, *Novelle Rusticane*, and *Vagabondaggio*. They open out another world at once, the southern, sun-beaten island whose every outline is like pure memory. Then there is a small novel about a girl who is condemned to a convent: *Storia di una Capinera*. And finally, there are the two great novels, *I Malavoglia* and *Mastro-don Gesualdo*. The sketches in *Cavalleria Rusticana* had already established Verga's fame. But it was *I Malavoglia* that was hailed as a masterpiece, in Paris as well as in Italy. It was translated into French by Jose-Maria de Heredia, and after that, into English by an American lady. The English translation, which weakens the book very much, came out in America in the 'nineties, under the title *The House by the Medlar Tree*, and can still be procured.

Speaking, in conversation, the other day about Giovanni Verga, in Rome, one of the most brilliant young Italian literary men said: There is Verga, ah yes! *Some* of his things! But a thing like the *Storia di una Capinera*, now, that is ridiculous.—And it was so obvious, the young man thought all Verga a little ridiculous. Because Verga *doesn't* write about lunatics and maniacs, like Pirandello,* therefore he is ridiculous. It is the attitude of the smart young. They find Tolstoi ridiculous, George Eliot ridiculous, everybody ridiculous who is not 'disillusioned'.

The *Story of a Blackcap* is indeed sentimental and overloaded with emotion. But so is Dickens' *Christmas Carol*, or *Silas Marner.** They do not therefore become ridiculous.

It is a fault in Verga, partly owing to the way he had lived his life, and partly owing to the general tendency of all European literature of the eighteen-sixties and thereabouts, to pour too much emotion, and especially too much pity, over the humble poor. Verga's novel *I Malavoglia* is really spoilt by this, and by his exaggeration of the tragic fate of his humble fisher-folk. But then it is characteristic of the southerner, that when he has an emotion he has it wholesale. And the tragic fate of the humble poor was the stunt of that day. *Les Misérables** stands as the great monument to this stunt. The poor have lately gone rather out of favour, so Hugo stands at a rather low figure, and Verga hardly exists. But when we

have got over our reaction against the pity-the-poor stunt, we shall
see that there is a good deal of fun in Hugo, and that *I Malavoglia*
is really a very great picture of Sicilian sea-coast life, far more
human and *valid* than Victor Hugo's picture of Paris.

The trouble with the Italians is, they do tend to take over other
people's stunts and exaggerate them. Even when they invent a
stunt of their own, for some mysterious reason it *seems* second-
hand. Victor Hugo's pity-the-poor was a real Gallic gesture.
Verga's pity-the-poor is just a bit too much of a good thing, and it
doesn't seem to come *quite* spontaneously from him. He had been
inoculated. Or he had reacted.

In his last novel, *Mastro-don Gesualdo*, Verga has slackened off
in his pity-the-poor. But he is still a realist, in the grim Flaubertian
sense of the word. A realism which, as every one now knows, has
no more to do with reality than romanticism has. Realism is just
one of the arbitrary views man takes of man. It sees us all as little
ant-like creatures toiling against the odds of circumstance, and
doomed to misery. It is a kind of aeroplane view. It became the
popular outlook, and so today we actually are, millions of us, little
ant-like creatures toiling against the odds of circumstance, and
doomed to misery; until we take a different view of ourselves. For
man always becomes what he passionately thinks he is; since he is
capable of becoming almost anything.

Mastro-don Gesualdo is a great realistic novel of Sicily, as
Madame Bovary is a great realistic novel of France. They both
suffer from the defects of the realistic method. I think the inherent
flaw in *Madame Bovary*—though I hate talking about flaws in great
books; but the charge is really against the realistic method—is that
individuals like Emma and Charles Bovary are too insignificant to
carry the full weight of Gustave Flaubert's profound sense of
tragedy; or, if you will, of tragic futility. Emma and Charles Bovary
are two ordinary persons, chosen because they *are* ordinary. But
Flaubert is by no means an ordinary person. Yet he insists on
pouring his own deep and bitter tragic consciousness into the little
skins of the country doctor and his dissatisfied wife. The result is a
certain discrepancy, even a certain dishonesty in the attempt to be
too honest. By choosing *ordinary* people as the vehicles of an
extraordinarily passionate feeling of bitterness, Flaubert loads the
dice, and wins by a trick which is sure to be found out against him.

Because a great soul like Flaubert's has a pure satisfaction and joy in its own consciousness, even if the consciousness be only of ultimate tragedy or misery. But the very fact of being so marvellously and vividly *aware*, awake, as Flaubert's soul was, is in itself a refutation of the all-is-misery doctrine. Since the human soul has supreme joy in true, vivid consciousness. And Flaubert's soul has this joy. But Emma Bovary's soul does not, poor thing, because she was deliberately chosen because her soul was ordinary. So Flaubert cheats us a little, in his doctrine, if not in his art. And his art is biased by his doctrine as much as any artist's is.

The same is true of *Mastro-don Gesualdo*. Gesualdo is a peasant's son, who becomes rich in his own tiny town through his own force and sagacity. He is allowed the old heroic qualities of force and sagacity. Even Emma Bovary has a certain extraordinary female energy of restlessness and unsatisfied desire. So that both Flaubert and Verga allow their heroes something of the hero, after all. The one thing they deny them is the consciousness of heroic effort.

Now Flaubert and Verga alike were aware of their own heroic effort to be truthful, to show things as they are. It was the heroic impulse which made them write their great books. Yet they deny to their protagonists any inkling of the heroic effort. It is in this sense that Emma Bovary and Gesualdo Motta are 'ordinary'. Ordinary people don't have much sense of heroic effort in life; and by the heroic effort we mean that instinctive fighting for more life to come into being, which is a basic impulse in more men than we like to admit; women too. Or it used to be. The discrediting of the heroic effort has almost extinguished that effort in the young, hence the appalling 'flatness' of their lives. It is the parents' fault. Life without the heroic effort, and without *belief* in the subtle, life-long validity of the heroic impulse, is just stale, flat and unprofitable. As the great realistic novels will show you.

Gesualdo Motta has the makings of a hero. Verga had to grant him something. I think it is in *Novelle Rusticane** that we find the long sketch or story of the little fat peasant who has become enormously rich by grinding his labourers and bleeding the Barons. It is a marvellous story, reeling with the hot atmosphere of Sicily, and the ironic fatalism of the Sicilians. And that little fat peasant must have been an actual man whom Verga knew—Verga wasn't good at inventing, he always had to have a core of actuality —and who served as the idea-germ for Gesualdo. But Gesualdo is much more attractive, much nearer the true hero. In fact, with all his energy and sagacity *and* his natural humaneness, we don't see how Gesualdo quite escaped the heroic consciousness. The original little peasant, the prototype, was a mere frog, a grabber and nothing else. He had none of Gesualdo's large humaneness. So that Verga brings Gesualdo much nearer to the hero, yet denies him still any spark of the heroic consciousness, any spark of awareness of a greater impulse within him. Men naturally have this spark, if they are the tiniest bit uncommon. The curious thing is, the moment you deny the spark, it dies, and then the heroic impulse dies with it.

It is probably true that, since the extinction of the pagan gods, the countries of the Mediterranean have never been aware of the heroic impulse in themselves, and so it has died down very low, in them. In Sicily, even now, and in the remoter Italian villages, there is what we call a low level of life, appalling. Just a squalid, un-imaginative, heavy, petty-fogging, grubby sort of existence, without light or flame. It is the absence of the heroic awareness, the heroic hope.

The northerners have got over the death of the old Homeric idea of the hero, by making the hero self-conscious, and a hero by virtue of suffering and awareness of suffering. The Sicilians may have little spasms of this sort of heroic feeling, but it never lasts. It is not natural to them.

The Russians carry us to great lengths of introspective heroism. They escape the non-heroic dilemma of our age by making every man his own introspective hero. The merest scrub of a pickpocket is so phenomenally aware of his own soul, that we are made to bow down before the imaginary coruscations of suffering and sympathy that go on inside him. So is Russian literature.

Of course, your soul will coruscate with suffering and sympathy, if you think it does: since the soul is capable of anything, and is no doubt full of unimaginable coruscations which far-off future civilizations will wake up to. So far, we have only lately wakened up to the sympathy-suffering coruscation, so we are full of it. And that is why the Russians are so popular. No matter how much of a shabby little slut you may be, you can learn from Dostoevsky and

Tchekov* that you have got the most tender, unique soul on earth, coruscating with sufferings and impossible sympathies. And so you may be most vastly important to yourself, introspectively. Outwardly, you will say: Of course I'm an ordinary person, like everybody else.—But your very saying it will prove that you think the opposite: namely, that everybody on earth is ordinary, *except* yourself.

This is our northern way of heroism, up to date. The Sicilian hasn't yet got there. Perhaps he never will. Certainly he was nowhere near it in Gesualdo Motta's day, the mediaeval Sicilian day of the middle of the last century, before Italy existed, and Sicily was still part of the Bourbon kingdom of Naples, and about as remote as the kingdom of Dahomey.

The Sicilian has no soul, except that funny little naked man who hops on hot bricks, in purgatory, and howls to be prayed out into paradise; and is in some mysterious way an *alter ego*, my me beyond the grave. This is the catholic soul, and there is nothing to do about it but to pay, and get it prayed into paradise.

For the rest, in our sense of the word, the Sicilian doesn't have any soul. He can't be introspective, because his consciousness, so to speak, doesn't have any inside to it. He can't look inside himself, because he is, as it were, solid. When Gesualdo is tormented by mean people, atrociously, all he says is: I've got bitter in my mouth.—And when he is dying, and has some awful tumour inside, he says: It is all the bitterness I have known, swelled up inside me.—That is all: a physical fact! Think what even Dmitri Karamazov* would have made of it! And Dmitri Karamazov doesn't go half the lengths of the other Russian soul-twisters. Neither is he half the man Gesualdo is, although he may be much more 'interesting', if you like soul-twisters.

In *Mastro-don Gesualdo* you have, in a sense, the same sort of tragedy as in the Russians, yet anything more un-Russian could not be imagined. Un-Russian almost as Homer. But Verga will have gods neither above nor below.

The Sicilians today are supposed to be the nearest descendants of the classic Greeks, and the nearest thing to the classic Greeks in life and nature. And perhaps it is true. Like the classic Greeks, the Sicilians have no insides, introspectively speaking. But, alas, outside they have no busy gods. It is their great loss. Because Jesus is to them only a wonder-man who was killed by foreigners and villains, and who will help you to get out of Hell, perhaps.

In the true sense of the word, the Sicily of Gesualdo is drearily godless. It needs the bright and busy gods outside. The inside gods, gods who have to be inside a man's soul, are distasteful to people who live in the sun. Once you get to Ceylon, you see that even Buddha is purely an outside god, purely objective to the natives. They have no conception of his being inside themselves.

It was the same with the Greeks, it is the same today with the Sicilians. They aren't *capable* of introspection and the inner Jesus. They leave it all to us and the Russians.

Save that he has no bright outside gods, Gesualdo is very like an old Greek: the same energy and quickness of response, the same vivid movement, the same ambition and real passion for wealth, the same easy conscience, the same queer openness, without ever really openly committing himself, and the same ancient astuteness. He is prouder, more fearless, more frank, yet more subtle than an Italian; more on his own. He is like a Greek or a traditional Englishman, in the way he just goes ahead by himself. And in that, he is Sicilian, not Italian.

And he is Greek above all, in having no inside, in the Russian sense of the word.

The tragedy is, he has no heroic gods or goddesses to fix his imagination. He has nothing, not even a country. Even his Greek ambitious desire to come out splendidly, with a final splendid look of the thing and a splendid final ring of words, turns bitter. The Sicilian aristocracy was an infinitely more paltry thing than Gesualdo himself.

It is the tragedy of a man who is forced to be ordinary, because all visions have been taken away from him. It is useless to say he should have had the northern inwardness and the Russianizing outlet. You might as well say the tall and reckless asphodel of Magna Graecia should learn to be a snowdrop. 'I'll learn you to be a toad!'

But a book exists by virtue of the vividness, the aliveness and powerful pulsing of its life-portrayal, and not by virtue of the pretty or unpretty things it portrays. *Mastro-don Gesualdo* is a great undying book, one of the great novels of Europe. If you cannot read it because it is *à terre*,* and has neither nervous uplift nor nervous hysteria, you condemn yourself.

As a picture of Sicily in the middle of the last century, it is marvellous. But it is a picture done from the inside. There are no picture-postcard effects. The thing is a heavy, earth-adhering organic whole. There is nothing showy.

Sicily in the middle of the last century was an incredibly poor, lost, backward country. Spaniards, Bourbons, one after the other they had killed the life in her. The Thousand and Garibaldi had not risen over the horizon, neither had the great emigration to America begun, nor the great return, with dollars and a newish outlook. The mass of the people were poorer even than the poor Irish of the same period, and save for climate, their conditions were worse. There were some great and wealthy landlords, dukes and barons still. But they lived in Naples, or in Palermo at the nearest. In the country, there were no roads at all for wheeled vehicles, consequently no carts, nothing but donkeys and pack-mules on the trails, or a sick person in a mule litter, or armed men on horseback, or men on donkeys. The life was mediaeval as in Russia. But whereas the Russia of 1850 is a vast flat country with a most picturesque life of nobles and serfs and soldiers, open and changeful, Sicily is a most beautiful country, but hilly, steep, shut-off, and abandoned, and the life is, or was, grimly unpicturesque in its dead monotony. The great nobles shunned the country, as in Ireland. And the people were sunk in bigotry, suspicion, and gloom. The life of the villages and small towns was of an incredible spiteful meanness, as life always is when there is not enough change and fresh air; and the conditions were sordid, dirty, as they always are when the human spirits sink below a certain level. It is not in such places that one looks for passion and colour. The passion and colour in Verga's stories come in the villages near the east coast, where there is change since Ulysses sailed that way. Inland, in the isolation, the lid is on, and the intense watchful malice of neighbours is infinitely worse than any police system, infinitely more killing to the soul and the passionate body.

The picture is a bitter and depressing one, while ever we stay in the dense and smelly little streets. Verga wrote what he knew and felt. But when we pass from the habitations of sordid man, into the light and marvellous open country, then we feel at once the undying beauty of Sicily and the Greek world, a morning beauty, that has something miraculous in it, of purple anemones and cyclamens, and sumach and olive trees, and the place where Persephone came above-world, bringing back spring.*

And we must remember that eight-tenths of the population of Sicily is maritime or agricultural, always has been, and therefore practically the whole day-life of the people passes in the open, in the splendour of the sun and the landscape, and the delicious, elemental aloneness of the old world. This is a great *unconscious* compensation. But what a compensation, after all!—even if you don't know you've got it; as even Verga doesn't quite. But he puts it in, all the same, and you can't read *Mastro-don Gesualdo* without feeling the marvellous glow and glamour of Sicily, and the people throbbing inside the glow and the glamour like motes in a sunbeam. Out of doors, in a world like that, what is misery, after all! The great freshness keeps the men still fresh. It is the women in the dens of houses who deteriorate most.

And perhaps it is because the outside world is so lovely, that men in the Greek regions have never become introspective. They had not been driven to *that* form of compensation. With them, life pulses outwards, and the positive reality is outside. There is no turning inwards. So man becomes purely objective. And this is what makes the Greeks so difficult to understand: even Socrates. We don't understand him. We just translate him into another thing, our own thing. He is so peculiarly *objective* even in his attitude to the soul, that we could never get him if we didn't translate him into something else, and thus 'make him our own'.

And the glorious objectivity of the old Greek world still persists, old and blind now, among the southern Mediterranean peoples. It is this decayed objectivity, not even touched by mediaeval mysticism, which makes a man like Gesualdo so simple, and yet so incomprehensible to us. We are apt to see him as just meaningless, just stupidly and meaninglessly getting rich, merely acquisitive. Yet, at the same time, we see him so patient with his family, with the phthisical Bianca, with his daughter, so humane, and yet so desperately enduring. In affairs, he has an unerring instinct, and he is a superb fighter. Yet in life, he seems to do the wrong thing every time. It is as if, in his life, he has no driving motive at all.

He should, of course, by every standard we know, have married Diodata. Bodily, she was the woman he turned to. She bore him sons. Yet he married her to one of his own hired men, to clear the way for his, Gesualdo's, marriage with the noble but merely pathetic Bianca Trao. And after he was married to Bianca, who was too weak for him, he still went back to Diodata, and paid her husband to accommodate him. And it never occurs to him to have any of this on his conscience. Diodata has his sons in her house, but Gesualdo, who has only one daughter by the frail Bianca, never seems to interest himself in his boys at all. There is the most amazing absence of a certain range of feeling in the man, especially feeling about himself. It is as if he had no inside. And yet we see that he most emphatically has. He has a warm and attractive presence. And he suffers bitterly, bitterly. Yet he blindly brings most of his sufferings on himself, by doing the wrong things to himself.

The idea of living for love is just entirely unknown to him, unknown as if it were a new German invention. So is the idea of living for sex. In that respect, woman is just the female of the species to him, as if he were a horse, that jumps in heat, and forgets. He never really thinks about women. Life means something else to him.

But what? What? It is so hard to see. Does he just want to *get on*, in our sense of the word? No, not even that. He has not the faintest desire to be mayor, or podesta, or that sort of thing. But he does make a duchess of his daughter. Yes, Mastro–don Gesualdo's daughter is a duchess of very aristocratic rank.

And what then? Gesualdo realizes soon enough that she is not happy. And now he is an elderly, dying man, and the impetuosity of his manhood is sinking, he begins to wonder what he should have done. What was it all about?

What *did* life mean to him, when he was in the impetuous tide of his manhood? What was he unconsciously driving at? Just blindly at nothing? Was that why he put aside Diodata, and brought on himself all that avalanche of spite, by marrying Bianca? Not that his marriage was a failure. Bianca was his wife, and he was unfailingly kind to her, fond of her, her death was bitter to him. Not being under the tyrannical sway of the idea of 'love', he could be fond of his wife, and he could be fond of D___ needn't get into a stew about any of them.

But what was he under the sway of? What was he blindly driving at? We ask, and we realize at last that it was the old Greek impulse towards splendour and self-enhancement. Not ambition, in our sense of the word, but something more personal, more individual. That which swayed Achilles and swayed Pericles and Alcibiades:* the passionate desire for individual splendour. We now call it vanity. But in the countries of the sun, where the whole outdoors consists in the splendour of the sun, it is a real thing to men, to try to make themselves splendid and like suns.

Gesualdo was blindly repeating, in his own confused way, the magnificent old gesture. But ours is not the age for splendour. We have changed all that. So Gesualdo's life amounts to nothing. Yet not, as far as I can see, to any less than the lives of the 'humble' Russians. At least he lived his life. If he thought too little about it, he helps to counterbalance all those people who think too much. Because he never has any 'profound' talk, he is not less a man than Myshkin or a Karamazov. He is possibly not more a man, either. But to me he is less distasteful. And because his life all ends in a mistake, he is not therefore any more meaningless than Tolstoi himself. And because he simply has no idea whatsoever of 'salvation', whether his own or anybody else's, he is not therefore a fool. Any more than Hector* and Achilles were fools; for neither of them had any idea of salvation.

The last forlorn remnant of the Greeks, blindly but brightly seeking for splendour and self-enhancement, instead of salvation, and choosing to surge blindly on, instead of retiring inside himself to twist his soul into knots, Gesualdo still has a lovable glow in his body, the very reverse of the cold marsh-gleam of Myshkin. His life ends in a tumour of bitterness. But it was a life, and I would rather have lived it than, the life of Tolstoi's Pierre,* or the life of any Dostoevskian hero. It was not Gesualdo's fault that the bright objective gods are dead, killed by envy and spite. It was not his fault that there was no real splendour left in our world for him to choose, once he had the means.

...s in Poetry

...... matter of words. And this is just as much
...... are a matter of paint, and frescoes a matter of
......ash. It is such a long way from being the whole
tru...... ....ghtly silly if uttered sententiously.

Poet...... matter of words. Poetry is a stringing together of
words into a ripple and jingle and a run of colours. Poetry is an
interplay of images. Poetry is the iridescent suggestion of an idea.
Poetry is all these things, and still it is something else. Given all
these ingredients, you have something very like poetry, something
for which we might borrow the old romantic name of poesy. And
poesy, like bric-à-brac, will for ever be in fashion. But poetry is still
another thing.

The essential quality of poetry is that it makes a new effort of
attention, and 'discovers' a new world within the known world.
Man, and the animals, and the flowers, all live within a strange and
for ever surging chaos. The chaos which we have got used to we
call a cosmos. The unspeakable inner chaos of which we are
composed we call consciousness, and mind, and even civilization.
But it is, ultimately, chaos, lit up by visions, or not lit up by visions.
Just as the rainbow may or may not light up the storm. And, like
the rainbow, the vision perisheth.

But man cannot live in chaos. The animals can. To the animal
all is chaos, only there are a few recurring motions and aspects
within the surge. And the animal is content. But man is not. Man
must wrap himself in a vision, make a house of apparent form and
stability, fixity. In his terror of chaos he begins by putting up an
umbrella between himself and the everlasting whirl. Then he
paints the under-side of his umbrella like a firmament. Then he
parades around, lives and dies under his umbrella. Bequeathed to
his descendants, the umbrella becomes a dome, a vault, and men at
last begin to feel that something is wrong.

Man fixes some wonderful erection of his own between himself
and the wild chaos, and gradually goes bleached and stifled under
his parasol. Then comes a poet, enemy of convention, and makes a
slit in the umbrella; and lo! the glimpse of chaos is a vision, a

window to the sun. But after a while, getting used to the vision, and not liking the genuine draught from chaos, commonplace man daubs a simulacrum of the window that opens on to chaos, and patches the umbrella with the painted patch of the simulacrum. That is, he has got used to the vision; it is part of his house-decoration. So that the umbrella at last looks like a glowing open firmament, of many aspects. But alas! it is all simulacrum, in innumerable patches. Homer and Keats, annotated and with glossary.

This is the history of poetry in our era. Someone sees Titans in the wild air of chaos, and the Titan becomes a wall between succeeding generations and the chaos they should have inherited. The wild sky moved and sang. Even that became a great umbrella between mankind and the sky of fresh air; then it became a painted vault, a fresco on a vaulted roof, under which men bleach and go dissatisfied. Till another poet makes a slit on to the open and windy chaos.

But at last our roof deceives us no more. It is painted plaster, and all the skill of all the human ages won't take us in. Dante or Leonardo, Beethoven or Whitman: lo! it is painted on the plaster of our vault. Like St Francis preaching to the birds in Assisi. Wonderfully like air and birdy space and chaos of many things—partly because the fresco is faded. But even so, we are glad to get out of that church, and into the natural chaos.

This is the momentous crisis for mankind, when we have to get back to chaos. So long as the umbrella serves, and poets make slits in it, and the mass of people can be gradually educated up to the vision in the slit: which means they patch it over with a patch that looks just like the vision in the slit: so long as this process can continue, and mankind can be educated up, and thus built in, so long will a civilization continue more or less happily, completing its own painted prison. It is called completing the consciousness.

The joy men had when Wordsworth, for example, made a slit and saw a primrose!* Till then, men had only seen a primrose dimly, in the shadow of the umbrella. They saw it through Wordsworth in the full gleam of chaos. Since then, gradually, we have come to see primavera* nothing but primrose. Which means, we have patched over the slit.

And the greater joy when Shakespeare made a big rent and saw emotional, wistful man outside in the chaos, beyond the conventional idea and painted umbrella of moral images and iron-bound paladins, which had been put up in the Middle Ages. But now, alas, the roof of our vault is simply painted dense with Hamlets and Macbeths, the side walls too, and the order is fixed and complete. Man can't be any different from his image. Chaos is all shut out.

The umbrella has got so big, the patches and plaster are so tight and hard, it can be slit no more. If it were slit, the rent would no more be a vision, it would only be an outrage. We should dab it over at once, to match the rest.

So the umbrella is absolute. And so the yearning for chaos becomes a nostalgia. And this will go on till some terrific wind blows the umbrella to ribbons, and much of mankind to oblivion. The rest will shiver in the midst of chaos. For chaos is always there, and always will be, no matter how we put up umbrellas of visions.

What about the poets, then, at this juncture? They reveal the inward desire of mankind. What do they reveal? They show the desire for chaos, and the fear of chaos. The desire for chaos is the breath of their poetry. The fear of chaos is in their parade of forms and technique. Poetry is made of words, they say. So they blow bubbles of sound and image, which soon burst with the breath of longing for chaos, which fills them. But the poetasters can make pretty shiny bubbles for the Christmas-tree, which never burst, because there is no breath of poetry in them, but they remain till we drop them.

What, then, of *Chariot of the Sun?* * It is a warlike and bronzy title for a sheaf of flimsies, almost too flimsy for real bubbles. But incongruity is man's recognition of chaos.

If one had to judge these little poems for their magic of words, as one judges Paul Valéry, * for example, they would look shabby. There is no obvious incantation of sweet noise; only too often the music of one line deliberately kills the next, breathlessly staccato. There is no particular jewellery of epithet. And no handsome handling of images. Where deliberate imagery is used, it is perhaps a little clumsy. There is no coloured thread of an idea; and no subtle ebbing of a theme into consciousness, no recognizable vision, new gleam of chaos let in to a world of order. There is only a repetition of sun, sun, sun, not really as a glowing symbol, more as a bewilderment and a narcotic. The images in 'Sun Rhapsody' shatter one another, line by line. For the sun,

> it is a forest without trees
> it is a lion in a cage of breeze
> it is the roundness of her knees
> great Hercules
> and all the seas
> and our soliloquies

The rhyme is responsible for a great deal. The lesser symbols are as confusing: sunmaids who are naiads of the water world, hiding in a cave. Only the forest becomes suddenly logical.

I am a tree whose roots are tangled in the sun
All men and women are trees whose roots are tangled in the sun
Therefore humanity is the forest of the sun.

What is there, then, in this poetry, where there seems to be nothing? For if there is nothing, it is merely nonsense.

And, almost, it is nonsense. Sometimes, as in the 'verse' beginning: 'sthhe fous on ssu eod', since I at least can make no head or tail of it, and the mere sound is impossible, and the mere look of it is not inspiring, to me it is just nonsense. But in a world overloaded with shallow 'sense', I can bear a page of nonsense, just for a pause.

For the rest, what is there? Take, at random, the poem called 'Néant':

> Red sunbeams from an autumn sun
>> Shall be the strongest wall
> To shield the sunmaids of my soul
>> From worlds inimical.
>
> Yet sunflakes falling in the sea
>> Beyond the outer shore
> Reduplicate their epitaph
>> To kill the conqueror.

It is a tissue of incongruity, in sound and sense. It means nothing, and it says nothing. And yet it has something to say. It even carries a dim suggestion of that which refuses to be said.

And therein lies the charm. It is a glimpse of chaos not reduced to order. But the chaos *alive,* not the chaos of matter. A glimpse of the living, untamed chaos. For the grand chaos is all alive, and everlasting. From it we draw our breath of life. If we shut ourselves off from it, we stifle. The animals live with it, as they live in grace. But when man became conscious, and aware of *himself,* his own littleness and puniness in the whirl of the vast chaos of God, he took fright, and began inventing God in his own image.*

Now comes the moment when the terrified but inordinately conceited human consciousness must at last submit, and own itself part of the vast and potent living chaos. We must keep true to ourselves. But we must breathe in life from the living and unending chaos. We shall put up more umbrellas. They are a necessity of our consciousness. But never again shall we be able to put up The Absolute Umbrella, either religious or moral or rational or scientific or practical. The vast parasol of our conception of the universe, the cosmos, the firmament of suns and stars and space, this we can roll up like any other green sunshade, and bring it forth again when we want it. But we mustn't imagine it always spread above us. It is no more absolutely there than a green sunshade is absolutely there. It is casually there, only; because it is as much a contrivance and invention of our mind as a green sunshade is. Likewise the grand conception of God: this already shuts up like a Japanese parasol, rather clumsily, and is put by for Sundays, or bad weather, or a 'serious' mood.

Now we see the charm of *Chariot of the Sun*. It shuts up all the little and big umbrellas of poesy and importance, has no out-standing melody or rhythm or image or epithet or even sense. And we feel a certain relief. The sun is very much in evidence, certainly, but it is a bubble reality that always explodes before you can really look at it. And it upsets all the rest of things with its disappearing.

Hence the touch of true poetry in this sun. It bursts all the bubbles and umbrellas of reality, and gives us a breath of the live chaos. We struggle out into the fathomless chaos of things passing and coming, and many suns and different darknesses. There is a bursting of bubbles of reality, and the pang of extinction that is also liberation into the roving, uncaring chaos which is all we shall ever know of God.

To me there is a breath of poetry, like an uneasy waft of fresh air at dawn, before it is light. There is an acceptance of the limitations of consciousness, and a leaning-up against the sun-imbued world of chaos. It is poetry at the moment of inception in the soul, before the germs of the known and the unknown have fused to begin a new body of concepts. And therefore it is useless to quote fragments. They are too nebulous and *not there.* Yet in the whole there is a breath of real poetry, the essential quality of poetry. It makes a new act of attention, and wakes us to a nascent world of inner and outer suns. And it has the poetic faith in the chaotic splendour of suns.

It is poetry of suns which are the core of chaos, suns which are fountains of shadow and pools of light and centres of thought and lions of passion. Since chaos has a core which is itself quint-essentially chaotic and fierce with incongruities. That such a sun should have a chariot makes it only more chaotic.

And in the chaotic re-echoing of the soul, wisps of sound curl round with curious soothing—

> Likewise invisible winds
> Drink fire, and all my heart is sun-consoled.

And a poem such as 'Water-Lilies' has a lovely suffusion in which the visual image passes at once into sense of touch, and back again, so that there is an iridescent confusion of sense-impression, sound and touch and sight all running into one another, blending into a vagueness which is a new world, a vagueness and a suffusion which liberates the soul, and lets a new flame of desire flicker delicately up from the numbed body.

The suffused fragments are the best, those that are only comprehensible with the senses, with visions passing into touch and to sound, then again touch, and the bursting of the bubble of an image. There is always sun, but there is also water, most palpably water. Even some of the suns are wetly so, wet pools that wet us with their touch. Then loose suns like lions, soft gold lions and white lions half-visible. Then again the elusive gleam of the sun of livingness, soft as gold and strange as the lion's eyes, the livingness that never ceases and never will cease. In this there is faith, soft, intangible, suffused faith that is the breath of all poetry, part of the breathing of the myriad sun in chaos. Such sun breathes its way into words, and the words become poetry, by suffusion. On the part of the poet it is an act of faith, pure attention and purified receptiveness. And without such faith there is no poetry. There is

even no life. The poetry of conceit is a dead-sea fruit.* The poetry
of sunless chaos is already a bore. The poetry of a regulated cosmos
is nothing but a wire bird-cage. Because in all living poetry the
living chaos stirs, sun-suffused and sun-impulsive, and most subtly
chaotic. All true poetry is most subtly and sensitively chaotic,
outlawed. But it is the impulse of the sun in chaos, not conceit.

> The Sun in unconcealed rage
> Glares down across the magic of the world.

The sun within us, that sways us incalculably.

> At night
> Swift to the Sun
> Deep imaged in my soul
> But during the long day black lands
> To cross

And it is faith in the incalculable sun, inner and outer, which
keeps us alive.

> Sunmaid
> Left by the tide
> I bring you a conch-shell
> That listening to the Sun you may
> Revive

And there is always the battle of the sun, against the corrosive acid
vapour of vanity and poisonous conceit, which is the breath of the
world.

> Dark clouds
> Are not so dark
> As our embittered thoughts
> Which carve strange silences within
> The Sun

That the next 'cinquain'* may not be poetry at all is perhaps
just as well, to keep us in mind of the world of conceit outside. It is
the expired breath, with its necessary carbonic acid. It is the cold
shadow across the sun, and saves us from the strain of the monos,
from homogeneity and exaltation and forcedness and all-of-a-
pieceness, which is the curse of the human consciousness. What
does it matter if half the time a poet fails in his effort at expression!

The failures make it real. The act of attention is not so easy. It is much easier to write poesy. Failure is part of the living chaos. And the groping reveals the act of attention, which suddenly passes into pure expression.

> But I shall not be frightened by a sound
> Of Something moving cautiously around.

Whims, and fumblings, and effort, and nonsense, and echoes from other poets, these all go to make up the living chaos of a little book of real poetry, as well as pure little poems like 'Sun-Ghost', 'To Those Who Return', 'Torse de Jeune Femme au Soleil', 'Poem for the Feet of Polia'. Through it all runs the intrinsic naïveté without which no poetry can exist, not even the most sophisticated. This naïveté is the opening of the soul to the sun of chaos, and the soul may open like a lily or a tiger-lily or a dandelion or a deadly nightshade or a rather paltry chickweed flower, and it will be poetry of its own sort. But open it must. This opening, and this alone, is the essential act of attention, the essential poetic and vital act. We may fumble in the act, and a hailstone may hit us. But it is in the course of things. In this act, and this alone, we truly *live*: in that innermost naïve opening of the soul, like a flower, like an animal, like a coloured snake, it does not matter, to the sun of chaotic livingness.

Now, after a long bout of conceit and self-assurance and flippancy, the young are waking up to the fact that they are starved of life and of essential sun, and at last they are being driven, out of sheer starvedness, to make the act of submission, the act of attention, to open into inner naïveté, deliberately and dauntlessly, admit the chaos and the sun of chaos. This is the new naïveté, chosen, recovered, regained. Round it range the white and golden soft lions of courage and the sun of dauntlessness, and the whorled ivory horn of the unicorn is erect and ruthless, as a weapon of defence. The naïve, open spirit of man will no longer be a victim, to be put on a cross, nor a beggar, to be scorned and given a pittance. This time it will be erect and a bright lord, with a heart open to the wild sun of chaos, but with the yellow lions of the sun's danger on guard in the eyes.

The new naïveté, erect, and ready, sufficiently sophisticated to wring the neck of sophistication, will be the new spirit of poetry and the new spirit of life. Tender, but purring like a leopard that may snarl, it may be clumsy at first, and make gestures of self-conscious crudity. But it is a real thing, the real creature of the inside of the soul. And to the young it is the essential reality, the liberation into the real self. The liberation into the wild air of chaos, the being part of the sun. A long course of merely negative 'freedom' reduces the soul and body both to numbness. They can feel no more and respond no more. Only the mind remains awake, and suffers keenly from the sense of nullity; to be young, and to feel you have every 'opportunity', every 'freedom' to live, and yet not to be able to live, because the responses have gone numb in the body and soul, this is the nemesis that is overtaking the young. It drives them silly.

But there is the other way, back to the sun, to faith in the speckled leopard of the mixed self. What is more chaotic than a dappled leopard trotting through dappled shade? And that is our life, really. Why try to whitewash ourselves?—or to camouflage ourselves into an artificially chaotic pattern? All we have to do is to accept the true chaos that we are, like the jaguar dappled with black suns in gold.

Review of
The Station: Athos, Treasures and Men by Robert Byron; *England and the Octopus* by Clough Williams-Ellis; *Comfortless Memory* by Maurice Baring; *Ashenden* by W. Somerset Maugham

ATHOS is an old place, and Mr Byron* is a young man. The combination for once is really happy. We can imagine ourselves being very bored by a book on ancient Mount Athos and its ancient monasteries with their ancient rule. Luckily Mr Byron belongs to the younger generation, even younger than the Sitwells,* who have shown him the way to be young. Therefore he is not more than becomingly impressed with ancientness. He never gapes in front of it. He settles on it like a butterfly, tastes it, is perfectly honest about the taste, and flutters on. And it is charming.

We confess that we find this youthful revelation of ancient Athos charming. It is all in the butterfly manner. But the butterfly, airy creature, is by no means a fool. And its interest is wide. It is amusing to watch a spangled beauty settle on the rose, then on a spat-out cherry-stone, then with a quiver of sunny attention, upon a bit of horse-droppings in the road. The butterfly tries them all, with equal concern. It is neither shocked nor surprised, though sometimes, if thwarted, it is a little exasperated. But it is still a butterfly, graceful, charming, and ephemeral. And, of course, the butterfly on its careless, flapping wings is just as immortal as some hooting and utterly learned owl. Which is to say, we are thankful Mr Byron is no more learned and serious than he is, and his description of Athos is far more vitally convincing than that, for example, of some heavy Gregorovius.*

The four young men set out from England with a purpose. The author wants to come into closer contact with the monks and monasteries, which he has already visited; and to write a book about it. He definitely sets out with the intention of writing a book about it. He has no false shame. David, the archaeologist, wants to photograph the Byzantine frescoes in the monastery buildings.

Mark chases and catches insects. And Reinecker looks at art and old pots. They are four young gentlemen with the echoes of Oxford still in their ears, light and frivolous as butterflies, but with an underneath tenacity of purpose and almost a grim determination *to do something*.

The butterfly and the Sitwellian manner need not deceive us. These young gentlemen are not simply gay. They are grimly in earnest to get something done. They are not young sports amusing themselves. They are young earnests making their mark. They are stoics rather than frivolous, and epicureans truly in the deeper sense, of undergoing suffering in order to achieve a higher pleasure.

For the monasteries of Mount Athos are no Paradise. The food which made the four young men shudder makes us shudder. The vermin in the beds are lurid. The obstinacy and grudging malice of some of the monks, whose one pleasure seems to have been in thwarting and frustrating the innocent desires of the four young men, make our blood boil too. We know exactly what sewage is like, spattering down from above on to leaves and rocks. And the tortures of heat and fatigue are very real indeed.

It is as if the four young men expected to be tormented at every hand's turn. Which is just as well, for tormented they were. Monks apparently have a special gift of tormenting people: though of course some of the monks were charming. But it is chiefly out of the torments of the young butterflies, always humorously and gallantly told, that we get our picture of Athos, its monasteries and its monks. And we are left with no desire at all to visit the holy mountain, unless we could go disembodied, in such state that no flea could bite us, and no stale fish could turn our stomachs.

Then, disembodied, we should like to go and see the unique place, the lovely views, the strange old buildings, the unattractive monks, the paintings, mosaics, frescoes of that isolated little Byzantine world.

For everything artistic is there purely Byzantine. Byzantine is to Mr Byron what Baroque is to the Sitwells. That is to say, he has a real feeling for it, and finds in it a real kinship with his own war-generation mood. Also, it is his own special elegant stone to sling at the philistine* world.

Perhaps, in a long book like this, the unfailing humoresque of the style becomes a little tiring. Perhaps a page or two here and there of honest-to-God simplicity might enhance the high light of the author's facetious impressionism. But then the book might have been undertaken by some honest-to-God professor, and we so infinitely prefer Mr Byron.

When we leave Mr Byron we leave the younger generation for the elder; at least as far as style and manner goes. Mr Williams-Ellis has chosen a thankless subject: *England and the Octopus:** the Octopus being the millions of little streets of mean little houses that are getting England in their grip, and devouring her. It is a depressing theme, and the author rubs it in. We see them all, those millions of beastly little red houses spreading like an eruption over the face of rural England. Look! Look! says Mr Williams-Ellis, till we want to shout: Oh, shut up! What's the good of our looking! We've looked and got depressed too often. Now leave us alone.

But Mr Williams-Ellis is honestly in earnest and has an honest sense of responsibility. This is the difference between the attitude of the younger and the older generations. The younger generation can't take anything very seriously, and refuses to feel responsible for humanity. The younger generation says in effect: I didn't make the world. I'm not responsible. All I can do is to make my own little mark and depart. But the elder generation still feels responsible for all humanity.

And Mr Williams-Ellis feels splendidly responsible for poor old England: the face of her, at least. As he says: You can be put in prison for uttering a few mere swear-words to a policeman, but you can disfigure the loveliest features of the English country-side, and probably be called a public benefactor. And he wants to alter all that.

And he's quite right. His little book is excellent: sincere, honest, and even passionate, the well-written, humorous book of a man who knows what he's writing about. Everybody ought to read it, whether we know all about it beforehand or not. Because in a question like this, of the utter and hopeless disfigurement of the English country-side by modern industrial encroachment, the point is not whether we can do anything about it or not, all in a hurry. The point is, that we should all become acutely conscious of what is happening, and of what has happened; and as soon as we are really awake to this, we can begin to arrange things differently.

Mr Williams-Ellis makes us conscious. He wakes up our age to our own immediate surroundings. He makes us able to look intelligently at the place we live in, at our own street, our own post-office or pub or bank or petrol pump-station. And when we begin to look around us critically and intelligently, it is fun. It is great fun. It is like analysing a bad picture and seeing how it could be turned into a good picture.

Mr Williams-Ellis's six questions which should be asked of every building ought to be printed on a card and distributed to every individual in the nation. Because, as a nation, it is our intuitive faculty for seeing beauty and ugliness which is lying dead in us. As a nation we are dying of ugliness.

Let us open our eyes, or let Mr Williams-Ellis open them for us, to houses, streets, railways, railings, paint, trees, roofs, petrol-pumps, advertisements, tea-shops, factory-chimneys, let us open our eyes and see them as they are, beautiful or ugly, mean and despicable, or grandiose, or pleasant. People who live in mean, despicable surroundings become mean and despicable. The chief thing is to become properly conscious of our environment.

But if some of the elder generation really take things seriously, some others only pretend. And this *pretending* to take things seriously is a vice, a real vice, and the young know it.

Mr Baring's book *Comfortless Memory** is, thank heaven, only a little book, but it is sheer pretence of taking seriously things which its own author can never for a moment consider serious. That is, it is faked seriousness, which is utterly boring. I don't know when Mr Baring wrote this slight novel. But he ought to have published it at least twenty years ago, when faked seriousness was more in the vogue. Mr Byron, the young author, says that progress is the appreciation of Reality. Mr Baring, the elderly author, offers us a piece of portentous unreality larded with Goethe, Dante, Heine,* hopelessly out of date, and about as exciting as stale restaurant cake.

A dull, stuffy elderly author makes faked love to a bewitching but slightly damaged lady who has 'lived' with a man she wasn't married to!! She is an enigmatic lady: very! For she falls in love, violently, virginally, deeply, passionately and exclusively, with the comfortably married stuffy elderly author. The stuffy elderly author himself tells us so, much to his own satisfaction. And the lovely, alluring, enigmatic, experienced lady actually expires, in her riding-habit, out of sheer love for the comfortably married elderly author. The elderly author assures us of it. If it were not quite so stale it would be funny.

Mr Somerset Maugham is even more depressing. His Mr Ashenden* is also an elderly author, who becomes an agent in the British Secret Service during the War. An agent in the Secret Service is a sort of spy. Spying is a dirty business, and Secret Service altogether is a world of underdogs, a world in which the meanest passions are given play.

And this is Mr Maugham's, or at least Mr Ashenden's world. Mr Ashenden is an elderly author, so he takes life seriously, and takes his fellow-men seriously, with a seriousness already a little out of date. He has a sense of responsibility towards humanity. It would be much better if he hadn't. For Mr Ashenden's sense of responsibility oddly enough is inverted. He is almost passionately concerned with proving that all men and all women are either dirty dogs or imbeciles. If they are clever men or women, they are crooks, spies, police-agents, and tricksters 'making good', living in the best hotels because they know that in a humble hotel they'll be utterly declassé, and showing off their base cleverness, and being dirty dogs, from Ashenden himself, and his mighty clever colonel, and the distinguished diplomat, down to the mean French porters.

If, on the other hand, you get a decent, straight individual, especially an individual capable of feeling love for another, then you are made to see that such a person is a despicable fool, encompassing his own destruction. So the American dies for his dirty washing, the Hindu dies for a blowsy woman who wants her wrist-watch back, the Greek merchant is murdered by mistake, and so on. It is better to be a live dirty dog than a dead lion,* says Mr Ashenden. Perhaps it is, to Mr Ashenden.

But these stories, being 'serious', are faked. Mr Maugham is a splendid observer. He can bring before us persons and places most excellently. But as soon as the excellently observed characters have to move, it is a fake. Mr Maugham gives them a humorous shove or two. We find they are nothing but puppets, instruments of the author's pet prejudice. The author's pet prejudice being 'humour', it would be hard to find a bunch of more ill-humoured stories, in which the humour has gone more rancid.

Introduction to These Paintings

THE reason the English produce so few painters is not that they are, as a nation, devoid of a genuine feeling for visual art: though to look at their productions, and to look at the mess which has been made of actual English landscape, one might really conclude that they were, and leave it at that. But it is not the fault of the God that made them. They are made with aesthetic sensibilities the same as anybody else. The fault lies in the English attitude to life.

The English, and the Americans following them, are paralysed by fear. That is what thwarts and distorts the Anglo-Saxon existence, this paralysis of fear. It thwarts life, it distorts vision, and it strangles impulse: this overmastering fear. And fear of what, in heaven's name? What is the Anglo-Saxon stock today so petrified with fear about? We have to answer that before we can understand the English failure in the visual arts: for, on the whole, it is a failure.

It is an old fear, which seemed to dig in to the English soul at the time of the Renaissance. Nothing could be more lovely and fearless than Chaucer. But already Shakespeare is morbid with fear, fear of consequences. That is the strange phenomenon of the English Renaissance: this mystic terror of the consequences, the consequences of action. Italy, too, had her reaction, at the end of the sixteenth century, and showed a similar fear. But not so profound, so over-mastering. Aretino* was anything but timorous: he was bold as any Renaissance novelist, and went one better.

What appeared to take full grip on the northern consciousness at the end of the sixteenth century was a terror, almost a horror of sexual life. The Elizabethans, grand as we think them, started it. The real 'mortal coil'* in Hamlet is all sexual; the young man's horror of his mother's incest, sex carrying with it a wild and nameless terror which, it seems to me, it had never carried before. Oedipus* and Hamlet are very different in this respect. In Oedipus there is no recoil in horror from sex itself: Greek drama never shows us that. The horror, when it is present in Greek tragedy, is against *destiny,* man caught in the toils of destiny. But with the Renaissance itself, particularly in England, the horror is sexual.

Orestes* is dogged by destiny and driven mad by the Eumenides. But Hamlet is overpowered by horrible revulsion from his physical connexion with his mother, which makes him recoil in similar revulsion from Ophelia, and almost from his father, even as a ghost. He is horrified at the merest suggestion of physical connexion, as if it were an unspeakable taint.

This, no doubt, is all in the course of the growth of the 'spiritual-mental' consciousness, at the expense of the instinctive-intuitive consciousness. Man came to have his own body in horror, especially in its sexual implications: and so he began to suppress with all his might his instinctive-intuitive consciousness, which is so radical, so physical, so sexual. Cavalier poetry, love poetry, is already devoid of body. Donne, after the exacerbated revulsion-attraction excitement of his earlier poetry, becomes a divine. 'Drink to me only with thine eyes,' sings the cavalier: an expression incredible in Chaucer's poetry. 'I could not love thee, dear, so much, loved I not honour more,'* sings the Cavalier lover. In Chaucer the 'dear' and the 'honour' would have been more or less identical.

But with the Elizabethans the grand rupture had started in the human consciousness, the mental consciousness recoiling in violence away from the physical, instinctive-intuitive. To the Restoration dramatist sex is, on the whole, a dirty business, but they more or less glory in the dirt. Ielding tries in vain to defend the Old Adam.* Richardson with his calico purity and his underclothing excitements sweeps all before him. Swift goes mad with sex and excrement revulsion. Sterne* flings a bit of the same excrement humorously around. And physical consciousness gives a last song in Burns, then is dead. Wordsworth, Keats, Shelley, the Brontës, all are post-mortem poets. The essential instinctive-intuitive body is dead, and worshipped in death—all very unhealthy. Till Swinburne and Oscar Wilde try to start a revival from the mental field. Swinburne's 'white thighs'* are purely mental.

Now, in England—and following, in America—the physical self was not just fig-leafed over or suppressed in public, as was the case in Italy and on most of the Continent. In England it excited a strange horror and terror. And this extra morbidity came, I believe, from the great shock of syphilis and the realization of the consequences of the disease. Wherever syphilis, or 'pox', came from, it was fairly new in England at the end of the fifteenth century. But by the end of the sixteenth, its ravages were obvious, and the shock of them had just penetrated the thoughtful and the imaginative consciousness. The royal families of England and Scotland were syphilitic; Edward VI and Elizabeth born with the inherited consequences of the disease. Edward VI died of it, while still a boy. Mary died childless and in utter depression. Elizabeth had no eyebrows, her teeth went rotten; she must have felt herself, somewhere, utterly unfit for marriage, poor thing. That was the grisly horror that lay behind the glory of Queen Bess. And so the Tudors died out: and another syphilitic-born unfortunate came to the throne, in the person of James I. Mary Queen of Scots had no more luck than the Tudors, apparently. Apparently Darnley* was reeking with the pox, though probably at first she did not know it. But when the Archbishop of St Andrews was christening her baby James, afterwards James I of England, the old clergyman was so dripping with pox that she was terrified lest he should give it to the infant. And she need not have troubled, for the wretched infant had brought it into the world with him, from that fool Darnley. So James I of England slobbered and shambled, and was the wisest fool in Christendom,* and the Stuarts likewise died out, the stock enfeebled by the disease.

With the royal families of England and Scotland in this condition, we can judge what the noble houses, the nobility of both nations, given to free living and promiscuous pleasure, must have been like. England traded with the East and with America; England, unknowing, had opened her doors to the disease. The English aristocracy travelled and had curious taste in loves. And pox entered the blood of the nation, particularly of the upper classes, who had more chance of infection. And after it had entered the blood, it entered the consciousness, and hit the vital imagination.

It is possible that the effects of syphilis and the conscious realization of its consequences gave a great blow also to the Spanish psyche, precisely at this period. And it is possible that Italian society, which was on the whole so untravelled, had no connexion with America, and was so privately self-contained, suffered less from the disease. Someone ought to make a thorough study of the effects of 'pox' on the minds and the emotions and imaginations of the various nations of Europe, at about the time of our Elizabethans.

The apparent effect on the Elizabethans and the Restoration wits is curious. They appear to take the whole thing as a joke. The common oath, 'Pox on you!' was almost funny. But how common the oath was! How the word 'pox' was in every mind and in every mouth. It is one of the words that haunt Elizabethan speech. Taken very manly, with a great deal of Falstaffian bluff, treated as a huge joke! Pox! Why, he's got the pox! Ha-ha! What's he been after?

There is just the same attitude among the common run of men today with regard to the minor sexual diseases. Syphilis is no longer regarded as a joke, according to my experience. The very word itself frightens men. You could joke with the word 'pox'. You can't joke with the word 'syphilis'. The change of word has killed the joke. But men still joke about *clap!* which is a minor sexual disease. They pretend to think it manly, even, to have the disease, or to have had it. 'What! never had a shot of clap!' cries one gentleman to another. 'Why, where have you been all your life?' If we change the word and insisted on 'gonorrhoea', or whatever it is, in place of 'clap', the joke would die. And anyhow I have had young men come to me green and quaking, afraid they've caught a 'shot of clap'.

Now, in spite of all the Elizabethan jokes about pox, pox was no joke to them. A joke may be a very brave way of meeting a calamity, or it may be a very cowardly way. Myself, I consider the Elizabethan pox joke a purely cowardly attitude. They didn't think it funny, for by God it *wasn't* funny. Even poor Elizabeth's lack of eyebrows and her rotten teeth were not funny. And they all knew it. They may not have known it was the direct result of pox: though probably they did. This fact remains, that no man can contract syphilis, or any deadly sexual disease, without feeling the most shattering and profound terror go through him, through the very roots of his being. And no man can look without a sort of horror on the effects of a sexual disease in another person. We are so constituted that we are all at once horrified and terrified. The fear and dread has been so great that the pox joke was invented as an evasion, and following that, the great hush! hush! was imposed. Man was *too* frightened: that's the top and bottom of it.

But now, with remedies discovered, we need no longer be *too* frightened. We can begin, after all these years, to face the matter. After the most fearful damage has been done.

For an overmastering fear is poison to the human psyche. And this overmastering fear, like some horrible secret tumour, has been poisoning our consciousness ever since the Elizabethans, who first woke up with dread to the entry of the original syphilitic poison into the blood.

I know nothing about medicine and very little about diseases, and my facts are such as I have picked up in casual reading. Nevertheless I am convinced that the secret awareness of syphilis, and the utter secret terror and horror of it, has had an enormous and incalculable effect on the English consciousness and on the American. Even when the fear has never been formulated, there it has lain, potent and overmastering. I am convinced that *some* of Shakespeare's horror and despair, in his tragedies, arose from the shock of his consciousness of syphilis. I don't suggest for one moment Shakespeare ever contracted syphilis. I have never had syphilis myself. Yet I know and confess how profound is my fear of the disease, and more than fear, my horror. In fact, I don't think I am so very much afraid of it. I am more horrified, inwardly and deeply, at the idea of its existence.

All this sounds very far from the art of painting. But it is not so far as it sounds. The appearance of syphilis in our midst gave a fearful blow to our sexual life. The real natural innocence of Chaucer was impossible after that. The very sexual act of procreation might bring as one of its consequences a foul disease, and the unborn might be tainted from the moment of conception. Fearful thought! It is truly a fearful thought, and all the centuries of getting used to it won't help us. It remains a fearful thought, and to free ourselves from this fearful dread we should use all our wits and all our efforts, not stick our heads in the sand of some idiotic joke, or still more idiotic don't-mention-it. The fearful thought of the consequences of syphilis, or of any sexual disease, upon the unborn gives a shock to the impetus of fatherhood in any man, even the cleanest. Our consciousness is a strange thing, and the knowledge of a certain fact may wound it mortally, even if the fact does not touch us directly. And so I am certain that *some* of Shakespeare's father-murder complex, *some* of Hamlet's horror of his mother, of his uncle, of all old men came from the feeling that fathers may transmit syphilis, or syphilis-consequences, to children. I don't know even whether Shakespeare was actually aware of the consequences to a child born of a syphilitic father or mother. He may not have been, though most probably he was. But he certainly was aware of the effects of syphilis itself, especially on men. And this awareness struck at his deep sex imagination, at his instinct for fatherhood, and brought in an element of terror and abhorrence there where men should feel anything but terror and abhorrence, into the procreative act.

The terror-horror element which had entered the imagination with regard to the sexual and procreative act was at least partly responsible for the rise of Puritanism, the beheading of the king-father Charles,* and the establishment of the New England colonies. If America really sent us syphilis, she got back the full recoil of the horror of it, in her puritanism.

But deeper even than this, the terror-horror element led to the crippling of the consciousness of man. Very elementary in man is his sexual and procreative being, and on his sexual and procreative being depend many of his deepest instincts and the flow of his intuition. A deep instinct of kinship joins men together, and the kinship of flesh-and-blood keeps the warm flow of intuitional awareness streaming between human beings. Our true awareness of one another is intuitional, not mental. Attraction between people is really instinctive and intuitional, not an affair of judgment. And in mutual attraction lies perhaps the deepest pleasure in life, mutual attraction which may make us 'like' our travelling companion for the two or three hours we are together, then no more; or mutual attraction that may deepen to powerful love, and last a life-time.

The terror-horror element struck a blow at our feeling of physical communion. In fact, it almost killed it. We have become ideal beings, creatures that exist in idea, to one another, rather than flesh-and-blood kin. And with the collapse of the feeling of physical, flesh-and-blood kinship, and the substitution of our ideal, social or political oneness, came the failing of our intuitive awareness, and the great unease, the *nervousness* of mankind. We are *afraid* of the instincts. We are *afraid* of the intuition within us. We suppress the instincts, and we cut off our intuitional awareness from one another and from the world. The reason being some great shock to the procreative self. Now we know one another only as ideal or social or political entities, fleshless, bloodless, and cold, like Bernard Shaw's creatures. Intuitively we are dead to one another, we have all gone cold.

But by intuition alone can man *really* be aware of man, or of the living, substantial world. By intuition alone can man live and know either woman or world, and by intuition alone can he bring forth again images of magic awareness which we call art. In the past men brought forth images of magic awareness, and now it is the convention to admire these images. The convention says, for example, we must admire Botticelli or Giorgione, so Baedeker* stars the pictures, and we admire them. But it is all a fake. Even those that get a thrill, even when they call it ecstasy, from these old pictures are only undergoing cerebral excitation. Their deeper responses, down in the intuitive and instinctive body, are not touched. They cannot be, because they are dead. A dead intuitive body stands there and gazes at the corpse of beauty: and usually it is completely and honestly bored. Sometimes it feels a mental coruscation which it calls an ecstasy or an aesthetic response.

Modern people, but particularly English and Americans, *cannot* feel anything with the whole imagination. They can see the living body of imagery as little as a blind man can see colour. The imaginative vision, which includes physical, intuitional perception, they *have not got*. Poor things, it is dead in them. And they stand in front of a Botticelli Venus, which they know as conventionally 'beautiful', much as a blind man might stand in front of a bunch of roses and pinks and monkey-musk, saying: 'Oh, do tell me which is red; let me feel red! Now let me feel white! Oh, let me feel it! What is this I am feeling? Monkey-musk? Is it white? Oh, do you say it is yellow blotched with orange-brown? Oh, but I can't feel it! What *can* it be? Is white velvety, or just silky?'

So the poor blind man! Yet he may have an acute perception of alive beauty. Merely by touch and scent, his intuitions being alive, the blind man may have a genuine and soul-satisfying experience of imagery. But not pictorial images. These are for ever beyond him.

So those poor English and Americans in front of the Botticelli Venus.* They stare so hard; they do so *want* to see. And their eyesight is perfect. But all they can see is a sort of nude woman on a sort of shell on a sort of pretty greenish water. As a rule they rather dislike the 'unnaturalness' or 'affectation' of it. If they are high-brows they may get a little self-conscious thrill of aesthetic excitement. But real imaginative awareness, which is so largely physical, is denied them. *Ils n'ont pas de quoi,** as the Frenchman said of the angels, when asked if they made love in heaven.

Ah, the dear high-brows who gaze in a sort of ecstasy and get a correct mental thrill! Their poor high-brow bodies stand there as dead as dust-bins, and can no more feel the sway of complete imagery upon them than they can feel any other real sway. *Ils n'ont pas de quoi.* The instincts and the intuitions are so nearly dead in them, and they fear even the feeble remains. Their fear of the instincts and intuitions is even greater than that of the English Tommy who calls: 'Eh, Jack! Come an' look at this girl standin' wi' no clothes on, an' two blokes spittin' at 'er.' That is his vision of Botticelli's Venus. It is, for him, complete, for he is void of the image-seeing imagination. But at least he doesn't have to work up a cerebral excitation, as the high-brow does, who is really just as void.

All alike, cultured and uncultured, they are still dominated by that unnamed, yet overmastering dread and hate of the instincts deep in the body, dread of the strange intuitional awareness of the body, dread of anything but ideas, which *can't* contain bacteria. And the dread all works back to a dread of the procreative body, and is partly traceable to the shock of the awareness of syphilis.

The dread of the instincts included the dread of intuitional awareness. 'Beauty is a snare'—'Beauty is but skin-deep'—'Handsome is as handsome does'—'Looks don't count'—'Don't judge by appearances'—if we only realized it, there are thousands of these vile proverbs which have been dinned into us for over two hundred years. They are all of them false. Beauty is not a snare, nor is it skin-deep, since it always involves a certain loveliness of modelling, and handsome doers are often ugly and objectionable people, and if you ignore the look of the thing you plaster England with slums and produce at last a state of spiritual depression that is suicidal, and if you don't judge by appearances, that is, if you can't trust the impression which things make on you, you are a fool. But all these base-born proverbs, born in the cash-box, hit direct against the intuitional consciousness. Naturally, man gets a great deal of his life's satisfaction from beauty, from a certain sensuous pleasure in the look of the thing. The old Englishman built his hut of a cottage with a childish joy in its appearance, purely intuitional and direct. The modern Englishman has a few borrowed ideas, simply doesn't know *what* to feel, and makes a silly mess of it: though perhaps he is improving, hopefully, in this field of architecture and housebuilding. The intuitional faculty, which alone relates us in direct awareness to physical things and substantial presences, is atrophied and dead, and we don't know *what* to feel. We know we ought to feel something, but what?—Oh, tell us what! And this is true of all nations, the French and Italians as much as the English. Look at new French suburbs! Go through the crockery and furniture departments in the *Dames de France* or any big shop. The blood in the body stands still, before such *crétin** ugliness. One has to decide that the modern bourgeois is a *crétin*.

This movement against the instincts and the intuition took on a moral tone in all countries. It started in hatred. Let us never forget that modern morality has its roots in hatred, a deep, evil hate of the instinctive, intuitional, procreative body. This hatred is made more virulent by fear, and an extra poison is added to the fear by unconscious horror of syphilis. And so we come to modern bourgeois consciousness, which turns upon the secret poles of fear and hate. That is the real pivot of all bourgeois consciousness in all countries: fear and hate of the instinctive, intuitional, procreative body in man or woman. But of course this fear and hate had to take on a righteous appearance, so it became moral, said that the instincts, intuitions and all the activities of the procreative body were evil, and promised a *reward* for their suppression. That is the great clue to bourgeois psychology: the reward business. It is screamingly obvious in Maria Edgeworth's tales,* which must have done unspeakable damage to ordinary people. Be good, and you'll have money. Be wicked, and you'll be utterly penniless at last, and the good ones will have to offer you a little charity. This is sound working morality in the world. And it makes one realize that, even to Milton, the true hero of *Paradise Lost* must be Satan.* But by this baited morality the masses were caught and enslaved to industrialism before ever they knew it; the good got hold of the goods, and our modern 'civilization' of money, machines, and wage-slaves was inaugurated. The very pivot of it, let us never forget, being fear and hate, the most intimate fear and hate, fear and hate of one's own instinctive, intuitive body, and fear and hate of every other man's and every other woman's warm, procreative body and imagination.

Now it is obvious what result this will have on the plastic arts, which depend entirely on the representation of substantial bodies, and on the intuitional perception of the *reality* of substantial bodies. The reality of substantial bodies can only be perceived by the imagination, and the imagination is a kindled state of consciousness in which intuitive awareness predominates. The plastic arts are all imagery, and imagery is the body of our imaginative life, and our imaginative life is a great joy and fulfilment to us, for the imagination is a more powerful and more comprehensive flow of consciousness than our ordinary flow. In the flow of true imagination we know in full, mentally and physically at once, in a greater, enkindled awareness. At the maximum of our imagination we are religious. And if we deny our imagination, and have no imaginative life, we are poor worms who have never lived.

In the seventeenth and eighteenth centuries we have the deliberate denial of intuitive awareness, and we see the results on the arts. Vision became more optical, less intuitive and painting began to flourish. But what painting! Watteau, Ingres, Poussin, Chardin* have some real imaginative glow still. They are still somewhat free. The puritan and the intellectual has not yet struck them down with his fear and hate obsession. But look at England! Hogarth, Reynolds, Gainsborough,* they all are already bourgeois. The coat is really more important than the man. It is amazing how important clothes suddenly become, how they *cover* the subject. An old Reynolds colonel in a red uniform is much more a uniform than an individual, and as for Gainsborough, all one can say is: What a lovely dress and hat! What really expensive Italian silk! This painting of garments continued in vogue, till pictures like Sargent's* seem to be nothing but yards and yards of satin from the most expensive shops, having some pretty head popped on the top. The imagination is quite dead. The optical vision, a sort of flashy coloured photography of the eye, is rampant.

In Titian, in Velasquez,* in Rembrandt the people are there inside their clothes all right, and the clothes are imbued with the life of the individual, the gleam of the warm procreative body comes through all the time, even if it be an old, half-blind woman or a weird, ironic little Spanish princess. But modern people are nothing inside their garments, and a head sticks out at the top and hands stick out of the sleeves, and it is a bore. Or, as in Lawrence or Raeburn,* you have something very pretty but almost a mere cliché, with very little instinctive or intuitional perception to it.

After this, and apart from landscape and water-colour, there is strictly no English painting that exists. As far as I am concerned, the pre-Raphaelites don't exist; Watts doesn't, Sargent doesn't, and none of the moderns.

There is the exception of Blake. Blake is the only painter of imaginative pictures, apart from landscape, that England has produced. And unfortunately there is so little Blake, and even in that little the symbolism is often artificially imposed. Nevertheless, Blake paints with real intuitional awareness and solid instinctive feeling. He dares handle the human body, even if he sometimes makes it a mere ideograph. And no other Englishman has even dared handle it with alive imagination. Painters of composition-pictures in England, of whom perhaps the best is Watts, never quite get beyond the level of cliché, sentimentalism, and *funk*. Even Watts is a failure, though he made some sort of try: even Etty's nudes in York fail imaginatively, though they have some feeling for flesh. And the rest, the Leightons,* even the moderns don't really do anything. They never get beyond studio models and clichés of the nude. The image never gets across to us, to seize us intuitively. It remains merely optical.

Landscape, however, is different. Here the English exist and hold their own. But, for me, personally, landscape is always waiting for something to occupy it. Landscape seems to be *meant* as a background to an intenser vision of life, so to my feeling painted landscape is background with the real subject left out.

Nevertheless, it can be very lovely, especially in water-colour, which is a more bodiless medium, and doesn't aspire to very substantial existence, and is so small that it doesn't try to make a very deep seizure on the consciousness. Water-colour will always be more of a statement than an experience.

And landscape, on the whole, is the same. It doesn't call up the more powerful responses of the human imagination, the sensual, passional responses. Hence it is the favourite modern form of expression in painting. There is no deep conflict. The instinctive and intuitional consciousness is called into play, but lightly, superficially. It is not confronted with any living, procreative body.

Hence the English have delighted in landscape, and have succeeded in it well. It is a form of escape for them, from the actual human body they so hate and fear, and it is an outlet for their perishing aesthetic desires. For more than a century we have produced delicious water-colours, and Wilson, Crome, Constable, Turner* are all great landscape-painters. Some of Turner's landscape compositions are, to my feelings, among the finest that exist. They still satisfy me more even than Van Gogh's or Cézanne's landscapes, which make a more violent assault on the emotions, and repel a little for that reason. Somehow I don't want landscape to make a violent assault on my feelings. Landscape is background with the figures left out or reduced to minimum, so let it stay back. Van Gogh's surging earth and Cézanne's explosive or rattling planes worry me. Not being profoundly interested in landscape, I prefer it to be rather quiet and unexplosive.

But, of course, the English delight in landscape is a delight in escape. It is always the same. The northern races are so innerly afraid of their own bodily existence, which they believe fantastically to be an evil thing—you could never find them feel anything but uneasy shame, or an equally shameful gloating, over the fact that a man was having intercourse with his wife, in his house next door—that all they cry for is an escape. And, especially, art must provide that escape.

It is easy in literature. Shelley is pure escape: the body is sublimated into sublime gas. Keats is more difficult—the body can still be *felt* dissolving in waves of successive death—but the death-business is very satisfactory. The novelists have even a better time. You can get some of the lasciviousness of Hetty Sorrell's 'sin', and you can enjoy condemning her to penal servitude for life. You can thrill to Mr Rochester's *passion,* and you can enjoy having his eyes burnt out.* So it is, all the way: the novel of 'passion'!

But in paint it is more difficult. You cannot paint Hetty Sorrell's sin or Mr Rochester's passion without being really shocking. And you *daren't* be shocking. It was this fact that unsaddled Watts and Millais.* Both might have been painters if they hadn't been Victorians. As it is, each of them is a wash-out.

Which is the poor, feeble history of art in England, since we can lay no claim to the great Holbein. And art on the continent, in the last century? It is more interesting, and has a fuller story. An artist *can* only create what he really religiously *feels* is truth, religious truth really *felt*, in the blood and the bones. The English could never think anything connected with the body *religious*—unless it were the eyes. So they painted the social appearance of human beings, and hoped to give them wonderful eyes. But they *could* think landscape religious, since it had no sensual reality. So they felt religious about it and painted it as well as it could be painted, maybe, from their point of view.

And in France? In France it was more or less the same, but with a difference. The French, being more rational, decided that the body had its place, but that it should be rationalized. The Frenchman of today has the most reasonable and rationalized body possible. His conception of sex is basically hygienic. A certain amount of copulation is good for you. *Ça fait du bien au corps!** sums up the physical side of a Frenchman's idea of love, marriage, food, sport, and all the rest. Well, it is more sane, anyhow, than the Anglo-Saxon terrors. The Frenchman is afraid of syphilis and afraid of the procreative body, but not quite so deeply. He has known for a long time that you can take precautions. And he is not profoundly imaginative.

Therefore he has been able to paint. But his tendency, just like that of all the modern world, has been to get away from the body, while still paying attention to its hygiene, and still not violently quarrelling with it. Puvis de Chavannes* is really as sloppy as all the other spiritual sentimentalizers. Renoir is jolly: *ça fait du bien au corps!* is his attitude to the flesh. If a woman didn't have buttocks and breasts, she wouldn't be paintable, he said, and he was right. *Ça fait du bien au corps!* What do you paint with, Maître— With my penis,* and be damned! Renoir didn't try to get away from the body. But he had to dodge it in some of its aspects, rob it of its natural terrors, its natural demonishness. He is delightful, but a trifle banal. *Ça fait du bien au corps!* Yet how infinitely much better he is than any English equivalent.

Courbet, Daumier, Dégas, they all painted the human body. But Daumier satirized it, Courbet saw it as a toiling thing, Dégas saw it as a wonderful instrument.* They all of them deny it its finest qualities, its deepest instincts, its purest intuitions. They prefer, as it were, to industrialize it. They deny it the best imaginative existence.

And the real grand glamour of modern French art, the real outburst of delight came when the body was at last dissolved of its substance, and made part and parcel of the sunlight-and-shadow scheme. Let us say what we will, but the real grand thrill of modern French art was the discovery of light, the discovery of light, and all the subsequent discoveries of the impressionists, and of the post-impressionists, even Cézanne. No matter how Cézanne may have reacted from the impressionists, it was they, with their deliriously joyful discovery of light and 'free' colour, who really opened his eyes. Probably the most joyous moment in the whole history of painting was the moment when the incipient impressionists discovered light, and with it, colour. Ah, then they made the grand, grand escape into freedom, into infinity, into light and delight. They escaped from the tyranny of solidity and the menace of mass-form. They escaped, they escaped from the dark procreative body which so haunts a man, they escaped into the open air, *plein air* and *plein soleil:** light and almost ecstasy.

Like every other human escape, it meant being hauled back later with the tail between the legs. Back comes the truant, back to the old doom of matter, of corporate existence, of the body sullen and stubborn and obstinately refusing to be transmuted into pure light, pure colour, or pure anything. It is not concerned with purity. Life isn't. Chemistry and mathematics and ideal religion are, but these are only small bits of life, which is itself bodily, and hence neither pure nor impure.

After the grand escape into impressionism and pure light, pure colour, pure bodilessness—for what is the body but a shimmer of lights and colours!—poor art came home truant and sulky, with its tail between its legs. And it is this return which now interests us. We know the escape was illusion, illusion, illusion. The cat had to come back. So now we despise the 'light' blighters too much. We haven't a good word for them. Which is nonsense, for they too are wonderful, even if their escape was into *le grand néant*, the great nowhere.

But the cat came back. And it is the home-coming tom that now has our sympathy: Renoir, to a certain extent, but mostly Cézanne, the sublime little grimalkin, who is followed by Matisse and

Gauguin and Derain and Vlaminck and Braque* and all the host of other defiant and howling cats that have come back, perforce, to form and substance and *thereness,* instead of delicious nowhereness.

Without wishing to labour the point, one cannot help being amused at the dodge by which the impressionists made the grand escape from the body. They metamorphosed it into a pure assembly of shifting lights and shadows, all coloured. A web of woven, luminous colour was a man, or a woman—and so they painted her, or him: a web of woven shadows and gleams. Delicious! and quite true as far as it goes. A purely optical, *visual* truth: which paint is supposed to be. And they painted delicious pictures: a little too delicious. They bore us, at the moment. They bore people like the very modern critics intensely. But very modern critics need not be so intensely bored. There is something very lovely about the good impressionist pictures. And ten years hence critics will be bored by the present run of post-impressionists, though not so passionately bored, for these post-impressionists don't move us as the impressionists moved our fathers. We have to persuade ourselves, and we have to persuade one another to be impressed by the post-impressionists, on the whole. On the whole, they rather depress us. Which is perhaps good for us.

But modern art criticism is in a curious hole. Art has suddenly gone into rebellion, against all the canons of accepted religion, accepted good form, accepted everything. When the cat came back from the delicious impressionist excursion, it came back rather tattered, but bristling and with its claws out. The glorious escape was all an illusion. There *was* substance still in the world, a thousand times be damned to it! There *was* the body, the great lumpy body. There it was. You had it shoved down your throat. What really existed was lumps, lumps. Then paint 'em. Or else paint the thin 'spirit' with gaps in it and looking merely dishevelled and 'found out'. Paint had found the spirit out.

This is the sulky and rebellious mood of the post-impressionists. They still hate the body—hate it. But, in a rage, they admit its existence, and paint it as huge lumps, tubes, cubes, planes, volumes, spheres, cones, cylinders, all the 'pure' or mathematical forms of substance. As for landscape, it comes in for some of the same rage. It has also suddenly gone lumpy. Instead of being nice and ethereal and non-sensual, it was discovered by Van

Gogh to be heavily, overwhelmingly substantial and sensual. Van Gogh took up landscape in heavy spadefuls. And Cézanne had to admit it. Landscape, too, after being, since Claude Lorrain,* a thing of pure luminosity and floating shadow, suddenly exploded, and came tumbling back on to the canvases of artists in lumps. With Cézanne, landscape 'crystallized', to use one of the favourite terms of the critics, and it has gone on crystallizing into cubes, cones, pyramids, and so forth ever since.

The impressionists brought the world at length, after centuries of effort, into the delicious oneness of light. At last, at last! Hail, holy Light!* the great natural One, the universal, the universalizer! We are not divided, all one body we—one in Light, lovely light! No sooner had this paean gone up than the post-impressionists, like Judas, gave the show away. They exploded the illusion, which fell back to the canvas of art in a chaos of lumps.

This new chaos, of course, needed new apologists, who therefore rose up in hordes to apologize, almost, for the new chaos. They felt a little guilty about it, so they took on new notes of effrontery, defiant as any Primitive Methodists, which, indeed, they are: the Primitive Methodists* of art criticism. These evangelical gentlemen at once ran up their chapels, in a Romanesque or Byzantine shape, as was natural for a primitive and a methodist, and started to cry forth their doctrines in the decadent wilderness. They discovered once more that the aesthetic experience was an ecstasy, an ecstasy granted only to the chosen few, the elect, among whom said critics were, of course, the arch-elect. This was outdoing Ruskin. It was almost Calvin* come to art. But let scoffers scoff, the aesthetic ecstasy was vouchsafed only to the few, the elect, and even then only when they had freed their minds of false doctrine. They had renounced the mammon of 'subject' in pictures, they went whoring no more after the Babylon of painted 'interest', nor did they hanker after the flesh-pots of artistic 'representation'. Oh, purify yourselves, ye who would know the aesthetic ecstasy, and be lifted up to the 'white peaks of artistic inspiration'. Purify yourselves of all base hankering for a tale that is told, and of all low lust for likenesses. Purify yourselves, and know the one supreme way, the way of Significant Form.* I am the revelation and the way! I am Significant Form, and my unutterable name is Reality. Lo, I am Form and I am Pure, behold, I am Pure

Form. I am the revelation of Spiritual Life, moving behind the veil. I come forth and make myself known, and I am Pure Form, behold, I am Significant Form.

So the prophets of the new era in art cry aloud to the multitude, in exactly the jargon of the revivalists, for revivalists they are. They will revive the Primitive Method-brethren, the Byzantines, the Ravennese,* the early Italian and French primitives (which ones, in particular, we aren't told); these were Right, these were Pure, these were Spiritual, these were Real! And the builders of early Romanesque churches, O my brethren! these were holy men, before the world went a-whoring after Gothic. Oh, return, my brethren, to the Primitive Method. Lift up your eyes to Significant Form, and be saved.

Now myself, brought up a nonconformist as I was, I just was never able to understand the language of salvation. I never knew what they were talking about, when they raved about being saved, and safe in the arms of Jesus, and Abraham's bosom, and seeing the great light, and entering into glory: I just was puzzled, for what did it *mean*? It seemed to work out as a getting rather drunk on your own self-importance, and afterwards coming dismally sober again and being rather unpleasant. That was all I could see in actual experience of the entering-into-glory business. The term itself, like something which ought to mean something but somehow doesn't, stuck on my mind like an irritating bur, till I decided that it was just an artificial stimulant to the individual self-conceit. How could I enter into glory, when glory is just an abstraction of a human state, and not a separate reality at all? If glory means anything at all, it means the thrill a man gets when a great many people look up to him with mixed awe, reverence, delight. Today, it means Rudolph Valentino.* So that the cant about entering into glory is just used fuzzily to enhance the individual sense of self-importance—one of the rather cheap cocaine-phrases.

And I'm afraid 'aesthetic ecstasy' sounds to me very much the same, especially when accompanied by exhortations. It so sounds like another great uplift into self-importance, another apotheosis of personal conceit; especially when accompanied by a lot of jargon about the pure world of reality existing behind the veil of this vulgar world of accepted appearances, and of the entry of the elect through the doorway of visual art. Too evangelical altogether, too much chapel and Primitive Methodist, too obvious a trick for advertising one's own self-glorification. The ego, as an American says, shuts itself up and paints the inside of the walls sky-blue, and thinks it is in heaven.

And then the great symbols of this salvation. When the evangelical says: Behold the lamb of God!—what on earth does he want one to behold? Are we invited to look at a lamb, with woolly, muttony appearance, frisking and making its little pills? Awfully nice, but what *has* it got to do with God or my soul? Or the cross? What *do* they expect us to see in the cross? A sort of gallows? Or the mark we use to cancel a mistake?—cross it out! That the cross by itself was supposed to *mean* something always mystified me. The same with the Blood of the Lamb.—Washed in the Blood of the Lamb! always seemed to me an extremely unpleasant suggestion. And when Jerome* says: He who has once washed in the blood of Jesus need never wash again!—I feel like taking a hot bath at once, to wash off even the suggestion.

And I find myself equally mystified by the cant phrases like Significant Form and Pure Form. They are as mysterious to me as the Cross and the Blood of the Lamb. They are just the magic jargon of invocation, nothing else. If you want to invoke an aesthetic ecstasy, stand in front of a Matisse and whisper fervently under your breath: 'Significant Form! Significant Form!' and it will come. It sounds to me like a form of masturbation, an attempt to make the body react to some cerebral formula.

No, I am afraid modern criticism has done altogether too much for modern art. If painting survives this outburst of ecstatic evangelicism, which it will, it is because people do come to their senses, even after the silliest vogue.

And so we can return to modern French painting, without having to quake before the bogy, or the Holy Ghost of Significant Form: a bogy which doesn't exist if we don't mind leaving aside our self-importance when we look at a picture.

The actual fact is that in Cézanne modern French art made its first tiny step back to real substance, to objective substance, if we may call it so. Van Gogh's earth was still subjective earth, himself projected into the earth. But Cézanne's apples are a real attempt to let the apple exist in its own separate entity, without transfusing it with personal emotion. Cézanne's great effort was, as it were, to shove the apple away from him, and let it live of itself. It seems a small thing to do: yet it is the first real sign that man has made for several thousands of years that he is willing to admit that matter *actually* exists. Strange as it may seem, for thousands of years, in short, ever since the mythological 'Fall', man has been preoccupied with the constant preoccupation of the denial of the existence of matter, and the proof that matter is only a form of spirit. And then, the moment it is done, and we realize finally that matter is only a form of energy, whatever that may be, in the same instant matter rises up and hits us over the head and makes us realize that it exists absolutely, since it is compact energy itself.

Cézanne felt it in paint, when he felt for the apple. Suddenly he felt the tyranny of mind, the white, worn-out arrogance of the spirit, the mental consciousness, the enclosed ego in its sky-blue heaven self-painted. He felt the sky-blue prison. And a great conflict started inside him. He was dominated by his old mental consciousness, but he wanted terribly to escape the domination. He wanted to *express* what he suddenly, convulsedly knew! the existence of matter. He terribly wanted to paint the real existence of the body, to make it artistically palpable. But he couldn't. He hadn't got there yet. And it was the torture of his life. He wanted to be himself in his own procreative body—and he couldn't. He was, like all the rest of us, so intensely and exclusively a mental creature, or a spiritual creature, or an egoist, that he could no longer identify himself with his intuitive body. He wanted to, terribly. At first he determined to do it by sheer bravado and braggadocio. But no good; it couldn't be done that way. He had, as one critic says, to become humble. But it wasn't a question of becoming humble. It was a question of abandoning his cerebral conceit and his 'willed ambition'* and coming down to brass tacks. Poor Cézanne, there he is in his self-portraits, even the early showy ones, peeping out like a mouse and saying: I *am* a man of flesh, am I not? For he was not quite, as none of us are. The man of flesh has been slowly destroyed through centuries, to give place to the man of spirit, the mental man, the ego, the self-conscious I. And in his artistic soul Cézanne knew it, and wanted to rise in the flesh. He couldn't do it, and it embittered him. Yet, with his apple, he did shove the stone from the door of the tomb.*

He wanted to be a man of flesh, a real man: to get out of the sky-blue prison into real air. He wanted to live, really live in the body, to know the world through his instincts and his intuitions, and to be himself in his procreative blood, not in his mere mind and spirit. He wanted it, he wanted it terribly. And whenever he tried, his mental consciousness, like a cheap fiend, interfered. If he wanted to paint a woman, his mental consciousness simply overpowered him and wouldn't let him paint the woman of flesh, the first Eve who lived before any of the fig-leaf nonsense. He couldn't do it. If he wanted to paint people intuitively and instinctively, he couldn't do it. His mental concepts shoved in front, and these he *wouldn't* paint—mere representations of what the *mind* accepts, not what the intuitions gather—and they, his mental concepts, wouldn't let him paint from intuition; they shoved in between all the time, so he painted his conflict and his failure, and the result is almost ridiculous.

Woman he was not allowed to know by intuition; his mental self, his ego, that bloodless fiend, forbade him. Man, other men, he was likewise not allowed to know—except by a few, few touches. The earth likewise he was not allowed to know: his landscapes are mostly acts of rebellion against the mental concept of landscape. After a fight tooth-and-nail for forty years, he did succeed in knowing an apple, fully; and, not quite as fully, a jug or two. That was all he achieved.

It seems little, and he died embittered. But it is the first step that counts, and Cézanne's apple is a great deal, more than Plato's Idea.* Cézanne's apple rolled the stone from the mouth of the tomb, and if poor Cézanne couldn't unwind himself from his cerements and mental winding-sheet, but had to lie still in the tomb, till he died, still he gave us a chance.

The history of our era is the nauseating and repulsive history of the crucifixion of the procreative body for the glorification of the spirit, the mental consciousness. Plato was an arch-priest of this crucifixion. Art, that handmaid, humbly and honestly served the vile deed, through three thousand years at least. The Renaissance put the spear through the side of the already crucified body, and syphilis put poison into the wound made by the imaginative spear. It took still three hundred years for the body to finish: but in the eighteenth century it became a corpse, a corpse with an abnormally active mind: and today it stinketh.*

We, dear reader, you and I, we were born corpses, and we are corpses. I doubt if there is even one of us who has ever known so much as an apple, a whole apple. All we know is shadows, even of apples. Shadows of everything, of the whole world, shadows even of ourselves. We are inside the tomb, and the tomb is wide and shadowy like hell, even if sky-blue by optimistic paint, so we think it is all the world. But our world is a wide tomb full of ghosts, replicas. We are all spectres, we have not been able to touch even so much as an apple. Spectres we are to one another. Spectre you are to me, spectre I am to you. Shadow you are even to yourself. And by shadow I mean idea, concept, the abstracted reality, the ego. We are not solid. We don't live in the flesh. Our instincts and intuitions are dead, we live wound round with the winding-sheet of abstraction. And the touch of anything solid hurts us. For our instincts and intuitions, which are our feelers of touch and knowing through touch, they are dead, amputated. We walk and talk and eat and copulate and laugh and evacuate wrapped in our winding-sheets, all the time wrapped in our winding-sheets.

So that Cézanne's apple hurts. It made people shout with pain. And it was not till his followers had turned him again into an abstraction that he was ever accepted. Then the critics stepped forth and abstracted his good apple into Significant Form, and henceforth Cézanne was saved. Saved for democracy. Put safely in the tomb again, and the stone rolled back. The resurrection was postponed once more.

As the resurrection will be postponed *ad infinitum* by the good bourgeois corpses in their cultured winding-sheets. They will run up a chapel to the risen body, even if it is only an apple, and kill it on the spot. They are wide awake, are the corpses, on the alert. And a poor mouse of a Cézanne is alone in the years. Who else shows a spark of awakening life, in our marvellous civilized cemetery? All is dead, and dead breath preaching with phosphorescent effulgence about aesthetic ecstasy and Significant Form. If only the dead would bury their dead.* But the dead are not dead for nothing. Who buries his own sort? The dead are cunning and alert to pounce on any spark of life and bury *it*, even as they have already buried Cézanne's apple and put up to it a white tombstone of Significant Form.

For who of Cézanne's followers does anything but follow at the triumphant funeral of Cézanne's achievement? They follow him in order to bury him, and they succeed. Cézanne is deeply buried under all the Matisses and Vlamincks of his following, while the critics read the funeral homily.

It is quite easy to accept Matisse and Vlaminck and Friesz* and all the rest. They are just Cézanne abstracted again. They are all just tricksters, even if clever ones. They are all mental, mental, egoists, egoists, egoists. And therefore they are all acceptable now to the enlightened corpses of connoisseurs. You needn't be afraid of Matisse and Vlaminck and the rest. They will never give your corpse-anatomy a jar. They are just shadows, minds mounte-banking and playing charades on canvas. They may be quite amusing charades, and I am all for the mountebank. But of course it is all games inside the cemetery, played by corpses and *hommes d'esprit*, even *femmes d'esprit*, like Mademoiselle Laurencin.* As for *l'esprit*, said Cézanne, I don't give a fart for it. Perhaps not! But the connoisseurs will give large sums of money. Trust the dead to pay for their amusement, when the amusement is deadly!

The most interesting figure in modern art, and the only really interesting figure, is Cézanne: and that, not so much because of his achievement as because of his struggle. Cézanne was born at Aix in Provence in 1839: small, timorous, yet sometimes bantam defiant, sensitive, full of grand ambition, yet ruled still deeper by a naïve, Mediterranean sense of truth or reality, imagination, call it what you will. He is not a big figure. Yet his struggle is truly heroic. He was a bourgeois, and one must never forget it. He had a moderate bourgeois income. But a bourgeois in Provence is much more real and human than a bourgeois in Normandy. He is much nearer the actual people, and the actual people are much less subdued by awe of his respectable bourgeois money.

Cézanne was naïve to a degree, but not a fool. He was rather in-significant, and grandeur impressed him terribly. Yet still stronger in him was the little flame of life where he *felt* things to be true. He didn't betray himself in order to get success, because he couldn't: to his nature it was impossible: he was too pure to be able to betray his own small real flame for immediate rewards. Perhaps that is the best one can say of a man, and it puts Cézanne, small and in-significant as he is, among the heroes. He would *not* abandon his own vital imagination.

He was terribly impressed by physical splendour and flamboyancy, as people usually are in the lands of the sun. He admired terribly the splendid virtuosity of Paul Veronese and Tintoretto*, and even of later and less good baroque painters. He wanted to be like that—terribly he wanted it. And he tried very, very hard, with bitter effort. And he always failed. It is a cant phrase with the critics to say 'he couldn't draw'. Mr Fry* says: 'With all his rare endowments, he happened to lack the comparatively common gift of illustration, the gift that any draughtsman for the illustrated papers learns in a school of commercial art.'

Now this sentence gives away at once the hollowness of modern criticism. In the first place, can one learn a 'gift' in a school of commercial art, or anywhere else? A gift surely is given, we tacitly assume, by God or Nature or whatever higher power we hold responsible for the things we have no choice in.

Was, then, Cézanne devoid of this gift? Was he simply incapable of drawing a cat so that it would look like a cat? Nonsense! Cézanne's work is full of accurate drawing. His more trivial pictures, suggesting copies from other masters, are perfectly well drawn—that is, conventionally: so are some of the landscapes, so even is that portrait of M. Geffroy and his books,* which is, or was, so famous. Why these cant phrases about not being able to draw? Of course Cézanne could draw, as well as anybody else. And he had learned everything that was necessary in the art-schools.

He *could* draw. And yet, in his terrifically earnest compositions in the late Renaissance or baroque manner, he drew so badly. Why? Not because he couldn't. And not because he was sacrificing 'significant form' to 'insignificant form', or mere slick representation, which is apparently what artists themselves mean when they talk about drawing. Cézanne knew all about drawing: and he surely knew as much as his critics do about significant form. Yet he neither succeeded in drawing so that things looked right, nor combining his shapes so that he achieved real form. He just failed.

He failed, where one of his little slick successors would have succeeded with one eye shut. And why? Why did Cézanne fail in his early pictures? Answer that, and you'll know a little better what art is. He didn't fail because he understood nothing about drawing or significant form or aesthetic ecstasy. He knew about them all, and didn't give a spit for them.

Cézanne failed in his earlier pictures because he was trying with his mental consciousness to do something which his living Provençal body didn't want to do, or couldn't do. He terribly wanted to do something grand and voluptuous and sensuously satisfying, in the Tintoretto manner. Mr Fry calls that his 'willed ambition', which is a good phrase, and says he had to learn humility, which is a bad phrase.

The 'willed ambition' was more than a mere willed ambition—it was a genuine desire. But it was a desire that thought it would be satisfied by ready-made baroque expressions, whereas it needed to achieve a whole new marriage of mind and matter. If we believed in reincarnation, then we should have to believe that after a certain number of new incarnations into the body of an artist, the soul of Cézanne *would* produce grand and voluptuous and sensually rich pictures—but not at all in the baroque manner. Because the pictures he actually did produce with undeniable success are the first steps in that direction, sensual and rich, with not the slightest hint of baroque, but new, the man's new grasp of substantial reality.

There was, then, a certain discrepancy between Cézanne's *notion* of what he wanted to produce, and his other, intuitive knowledge of what he *could* produce. For whereas the mind works in possibilities, the intuitions work in actualities, and what you *intuitively* desire, that is possible to you. Whereas what you mentally or 'consciously' desire is nine times out of ten impossible: hitch your wagon to a star, and you'll just stay where you are.

So the conflict, as usual, was not between the artist and his medium, but between the artist's *mind* and the artist's *intuition* and *instinct*. And what Cézanne had to learn was not humility—cant word!—but honesty, honesty with himself. It was not a question of any gift or significant form or aesthetic ecstasy: it was a question of Cézanne being himself, just Cézanne. And when Cézanne is himself he is not Tintoretto, nor Veronese, nor anything baroque at all. Yet he is something *physical*, and even sensual: qualities which he had identified with the masters of virtuosity.

In passing, if we think of Henri Matisse, a real virtuoso, and imagine him possessed with a 'willed ambition' to paint grand and flamboyant baroque pictures, then we know at once that he would not have to 'humble' himself at all, but that he would start in and paint with great success grand and flamboyant modern-baroque pictures. He would succeed because he has the gift of virtuosity. And the gift of virtuosity simply means that you don't have to humble yourself, or even be honest with yourself, because you are a clever mental creature who is capable at will of making the intuitions and instincts subserve some mental concept: in short, you can prostitute your body to your mind, your instincts and intuitions you can prostitute to your 'willed ambition', in a sort of masturbation process, and you can produce the impotent glories of virtuosity. But Veronese and Tintoretto are real painters; they are not mere *virtuosi*, as some of the later men are.

The point is very important. Any creative act occupies the whole consciousness of a man. This is true of the great discoveries of science as well as of art. The truly great discoveries of science and real works of art are made by the whole consciousness of man working together in unison and oneness: instinct, intuition, mind, intellect all fused into one complete consciousness, and grasping what we may call a complete truth, or a complete vision, a complete revelation in sound. A discovery, artistic or otherwise, may be more or less intuitional, more or less mental; but intuition will have entered into it, and mind will have entered too. The whole consciousness is concerned in every case.—And a painting requires the activity of the whole imagination, for it is made of imagery, and the imagination is that form of complete consciousness in which predominates the intuitive awareness of forms, images, the *physical* awareness.

And the same applies to the genuine appreciation of a work of art, or the *grasp* of a scientific law, as to the production of the same. The whole consciousness is occupied, not merely the mind alone, or merely the body. The mind and spirit alone can never really grasp a work of art, though they may, in a masturbating fashion, provoke the body into an ecstasized response. The ecstasy will die out into ash and more ash. And the reason we have so many trivial scientists promulgating fantastic 'facts' is that so many modern scientists likewise work with the mind alone, and *force* the intuitions and instincts into a prostituted acquiescence. The very statement that water is H_2O is a mental *tour de force*. With our bodies we know that water is *not* H_2O, our intuitions and instincts both know it is not so. But they are bullied by the impudent mind. Whereas if we said that water, under certain circumstances, produces two volumes of hydrogen and one of oxygen, then the intuitions and instincts would agree entirely. But that water *is composed* of two volumes of hydrogen to one of oxygen we cannot physically believe. It needs something else. Something is missing. Of course, alert science does not ask us to believe the commonplace assertion of: *water* is H_2O, but school children have to believe it.

A parallel case is all this modern stuff about astronomy, stars, their distances and speeds and so on, talking of billions and trillions of miles and years and so forth: it is just occult. The mind is revelling in words, the intuitions and instincts are just left out, or prostituted into a sort of ecstasy. In fact, the sort of ecstasy that lies in absurd figures such as 2,000,000,000,000,000,000,000,000,000,000 miles or years or tons, figures which abound in modern *scientific* books on astronomy, is just the sort of aesthetic ecstasy that the over-mental critics of art assert they experience today from Matisse's pictures. It is all poppycock. The body is either stunned to a corpse, or prostituted to ridiculous thrills, or stands coldly apart.

When I read how far off the suns are, and what they are made of, and so on, and so on, I believe all I am *able* to believe, with the true imagination. But when my intuition and instinct can grasp no more, then I call my mind to a halt. I am not going to accept mere mental asseverations. The mind can assert anything, and pretend it has proved it. My beliefs I test on my body, on my intuitional consciousness, and when I get a response there, then I accept. The same is true of great scientific 'laws', like the law of evolution. After years of acceptance of the 'laws' of evolution—rather desultory or 'humble' acceptance—now I realize that my vital imagination makes great reservations. I find I can't, with the best will in the world, believe that the species have 'evolved' from one common life-form. I just can't feel it, I have to violate my intuitive and instinctive awareness of something else, to make myself believe it. But since I know that my intuitions and instincts may still be held back by prejudice, I seek in the world for someone to make me intuitively and instinctively feel the truth of the 'law'—and I don't find anybody. I find scientists, just like artists, asserting things they are *mentally* sure of, in fact cocksure, but about which they are much too egoistic and ranting to be *intuitively, instinctively* sure. When I find a man, or a woman, intuitively and instinctively sure of anything, I am all respect. But for scientific or artistic braggarts how can one have respect? The intrusion of the egoistic element is a sure proof of intuitive uncertainty. No man who is sure by instinct and intuition *brags*, though he may fight tooth and nail for his beliefs.

Which brings us back to Cézanne, why he couldn't draw, and why he couldn't paint baroque masterpieces. It is just because he was real, and could only believe in his own expression when it expressed a moment of wholeness or completeness of consciousness in himself. He could not prostitute one part of himself to the other. He *could* not masturbate, in paint or words. And that is saying a very great deal, today; today, the great day of the masturbating consciousness, when the mind prostitutes the sensitive responsive body, and just forces the reactions. The masturbating consciousness produces all kinds of novelties, which thrill for the moment, then go very dead. It cannot produce a single genuinely new utterance.

What we have to thank Cézanne for is not his humility, but for his proud, high spirit that refused to accept the glib utterances of his facile mental self. He wasn't poor-spirited enough to be facile— nor humble enough to be satisfied with visual and emotional clichés. Thrilling as the baroque masters were to him in themselves, he realized that as soon as he reproduced them he produced nothing but cliché. The mind is full of all sorts of memory, visual, tactile, emotional memory, memories, groups of memories, systems of memories. A cliché is just a worn-out memory that has no more emotional or intuitional root, and has become a habit. Whereas a novelty is just a new grouping of clichés, a new arrangement of accustomed memories. That is why a novelty is so easily accepted: it gives the little shock or thrill of surprise, but it does not *disturb* the emotional and intuitive self. It forces you to see nothing new. It is only a novel compound of clichés. The work of most of Cézanne's successors is just novel, just a new arrangement of clichés, soon growing stale. And the clichés are Cézanne clichés, just as in Cézanne's own earlier pictures the clichés were all, or mostly, baroque clichés.

Cézanne's early history as a painter is a history of his fight with his own cliché. His consciousness wanted a new realization. And his ready-made mind offered him all the time a ready-made expression. And Cézanne, far too inwardly proud and haughty to accept the ready-made clichés that came from his mental consciousness, stocked with memories, and which appeared mocking at him on his canvas, spent most of his time smashing his own forms to bits. To a true artist, and to the living imagination, the cliché is the deadly enemy. Cézanne had a bitter fight with it. He hammered it to pieces a thousand times. And still it reappeared.

Now again we can see why Cézanne's drawing was so bad. It was bad because it represented a smashed, mauled cliché, terribly knocked about. If Cézanne had been willing to accept his own baroque cliché, his drawing would have been perfectly conventionally 'all right', and not a critic would have had a word to say about it. But when his drawing was conventionally all right, to Cézanne himself it was mockingly all wrong, it was cliché. So he flew at it and knocked all the shape and stuffing out of it, and when it was so mauled that it was all wrong, and he was exhausted with it, he let it go; bitterly, because it still was not what he wanted. And here comes in the comic element in Cézanne's pictures. His rage with the cliché made him distort the cliché sometimes into parody, as we see in pictures like *The Pasha* and *La Femme*.* 'You *will* be cliché, will you?' he gnashes. 'Then *be* it!' And he shoves it in a frenzy of exasperation over into parody. And the sheer exasperation makes the parody still funny; but the laugh is a little on the wrong side of the face.

This smashing of the cliché lasted a long way into Cézanne's life; indeed, it went with him to the end. The way he worked over and over his forms was his nervous manner of laying the ghost of his cliché, burying it. Then when it disappeared perhaps from his forms themselves, it lingered in his composition, and he had to fight with the *edges* of his forms and contours, to bury the ghost there. Only his colour he knew was not cliché. He left it to his disciples to make it so.

In his very best pictures, the best of the still-life compositions, which seem to me Cézanne's greatest achievement, the fight with the cliché is still going on. But it was in the still-life pictures he learned his final method of *avoiding* the cliché: just leaving gaps through which it fell into nothingness. So he makes his landscape succeed.

In his art, all his life long, Cézanne was tangled in a twofold activity. He wanted to express something, and before he could do it he had to fight the hydra-headed cliché, whose last head he could never lop off. The fight with the cliché is the most obvious thing in his pictures. The dust of battle rises thick, and the splinters fly wildly. And it is this dust of battle and flying of splinters which his imitators still so fervently imitate. If you give a Chinese dressmaker a dress to copy, and the dress happens to have a darned rent in it, the dressmaker carefully tears a rent in the new dress, and darns it in exact replica. And this seems to be the chief occupation of Cézanne's disciples, in every land. They absorb themselves reproducing imitation mistakes. He let off various explosions in order to blow up the stronghold of the cliché, and his followers make grand firework imitations of the explosions, without the faintest inkling of the true attack. They do, indeed, make an onslaught on representation, true-to-life representation: because the explosion in Cézanne's pictures blew them up. But I am convinced that what Cézanne himself wanted *was* representation. He *wanted* true-to-life representation. Only he wanted it *more* true to life. And once you have got photography, it is a very, very difficult thing to get representation *more* true-to-life: which it has to be.

Cézanne was a realist, and he wanted to be true to life. But he would not be content with the optical cliché. With the impressionists, purely optical vision perfected itself and fell *at once* into cliché, with a startling rapidity. Cézanne saw this. Artists like Courbet and Daumier were not purely optical, but the other element in these two painters, the intellectual element, was cliché. To the optical vision they added the concept of force-pressure, almost like an hydraulic brake, and this force-pressure concept is mechanical, a cliché, though still popular. And Daumier added mental satire, and Courbet added a touch of a sort of socialism: both cliché and unimaginative.

Cézanne wanted something that was neither optical nor mechanical nor intellectual. And to introduce into our world of vision something which is neither optical nor mechanical nor intellectual-psychological requires a real revolution. It was a revolution Cézanne began, but which nobody, apparently, has been able to carry on.

He wanted to touch the world of substance once more with the intuitive touch, to be aware of it with the intuitive awareness, and to express it in intuitive terms. That is, he wished to displace our present mode of mental-visual consciousness, the consciousness of mental concepts, and substitute a mode of consciousness that was predominantly intuitive, the awareness of touch. In the past the primitives painted intuitively, but *in the direction* of our present mental-visual, conceptual form of consciousness. They were working away from their own intuition. Mankind has never been able to trust the intuitive consciousness, and the decision to accept that trust marks a very great revolution in the course of human development.

Without knowing it, Cézanne, the timid little conventional man sheltering behind his wife and sister and the Jesuit father, was a pure revolutionary. When he said to his models: 'Be an apple! Be an apple!' he was uttering the foreword to the fall not only of Jesuits and the Christian idealists altogether, but to the collapse of our whole way of consciousness, and the substitution of another way. If the human being is going to be primarily an apple, as for Cézanne it was, then you are going to have a new world of men: a world which has very little to say, men that can sit still and just be physically there, and be truly non-moral. That was what Cézanne meant with his: 'Be an apple!' He knew perfectly well that the moment the model began to intrude her personality and her 'mind', it would be cliché and moral, and he would have to paint cliché. The only part of her that was not banal, known *ad nauseam*, living cliché, the only part of her that was not living cliché was her appleyness. Her body, even her very sex, was known, nauseously: *connu,** *connu!* the endless chance of known cause-and-effect, the infinite web of the hated cliché which nets us all down in utter boredom. He knew it all, he hated it all, he refused it all, this timid and 'humble' little man. He knew, as an artist, that the only bit of a woman which nowadays escapes being ready-made and ready-known cliché is the appley part of her. Oh, be an apple, and leave out all your thoughts, all your feelings, all your mind and all your personality, which we know all about and find boring beyond endurance. Leave it all out—and be an apple! It is the appleyness of the portrait of Cézanne's wife that makes it so permanently interesting: the appleyness, which carries with it also the feeling of knowing the other side as well, the side you don't see, the hidden side of the moon. For the intuitive apperception of the apple is so *tangibly* aware of the apple that it is aware of it *all round*, not only just of the front. The eye sees only fronts, and the mind, on the whole, is satisfied with fronts. But intuition needs all-aroundness, and instinct needs insideness. The true imagination is for ever curving round to the other side, to the back of presented appearance.

So to my feeling the portraits of Madame Cézanne, particularly the portrait in the red dress,* are more interesting than the portrait of M. Geffroy, or the portraits of the housekeeper or the gardener. In the same way the *Card-Players** with two figures please me more than those with four.

But we have to remember, in his figure-paintings, that while he was painting the appleyness he was also deliberately painting *out* the so-called humanness, the personality, the 'likeness', the physical cliché. He had deliberately to paint it out, deliberately to make the hands and face rudimentary, and so on, because if he had painted them in fully they would have been cliché. He *never* got over the cliché denominator, the intrusion and interference of the ready-made concept, when it came to people, to men and women. Especially to women he could only give a cliché response—and that maddened him. Try as he might, women remained a known, ready-made cliché object to him, and he *could not* break through the concept obsession to get at the intuitive awareness of her. Except with his wife—and in his wife he did at least know the appleyness. But with his housekeeper he failed somewhat. She was a bit cliché, especially the face. So really is M. Geffroy.

With men Cézanne often dodged it by insisting on the clothes, those stiff cloth jackets bent into thick folds, those hats, those blouses, those curtains. Some of the *Card-Players*, the big ones with four figures, seem just a trifle banal, so much occupied with painted stuff, painted clothing, and the humanness a bit cliché. Nor good colour, nor clever composition, nor 'planes' of colour, nor anything else will save an emotional cliché from being an emotional cliché, though they may, of course, garnish it and make it more interesting.

Where Cézanne did sometimes escape the cliché altogether and really give a complete intuitive interpretation of actual objects is in some of the still-life compositions. To me these good still-life scenes are purely representative and quite true to life. Here Cézanne did what he wanted to do: he made the things quite real, he didn't deliberately leave anything out, and yet he gave us a triumphant and rich intuitive vision of a few apples and kitchen pots. For once his intuitive consciousness triumphed, and broke into utterance. And here he is inimitable. His imitators imitate his accessories of tablecloths folded like tin, etc.—the unreal parts of his pictures—but they don't imitate the pots and apples, because they can't. It's the real appleyness, and you can't imitate it. Every man must create it new and different out of himself: new and different. The moment it looks 'like' Cézanne, it is nothing.

But at the same time Cézanne was triumphing with the apple and appleyness he was still fighting with the cliché. When he makes Madame Cézanne most *still*, most appley, he starts making the universe slip uneasily about her. It was part of his desire: to make the human form, the *life* form, come to rest. Not static—on the contrary. Mobile but come to rest. And at the same time he set the unmoving material world into motion. Walls twitch and slide, chairs bend or rear up a little, cloths curl like burning paper. Cézanne did this partly to satisfy his intuitive feeling that nothing is really *statically* at rest—a feeling he seems to have had strongly—as when he watched the lemons shrivel or go mildewed, in his still-life group, which he left lying there so long so that he *could* see that gradual flux of change: and partly to fight the cliché, which says that the inanimate world *is* static, and that walls *are* still. In his fight with the cliché he denied that walls are still and chairs are static. In his intuitive self he *felt* for their changes.

And these two activities of his consciousness occupy his later landscapes. In the best landscapes we are fascinated by the mysterious *shiftiness* of the scene under our eyes; it shifts about as we watch it. And we realize, with a sort of transport, how intuitively *true* this is of landscape. It is *not* still. It has its own weird anima, and to our wide-eyed perception it changes like a living animal under our gaze. This is a quality that Cézanne sometimes got marvellously.

Then again, in other pictures he seems to be saying: Landscape is not like this and not like this and not like this and not ... etc.— and every *not* is a little blank space in the canvas, defined by the remains of an assertion. Sometimes Cézanne builds up a landscape essentially out of omissions. He puts fringes on the complicated vacuum of the cliché, so to speak, and offers us that. It is interesting in a *repudiative* fashion, but it is not the new thing. The appleyness, the intuition has gone. We have only a mental repudiation. This occupies many of the later pictures: and ecstasizes the critics.

And Cézanne was bitter. He had never, as far as his *life* went, broken through the horrible glass screen of the mental concepts, to the actual *touch* of life. In his art he had touched the apple, and that was a great deal. He had intuitively known the apple and intuitively brought it forth on the tree of his life, in paint. But when it came to anything beyond the apple, to landscape, to people, and above all to nude woman, the cliché had triumphed over him. The cliché had triumphed over him, and he was bitter, misanthropic. How not to be misanthropic when men and women are just clichés to you, and you hate the cliché? Most people, of course, love the cliché— because most people *are* the cliché. Still, for all that, there is perhaps more appleyness in man, and even in nude woman, than Cézanne was able to get at. The cliché obtruded, so he just abstracted away from it. Those last water-colour landscapes are just abstractions from the cliché. They are blanks, with a few pearly-coloured sort of edges. The blank is vacuum, which was Cézanne's last word against the cliché. It is a vacuum, and the edges are there to assert the vacuity.

And the very fact that we can reconstruct almost instantly a whole landscape from the few indications Cézanne gives, shows what a cliché the landscape is, how it exists already, ready-made, in our minds, how it exists in a pigeon-hole of the consciousness, so to speak, and you need only be given its number to be able to get it out, complete. Cézanne's last water-colour landscapes, made up of a few touches on blank paper, are a satire on landscape altogether. *They leave so much to the imagination!*—that immortal cant phrase, which means they give you the clue to a cliché and the cliché comes. That's what the cliché exists for. And that sort of imagination is just a rag-bag memory stored with thousands and thousands of old and really worthless sketches, images, etc., clichés.

We can see what a fight it means, the escape from the domination of the ready-made mental concept, the mental con-sciousness stuffed full of clichés that intervene like a complete screen between us and life. It means a long, long fight, that will probably last for ever. But Cézanne did get as far as the apple. I can think of nobody else who has done anything.

When we put it in personal terms, it is a fight in a man between his own ego, which is his ready-made mental self which inhabits either a sky-blue, self-tinted heaven or a black, self-tinted hell, and his other free intuitive self. Cézanne never freed himself from his ego, in his life. He haunted the fringes of experience. 'I who am so feeble in life'—but at least he knew it. At least he had the greatness to feel bitter about it. Not like the complacent bourgeois who now 'appreciate' him!

So now perhaps it is the English turn. Perhaps this is where the English will come in. They have certainly stayed out very completely. It is as if they had received the death-blow to their instinctive and intuitive bodies in the Elizabethan age, and since then they have steadily died, till now they are complete corpses. As a young English painter, an intelligent and really modest young man, said to me: 'But I do think we ought to begin to paint good pictures, now that we know pretty well all there is to know about how a picture should be made. You do agree, don't you, that technically we know almost all there is to know about painting?'

I looked at him in amazement. It was obvious that a new-born babe was as fit to paint pictures as he was. He knew technically all there was to know about pictures: all about two-dimensional and three-dimensional composition, also the colour-dimension and the dimension of values in that view of composition which exists apart from form: all about the value of planes, the value of the angle in planes, the different values of the same colour on different planes: all about edges, visible edges, tangible edges, intangible edges: all about the nodality of form-groups, the constellating of mass-centres: all about the relativity of mass, the gravitation and the centrifugal force of masses, the resultant of the complex impinging of masses, the isolation of a mass in the line of vision: all about pattern, line pattern, edge pattern, tone pattern, colour pattern, and the pattern of moving planes: all about texture, impasto, surface, and what happens at the edge of the canvas: also which is the aesthetic centre of the canvas, the dynamic centre, the effulgent centre, the kinetic centre, the mathematical centre, and the Chinese centre: also the points of departure in the foreground, and the

points of disappearance in the background, together with the
various routes between these points, namely, as the crow flies, as
the cow walks, as the mind intoxicated with knowledge reels and
gets there: all about spotting, what you spot, which spot, on the
spot, how many spots, balance of spots, recedence of spots, spots
on the explosive vision and spots on the co-ordinative vision: all
about literary interest and how to hide it successfully from the
policeman: all about photographic representation, and which
heaven it belongs to, and which hell: all about the sex-appeal of a
picture, and when you can be arrested for solicitation, when for
indecency: all about the psychology of a picture, which section of
the mind it appeals to, which mental state it is intended to
represent, how to exclude the representation of all other states of
mind from the one intended, or how, on the contrary, to give a hint
of complementary states of mind fringing the state of mind
portrayed: all about the chemistry of colours, when to use Winsor
& Newton and when not, and the relative depth of contempt to
display for Lefranc:* on the history of colour, past and future,
whether cadmium will really stand the march of ages, whether
viridian will go black, blue, or merely greasy, and the effect on our
great-great-grandsons of the flake white and zinc white and white
lead we have so lavishly used: on the merits and demerits of leaving
patches of bare, prepared canvas, and which preparation will
bleach, which blacken: on the mediums to be used, the vice of
linseed oil, the treachery of turps, the meanness of gums, the
innocence or the unspeakable crime of varnish: on allowing your
picture to be shiny, on insisting that it should be shiny, on weeping
over the merest suspicion of gloss and rubbing it with a raw potato:
on brushes, and the conflicting length of the stem, the best of the
hog, the length of bristle most to be desired on the many varying
occasions, and whether to slash in one direction only: on the
atmosphere of London, on the atmosphere of Glasgow, on the
atmosphere of Rome, on the atmosphere of Paris, and the peculiar
action of them all upon vermilion, cinnabar, pale cadmium yellow,
mid-chrome, emerald green, Veronese green, linseed oil, turps, and
Lyall's perfect medium: on quality, and its relation to light, and its
ability to hold its own in so radical a change of light as that from
Rome to London—all these things the young man knew—and out
of it, God help him, he was going to make pictures.

Now, such innocence and such naïveté, coupled with true modesty, must make us believe that we English have indeed, at least as far as paint goes, become again as little children:* very little children: tiny children: babes: nay, babes unborn. And if we have really got back to the state of the unborn babe, we are perhaps almost ready to be born. The English *may* be born again, pictorially. Or, to tell the truth, they may begin for the first time to be born: since as painters of composition pictures they don't really exist. They have reached the stage where their innocent egos are entirely and totally enclosed in pale-blue glass bottles of insulated inexperience. Perhaps now they *must* hatch out!

'Do you think we may be on the brink of a Golden Age again in England?' one of our most promising young writers asked me, with that same half-timorous innocence and naïveté of the young painter. I looked at him—he was a sad young man—and my eyes nearly fell out of my head. A golden age! He looked so ungolden, and though he was twenty years my junior, he felt also like my grandfather. A golden age! in England! a golden age! now, when even money is paper! when the enclosure in the ego is final, when they are hermetically sealed and insulated from all experience, from any *touch*, from anything *solid*.

'I suppose it's up to *you*,' said I.

And he quietly accepted it.

But such innocence, such naïveté must be a prelude to something. It's a *ne plus ultra*. So why shouldn't it be a prelude to a golden age? If the innocence and naïveté as regards artistic expression doesn't become merely idiotic, why shouldn't it become golden? The young might, out of a sheer sort of mental blankness, strike the oil of their live intuition, and get a gusher. Why not? A golden gush of artistic expression! 'Now we know pretty well everything that can be known about the technical side of pictures.' A golden age!

Introduction to *Pansies*

THIS little bunch of fragments is offered as a bunch of *pensées*, *anglicé* pansies; a handful of thoughts. Or, if you will have the other derivation of pansy, from *panser*, to dress or soothe a wound, these are my tender administrations to the mental and emotional wounds we suffer from. Or you can have heartsease if you like, since the modern heart could certainly do with it.

Each little piece is a thought; not a bare idea or an opinion or a didactic statement, but a true thought, which comes as much from the heart and the genitals as from the head. A thought, with its own blood of emotion and instinct running in it like the fire in a fire-opal, if I may be so bold. Perhaps if you hold up my pansies properly to the light, they may show a running vein of fire. At least, they do not pretend to be half-baked lyrics or melodies in American measure. They are thoughts which run through the modern mind and body, each having its own separate existence, yet each of them combining with all the others to make up a complete state of mind.

It suits the modern temper better to have its state of mind made up of apparently irrelevant thoughts that scurry in different directions, yet belong to the same nest; each thought trotting down the page like an independent creature, each with its own small head and tail, trotting its own little way, then curling up to sleep. We prefer it, at least the young seem to prefer it to those solid blocks of mental pabulum packed like bales in the pages of a proper heavy book. Even we prefer it to those slightly didactic opinions and slices of wisdom which are laid horizontally across the pages of Pascal's *Pensées* or La Bruyère's *Caractères*, separated only by *pattes de mouches*,.. like faint sprigs of parsley. Let every *pensée* trot on its own little paws, not be laid like a cutlet trimmed with a *patte de mouche*.

Live and let live, and each pansy will tip you its separate wink. The fairest thing in nature, a flower, still has its roots in earth and manure; and in the perfume there hovers still the faint strange scent of earth, the under-earth in all its heavy humidity and darkness. Certainly it is so in pansy-scent, and in violet-scent;

mingled with the blue of the morning the black of the corrosive humus. Else the scent would be just sickly sweet.

So it is: we all have our roots in earth. And it is our roots that now need a little attention, need the hard soil eased away from them, and softened so that a little fresh air can come to them, and they can breathe. For by pretending to have no roots, we have trodden the earth so hard over them that they are starving and stifling below the soil. We have roots, and our roots are in the sensual, instinctive and intuitive body, and it is here we need fresh air of open consciousness.

I am abused most of all for using the so-called 'obscene' words. Nobody quite knows what the word 'obscene' itself means, or what it is intended to mean: but gradually all the *old* words that belong to the body below the navel, have come to be judged obscene. Obscene means today that the policeman thinks he has a right to arrest you, nothing else.

Myself, I am mystified at this horror over a mere word, a plain simple word that stands for a plain simple thing. 'In the beginning was the Word, and the Word was God and the Word was with God.'.. If that is true, then we are very far from the beginning. When did the Word 'fall'? When did the Word become unclean 'below the navel'? Because today, if you suggest that the word arse was in the beginning and was God and was with God, you will just be put in prison at once. Though a doctor might say the same of the word *ischial tuberosity*,.. and all the old ladies would piously murmur 'Quite!' Now that sort of thing is idiotic and humiliating. Whoever the God was that made us, He made us complete. He didn't stop at the navel and leave the rest to the devil. It is too childish. And the same with the Word which is God. If the Word is God—which in the sense of the human it is—then you can't suddenly say that all the words which belong below the navel are obscene. The word arse is as much god as the word face. It must be so, otherwise you cut off your god at the waist.

What is obvious is that the words in these cases have been dirtied by the mind, by unclean mental associations. The words themselves are clean, so are the things to which they apply. But the mind drags in a filthy association, calls up some repulsive emotion. Well, then, cleanse the mind, that is the real job. It is the mind which is the Augean stables,.. not language. The word arse is clean enough. Even the part of the body it refers to is just as much me as my hand and my brain are me. It is not for *me* to quarrel with my own natural make-up. If I am, I am all that I am. But the impudent and dirty mind won't have it. It hates certain parts of the body, and makes the words representing these parts scapegoats. It pelts them out of the consciousness with filth, and there they hover, never dying, never dead, slipping into the consciousness again unawares, and pelted out again with filth, haunting the margins of the consciousness like jackals or hyenas. And they refer to parts of our own living bodies, and to our most essential acts. So that man turns himself into a thing of shame and horror. And his consciousness shudders with horrors that he has made for himself.

That sort of thing has got to stop. We can't have the consciousness haunted any longer by repulsive spectres which are no more than poor simple scapegoat words representing parts of man himself; words that the cowardly and unclean mind has driven out into the limbo of the unconscious, whence they return upon us looming and magnified out of all proportion, frightening us beyond all reasons. We must put an end to that. It is the self divided against itself most dangerously. The simple and natural 'obscene' words must be cleaned up of all their depraved fear-associations, and re-admitted into the consciousness to take their natural place. Now they are magnified out of all proportion, so is the mental fear they represent. We must accept the word arse as we accept the word face, since arses we have and always shall have. We can't start cutting off the buttocks of unfortunate mankind, like the ladies in the Voltaire story,.. just to fit the mental expulsion of the word.

This scapegoat business does the mind itself so much damage. There is a poem of Swift's which should make us pause. It is written to Celia, his Celia—and every verse ends with the mad, maddened refrain: 'But—Celia, Celia, Celia shits!'.. Now that, stated baldly, is so ridiculous it is almost funny. But when one remembers the gnashing insanity to which the great mind of Swift was reduced by that and similar thoughts, the joke dies away. Such thoughts poisoned him, like some terrible constipation. They poisoned his mind. And why, in heaven's name? The *fact* cannot have troubled him, since it applied to himself and to all of us. It was not the fact that Celia shits which so deranged him, it was the *thought*. His mind couldn't bear the thought. Great wit as he was, he could not see how ridiculous his revulsions were. His arrogant mind over-bore him. He couldn't even see how much worse it would be if Celia didn't shit. His physical sympathies were too weak, his guts were too cold to sympathize with poor Celia in her natural functions. His insolent and sicklily squeamish mind just turned her into a thing of horror, because she was merely natural and went to the w.c. It is monstrous! One feels like going back across all the years to poor Celia, to say to her: It's all right, don't you take any notice of that mental lunatic.

And Swift's form of madness is very common today. Men with cold guts and over-squeamish minds are always thinking those things and squirming. Wretched man is the victim of his own little revulsions, which he magnifies into great horrors and terrifying taboos. We are all savages, we all have taboos. The Australian black may have the kangaroo for his taboo. And then he will probably die of shock and terror if a kangaroo happens to touch him. Which is what I would call a purely unnecessary death. But modern men have even more dangerous taboos. To us, certain words, certain ideas are taboo, and if they come upon us and we can't drive them away, we die or go mad with a degraded sort of terror. Which is what happened to Swift. He was such a great wit. And the modern mind altogether is falling into this form of degraded taboo-insanity. I call it a waste of sane human consciousness. But it is very dangerous, dangerous to the individual and utterly dangerous to society as a whole. Nothing is so fearful in a mass-civilization like ours as a mass-insanity.

The remedy is, of course, the same in both cases: lift off the taboo. The kangaroo is a harmless animal, the word shit is a harmless word. Make either into a taboo, and it becomes more dangerous. The result of taboo is insanity. And insanity, especially mob-insanity, mass-insanity, is the fearful danger that threatens our civilization. There are certain persons with a sort of rabies, who live only to infect the mass. If the young do not watch out, they will find themselves, before so very many years are past, engulfed in a howling manifestation of mob-insanity, truly terrifying to think of. It will be better to be dead than to live to see it. Sanity, wholeness, is everything. In the name of piety and purity, what a mass of disgusting insanity is spoken and written. We shall have to fight the mob, in order to keep sane, and to keep society sane.

Making Pictures

ONE has to eat one's own words. I remember I used to assert, perhaps I even wrote it: Everything that can possibly be painted has been painted, every brush-stroke that can possibly be laid on canvas has been laid on. The visual arts are at a dead end. Then suddenly, at the age of forty, I begin painting myself and am fascinated.

Still, going through the Paris picture shops this year of grace, and seeing the Dufys and Chiricos, etc., and the Japanese Ito* with his wish-wash nudes with pearl-button eyes, the same weariness comes over one. They are all so would-be, they make such efforts. They at least have nothing to paint. In the midst of them a graceful Friesz flower-piece, or a blotting-paper Laurencin,* seems a masterpiece. At least here is a bit of *natural* expression in paint. Trivial enough, when compared to the big painters, but still, as far as they go, real.

What about myself, then! What am I doing, bursting into paint? I am a writer, I ought to stick to ink. I have found my medium of expression; why, at the age of forty, should I suddenly want to try another?

Things happen, and we have no choice. If Maria Huxley* hadn't come rolling up to our house near Florence with four rather large canvases, one of which she had busted, and presented them to me because they had been abandoned in her house, I might never have started in on a real picture in my life. But those nice stretched canvases were too tempting. We had been painting doors and window-frames in the house, so there was a little stock of oil, turps and colour in powder, such as one buys from an Italian drogheria. There were several brushes for house-painting. There was a canvas on which the unknown owner had made a start—mud-grey, with the beginnings of a red-haired man. It was a grimy and ugly beginning, and the young man who had made it had wisely gone no further. He certainly had had no inner compulsion: nothing in him, as far as paint was concerned, or if there was anything in him, it had stayed in, and only a bit of the mud-grey 'group' had come out.

So for the sheer fun of covering a surface and obliterating that mud-grey, I sat on the floor with the canvas propped against a chair—and with my house-paint brushes and colours in little casseroles, I disappeared into that canvas. It is to me the most exciting moment—when you have a blank canvas and a big brush full of wet colour, and you plunge. It is just like diving into a pond—then you start frantically to swim. So far as I am concerned, it is like swimming in a baffling current and being rather frightened and very thrilled, gasping and striking out for all you're worth. The knowing eye watches sharp as a needle; but the picture comes clean out of instinct, intuition and sheer physical action. Once the instinct and intuition gets into the brush-tip, the picture *happens*, if it is to be a picture at all.

At least, so my first picture happened—the one I have called 'A Holy Family'. In a couple of hours there it all was, man, woman, child, blue shirt, red shawl, pale room—all in the rough, but, as far as I am concerned, a picture. The struggling comes later. But the picture itself comes in the first rush, or not at all. It is only when the picture has come into being that one can struggle and make it *grow* to completion.

Ours is an excessively conscious age. We *know* so much, we feel so little. I have lived enough among painters and around studios to have had all the theories—and how contradictory they are— rammed down my throat. A man has to have a gizzard like an ostrich to digest all the brass-tacks and wire nails of modern art theories. Perhaps all the theories, the utterly indigestible theories, like nails in an ostrich's gizzard, do indeed help to grind small and make digestible all the emotional and aesthetic pabulum that lies in an artist's soul. But they can serve no other purpose. Not even corrective. The modern theories of art make real pictures impossible. You only get these expositions, critical ventures in paint, and fantastic negations. And the bit of fantasy that may lie in the negation—as in a Dufy or a Chirico—is just the bit that has escaped theory and perhaps saves the picture. Theorize, theorize all you like—but when you start to paint, shut your theoretic eyes and go for it with instinct and intuition.

Myself, I have always loved pictures, the pictorial art. I never went to an art school, I have had only one real lesson in painting in all my life. But of course I was thoroughly drilled in 'drawing', the solid-geometry sort, and the plaster-cast sort, and the pin-wire sort. I think the solid-geometry sort, with all the elementary laws of perspective, was valuable. But the pin-wire sort and the plaster-cast light-and-shade sort was harmful. Plaster-casts and pin-wire outlines were always so repulsive to me, I quite early decided I 'couldn't draw'. I couldn't draw, so I could never do anything on my own. When I did paint jugs of flowers or bread and potatoes, or cottages in a lane, copying from Nature, the result wasn't very thrilling. Nature was more or less of a plaster-cast to me—those plaster-cast heads of Minerva or figures of Dying Gladiators* which so unnerved me as a youth. The 'object', be it what it might, was always slightly repulsive to me once I sat down in front of it, to paint it. So, of course, I decided I couldn't really paint. Perhaps I can't. But I verily believe I can make pictures, which is to me all that matters in this respect. The art of painting consists in making pictures—and so many artists accomplish canvases without coming within miles of painting a picture.

I learnt to paint from copying other pictures—usually reproductions, sometimes even photographs. When I was a boy, how I concentrated over it! Copying some perfectly worthless scene reproduction in some magazine. I worked with almost dry watercolour, stroke by stroke, covering half a square-inch at a time, each square-inch perfect and completed, proceeding in a kind of mosaic advance, with no idea at all of laying on a broad wash. Hours and hours of intense concentration, inch by inch progress, in a method entirely wrong—and yet those copies of mine managed, when they were finished, to have a certain something that delighted me: a certain glow of life, which was beauty to me. A picture lives with the life you put into it. If you put no *life* into it—no thrill, no concentration of delight or exaltation of visual discovery—then the picture is dead, like so many canvases, no matter how much thorough and scientific work is put into it. Even if you only copy a purely banal reproduction of an old bridge, some sort of keen, delighted awareness of the old bridge or of its atmosphere, or the image it has kindled inside you, can go over on to the paper and give a certain touch of life to a banal conception.

It needs a certain purity of spirit to be an artist, of any sort. The motto which should be written over every School of Art is: 'Blessed are the pure in spirit, for theirs is the kingdom of heaven.'* But by 'pure in spirit' we mean pure in spirit. An artist may be a profligate and, from the social point of view, a scoundrel. But if he can paint a nude woman, or a couple of apples, so that they are a living image, then he was pure in spirit, and, for the time being, his was the kingdom of heaven. This is the beginning of all art, visual or literary or musical: be pure in spirit. It isn't the same as goodness. It is much more difficult and nearer the divine. The divine isn't only good, it is all things.

One may see the divine in natural objects; I saw it today, in the frail, lovely little camellia flowers on long stems, here on the bushy and splendid flower-stalls of the Ramblas* in Barcelona. They were different from the usual fat camellias, more like gardenias, poised delicately, and I saw them like a vision. So now, I could paint them. But if I had bought a handful, and started in to paint them 'from nature', then I should have lost them. By staring at them I should have lost them. I have learnt by experience. It is personal experience only. Some men can only get at a vision by staring themselves blind, as it were: like Cézanne; but staring kills my vision. That's why I could never 'draw' at school. One was supposed to draw what one stared at.

The only thing one can look into, stare into, and see only vision, is the vision itself: the visionary image. That is why I am glad I never had any training but the self-imposed training of copying other men's pictures. As I grew more ambitious, I copied Leader's landscapes, and Frank Brangwyn's cartoon-like pictures, then Peter de Wint and Girtin* water-colours. I can never be sufficiently grateful for the series of English water-colour painters, published by the *Studio* in eight parts, when I was a youth. I had only six of the eight parts, but they were invaluable to me. I copied them with the greatest joy, and found some of them extremely difficult. Surely I put as much labour into copying from those water-colour reproductions as most modern art students put into all their years of study. And I had enormous profit from it. I not only acquired a considerable technical skill in handling water-colours—let any man try copying the English water-colour artists, from Paul Sandby* and Peter de Wint and Girtin, up to Frank Brangwyn and the impressionists like Brabazon,* and he will see how much skill he requires—but also I developed my visionary awareness. And I believe one can only develop one's visionary awareness by close contact with the vision itself: that is, by knowing pictures, real vision pictures, and by dwelling on them, and really dwelling in them. It is a great delight, to dwell in a picture. But it needs a purity of spirit, a sloughing of vulgar sensation and vulgar interest, and above all, vulgar contact, that few people know how to perform. Oh, if art schools only taught that! If, instead of saying: This drawing is wrong, incorrect, badly drawn, etc., they would say: Isn't this in bad taste? isn't it insensitive? isn't that an insentient curve with none of the delicate awareness of life in it?— But art is treated all wrong. It is treated as if it were a science, which it is not. Art is a form of religion, minus the Ten Commandment business, which is sociological. Art is a form of supremely delicate awareness and atonement—meaning at-oneness, the state of being at one with the object. But is the great atonement in delight?—for I can never look on art save as a form of delight.

All my life I have from time to time gone back to paint, because it gave me a form of delight that words can never give. Perhaps the joy in words goes deeper and is for that reason more unconscious. The *conscious* delight is certainly stronger in paint. I have gone back to paint for real pleasure—and by paint I mean copying, copying either in oils or waters. I think the greatest pleasure I ever got came from copying Fra Angelico's 'Flight into Egypt' and Lorenzetti's big picture of the Thebaid, in each case working from photographs and putting in my own colour; or perhaps even more a Carpaccio* picture in Venice. Then I *really* learned what life, what powerful life has been put into every curve, every motion of a great picture. Purity of spirit, sensitive awareness, intense eagerness to portray an inward vision, how it all comes. The English water-colours are frail in comparison—and the French and the Flemings are shallow. The great Rembrandt I never tried to copy, though I loved him intensely, even more than I do now; and Rubens I never tried, though I always liked him so much, only he seemed so spread out. But I have copied Peter de Hooch, and Vandyck,* and others that I forget. Yet none of them gave me the deep thrill of the Italians, Carpaccio, or the lovely 'Death of Procris' in the National Gallery, or that 'Wedding' with the scarlet legs, in the Uffizi, or a Giotto from Padua.* I must have made many copies in my day, and got endless joy out of them.

Then suddenly, by having a blank canvas, I discovered I could

make a picture myself. That is the point, to make a picture on a
blank canvas. And I was forty before I had the real courage to try.
Then it became an orgy, making pictures.

I have learnt now not to work from objects, not to have models,
not to have a technique. Sometimes, for a water-colour, I have
worked direct from a model. But it always spoils the *picture*. I can
only use a model when the picture is already made; then I can look
at the model to get some detail which the vision failed me with, or
to modify something which I *feel* is unsatisfactory and I don't know
why. Then a model may give a suggestion. But at the beginning, a
model only spoils the picture. The picture must all come out of the
artist's inside, awareness of forms and figures. We can call it
memory, but it is more than memory. It is the image as it lives in
the consciousness, alive like a vision, but unknown. I believe many
people have, in their consciousness, living images that would give
them the greatest joy to bring out. But they don't know how to go
about it. And teaching only hinders them.

To me, a picture has delight in it, or it isn't a picture. The
saddest pictures of Piero della Francesca or Sodoma or Goya,* have
still that indescribable delight that goes with the real picture.
Modern critics talk a lot about ugliness, but I never saw a real
picture that seemed to me ugly. The theme may be ugly, there may
be a terrifying, distressing, almost repulsive quality, as in El
Greco.* Yet it is all, in some strange way, swept up in the delight of
a picture. No artist, even the gloomiest, ever painted a picture
without the curious delight in image-making.

Pornography and Obscenity

WHAT they are depends, as usual, entirely on the individual. What is pornography to one man is the laughter of genius to another.

The word itself, we are told, means 'pertaining to harlots'—the graph of the harlot. But nowadays, what is a harlot? If she was a woman who took money from a man in return for going to bed with him—really, most wives sold themselves, in the past, and plenty of harlots gave themselves, when they felt like it, for nothing. If a woman hasn't got a tiny streak of a harlot in her, she's a dry stick as a rule. And probably most harlots had somewhere a streak of womanly generosity. Why be so cut and dried? The law is a dreary thing, and its judgments have nothing to do with life.

The same with the word *obscene:* nobody knows what it means. Suppose it were derived from *obscena:* that which might not be represented on the stage; how much further are you? None! What is obscene to Tom is not obscene to Lucy or Joe, and really, the meaning of a word has to wait for majorities to decide it. If a play shocks ten people in an audience, and doesn't shock the remaining five hundred, then it is obscene to ten and innocuous to five hundred; hence, the play is not obscene, by majority. But *Hamlet* shocked all the Cromwellian Puritans, and shocks nobody today, and some of Aristophanes* shocks everybody today, and didn't galvanize the later Greeks at all, apparently. Man is a changeable beast, and words change their meanings with him, and things are not what they seemed, and what's what becomes what isn't, and if we think we know where we are it's only because we are so rapidly being translated to somewhere else. We have to leave everything to the majority, everything to the majority, everything to the mob, the mob, the mob. They know what is obscene and what isn't, they do. If the lower ten million doesn't know better than the upper ten men, then there's something wrong with mathematics. Take a vote on it! Show hands, and prove it by count! *Vox populi, vox Dei. Odi profanum vulgum!* Profanum vulgum.*

So it comes down to this: if you are talking to the mob, the meaning of your words is the mob-meaning, decided by majority. As somebody wrote to me: the American law on obscenity is very plain, and America is going to enforce the law. Quite, my dear, quite, quite, quite! The mob knows all about obscenity. Mild little words that rhyme with spit or farce are the height of obscenity. Supposing a printer put 'h' in the place of 'p' by mistake, in that mere word spit? Then the great American public knows that this man has committed an obscenity, an indecency, that his act was lewd, and as a compositor he was pornographical. You can't tamper with the great public, British or American. *Vox populi, vox Dei,* don't you know. If you don't we'll let you know it. At the same time, this *vox Dei* shouts with praise over moving-pictures and books and newspaper accounts that seem, to a sinful nature like mine, completely disgusting and obscene. Like a real prude and Puritan, I have to look the other way. When obscenity becomes mawkish, which is its palatable form for the public, and when the *Vox populi, vox Dei* is hoarse with sentimental indecency, then I have to steer away, like a Pharisee, afraid of being contaminated. There is a certain kind of sticky universal pitch that I refuse to touch.

So again, it comes down to this: you accept the majority, the mob, and its decisions, or you don't. You bow down before the *Vox populi, vox Dei,* or you plug your ears not to hear its obscene howl. You perform your antics to please the vast public, *Deus ex machina,* or you refuse to perform for the public at all, unless now and then to pull its elephantine and ignominious leg.

When it comes to the meaning of anything, even the simplest word, then you must pause. Because there are two great categories of meaning, for ever separate. There is mob-meaning, and there is individual meaning. Take even the word *bread*. The mob-meaning is merely: stuff made with white flour into loaves that you eat. But take the individual meaning of the word bread: the white, the brown, the corn-pone, the home-made, the smell of bread just out of the oven, the crust, the crumb, the unleavened bread, the shew-bread, the staff of life, sour-dough bread, cottage loaves, French bread, Viennese bread, black bread, a yesterday's loaf, rye, graham, barley, rolls, *Bretzeln, Kringeln,* scones, damper, matsen—there is no end to it all, and the word bread will take you to the ends of time and space, and far-off down avenues of memory. But this is individual. The word bread will take the individual off on his own journey, and its meaning will be his own meaning, based on his own genuine imagination reactions. And when a word comes to us in its individual character, and starts in us the individual responses, it is great pleasure to us. The American advertisers have discovered this, and some of the cunningest American literature is to be found in advertisements of soap-suds, for example. These advertisements are *almost* prose-poems. They give the word soap-suds a bubbly, shiny individual meaning, which is very skilfully poetic, would, perhaps, be quite poetic to the mind which could forget that the poetry was bait on a hook.

Business is discovering the individual, dynamic meaning of words, and poetry is losing it. Poetry more and more tends to far-fetch its word-meanings, and this results once again in mob-meanings, which arouse only a mob-reaction in the individual. For every man has a mob-self and an individual self, in varying proportions. Some men are almost all mob-self, incapable of imaginative individual responses. The worst specimens of mob-self are usually to be found in the professions, lawyers, professors, clergymen and so on. The business man, much maligned, has a tough outside mob-self, and a scared, floundering yet still alive individual self. The public, which is feeble-minded like an idiot, will never be able to preserve its individual reactions from the tricks of the exploiter. The public is always exploited and always will be exploited. The methods of exploitation merely vary. Today the public is tickled into laying the golden egg.* With imaginative words and individual meanings it is tricked into giving the great goose-cackle of mob-acquiescence. *Vox populi, vox Dei.* It has always been so, and will always be so. Why? Because the public has not enough wit to distinguish between mob-meanings and individual meanings. The mass is for ever vulgar, because it can't distinguish between its own original feelings and feelings which are diddled into existence by the exploiter. The public is always profane, because it is controlled from the outside, by the trickster, and never from the inside, by its own sincerity. The mob is always obscene, because it is always second-hand.

Which brings us back to our subject of pornography and obscenity. The reaction to any word may be, in any individual, either a mob-reaction or an individual reaction. It is up to the individual to ask himself: Is my reaction individual, or am I merely reacting from my mob-self?

When it comes to the so-called obscene words, I should say that hardly one person in a million escapes mob-reaction. The first reaction is almost sure to be mob-reaction, mob-indignation, mob-condemnation. And the mob gets no further. But the real individual has second thoughts and says: Am I really shocked? Do I *really* feel outraged and indignant? And the answer of any individual is bound to be: No, I am not shocked, not outraged, nor indignant. I know the word, and take it for what it is, and I am not going to be jockeyed into making a mountain out of a mole-hill, not for all the law in the world.

Now if the use of a few so-called obscene words will startle man or woman out of a mob-habit into an individual state, well and good. And word prudery is so universal a mob-habit that it is time we were startled out of it.

But still we have only tackled obscenity, and the problem of pornography goes even deeper. When a man is startled into his individual self, he still may not be able to know, inside himself, whether Rabelais is or is not pornographic: and over Aretino or even Boccaccio* he may perhaps puzzle in vain, torn between different emotions.

One essay on pornography, I remember, comes to the conclusion that pornography in art is that which is calculated to arouse sexual desire, or sexual excitement. And stress is laid on the fact, whether the author or artist *intended* to arouse sexual feelings. It is the old vexed question of intention, become so dull today, when we know how strong and influential our unconscious intentions are. And why a man should be held guilty of his conscious intentions, and innocent of his unconscious intentions, I don't know, since every man is more made up of unconscious intentions than of conscious ones. I am what I am, not merely what I think I am.

However! We take it, I assume, that *pornography* is something base, something unpleasant. In short, we don't like it. And why don't we like it? Because it arouses sexual feelings?

I think not. No matter how hard we may pretend otherwise, most of us rather like a moderate rousing of our sex. It warms us, stimulates us like sunshine on a grey day. After a century or two of Puritanism, this is still true of most people. Only the mob-habit of condemning any form of sex is too strong to let us admit it naturally. And there are, of course, many people who are genuinely repelled by the simplest and most natural stirrings of sexual feeling. But these people are perverts who have fallen into hatred of their fellow men: thwarted, disappointed, unfulfilled people, of whom, alas, our civilization contains so many. And they nearly always enjoy some unsimple and unnatural form of sex excitement, secretly.

Even quite advanced art critics would try to make us believe that any picture or book which had 'sex appeal' was *ipso facto* a bad book or picture. This is just canting hypocrisy. Half the great poems, pictures, music, stories of the whole world are great by virtue of the beauty of their sex appeal. Titian or Renoir, the Song of Solomon or *Jane Eyre*, Mozart or 'Annie Laurie',* the loveliness is all interwoven with sex appeal, sex stimulus, call it what you will. Even Michelangelo, who rather hated sex, can't help filling the Cornucopia with phallic acorns.* Sex is a very powerful, beneficial and necessary stimulus in human life, and we are all grateful when we feel its warm, natural flow through us, like a form of sunshine.

So we can dismiss the idea that sex appeal in art is pornography. It may be so to the grey Puritan, but the grey Puritan is a sick man, soul and body sick, so why should we bother about his hallucinations? Sex appeal, of course, varies enormously. There are endless different kinds, and endless degrees of each kind. Perhaps it may be argued that a mild degree of sex appeal is not pornographical, whereas a high degree is. But this is a fallacy. Boccaccio at his hottest seems to me less pornographical than *Pamela* or *Clarissa Harlowe* or even *Jane Eyre*, or a host of modern books or films which pass uncensored. At the same time Wagner's *Tristan and Isolde** seems to me very near to pornography, and so, even, do some quite popular Christian hymns.

What is it, then? It isn't a question of sex appeal, merely: nor even a question of deliberate intention on the part of the author or artist to arouse sexual excitement. Rabelais sometimes had a deliberate intention, so in a different way, did Boccaccio. And I'm sure poor Charlotte Brontë, or the authoress of *The Sheik*,* did not have any deliberate intention to stimulate sex feelings in the reader. Yet I find *Jane Eyre* verging towards pornography and Boccaccio seems to me always fresh and wholesome.

The late British Home Secretary,* who prides himself on being a very sincere Puritan, grey, grey in every fibre, said with indignant sorrow in one of his outbursts on improper books: '—and these two young people, who had been perfectly pure up till that time, after reading this book went and had sexual intercourse together!!!' *One up to them!* is all we can answer. But the grey Guardian of British Morals seemed to think that if they had murdered one another, or worn each other to rags of nervous prostration, it would have been much better. The grey disease!

Then what is pornography, after all this? It isn't sex appeal or sex stimulus in art. It isn't even a deliberate intention on the part of the artist to arouse or excite sexual feelings. There's nothing wrong with sexual feelings in themselves, so long as they are straightforward and not sneaking or sly. The right sort of sex stimulus is invaluable to human daily life. Without it the world grows grey. I would give everybody the gay Renaissance stories to read, they would help to shake off a lot of grey self-importance, which is our modern civilized disease.

But even I would censor genuine pornography, rigorously. It would not be very difficult. In the first place, genuine pornography is almost always underworld, it doesn't come into the open. In the second, you can recognize it by the insult it offers, invariably, to sex, and to the human spirit.

Pornography is the attempt to insult sex, to do dirt on it. This is unpardonable. Take the very lowest instance, the picture post-card sold under hand, by the underworld, in most cities. What I have seen of them have been of an ugliness to make you cry. The insult to the human body, the insult to a vital human relationship! Ugly and cheap they make the human nudity, ugly and degraded they make the sexual act, trivial and cheap and nasty.

It is the same with the books they sell in the underworld. They are either so ugly they make you ill, or so fatuous you can't imagine anybody but a cretin or a moron reading them, or writing them.

It is the same with the dirty limericks that people tell after dinner, or the dirty stories one hears commercial travellers telling each other in a smoke-room. Occasionally there is a really funny one, that redeems a great deal. But usually they are just ugly and repellent, and the so-called 'humour' is just a trick of doing dirt on sex.

Now the human nudity of a great many modern people is just ugly and degraded, and the sexual act between modern people is just the same, merely ugly and degrading. But this is nothing to be proud of. It is the catastrophe of our civilization. I am sure no other civilization, not even the Roman, has showed such a vast proportion of ignominious and degraded nudity, and ugly, squalid dirty sex. Because no other civilization has driven sex into the underworld, and nudity to the w.c.

The intelligent young, thank heaven, seem determined to alter in these two respects. They are rescuing their young nudity from the stuffy, pornographical hole-and-corner underworld of their elders, and they refuse to sneak about the sexual relation. This is a change the elderly grey ones of course deplore, but it is in fact a very great change for the better, and a real revolution.

But it is amazing how strong is the will in ordinary, vulgar people, to do dirt on sex. It was one of my fond illusions, when I was young, that the ordinary healthy-seeming sort of men, in railway carriages, or the smoke-room of an hotel or a pullman, were healthy in their feelings and had a wholesome rough devil-may-care attitude towards sex. All wrong! All wrong! Experience teaches that common individuals of this sort have a disgusting attitude towards sex, a disgusting contempt of it, a disgusting desire to insult it. If such fellows have intercourse with a woman, they triumphantly feel that they have done her dirt, and now she is lower, cheaper, more contemptible than she was before.

It is individuals of this sort that tell dirty stories, carry indecent picture post-cards, and know the indecent books. This is the great pornographical class—the really common men-in-the-street and women-in-the-street. They have as great a hate and contempt of sex as the greyest Puritan, and when an appeal is made to them, they are always on the side of the angels.* They insist that a film-heroine shall be a neuter, a sexless thing of washed-out purity. They insist that real sex-feeling shall only be shown by the villain or villainess, low lust. They find a Titian or a Renoir really indecent, and they don't want their wives and daughters to see it.

Why? Because they have the grey disease of sex-hatred, coupled with the yellow disease of dirt-lust. The sex functions and the excrementory functions in the human body work so close together, yet they are, so to speak, utterly different in direction. Sex is a creative flow, the excrementory flow is towards dissolution, de-creation, if we may use such a word. In the really healthy human being the distinction between the two is instant, our profoundest instincts are perhaps our instincts of opposition between the two flows.

But in the degraded human being the deep instincts have gone dead, and then the two flows become identical. *This* is the secret of really vulgar and of pornographical people: the sex flow and the excrement flow is the same to them. It happens when the psyche deteriorates, and the profound controlling instincts collapse. Then sex is dirt and dirt is sex, and sexual excitement becomes a playing with dirt, and any sign of sex in a woman becomes a show of her dirt. This is the condition of the common, vulgar human being whose name is legion, and who lifts his voice and it is the *Vox populi, vox Dei*. And this is the source of all pornography.

And for this reason we must admit that *Jane Eyre* or Wagner's *Tristan* are much nearer to pornography than is Boccaccio. Wagner and Charlotte Brontë were both in the state where the strongest instincts have collapsed, and sex has become something slightly obscene, to be wallowed in, but despised. Mr Rochester's sex passion is not 'respectable' till Mr Rochester is burned, blinded, disfigured, and reduced to helpless dependence. Then, thoroughly humbled and humiliated, it may be merely admitted. All the previous titillations are slightly indecent, as in *Pamela* or *The Mill on the floss** or *Anna Karenina*. As soon as there is sex excitement with a desire to spite the sexual feeling, to humiliate it and degrade it, the element of pornography enters.

For this reason, there is an element of pornography in nearly all nineteenth century literature and very many so-called pure people have a nasty pornographical side to them, and never was the pornographical appetite stronger than it is today. It is a sign of a diseased condition of the body politic. But the way to treat the disease is to come out into the open with sex and sex stimulus. The real pornographer truly dislikes Boccaccio, because the fresh healthy naturalness of the Italian story-teller makes the modern pornographical shrimp feel the dirty worm he is. Today Boccaccio should be given to everybody young or old, to read if they like. Only a natural fresh openness about sex will do any good, now we are being swamped by secret or semi-secret pornography. And perhaps the Renaissance story-tellers, Boccaccio, Lasca,* and the rest, are the best antidote we can find now, just as more plasters of Puritanism are the most harmful remedy we can resort to.

The whole question of pornography seems to me a question of secrecy. Without secrecy there would be no pornography. But secrecy and modesty are two utterly different things. Secrecy has always an element of fear in it, amounting very often to hate. Modesty is gentle and reserved. Today, modesty is thrown to the winds, even in the presence of the grey guardians. But secrecy is hugged, being a vice in itself. And the attitude of the grey ones is: Dear young ladies, you may abandon all modesty, so long as you hug your dirty little secret.

This 'dirty little secret' has become infinitely precious to the mob of people today. It is a kind of hidden sore or inflammation which, when rubbed or scratched, gives off sharp thrills that seem delicious. So the dirty little secret is rubbed and scratched more and more, till it becomes more and more secretly inflamed, and the nervous and psychic health of the individual is more and more impaired. One might easily say that half the love novels and half the love films today depend entirely for their success on the secret rubbing of the dirty little secret. You can call this sex excitement if you like, but it is sex excitement of a secretive, furtive sort, quite special. The plain and simple excitement, quite open and wholesome, which you find in some Boccaccio stories is not for a minute to be confused with the furtive excitement aroused by rubbing the dirty little secret in all secrecy in modern best-sellers. This furtive, sneaking, cunning rubbing of an inflamed spot in the imagination is the very quick of modern pornography, and it is a beastly and very dangerous thing. You can't so easily expose it, because of its very furtiveness and its sneaking cunning. So the cheap and popular modern love novel and love film flourishes and is even praised by moral guardians, because you get the sneaking thrill fumbling under all the purity of dainty underclothes, without one single gross word to let you know what is happening.

Without secrecy there would be no pornography. But if pornography is the result of sneaking secrecy, what is the result of pornography? What is the effect on the individual?

The effect on the individual is manifold, and always pernicious. But one effect is perhaps inevitable. The pornography of today, whether it be the pornography of the rubber-goods shop or the pornography of the popular novel, film, and play, is an invariable stimulant to the vice of self-abuse, onanism, masturbation, call it what you will. In young or old, man or woman, boy or girl, modern pornography is a direct provocative of masturbation. It cannot be otherwise. When the grey ones wail that the young man and the young woman went and had sexual intercourse, they are bewailing the fact that the young man and the young woman didn't go separately and masturbate. Sex must go somewhere, especially in young people. So, in our glorious civilization, it goes in masturbation. And the mass of our popular literature, the bulk of our popular amusements just exists to provoke masturbation. Masturbation is the one thoroughly secret act of the human being, more secret even than excrementation. It is the one functional result of sex-secrecy, and it is stimulated and provoked by our glorious popular literature of pretty pornography, which rubs on the dirty secret without letting you know what is happening.

Now I have heard men, teachers and clergymen, commend maturbation as the solution of an otherwise insoluble sex problem. This at least is honest. The sex problem is there, and you can't just will it away. There it is, and under the ban of secrecy and taboo in mother and father, teacher, friend, and foe, it has found its own solution, the solution of masturbation.

But what about the solution? Do we accept it? Do all the grey ones of this world accept it? If so, they must now accept it openly. We can none of us pretend any longer to be blind to the fact of masturbation, in young and old, man and woman. The moral guardians who are prepared to censor all open and plain portrayal of sex must now be made to give their only justification: We prefer that the people shall masturbate. If this preference is open and declared, then the existing forms of censorship are justified. If the moral guardians prefer that the people shall masturbate, then their present behaviour is correct, and popular amusements are as they should be. If sexual intercourse is deadly sin, and masturbation is comparatively pure and harmless, then all is well. Let things continue as they now are.

Is masturbation so harmless, though? Is it even comparatively pure and harmless? Not to my thinking. In the young, a certain amount of masturbation is inevitable, but not therefore natural. I think, there is no boy or girl who masturbates without feeling a sense of shame, anger, and futility. Following the excitement comes the shame, anger, humiliation, and the sense of futility. This sense of futility and humiliation deepens as the years go on, into a suppressed rage, because of the impossibility of escape. The one thing that it seems impossible to escape from, once the habit is formed, is masturbation. It goes on and on, on into old age, in spite of marriage or love affairs or anything else. And it always carries this secret feeling of futility and humiliation, futility and humiliation. And this is, perhaps, the deepest and most dangerous cancer of our civilization. Instead of being a comparatively pure and harmless vice, masturbation is certainly the most dangerous sexual vice that a society can be afflicted with, in the long run. Comparatively pure it may be—purity being what it is. But harmless!!!

The great danger of masturbation lies in its merely exhaustive nature. In sexual intercourse, there is a give and take. A new stimulus enters as the native stimulus departs. Something quite new is added as the old surcharge is removed. And this is so in all sexual intercourse where two creatures are concerned, even in the homosexual intercourse. But in masturbation there is nothing but loss. There is no reciprocity. There is merely the spending away of a certain force, and no return. The body remains, in a sense, a corpse, after the act of self-abuse. There is no change, only deadening. There is what we call dead loss. And this is not the case in any act of sexual intercourse between two people. Two people may destroy one another in sex. But they cannot just produce the null effect of masturbation.

The only positive effect of masturbation is that it seems to release a certain mental energy, in some people. But it is mental energy which manifests itself always in the same way, in a vicious circle of analysis and impotent criticism, or else a vicious circle of false and easy sympathy, sentimentalities. The sentimentalism and the niggling analysis, often self-analysis, of most of our modern literature, is a sign of self-abuse. It is the manifestation of masturbation, the sort of conscious activity stimulated by masturbation, whether male or female. The outstanding feature of such consciousness is that there is no real object, there is only subject. This is just the same whether it be a novel or a work of science. The author never escapes from himself, he pads along within the vicious circle of himself. There is hardly a writer living who gets out of the vicious circle of himself—or a painter either. Hence the lack of creation, and the stupendous amount of production. It is a masturbation result, within the vicious circle of the self. It is self-absorption made public.

And of course the process is exhaustive. The real masturbation of Englishmen began only in the nineteenth century. It has continued with an increasing emptying of the real vitality and the real *being* of men, till now people are little more than shells of people. Most of the responses are dead, most of the awareness is dead, nearly all the constructive activity is dead, and all that remains is a sort of shell, a half-empty creature fatally self-preoccupied and incapable of either giving or taking. Incapable either of giving or taking, in the vital self. And this is masturbation result. Enclosed within the vicious circle of the self, with no vital contacts outside, the self becomes emptier and emptier, till it is almost a nullus, a nothingness.

But null or nothing as it may be, it still hangs on to the dirty little secret, which it must still secretly rub and inflame. For ever the vicious circle. And it has a weird, blind will of its own.

One of my most sympathetic critics* wrote: 'If Mr Lawrence's attitude to sex were adopted, then two things would disappear, the love lyric and the smoking-room story.' And this, I think, is true. But it depends on which love lyric he means. If it is the: *Who is Sylvia, what is she?*—then it may just as well disappear. All that pure and noble and heaven-blessed stuff is only the counterpart to the smoking-room story. *Du bist wie eine Blume!* Jawohl!* One can see the elderly gentleman laying his hands on the head of the pure maiden and praying God to keep her for ever so pure, so clean and beautiful. Very nice for him! Just pornography! Tickling the dirty little secret and rolling his eyes to heaven! He knows perfectly well that if God keeps the maiden so clean and pure and beautiful*—in his vulgar sense of clean and pure—for a few more years, then she'll be an unhappy old maid, and not pure nor beautiful at all, only stale and pathetic. Sentimentality is a sure sign of pornography. Why should 'sadness strike through the heart'* of the old gentleman, because the maid was pure and beautiful? Anybody but a masturbator would have been glad and would have thought: What a lovely bride for some lucky man!—But no, not the self-enclosed, pornographic masturbator. Sadness has to strike into his beastly heart!—Away with such love lyrics, we've had too much of their pornographic poison, tickling the dirty little secret and rolling the eyes to heaven.

But if it is a question of the sound love lyric, *My love is like a red, red rose—!** then we are on other ground. My love is like a red, red rose only when she's not like a pure, pure lily. And nowadays the pure, pure lilies are mostly festering,* anyhow. Away with them and their lyrics. Away with the pure, pure lily lyric, along with the smoking-room story. They are counterparts, and the one is as pornographic as the other. *Du bist wie eine Blume* is really as pornographic as a dirty story: tickling the dirty little secret and rolling the eyes to heaven. But oh, if only Robert Burns had been accepted for what he is, then love might still have been like a red, red rose.

The vicious circle, the vicious circle! The vicious circle of masturbation! The vicious circle of self-consciousness that is never *fully* self-conscious, never fully and openly conscious, but always harping on the dirty little secret. The vicious circle of secrecy, in parents, teachers, friends—everybody. The specially vicious circle of family. The vast conspiracy of secrecy in the press, and at the same time, the endless tickling of the dirty little secret. The needless masturbation! and the endless purity! The vicious circle!

How to get out of it? There is only one way: Away with the secret! No more secrecy! The only way to stop the terrible mental itch about sex is to come out quite simply and naturally into the open with it. It is terribly difficult, for the secret is cunning as a crab. Yet the thing to do is to make a beginning. The man who said to his exasperating daughter: 'My child, the only pleasure I ever had out of you was the pleasure I had in begetting you' has already done a great deal to release both himself and her from the dirty little secret.

How to get out of the dirty little secret! It is, as a matter of fact, extremely difficult for us secretive moderns. You can't do it by being wise and scientific about it, like Dr Marie Stopes:* though to be wise and scientific like Dr Marie Stopes is better than to be utterly hypocritical, like the grey ones. But by being wise and scientific in the serious and earnest manner you only tend to disinfect the dirty little secret, and either kill sex altogether with too much seriousness and intellect, or else leave it a miserable disinfected secret. The unhappy 'free and pure' love of so many people who have taken out the dirty little secret and thoroughly disinfected it with scientific words is apt to be more pathetic even than the common run of dirty-little-secret love. The danger is, that in killing the dirty little secret, you kill dynamic sex altogether, and leave only the scientific and deliberate mechanism.

This is what happens to many of those who become seriously 'free' in their sex, free and pure. They have mentalized sex till it is nothing at all, nothing at all but a mental quantity. And the final result is disaster, every time.

The same is true, in an even greater proportion, of the emancipated bohemians: and very many of the young are bohemian today, whether they ever set foot in Bohemia or not. But the bohemian is 'sex free'. The dirty little secret is no secret either to him or her. It is, indeed, a most blatantly open question. There is nothing they don't say: everything that can be revealed is revealed. And they do as they wish.

And then what? They have apparently killed the dirty little secret, but somehow, they have killed everything else too. Some of the dirt still sticks, perhaps; sex remains still dirty. But the thrill of secrecy is gone. Hence the terrible dreariness and depression of modern Bohemia, and the inward dreariness and emptiness of so many young people of today. They have killed, they imagine, the dirty little secret. The thrill of secrecy is gone. Some of the dirt remains. And for the rest, depression, inertia, lack of life. For sex is the fountain-head of our energetic life, and now the fountain ceases to flow.

Why? For two reasons. The idealists along the Marie Stopes line, and the young bohemians of today have killed the dirty little secret as far as their personal self goes. But they are still under its dominion socially. In the social world, in the press, in literature, film, theatre, wireless, everywhere purity and the dirty little secret reign supreme. At home, at the dinner table, it is just the same. It is the same wherever you go. The young girl, and the young woman is by tacit assumption pure, virgin, sexless. *Du bist wie eine Blume.* She, poor thing, knows quite well that flowers, even lilies, have tippling yellow anthers and a sticky stigma, sex, rolling sex. But to the popular mind flowers are sexless things, and when a girl is told she is like a flower, it means she is sexless and ought to be sexless.

She herself knows quite well she isn't sexless and she isn't merely like a flower. But how bear up against the great social life forced on her? She can't! She succumbs, and the dirty little secret triumphs. She loses her interest in sex, as far as men are concerned, but the vicious circle of masturbation and self-consciousness encloses her even still faster.

This is one of the disasters of young life today. Personally, and among themselves, a great many, perhaps a majority of the young people of today have come out into the open with sex and laid salt on the tail of the dirty little secret. And this is a very good thing. But in public, in the social world, the young are still entirely under the shadow of the grey elderly ones. The grey elderly ones belong to the last century, the eunuch century, the century of the mealy-mouthed lie, the century that has tried to destroy humanity, the nineteenth century. All our grey ones are left over from this century. And they rule us. They rule us with the grey, mealy-mouthed, canting lie of that great century of lies which, thank God, we are drifting away from. But they rule us still with the lie, for the lie, in the name of the lie. And they are too heavy and too numerous, the grey ones. It doesn't matter what government it is. They are all grey ones, left over from the last century, the century of mealy-mouthed liars, the century of purity and the dirty little secret.

So there is one cause for the depression of the young: the public reign of the mealy-mouthed lie, purity and the dirty little secret, which they themselves have privately overthrown. Having killed a good deal of the lie in their own private lives, the young are still enclosed and imprisoned within the great public lie of the grey ones. Hence the excess, the extravagance, the hysteria, and then the weakness, the feebleness, the pathetic silliness of the modern youth. They are all in a sort of prison, the prison of a great lie and a society of elderly liars. And this is one of the reasons, perhaps the main reason why the sex-flow is dying out of the young, the real energy is dying away. They are enclosed within a lie, and the sex won't flow. For the length of a complete lie is never more than three generations, and the young are the fourth generation of the nineteenth century lie.

The second reason why the sex-flow is dying is of course, that the young, in spite of their emancipation, are still enclosed within the vicious circle of self-conscious masturbation. They are thrown back into it, when they try to escape, by the enclosure of the vast public lie of purity and the dirty little secret. The most emancipated bohemians, who swank most about sex, are still utterly self-conscious and enclosed within the narcissus-masturbation circle. They have perhaps less sex even than the grey ones. The whole thing has been driven up into their heads. There isn't even the lurking hole of a dirty little secret. Their sex is more mental than their arithmetic; and as vital physical creatures they are more non-existent than ghosts. The modern bohemian is indeed a kind of ghost, not even narcissus, only the image of narcissus reflected on the face of the audience. The dirty little secret is most difficult to kill. You may put it to death publicly a thousand times, and still it reappears, like a crab, stealthily from under the submerged rocks of the personality. The French, who are supposed to be so open about sex, will perhaps be the last to kill the dirty little secret. Perhaps they don't want to. Anyhow, mere publicity won't do it.

You may parade sex abroad, but you will not kill the dirty little secret. You may read all the novels of Marcel Proust, with everything there in all detail. Yet you will not kill the dirty little secret. You will perhaps only make it more cunning. You may even bring about a state of utter indifference and sex-inertia, still without killing the dirty little secret. Or you may be the most wispy and enamoured little Don Juan of modern days, and still the core of your spirit merely be the dirty little secret. That is to say, you will still be in the narcissus-masturbation circle, the vicious circle of self-enclosure. For whenever the dirty little secret exists, it exists as the centre of the vicious circle of masturbation self-enclosure. And whenever you have the vicious circle of masturbation self-enclosure, you have at the core the dirty little secret. And the most high-flown sex-emancipated young people today are perhaps the most fatally and nervously enclosed within the masturbation self-enclosure. Nor do they want to get out of it, for there would be nothing left to come out.

But some people surely do want to come out of the awful self-enclosure. Today, practically everybody is self-conscious and imprisoned in self-consciousness. It is the joyful result of the dirty little secret. Vast numbers of people don't want to come out of the prison of their self-consciousness: they have so little left to come out with. But some people, surely, want to escape this doom of self-enclosure which is the doom of our civilization. There is surely a proud minority that wants once and for all to be free of the dirty little secret.

And the way to do it is, first, to fight the sentimental lie of purity and the dirty little secret wherever you meet it, inside yourself or in the world outside. ght the great lie of the nineteenth century, which has soaked through our sex and our bones. It means fighting with almost every breath, for the lie is ubiquitous.

Then secondly, in his adventure of self-consciousness a man must come to the limits of himself and become aware of something beyond him. A man must be self-conscious enough to know his own limits, and to be aware of that which surpasses him. What surpasses me is the very urge of life that is within me, and this life urges me to forget myself and to yield to the stirring half-born impulse to smash up the vast lie of the world, and make a new world. If my life is merely to go on in a vicious circle of self-enclosure, masturbating self-consciousness, it is worth nothing to me. If my individual life is to be enclosed within the huge corrupt lie of society today, purity and the dirty little secret, then it is worth not much to me. Freedom is a very great reality. But it means, above all things, freedom from lies. It is first, freedom from myself, from the lie of myself, from the lie of my all-importance, even to myself; it is freedom from the self-conscious masturbating thing I am, self-enclosed. And second, freedom from the vast lie of the social world, the lie of purity and the dirty little secret. All the other monstrous lies lurk under the cloak of this one primary lie. The monstrous lie of money lurks under the cloak of purity. Kill the purity-lie, and the money-lie will be defenceless.

We have to be sufficiently conscious, and self-conscious, to know our own limits and to be aware of the greater urge within us and beyond us. Then we cease to be primarily interested in ourselves. Then we learn to leave ourselves alone, in all the affective centres: not to force our feelings in any way, and never to force our sex. Then we make the great onslaught on to the outside lie, the inside lie being settled. And that is freedom and the fight for freedom.

The greatest of all lies in the modern world is the lie of purity and the dirty little secret. The grey ones left over from the nineteenth century are the embodiment of this lie. They dominate in society, in the press, in literature, everywhere. And, naturally, they lead the vast mob of the general public along with them.

Which means, of course, perpetual censorship of anything that would militate against the lie of purity and the dirty little secret, and perpetual encouragement of what may be called permissible pornography, pure, but tickling the dirty little secret under the delicate underclothing. The grey ones will pass and will commend floods of evasive pornography, and will suppress every outspoken word.

The law is a mere figment. In his article on the 'Censorship of Books', in the *Nineteenth Century*, Viscount Brentford, the late Home Secretary, says: 'Let it be remembered that the publishing of an obscene book, the issue of an obscene post-card or pornographic photograph—are all offences against the law of the land, and the Secretary of State who is the general authority for the maintenance of law and order most clearly and definitely cannot discriminate between one offence and another in discharge of his duty.'

So he winds up, *ex cathedra* and infallible. But only ten lines above he has written: 'I agree, that if the law were pushed to its logical conclusion, the printing and publication of such books as *The Decameron*, Benvenuto Cellini's *Life*, and Burton's *Arabian Nights** might form the subject of proceedings. But the ultimate sanction of all law is public opinion, and I do not believe for one moment that prosecution in respect of books that have been in circulation for many centuries would command public support.'*

Ooray then for public opinion! It only needs that a few more years shall roll. But now we see that the Secretary of State most clearly and definitely *does* discriminate between one offence and another in discharge of his duty. Simple and admitted discrimination on his part! Yet what is this public opinion? Just more lies on the part of the grey ones. They would suppress Benvenuto tomorrow, if they dared. But they would make laughing-stocks of themselves, because *tradition* backs up Benvenuto. It isn't public opinion at all. It is the grey ones afraid of making still bigger fools of themselves. But the case is simple. If the grey ones are going to be backed by a general public, then every new book that would smash the mealy-mouthed lie of the nineteenth century will be suppressed as it appears. Yet let the grey ones beware. The general

public is nowadays a very unstable affair, and no longer loves its
grey ones so dearly, with their old lie. And there is another public,
the small public of the minority, which hates the lie and the grey
ones that perpetuate the lie, and which has its own dynamic ideas
about pornography and obscenity. You can't fool all the people all
the time,* even with purity and a dirty little secret.

And this minority public knows well that the books of many
contemporary writers, both big and lesser fry, are far more
pornographical than the liveliest story in *The Decameron:* because
they tickle the dirty little secret and excite to private masturbation,
which the wholesome Boccaccio never does. And the minority
public knows full well that the most obscene painting on a Greek
vase—*Thou still unravished bride of quietness**—is not as pornographical as the close-up kisses on the film, which excite men and
women to secret and separate masturbation.

And perhaps one day even the general public will desire to look
the thing in the face, and see for itself the difference between the
sneaking masturbation pornography of the press, the film, and
present-day popular literature, and then the creative portrayals of
the sexual impulse that we have in Boccaccio or the Greek vase-
paintings or some Pompeian art, and which are necessary for the
fulfilment of our consciousness.

As it is, the public mind is today bewildered on this point, bewildered almost to idiocy. When the police raided my picture
show,* they did not in the least know what to take. So they took
every picture where the smallest bit of the sex organ of either man
or woman showed. Quite regardless of subject or meaning or anything else: they would allow anything, these dainty policemen in a
picture show, except the actual sight of a fragment of the human
pudenda. This was the police test. The dabbing on of a postage
stamp—especially a green one that could be called a leaf—would
in most cases have been quite sufficient to satisfy this 'public
opinion'.

It is, we can only repeat, a condition of idiocy. And if the
purity-with-a-dirty-little-secret lie is kept up much longer, the
mass society will really be an idiot, and a dangerous idiot at that.
For the public is made up of individuals. And each individual has
sex, and is pivoted on sex. And if, with purity and dirty little
secrets, you drive every individual into the masturbation self-

enclosure, and keep him there, then you will produce a state of general idiocy. For the masturbation self-enclosure produces idiots. Perhaps if we are all idiots, we shan't know it. But God preserve us.

Introduction to
The Dragon of the Apocalypse
by Frederick Carter*

IT is some years now since Frederick Carter first sent me the
manuscript of his *Dragon of the Apocalypse*. I remember it arrived
when I was staying in Mexico, in Chapala. The village post-master
sent for me to the post-office: Will the honourable Señor please
come to the post-office. I went, on a blazing April morning, there
in the northern tropics. The post-master, a dark, fat Mexican with
moustaches, was most polite: but also rather mysterious. There was
a packet—did I know there was a packet? No, I didn't. Well, after a
great deal of suspicious courtesy, the packet was produced; the
rather battered typescript of the *Dragon*, together with some of
Carter's line-engravings, mainly astrological, which went with it.
The post-master handled them cautiously. What was it? What was
it? It was a book, I said, the manuscript of a book, in English. Ah,
but what sort of a book? What was the book about? I tried to explain, in my hesitating Spanish, what the *Dragon* was about, with
its line-drawings. I didn't get far. The post-master looked darker
and darker, more uneasy. At last he suggested, was it *magic*? I held
my breath. It seemed like the Inquisition again. Then I tried to
accommodate him. No, I said, it was not magic, but the *history* of
magic. It was the history of what magicians had thought, in the
past, and these were the designs they had used. Ah! The postman
was relieved. The history of magic! A scholastic work! And these
were the designs they had used! He fingered them gingerly, but
fascinated.

And I walked home at last, under the blazing sun, with the
bulky package under my arm. And then, in the cool of the patio, I
read the beginning of the first *Dragon*.

The book was not then what it is now. Then, it was nearly all
astrology, and very little argument. It was confused: it was, in a
sense, a chaos. And it hadn't very much to do with St John's
Revelation. But that didn't matter to me. I was very often
smothered in words. And then would come a page, or a chapter,
that would release my imagination and give me a whole great sky to

move in. For the first time I strode forth into the grand fields of the sky. And it was a real experience, for which I have been always grateful. And always the sensation comes back to me, of the dark shade on the veranda in Mexico, and the sudden release into the great sky of the old world, the sky of the zodiac.

I have read books of astronomy which made me dizzy with the sense of illimitable space. But the heart melts and dies—it is the disembodied mind alone which follows on through this horrible hollow void of space, where lonely stars hang in awful isolation. And this is not a release. It is a strange thing, but when science extends space *ad infinitum*, and we get the terrible sense of limitlessness, we have at the same time a secret sense of imprisonment. Three-dimensional space is homogeneous, and no matter *how* big it is, it is a kind of prison. No matter how vast the range of space, there is no release.

Why then, this sense of release, of marvellous release, in reading the *Dragon*? I don't know. But anyhow, the *whole* imagination is released, not a part only. In astronomical space, one can only *move*, one cannot be. In the astrological heavens, that is to say, the ancient zodiacal heavens, the whole man is set free, once the imagination crosses the border. The whole man, bodily and spiritual, walks in the magnificent fields of the stars, and the stars have names, and the feet tread splendidly upon—we know not what, but the heavens, instead of untreadable space.

It is an experience. To enter the astronomical sky of space is a great sensational experience. To enter the astrological sky of the zodiac and the living, roving planets is another experience, another *kind* of experience; it is truly imaginative, and to me, more valuable. It is not a mere extension of what we know: an extension that becomes awful, then appalling. It is the entry into another world, another kind of world, measured by another dimension. And we find some prisoned self in us coming forth to live in this world.

Now it is ridiculous for us to deny any experience. I well remember my first real experience of space, reading a book of modern astronomy. It was rather awful, and since then I rather hate the mere suggestion of illimitable space.

But I also remember very vividly my first experience of the astrological heavens, reading Frederick Carter's *Dragon*: the sense of being the Macrocosm, the great sky with its meaningful stars and its profoundly meaningful motions, its wonderful bodily vastness, not empty, but all alive and doing. And I value this experience more. For the sense of astronomical space merely paralyses me. But the sense of the living astrological heavens gives me an extension of my being, I become big and glittering and vast with a sumptuous vastness. I am the Macrocosm, and it is wonderful. And since I am not afraid to feel my own nothingness in front of the vast void of astronomical space, neither am I afraid to feel my own splendidness in the zodiacal heavens.

The *Dragon* as it exists now is no longer the *Dragon* which I read in Mexico. It has been made more—more argumentative, shall we say. Give me the old manuscript and let me write an introduction to that! I urge. But: No, says Carter. It isn't *sound*.

Sound what? He means his old astrological theory of the Apocalypse was not sound, as it was exposed in the old manuscript. But who cares? We do not care, vitally, about theories of the Apocalypse: what the Apocalypse means. What we care about is the release of the imagination. A real release of the imagination renews our strength and our vitality, makes us feel stronger and happier. Scholastic works don't release the imagination: at the best, they satisfy the intellect, and leave the body an unleavened lump. But when I get the release into the zodiacal cosmos my very feet feel lighter and stronger, my very knees are glad.

What does the Apocalypse matter, unless in so far as it gives us imaginative release into another vital world? After all, what meaning *has* the Apocalypse? For the ordinary reader, not much. For the ordinary student and biblical student, it means a prophetic vision of the martyrdom of the Christian Church, the Second Advent, the destruction of worldly power, particularly the power of the great Roman Empire, and then the institution of the Millenium, the rule of the risen Martyrs of Christendom for the space of one thousand years: after which, the end of everything, the Last Judgment, and souls in heaven; all earth, moon and sun being wiped out, all stars and all space. The New Jerusalem, and Finis!

This is all very fine, but we know it pretty well by now, so it offers no imaginative release to most people. It is the orthodox interpretation of the Apocalypse, and probably it is the true superficial meaning, or the final intentional meaning of the work.

But what of it? It is a bore. Of all the stale buns, the New Jerusalem is one of the stalest. At the best, it was only invented for the Aunties of this world.

Yet when we read Revelation, we feel at once there are meanings behind meanings. The visions that we have known since childhood are not so easily exhausted by the orthodox commentators. And the phrases that have haunted us all our life, like: And I saw heaven opened, and behold! A white horse!*—these are not explained quite away by orthodox explanations. When all is explained and expounded and commented upon, still there remains a curious fitful, half-spurious and half-splendid wonder in the work. Sometimes the great figures loom up marvellous. Sometimes there is a strange sense of incomprehensible drama. Sometimes the figures have a life of their own, inexplicable, which cannot be explained away or exhausted.

And gradually we realize that we are in the world of symbol as well as of allegory. Gradually we realize the book has no one meaning. It has meanings. Not meaning *within* meaning: but rather, meaning against meaning. No doubt the last writer left the Apocalypse as a sort of complete Christian allegory, a Pilgrim's Progress to the Judgment Day and the New Jerusalem: and the orthodox critics can explain the allegory fairly satisfactorily. But the Apocalypse is a compound work. It is no doubt the work of different men, of different generations and even different centuries.

So that we don't have to look for a meaning, as we can look for meaning in an allegory like *Pilgrim's Progress*, or even like Dante.* John of Patmos didn't *compose* the Apocalypse. The Apocalypse is the work of no one man. The Apocalypse began probably two centuries before Christ, as some small book, perhaps, of Pagan ritual, or some small pagan-Jewish Apocalypse written in symbols. It was written over by other Jewish apocalyptists, and finally came down to John of Patmos. He turned it more or less, rather less than more, into a Christian allegory. And later scribes trimmed up his work.

So the ultimate intentional, Christian meaning of the book is, in a sense, only plastered over. The great images incorporated are like the magnificent Greek pillars plastered into the Christian Church in Sicily: they are not merely allegorical figures: they are symbols, they belong to a bigger age than that of John of Patmos. And as symbols they defy John's superficial allegorical meaning. You can't give a great symbol a 'meaning' any more than you can give a cat a 'meaning'. Symbols are organic units of consciousness with a life of their own, and you can never explain them away, because their value is dynamic, emotional, belonging to the sense-consciousness of the body and soul, and not simply mental. An allegorical image has a *meaning*. Mr Facing-both-ways has a meaning. But I defy you to lay your finger on the full meaning of Janus,* who is a symbol.

It is necessary for us to realize very definitely the difference between allegory and symbol. Allegory is narrative description using, as a rule, images to express certain definite qualities. Each image means something, and is a term in the argument and nearly always for a moral or didactic purpose, for under the narrative of an allegory lies a didactic argument, usually moral. Myth likewise is descriptive narrative using images. But myth is never an argument, it never has a didactic nor a moral purpose, you can draw no conclusion from it. Myth is an attempt to narrate a whole human experience, of which the purpose is too deep, going too deep in the blood and soul, for mental explanation or description. We *can* expound the myth of Chronos* very easily. We can explain it, we can even draw the moral conclusion. But we only look a little silly. The myth of Chronos lives on beyond explanation, for it describes a profound experience of the human body and soul, an experience which is never exhausted and never will be exhausted, for it is being felt and suffered now, and it will be felt and suffered while man remains man. You may explain the myths away: but it only means you go on suffering blindly, stupidly, 'in the unconscious', instead of healthily and with the imaginative comprehension playing upon the suffering.

And the images of myth are symbols. They don't 'mean something'. They stand for units of human *feeling*, human experience. A complex of emotional experience is a symbol. And the power of the symbol is to arouse the deep emotional self, and the dynamic self, beyond comprehension. Many ages of accumulated experience still throb within a symbol. And we throb in response. It takes centuries to create a really significant symbol: even the symbol of the Cross, or of the horse-shoe, or the horns. No man can invent symbols. He can invent an emblem, made up of images: or metaphors: or images: but not symbols. Some images, in the course of many generations of men, become symbols, embedded in the soul and ready to start alive when touched, carried on in the human consciousness for centuries. And again, when men become unresponsive and half dead, symbols die.

Now the Apocalypse has many splendid old symbols, to make us throb. And symbols suggest schemes of symbols. So the Apocalypse, with its symbols, suggests schemes of symbols, deep underneath its Christian, allegorical surface meaning of the Church of Christ.

And one of the chief schemes of symbols which the Apocalypse will suggest to any man who has a feeling for symbols, as contrasted with the orthodox feeling for allegory, is the astrological scheme. Again and again the symbols of the Apocalypse are astrological, the movement is star-movement, and these suggest an astrological scheme. Whether it is worth while to work out the astrological scheme from the impure text of the Apocalypse depends on the man who finds it worth while. Whether the scheme *can* be worked out remains for us to judge. In all probability there was once an astrological scheme there.

But what is certain is that the astrological symbols and suggestions are still there, they give us the lead. And the lead leads us sometimes out into a great imaginative world where we feel free and delighted. At least, that is my experience. So what does it matter whether the astrological scheme can be restored intact or not? Who cares about explaining the Apocalypse, either allegorically or astrologically or historically or any other way. All ones cares about is the lead, the lead that the symbolic figures give us, and their dramatic movement: the lead, and where it will lead us to. If it leads to a release of the imagination into some new sort of world, then let us be thankful, for that is what we want. It matters so little to us who care more about life than about scholarship, what is correct or what is not correct. What does 'correct' mean, anyhow? *Sanahorias** is the Spanish for carrots: I hope I am correct. But what are carrots correct for?

What the ass wants is carrots; not the idea of carrots, nor thought-forms of carrots, but carrots. The Spanish ass doesn't even know that he is eating *sanahorias.* He just eats and feels blissfully full of carrot. Now does *he* have more of the carrot, who eats it, or do I, who know that in Spanish it is called a *sanahoria* (I hope I am correct) and in botany it belongs to the *umbelliferae*?

We are full of the wind of thought-forms, and starved for a good carrot. I don't care *what* a man sets out to prove, so long as he will interest me and carry me away. I don't in the least care whether he proves his point or not, so long as he has given me a real imaginative experience by the way, and not another set of bloated thought-forms. We are starved to death, fed on the eternal sodom-apples* of thought-forms. What we want is *complete* imaginative experience, which goes through the whole soul and body. Even at the expense of reason we want imaginative experience. For reason is certainly not the final judge of life.

Though, if we pause to think about it, we shall realize that it is not Reason herself whom we have to defy, it is her myrmidons, our accepted ideas and thought-forms. Reason can adjust herself to almost anything, if we will only free her from her crinoline and powdered wig, with which she was invested in the eighteenth and nineteenth centuries. Reason is a supple nymph, and slippery as a fish by nature. She had as leave give her kiss to an absurdity any day, as to syllogistic truth. The absurdity may turn out truer.

So we need not feel ashamed of flirting with the zodiac. The zodiac is well worth flirting with. But not in the rather silly modern way of horoscopy and telling your fortune by the stars. Telling your fortune by the stars, or trying to get a tip from the stables, before a horse-race. You want to know what horse to put your money on. Horoscopy is just the same. They want their 'fortune' told: never their misfortune.

Surely one of the greatest imaginative experiences the human race has ever had was the Chaldean* experience of the stars, including the sun and moon. Sometimes it seems it must have been greater experience than any God-experience. For God is only a great imaginative experience. And sometimes it seems as if the experience of the living heavens, with a living yet not human sun, and brilliant living stars in *live* space must have been the most magnificent of all experiences, greater than any Jehovah or Baal, Buddha or Jesus. It may seem an absurdity to talk of *live* space. But is it? While we are warm and well and 'unconscious' of our bodies, are we not all the time ultimately conscious of our bodies in the same way, as live or living space? And is not this the reason why void space so terrifies us?

I would like to know the stars again as the Chaldeans knew

them, two thousand years before Christ. I would like to be able to put my ego into the sun, and my personality into the moon, and my character into the planets, and live the life of the heavens, as the early Chaldeans did. The human consciousness is really homogeneous. There is no complete forgetting, even in death. So that somewhere within us the old experience of the Euphrates, Mesopotamia* between the rivers, lives still. And in my Mesopotamian self I long for the sun again, and the moon and stars, for the Chaldean sun and the Chaldean stars. I long for them terribly. Because *our* sun and *our* moon are only thought-forms to us, balls of gas, dead globes of extinct volcanoes, things we *know* but never feel by experience. By *experience*, we should feel the sun as the savages feel him, we should 'know' him as the Chaldeans knew him, in a terrific embrace. But our experience of the sun is dead, we are cut off. All we have now is the thought-form of the sun. He is a blazing ball of gas, he has spots occasionally, from some sort of indigestion, and he makes you brown and healthy if you let him. The first two 'facts' we should never have known if men with telescopes, called astronomers, hadn't told us. It is obvious, they are mere thought-forms. The third 'fact' about being brown and healthy, we believe because the doctors have told us it is so. As a matter of fact, many neurotic people become more and more neurotic, the browner and 'healthier' they become by sun-baking. The sun can rot as well as ripen. So the third fact is also a thought-form.

And that is all we have, poor things, of the sun. Two or three cheap and inadequate thought-forms. Where, for us, is the great and royal sun of the Chaldeans? Where even, for us, is the sun of the Old Testament, coming forth like a strong man to run a race?* We have lost the sun. We have lost the sun, and we have found a few miserable thought-forms. A ball of blazing gas! With spots! He browns you!

To be sure, we are not the first to lose the sun. The Babylonians themselves began the losing of him. The great and living heavens of the Chaldeans deteriorated already in Belshazzar's* day to the fortune-telling disc of the night skies. But that was man's fault, not the heavens'. Man always deteriorates. And when he deteriorates he always becomes inordinately concerned about his 'fortune' and his fate. While life itself is fascinating, fortune is completely uninteresting, and the idea of fate does not enter. When men become poor in life then they become anxious about their fortune and frightened about their fate. By the time of Jesus, men had become so anxious about their fortunes and so frightened about their fates, that they put up the grand declaration that life was one long misery and you couldn't expect your fortune till you got to heaven; that is, till after you were dead. This was accepted by all men, and has been the creed till our day, Buddha and Jesus alike. It has provided us with a vast amount of thought-forms, and landed us in a sort of living death.

So now we want the sun again. Not the spotted ball of gas that browns you like a joint of meat, but the living sun, and the living moon of the old Chaldean days. Think of the moon, think of Artemis and Cybele,* think of the white wonder of the skies, so rounded, so velvety, moving so serene; and then think of the pock-marked horror of the scientific photographs of the moon!

But when we have seen the pock-marked face of the moon in scientific photographs, need that be the end of the moon for us? Even rationally? I think not. It is a great blow: but the imagination can recover from it. Even if we have to believe the pock-marked photograph, even if we believe in the cold and snow and utter deadness of the moon—which we *don't* quite believe—the moon is not therefore a dead nothing. The moon is a white strange world, great, white, soft-seeming globe in the night sky, and what she actually communicates to me across space I shall never fully know. But the moon that pulls the tides, and the moon that controls the menstrual periods of women, and the moon that touches the lunatics, she is not the mere dead lump of the astronomist. The moon is the great moon still, she gives forth her soft and feline influences, she sways us still, and asks for sympathy back again. In her so-called deadness there is enormous potency still, and power even over our lives. The Moon! Artemis! the great goddess of the splendid past of men! Are you going to tell me she is a dead lump?

She is not dead. But maybe we are dead, half-dead little modern worms stuffing our damp carcasses with thought-forms that have no sensual reality. When we describe the moon as dead, we are describing the deadness in ourselves. When we find space so hideously void, we are describing our own unbearable emptiness.

Do we imagine that we, poor worms with spectacles and telescopes and thought-forms, are really more conscious, more vitally aware of the universe than the men in the past were, who called the moon Artemis, or Cybele, or Astarte?* Do we imagine that we really, livingly know the moon better than they knew her? That our knowledge of the moon is more real, more 'sound'? Let us disabuse ourselves. We know the moon in terms of our own telescopes and our own deadness. We know everything in terms of our own deadness.

But the moon is Artemis still, and a dangerous goddess she is, as she always was. She throws her cold contempt on you as she passes over the sky, poor, mean little worm of a man who thinks she is nothing but a dead lump. She throws back the cold white vitriol of her angry contempt on to your mean, tense nerves, nervous man, and she is corroding you away. Don't think you can escape the moon, any more than you can escape breathing. She is on the air you breathe. She is active within the atom. Her sting is part of the activity of the electron.

Do you think you can put the universe apart, a dead lump here, a ball of gas there, a bit of fume somewhere else? How puerile it is, as if the universe were the back yard of some human chemical works! How gibbering man becomes, when he is really clever, and thinks he is giving the ultimate and final description of the universe! Can't he see that he is merely describing himself, and that the self he is describing is merely one of the more dead and dreary states that man can exist in? When man changes his state of being, he needs an entirely different description of the universe, and so the universe changes its nature to him entirely. Just as the nature of our universe is entirely different from the nature of the Chaldean Cosmos. The Chaldeans described the Cosmos as they found it: Magnificent. We describe the universe as we find it: mostly void, littered with a certain number of dead moons and unborn stars, like the back yard of a chemical works.

Is our description true? Not for a single moment, once you change your state of mind: or your state of soul. It is true for our present deadened state of mind. Our state of mind is becoming unbearable. We shall have to change it. And when we have changed it, we shall change our description of the universe entirely. We shall not call the moon Artemis, but the new name will be nearer to

Artemis than to a dead lump or an extinct globe. We shall not get back the Chaldean vision of the living heavens. But the heavens will come to life again for us, and the vision will express also the new men that we are.

And so the value of these studies in the Apocalypse. They wake the imagination and give us at moments a new universe to live in. We may think it is the old cosmos of the Babylonians, but it isn't. We can never recover an old vision, once it has been supplanted. But what we can do is to discover a new vision in harmony with the memories of old, far-off, far, far-off experience that lie within us. So long as we are not deadened or drossy, memories of Chaldean experience still live within us, at great depths, and can vivify our impulses in a new direction, once we awaken them.

Therefore we ought to be grateful for a book like this of the *Dragon*. What does it matter if it is confused? What does it matter if it repeats itself? What does it matter if in parts it is not very interesting, when in other parts it is intensely so, when it suddenly opens doors and lets out the spirit into a new world, even if it is a very old world! I admit that I cannot see eye to eye with Mr Carter about the Apocalypse itself. I cannot, myself, feel that old John of Patmos spent his time on his island lying on his back and gazing at the resplendent heavens; then afterwards writing a book in which all the magnificent cosmic and starry drama is deliberately wrapped up in Jewish-Christian moral threats and vengeances, sometimes rather vulgar.

But that, no doubt, is due to our different approach to the book. I was brought up on the Bible, and seem to have it in my bones. From early childhood I have been familiar with Apocalyptic language and Apocalyptic image: not because I spent my time reading Revelation, but because I was sent to Sunday School and to Chapel, to Band of Hope and to Christian Endeavour,* and was always having the Bible read at me or to me. I did not even listen attentively. But language has a power of echoing and re-echoing in my unconscious mind. I can wake up in the night and 'hear' things being said—or hear a piece of music—to which I had paid no attention during the day. The very sound itself registers. And so the sound of Revelation had registered in me very early, and I was as used to: 'I was in the Spirit on the Lord's day, and heard behind me a great voice, as of a trumpet, saying: I am Alpha and

Omega'*—as I was to a nursery rhyme like Little Bo-Peep! I didn't know the meaning, but then children so often prefer sound to sense. 'Alleluia: for the Lord God omnipotent reigneth.'* The Apocalypse is full of sounding phrases, beloved by the uneducated in the chapels for their true liturgical powers. 'And he treadeth the winepress of the fierceness and wrath of Almighty God.'*

No, for me the Apocalypse is altogether too full of fierce feeling, fierce and moral, to be a grand disguised star-myth. And yet it has intimate connexion with star-myths and the movement of the astrological heavens: a sort of submerged star-meaning. And nothing delights me more than to escape from the all too-moral chapel meaning of the book, to another wider, older, more magnificent meaning. In fact, one of the real joys of middle age is in coming back to the Bible, reading a new translation, such as Moffatt's,* reading the modern research and modern criticism of some Old Testament books, and of the Gospels, and getting a whole new conception of the Scriptures altogether. Modern research has been able to put the Bible back into its living connexions, and it is splendid: no longer the Jewish-moral book and a stick to beat an immoral dog, but a fascinating account of the adventure of the Jewish—or Hebrew or Israelite nation, among the great old civilized nations of the past, Egypt, Assyria, Babylon, and Persia: then on into the Hellenic world, the Seleucids,* and the Romans, Pompey and Anthony.* Reading the Bible in a new translation, with modern notes and comments, is more fascinating than reading Homer, for the adventure goes even deeper into time and into the soul, and continues through the centuries, and moves from Egypt to Ur and to Nineveh, from Sheba to Tarshish* and Athens and Rome. It is the very quick of ancient history.

And the Apocalypse, the last and presumably the latest of the books of the Bible, also comes to life with a great new life, once we look at its symbols and take the lead that they offer us. The text leads most easily into the great chaotic Hellenic world of the first century: Hellenic, not Roman. But the symbols lead much further back.

They lead Frederick Carter back to Chaldea and to Persia, chiefly, for his skies are the late Chaldean, and his mystery is chiefly Mithraic.* Hints, we have only hints from the outside. But the rest is within us, and if we can take a hint, it is extraordinary how far and into what fascinating worlds the hints can lead us. The orthodox critics will say: Fantasy! Nothing but fantasy! But then, thank God for fantasy, if it enhances our life.

And even so, the 'reproach' is not quite just. The Apocalypse has an old, submerged astrological meaning, and probably even an old astrological scheme. The hints are too obvious and too splendid: like the ruins of an old temple incorporated in a Christian chapel. Is it any more fantastic to try to reconstruct the embedded temple, than to insist that the embedded images and columns are mere rubble in the Christian building, and have no meaning? It is as fantastic to deny meaning when meaning is there, as it is to invent meaning when there is none. And it is much duller. For the invented meaning may still have a life of its own.

EXPLANATORY NOTES

(Though a number of these notes are cross-referenced, the Index lists occurrences of all individual references in the volume, the first of which is normally the one to be annotated.)

3 *Thomas Mann . . . Heinrich Mann . . . Jakob Wassermann*: Thomas Mann (1875–1955) remains more 'acclaimed' than his brother Heinrich (1871–1950) and Jakob Wassermann (1873–1934), both of whom combined social protest (to which Thomas Mann objected on artistic grounds) with lurid psychological and particularly erotic fantasy in fictions that were once sensationally popular, but are now less well known.

Gustave Flaubert: the great French novelist (1821–80) is one of Lawrence's favourite opponents, here attacked for his famed stylistic precision.

Novellen; *Königliche Hoheit . . . Der Tod in Venedig*: novellas or short novels; *Royal Highness* (1909); *Death in Venice* (1912).

Patrizier: patrician.

Alexander Pope: the Augustan poet (1688–1744) is taken here as an exemplar of the Age of Reason.

'Nothing outside . . . a maxim: i.e. nothing extraneous—the kind of literary dictum holding sway in the twentieth century but rejected by Lawrence.

the Russian painter girl: Lisabeta Ivanovna, a character to whom Tonio is speaking.

Sturm und Drang: 'Storm and Stress', a label for the fervent literary movement that began German Romanticism in the late eighteenth century, from the title of a romantic play (1776) by Friedrich Maximilian Klinger (1752–1831).

4 *fifty-three*: Mann in fact turned 38 in 1913, the year Lawrence wrote this.

Corot: Jean Baptiste Camille Corot (1796–1875), French landscape painter.

'Wählerisch . . . Geschmacks': 'Fastidious, select, precious, refined, irritated by the banal, and extremely sensitive in questions of tact and taste.'

Leitmotiv: 'leading motif' or recurring phrase in music or literature.

5 *He*: i.e. Aschenbach.

5 *'dass beinahe . . . gekommen sei'*: 'that almost everything great has come about in despite, in defiance of sorrow and pain, poverty, destitution, bodily weakness, vice, passion and a thousand obstructive circumstances.'

6 *Holbein Totentanz*: *The Dance of Death*, a series of woodcuts by the German painter Hans Holbein (1497–1543), first published in 1538.

dem allerliebsten . . . Liebchen': 'to everyone's beloved, to the beautiful darling'.

Hyacinth: a beautiful youth doomed, as Mann explains in the novella, because two gods, Apollo and Zephyr, were rivals for his love. *Künstler*: artist.

8 *Madame Bovary*: for more on Flaubert's novel (1857), see Lawrence's Introduction to *Mastro-don Gesualdo*, pp. 225–6 below.

10 *Ethelberta*: heroine of *The Hand of Ethelberta*; see next note.

11 *the Wessex novels*: the novels of Hardy's fictional 'Wessex' (SW England) were published in volume form as follows: *Desperate Remedies* (1871), *Under the Greenwood Tree* (1872), *A Pair of Blue Eyes* (1873), *Far from the Madding Crowd* (1874), *The Hand of Ethelberta* (1876), *The Return of the Native* (1878), *The Trumpet-Major* (1880), *A Laodicean* (1881), *Two on a Tower* (1882), *The Mayor of Casterbridge* (1886), *The Woodlanders* (1887), *Tess of the d'Urbervilles* (1891), *Jude the Obscure* (1896), *The Well-Beloved* (1897).

13 *Italian*: Eustacia's father is in fact Greek (ch. 7).

16 *'An inner . . . itself here'*: from *The Return of the Native*, bk. ii, ch. 6.

lived and . . . his being: from Acts 17: 28: 'in him we live, and move, and have our being.'

'he was . . . expected': adapted from *The Return of the Native*, bk. iii, ch. 1: 'He had been a lad of whom something was expected . . . in an original way.'

'As is . . . a ray': *The Return of the Native*, bk. ii, ch. 6.

17 *'to preach . . . themselves'*: *The Return of the Native*, bk. iii, ch. 2.

19 *Oedipus*: tragic hero of three plays by the Greek dramatist Sophocles (496–406 BC).

Anna Karenina: for more on Tolstoy's novel (1878), see 'The Novel', pp. 179–80, 183 below.

21 *'prédilection d'artiste'*: 'artist's preference.'

Archimedes . . . Stephenson: these famous engineers are the Greek mathematician (*c*.287–212 BC) who, among other things, constructed siege-engines against the Romans; Thomas Newcomen (1663–1729), inventor of the first practical steam-engine; James Watt (1736–1819), who improved Newcomen's machine; Thomas Telford (1757–1834), who constructed many bridges, roads, and canals; and George Stephenson (1781–1848), builder of locomotives and railways.

22 *Phidias . . . William of Wykeham*: these architects are, from Greece in the fifth century BC, the great sculptor (see note on p. 31, below), under whose superintendence Ictinus and Callicrates jointly designed the Parthenon, and Chersiphron, who designed the temple of Diana (Artemis) at Ephesus; the Roman Marcus Vitruvius Pollio (first century AD), who wrote the earliest surviving treatise on architecture; Villard de Honnecourt (fl. 1225–35), who was probably the master-mason of Cambrai Cathedral in France; and the English bishop and statesman (1324–1404) who established the perpendicular style of architecture.

prédilection de savant . . . prédilection d'economiste: scholar's preference; economist's preference (Lawrence's coinages).

25 *Agamemnon sacrifices . . . pledged wife*: a précis of the *Oresteia*, a tragic trilogy by the Greek playwright Aeschylus (525–456 BC), in which the hero, Orestes, avenges the murder of Agamemnon (his father) by Clytemnestra (his mother) and her lover.

26 *'Thou shalt not kill'*: Exodus 20: 13.

27 *Botticelli . . . the Saviour*: the *Mystic Nativity* by the Florentine painter Alessandro Botticelli (1444–1510).

Aphrodite: Greek goddess of love, the Roman Venus. Lawrence refers to Botticelli's *The Birth of Venus*, perhaps the most famous painting in the Uffizi, Florence; he returns to her exposure to the elements in 'Introduction to These Paintings', pp. 254–5 below.

the Song of Solomon: or 'The Song of Songs', a poetic and erotic book in the Old Testament, formerly attributed to King Solomon.

Correggio: Antonio Allegri da Correggio (1494–1534), the Italian painter.

29 *Dürer . . . Parthenon Friez*: Albrecht Dürer (1471–1528), the German artist; the fifth-century BC frieze from the Parthenon in Athens, now in the British Museum.

Andrea del Sarto . . . Michaelangelo: the famous painters here include the Florentine Andrea del Sarto (1486–1531), the Dutch Rembrandt van Rijn (1606–69), the Perugian Raphael (Raffaelo Sanzio, 1483–1520), and the Florentine Michelangelo Buonarroti (1475–1564).

Madonna degli Ansidei: altarpiece, now in the National Gallery, painted by Raphael for the Ansidei family in 1506.

30 *Fra Angelico*: 'Brother Angelico', Italian fresco painter and monk (Guido di Pietro, *c*.1400–55).

Primavera: 'Spring', now in the Uffizi.

Plato conception: in his Doctrine of Forms or Ideas, i.e. that abstract forms are the fundamental reality.

31 *Phidias*: Greek sculptor of the fifth century BC, who initiated the representation of perfect human forms.

Alcibiades, then Horace: for Alcibiades, see the note on p. 233 below; the Roman poet Quintus Horatius Flaccus (65–8 BC) was 'Someone who loves the golden mean' (*Odes* II. x. 5).

32 *Victor Hugo and Schiller*: the French poet, novelist, and dramatist (1802–85); Friedrich Schiller (1759–1805), the German dramatist, poet, and historian.

'Hail to thee ... wert': opening line of Shelley's ode 'To a Skylark'.

33 *Ewige Wiederkehr*: 'eternal recurrence', a phrase used by the German philosopher Friedrich Nietzsche (1844–1900) most frequently in *Thus Spake Zarathustra* (1883–5).

35 *Moses ... David ... slaves ... Madonna ... Adam*: these 'figures' include the sculptures of Moses for the tomb of Pope Julius II in Rome; of David, in the Accademia in Florence; and of two slaves, in the Louvre in Paris. Lawrence may intend various representations of the Madonna, but Adam is clearly from the ceiling of the Sistine Chapel in the Vatican.

36 *Boccioni ... through Space*: the sculpture by Umberto Boccioni (1882–1916), a leading light of the Italian Futurist movement in the arts, dates from 1912–13.

38 *Aeschylus ... Orestean trilogy*: see note on p. 25 above.

Euripides: the Greek tragic playwright (480–406 BC).

39 *Hail ... unpremeditated art*: continuation of the opening of 'To a Skylark'.

40 *Swinburne ... 'causae externae'*: the poet Algernon Charles Swinburne (1837–1909); 'love is a titillation, coupled with the idea of an external cause', from the *Ethics* (bk. iii) of the Dutch philosopher Baruch Spinoza (1632–77).

41 *Peter ... denied ... repented*: see Matthew 26: 69–75.

'What difficulty ... in it': from Count Ilya Tolstoy's *Reminiscences of Tolstoy*, trans. George Calderon (1914), 144–5.

Parable of the Sower: Matthew 13: 3–9.

42–3 *'Dost thou know ... and ashes'*: quotations from Job 37: 16–18, 37: 22, 39: 1–4, and 42: 3, 5–6.

43 *'Who made him in the womb'*: cf. Job 31: 15: 'he that made me in the womb'; Jude does not quote this, but does quote 'Why died I not from the womb' (Job 3: 11) as well as 'Let the day perish wherein I was born' (Job 3: 3) and other 'cursing' from the third chapter of Job.

Loxias: surname of Apollo, the Greek sun-god.

44 *created man in His Own Image*: Genesis 1: 27.

47 *Turner's*: i.e. Joseph Mallord William Turner (1775–1851), the English landscape painter whom Lawrence discusses further in 'Introduction to These Paintings' below, p. 259.

Darwin and Spencer and Huxley: three leading exponents of evolutionary theory, Charles Darwin (1809–82), Herbert Spencer (1820–1903), and Thomas Henry Huxley (1825–95).

50 *'Thou shalt love thy neighbour as thyself'*: Matthew 19: 19.

51 *'fools rush in'*: from Alexander Pope's 'Essay on Criticism' (1711), line 625.

53 *Wille zur Macht*: 'Will to Power', as in the title of Nietzsche's book (1906).

55 *daughters of men*: a phrase from Genesis 6: 2.

Fielding's Amelia to Dickens's Agnes: in *Amelia* (1751) by Henry Fielding (1707–54) and *David Copperfield* (1849–50) by Charles Dickens.

56 *Reynolds*: the portrait painter Sir Joshua Reynolds (1723–92).

58 *Cassandra*: daughter of King Priam of Troy, whose doom-laden prophecies were ignored.

59 *Gretchens . . . Turgenev heroines*: Gretchen is the heroine of *Faust*, the verse drama by Johann Wolfgang von Goethe (1749–1832); typical female portraits by the Russian novelist Ivan Sergeivich Turgenev (1818–83).

Aspasia: learned mistress of the fifth-century BC Athenian statesman Pericles.

Euripides: the playwright (see note to p. 38 above) has been praised for his sympathetic treatment of women.

62 *more blessed . . . to receive*: Acts 20: 35.

64 *Widow Edlin*: a mistake for Sue's Aunt Drusilla.

Thou hast . . . breath: Swinburne, 'Hymn to Proserpine' (1866), line 35.

65 *Pallas*: Athenian goddess of wisdom; see context on p. 43 above.

Mary of Bethany: for her love of Jesus, see John 11: 1–2 and 12: 1–3.

Venus Urania: goddess of sacred rather than profane love.

67 *fastened like Andromeda*: in Greek mythology, the jealous Nereids (sea-nymphs) persuaded Poseidon, god of the sea, to send a monster to which this beautiful maiden was, as declared by an oracle, to be offered; she was chained to a rock, but rescued by Perseus.

Saint Simon Stylites: he lived for thirty-six years from 423 on a pillar near Antioch.

68 *the Vestals*: virgin priestesses of the Roman goddess Vesta.

Frenchman . . . a corpse: in Flaubert's *La Légende de St Julien l'hospitalier* (1877), St Julien lies with a dying leper.

73 *Achilles*: the hero of the Greeks in Homer's *Iliad*.

77 *Whitman's*: Lawrence discusses the American poet Walt Whitman (1819–92), who published his poems as *Leaves of Grass* in nine different editions (1855–92), in the next essay.

'*old unhappy . . . the morning*': Wordsworth's 'The Solitary Reaper' (1805), line 19; Psalm 139:8 (Book of Common Prayer).

78 *serpent . . . own mouth*: a symbol developed in 'Him With His Tail in His Mouth', pp. 191–6, 198 below.

79 *vers libre*: free verse.

80 *Franklin*: Benjamin Franklin (1706–90), statesman and scientist, is one of Lawrence's 'Classic American' writers.

Crèvecœur . . . Holmes: the list includes, in addition to Whitman, another four of Lawrence's 'Classic American' writers: Hector St John de Crèvecœur (1735–1813), Nathaniel Hawthorne (1804–64), Edgar Allan Poe (1809–49) and Herman Melville (1819–91). 'Transcendentalists' such as Ralph Waldo Emerson (1803–82) formed a romantic idealistic literary movement in New England in the mid-nineteenth century. William Hickling Prescott (1796–1859) is best remembered for his *History of the Conquest of Mexico* (1843), Oliver Wendell Holmes (1809–94) for a humorous series of books beginning with *The Autocrat of the Breakfast-Table* (1858).

Baudelaire . . . Wilde: the French poet Charles Baudelaire (1821–67), the Belgian dramatist Maurice Maeterlinck (1862–1949), and the Irish writer Oscar Wilde (1854–1900) could all be described as symbolists as well as aesthetes.

Dostoevsky . . . underground: incorporates a punning allusion to *Notes from Underground* (1864) by the Russian novelist Fyodor Mikhailovich Dostoevsky (1821–81).

82 *Dana*: Richard Henry Dana (1815–82), the nautical writer, is another of Lawrence's 'Classic American' authors.

'*Whoever you . . . or know*': quoting respectively, Whitman's 'Starting from Paumanok', line 189; 'Song of Myself', line 329; the last line of 'City of Orgies' ('continual lovers'); the whole of 'I Am He that Aches with Love'.

83 '*And whoever . . . One Identity*': 'Song of Myself', line 1272; e.g. 'Our Old Feuillage', line 77 ('ONE IDENTITY').

in spite of Plato: Lawrence takes the same line as Plato's pupil Aristotle (384–322 BC), who argued against Plato's Doctrine of Forms or Ideas (see note on p. 30 above) that an individual is distinguished by essential characteristics that do not have a separate 'ideal' existence.

Sennacherib: King of Assyria 705–681 BC, whose downfall is described in 2 Chronicles 32.

84 *Nirvana*: a state of beatitude attained by the extinction of individuality.

85 *This is . . . and eat*: cf. Matthew 26: 26: 'Take, eat; this is my body.'

'*athletic mothers of these States*': 'these States' is a phrase used often by Whitman, but the closest he comes to 'athletic mothers' is the 'athletic American matron' in 'Our Old Feuillage', line 63, or the 'fierce and athletic girls' he hopes to breed in 'A Woman Waits for Me', line 34.

'*As I see . . . outlet again*—': 'I Sing the Body Electric', lines 72–4 and 64–5.

pour épater les bourgeois: to shock the middle-class.

86 '*Yet, you . . . you mean*—': 'Scented Herbage of my Breast', lines 10–16.

87 '*Whereto answering . . . death, death*—': 'Out of the Cradle Endlessly Rocking', lines 165–73. Lawrence quotes the first line of this poem at the end of the essay.

89 *Ave America!*: 'Hail America!'

90 *Lucretius or Apuleius . . . North Africa*: the Roman poet Lucretius does not fit here, either by date (*c.*99–59 BC) or birth, but the other four were all born and lived in North Africa: the Carthaginian Tertullian (*c.*160–*c.*220), St Augustine of Hippo (354–430), and the Alexandrian Athanasius (*c.*296–373) were theologians; Apuleius (second century) is famed for his satirical romance *The Golden Ass*.

91 *The Scarlet Letter*: Hawthorne's best-known novel (1850).

point a moral . . . a tale: Samuel Johnson (1709–84), 'The Vanity of Human Wishes' (1749), line 222.

92 *Pilgrim Fathers*: the English founders of Plymouth Colony, Massachusetts, in 1620.

93 *Ca Ca Caliban . . . new man*: adapted from Shakespeare, *The Tempest*, II. ii. 184–5: 'Ban, Ban, Cacaliban | Has a new master—get a new man.'

97 *Leatherstocking . . . white Americans*: i.e. turning from the 'White' novels, the subject of Lawrence's earlier essay on James Fenimore Cooper (1789–1851), to the five 'Leatherstocking' novels, deriving their generic title from the nickname of the hero, Natty Bumppo, who wears deerskin leggings. Their plot sequence, different from the order of publication, is *The Deerslayer* (1841), *The Last of the Mohicans* (1826), *The Pathfinder* (1840), *The Pioneers* (1823), and *The Prairie* (1827).

Eve Effingham: typically genteel Cooper heroine of the 'White' novels *Homeward Bound* and *Home as Found* (both 1838).

98 *CHINGACHGOOK*: 'Great Serpent', also known as John Mohegan; companion of Natty Bumppo and, after the death of Uncas, the last chief of the Mohicans, he is an idealized 'noble savage'.

99 *le grand écrivain américain*: 'the great American writer'.

99   *'West ... Apollo ... Mohawk'*: when visiting Rome, the American
     painter Benjamin West (1738–1820) was shown the Apollo Belvedere,
     an ancient marble statue of ideal masculine beauty, now in the
     Belvedere Gallery of the Vatican, and exclaimed, 'My God, how like it
     is to a young Mohawk warrior!' See John Galt, *The Life and Studies of
     Benjamin West* (London, 1816), 105.

100 *Odyssey ... Circes ... Ithacus*: in Homer's *Odyssey*, Circe is an
     enchantress who turns men into swine; 'Ithacus' represents the hero,
     Odysseus, a native of the island of Ithaca.

     Lake Champlain: in fact, the setting is Lake Otsego.

104 *Cooperstown*: in New York State, settled by Cooper's ancestors.

106 *The letter killeth*: 2 Corinthians 3: 6.

     Frank Norris's ... Bret Harte: novel (1901) by Frank Norris (1870–
     1902) about the struggles of wheatfarmers in California against the
     encroachments of the railroad; in the stories and poems of the West by
     Bret Harte (1836–1902).

107 *Ishmael ... Cyclops*: Ishmael Bush, named after the wild loner in
     Genesis 16: 12; one-eyed giants in Homer's *Odyssey*.

     the White Lily: Alice Munro.

108 *'lilies that fester'*: from the last line of Shakespeare's Sonnet 94: 'Lilies
     that fester smell far worse than weeds.'

111 *Dostoevsky's Idiot*: Prince Leo Myshkin, the title character in *The Idiot*
     (1868–9).

     a tale told by an idiot: Shakespeare's *Macbeth*, v. v. 25–6.

113 *Typee and Omoo*: *Typee* (1846) and its sequel, *Omoo* (1847), are short
     fictional narratives based on Melville's experiences in the Society
     Islands in 1842.

     personify the sea: as Swinburne does, e.g. in calling the sea 'the great
     sweet mother' and 'lover of men' in 'The Triumph of Time' (1866),
     lines 257–8.

     Lord Jim: the idealistic and emotional eponymous hero of the novel
     (1900) by Joseph Conrad (1857–1924).

     Allzu menschlich: 'all too human', from Nietzsche's *Human, All Too
     Human* (1878–80).

     Balder ... he stinketh: the god of the summer sun in Scandinavian
     mythology, killed by the blind god Hödur through the contriving of
     Loki, the spirit of evil; 'by this time he stinketh' is said of the dead
     Lazarus in John 11: 39.

114 *seal-woman*: as in 'The Seal-Woman's Song', set by Marjorie Kennedy-
     Fraser (1857–1930) in her *Songs of the Hebrides*, which Lawrence
     himself performed.

Woman, what . . . consummatum est: Christ's words in John 2: 4 and (in the English and Latin versions) 19: 30.

Basta: 'enough'.

Der Grosse oder Stille Ozean: 'the Great or Pacific Ocean'.

116 *a sleep and a forgetting . . . 'Trailing clouds of glory'*: phrases from Wordsworth's 'Ode: Intimations of Immortality' (1807), lines 58 and 64.

Delenda est Chicago: 'Chicago must be destroyed', punning adaptation of Cato's *Delenda est Carthago* ('Carthage must be destroyed') in Pliny's *Natural History*, bk. 15, ch. 74.

Rousseau's . . . Noble Savage: as in the *Discourse on the Origin of Inequality* (1755) of Jean Jacques Rousseau (1712–78), and *Atala* (1801) and *Les Natchez* (1826), romantic responses to American-Indian life by François René Chateaubriand (1768–1848).

117 *'This is . . . of me' . . . transubstantiation quibble*: words of the Eucharist derived from Matthew 26: 2–8 and Luke 22: 19–20; i.e. the theological argument concerning the extent (real or symbolic) of the conversion of bread and wine into Christ's body and blood.

Paradise . . . apple of knowledge: comparing the narrator's idyllic life with Fayaway, a Marquesan beauty, in *Typee*, to that of Adam and Eve before the Fall (Genesis 2).

118 *Gauguin*: Paul Gauguin (1848–1903), the French Post-Impressionist painter, likewise settled in the South Sea Islands.

119 *Noli me tangere*: 'Touch me not': Vulgate version of John 20: 17.

120 *The mills of God . . . exceeding small*: translation by the American poet Henry Wadsworth Longfellow (1807–82) of a line by the German epigrammatist Friedrich von Logau (1604–55), itself taken from an anonymous Latin verse.

121 *Fata Morgana*: a mirage or deception, supposedly caused by the enchantress Morgana or Morgan le Fay of Arthurian romance.

122 *White Jacket*: a semi-autobiographical novel (1850) based on Melville's service (1843–4) aboard the man-of-war *United States*.

123 *Pierre*: another semi-autobiographical novel (1852), in which the hero is destroyed by his ideals.

Dostoevsky's Idiot: see note on p. 111 above.

124 *half-sentimental love for Jack Chase*: Melville's 'best love' is addressed to this superhero in ch. 4.

Tous nos . . . être seuls: 'All our troubles come from the inability to be alone', adapted by Lawrence from Blaise Pascal (1623–62), *Pensées* (1669), ii. 139.

126 *Moby Dick . . . white Whale*: *Moby-Dick* was first published in London

as *The Whale* and in New York as *Moby-Dick*; *or, The Whale* (1851); 'White' seems to be Lawrence's addition.

126 *Leviathan . . . Hobbes*: alluding to *Leviathan* (1651), the famous political treatise by the English philosopher Thomas Hobbes (1588–1679).

transcendentalist . . . Hawthorne: see notes on pp. 81 and 120 above.

127 *au grand sérieux*: 'taking [things or oneself] extremely seriously'.

Dana: see note on p. 82 above.

Melville hugged . . . idol: as happens to the narrator of the novel in ch. 10.

128 *Ishmael*: named after the son of Abraham and Hagar in Genesis 16:12: 'he will be a wild man; his hand will be against every man, and every man's hand against him.'

'Hope': a beautiful boy, a South Sea Islander, in Dana's *Two Years before the Mast* (1840).

Benjamin Franklin: see note on p. 80 above. Lawrence ridicules Franklin's religious and moral platitudes in the essay on him.

129 *As I sat . . . loving pair*: all three quotations are from ch. 10.

'large, deep . . . Poe . . . 'clue': from ch. 10; Lawrence repeatedly asserts this in his essay on Poe (see note on p. 81 above).

Argonauts . . . hussies of the isles: the legendary sailors of the ship *Argo*, who sailed from Greece to Colchis in search of the Golden Fleece; in Homer's *Odyssey*, Circe, the sorceress who turns the companions of Odysseus (or Ulysses) into swine, is defeated by the hero's use of a magic herb, and he likewise escapes from island-dwelling 'hussies' like Calypso and Nausicaa.

I am the master . . . trip is done: final lines of 'Invictus' (1875), by William Ernest Henley (1849–1903); opening lines of Whitman's 'O Captain! My Captain!' from *Leaves of Grass* (see note on p. 77 above).

130 *'Fearless as fire . . . mechanical'*: adapted from ch. 134.

'the wondrous water-rat': from ch. 27.

Mr Wilson . . . Peace Conference: Woodrow Wilson (1856–1924; President 1912–21) and his 'efficient' American delegation played a leading role in negotiating the Treaty of Versailles at the end of the First World War.

132 *I remember . . . the spell*: footnote from ch. 42.

It was a cloudy . . . She blows!': both quotations are from ch. 47.

133 *'Give way . . . escaped*: from ch. 48.

It was while . . . the bow: from ch. 51.

134 *Steering north-eastward . . . else*: from ch. 58.

Slowly wading . . . disappeared again: both quotations are from ch. 59.

135 *'for I believe . . . spinal cord'*: both quotations are from ch. 80.

As the three . . . agony: from ch. 81.

136 *Broad on both . . . and delight*: both quotations are from ch. 87 ('The Grand Armada').

Uppermost . . . I thought: from ch. 96.

137 *How he . . . waning savage*: from ch. 110.

'To any . . . the world': from ch. 111.

It was far . . . worships fire: from ch. 116.

138 *Hither and . . . since Paradise*—: both quotations are from ch. 132.

Gethsemane: the Garden of Gethsemane, scene of Christ's agony and betrayal (Matthew 26: 36–46).

139 *'From this height . . . gliding whale*: both quotations are from ch. 133.

'The ship! . . . years ago: both quotations are from ch. 1340

140 *'Not so . . . astern'*: from ch. 96 (see fuller quotation on p. 136 above).

141 *Quien sabe . . . senor?*: 'Who knows? Who knows, sir?'

Vachel Lindsay: this American writer (1879–1931) uses the word 'Boom' repeatedly in one of his best-known poems, 'The Congo' (1914).

Jesus . . . Consummatum est: see note on p. 114 above.

Jesus . . . the Whale: extending the idea of Jesus as the Fish: see note on p. 155 below.

142 *Ulysses . . . Robert Chambers*: on the 'earnest' side of the modern novel that Lawrence depicts as Briareus, a giant with fifty heads and a hundred hands in Homer's *Iliad* I. 403, are *Ulysses* (1922) by James Joyce (1882–1941), Dorothy Richardson (1882–1957), whose *Pointed Roofs* begins her twelve-novel sequence *Pilgrimage* (1915–38), and Marcel Proust (1871–1922), author of the thirteen-volume *À la recherche du temps perdu* ('In search of times past', 1913–27); on the popular side are the best-selling *The Sheik* (1919) by Edith Maude Hull, Zane Grey (1875–1939) and his westerns, and Robert Chambers (1865–1933) and his long series of historical romances.

143 *chloro–coryambasis*: nonsense coined to indicate Lawrence's opinion of this 'answer'.

144 *Babbitts*: reference to *Babbitt* (1922), popular novel by the American author Sinclair Lewis (1885–1951).

If Winter Comes: popular novel by the American author Arthur Stuart Mentieth Hutchinson (1879–1971).

Cleopatra . . . 'Rose-coloured curtains': Mrs Skewton in Dickens's *Dombey and Son* (1847–8), ch. 41.

145 *Put away childish things*: 1 Corinthians 13: 11.

145 *Plato's Dialogues*: the twenty-five dialogues by the Athenian philosopher (*c.*429–347 BC).

Thomas Aquinas . . . beastly Kant: the foremost Roman Catholic theologian (1224/5–74); the German philosopher Immanuel Kant (1724–1804), an Idealist and Rationalist, did not appeal to Lawrence.

147 *A Second Contemporary Verse Anthology*: from this anthology (New York, 1923), selected by Charles Wharton Stork from issues of the magazine *Contemporary Verse* between 1920 and 1923, all Lawrence's quotations in this review are taken, unless otherwise identified. The poems he quotes have proved ephemeral, with the exception of 'Patterns', by his friend Amy Lowell (1874–1925), with its last line 'Christ! What are patterns for?' being as flippantly handled as all the others quoted.

Life . . . earnest . . . dust returneth: see note on p. 193 below; cf. Genesis 3: 19: 'dust thou art, and unto dust shalt thou return.'

148 *There be none . . . to me*: opening lines of 'Stanzas for Music' by George Gordon, Lord Byron (1788–1824).

Now fades . . . Save where—: from 'Elegy Written in a Country Churchyard' (lines 5–7) by Thomas Gray (1716–71).

When lilacs . . . bloomed—: first line of the first poem in the sequence entitled 'Memories of President Lincoln' in Whitman's *Leaves of Grass*.

'My heart aches', says Keats: in the opening words of his 'Ode to a Nightingale' (1819).

149 *roll up . . . Ezekiel*: Ezekiel's vision does begin when 'the heavens were opened' (1: 1), but the wording here is closer to Isaiah 34: 4 (and Revelation 6: 14), with the heavens 'rolled' together 'as a scroll'.

playboys . . . western world: playing on *The Playboy of the Western World* (1907), a play by the Irish writer John Millington Synge (1871–1909), much admired by Lawrence.

150 *nothing new under the sun*: from Ecclesiastes 1: 9: 'there is no new thing under the sun.'

151 *Vive la vie*: 'let life live'.

printanière: 'of spring'.

153 *no man lives . . . to sea*: these allusions, the second of which recurs, are to Swinburne's 'The Garden of Proserpine' (1866), in which the gods are thanked 'That no life lives for ever; That dead men rise up never; That even the weariest river Winds somewhere safe to sea' (lines 85–8).

'Know then thyself . . . Alexander Pope: Pope's *An Essay on Man* (1732–4), ii. 1–2.

'Love thy neighbour': Matthew 19: 19.

'Know thyself': this motto, inscribed on the temple of Apollo at Delphi, is attributed by Plato (*Protagoras* 343) to the Seven Wise Men.

Allons: 'let's go'.

155   *take the name . . . commit adultery*: selected from the Ten Commandments (Exodus 20: 3–17).

Oscar Wilde . . . succumbed to: cf. Wilde's *The Picture of Dorian Gray* (1891), ch. 2: 'The only way to get rid of a temptation is to yield to it.'

Jesus: The Fish. Pisces: the fish may have been adopted by early Christians as a symbol of Christ because the letters of the Greek 'fish' ('icthus') form an acrostic for 'Jesus Christ, Son of God, Saviour'; at the time of Christ, moreover, the sun entered the sign of the Fish, Pisces.

Ra or Ammon or Jupiter: Ra and Am(m)on were at different times the chief god of the Egyptians and were even combined as Ammon-Ra; the Greeks identified him with their own Zeus, the Roman Jupiter.

156   *Lloyd George . . . Poincaré*: of all politicians, David Lloyd George (1863–1945; Prime Minister 1916–22) was the most regular target of Lawrence's hatred; Raymond Poincaré (1860–1934), French President (1913–20) and Prime Minister (1912–13, 1922–4, 1926–9).

Oceanus: in Greek cosmology, the river supposed to circle the earth.

157   *the literature of perversity . . . playboys*: Lawrence is probably thinking of Joyce's *Ulysses*, primarily; apart from the allusion to Synge (see above), Lawrence has in mind a type of literature represented by David Garnett (1892–1981), whose popular fantasy *Lady into Fox* (1922) he described in a letter of 17 September 1922 to John Middleton Murry as 'piffle—just playboy stuff'.

St Paul . . . sensuality: St Paul's Epistles make notable attacks on 'the lusts of our flesh' (Ephesians 2: 3).

159   *John's*: St John of Patmos.

the four Prophets: Isaiah, Jeremiah, Ezekiel, and Daniel.

the two Women: the good woman, mother of righteous offspring, who is attacked by the dragon in ch. 12, and the wicked 'scarlet woman' or whore of Babylon in ch. 17.

161   *Pisgah*: mountain from which Moses saw the Promised Land, Canaan (Deuteronomy 346: 1–4).

Tampoco: 'not [that] either'.

Thomas Hardy . . . the Oversoul: Hardy's view of the 'Cosmic Spirit' is perhaps most clearly shown in *The Dynasts* (1903–8), with its 'Immanent Will' that rules the world and 'neither good nor evil knows'; 'Oversoul' is Emerson's term for the supreme animating spirit of the universe, as in 'The Over-Soul' in *Essays* (1841).

162   *'There's a good . . . time coming'*: from 'The Good Time Coming', popular song by the Scottish poet Charles Mackay (1814–89).

They climbed . . . down again: 'The Son of God goes forth to war', hymn by Bishop Reginald Heber (1783–1826), altering the line 'To follow in their train'.

162 *Pittsburgh*: archetypal American industrial city.

163 *Wrong turning . . . right one*: apparently a humorous play on right/left and right/wrong.

Ultimate Thule: Virgil's *ultima Thule* (*Georgics* I. 30), the place north of Britain regarded by the ancients as the limit of the world.

Everest . . . North Pole . . . Sahara: all were in the news in 1924 as objects of expeditions, the French crossing of the Sahara being in special 'caterpillar cars'.

the world well lost: from *All for Love, or The World Well Lost* (1678), play by John Dryden (1631–1700).

Homo sum . . . alienum puto: Lawrence's reversal ('I am a man. I consider everything human foreign to me') of '*Homo sum; humani nil a me alienum puto*' ('. . . nothing . . .'), from Terence (*c.*190–159 BC), *Heauton Timorumenos* I. I. 25.

Basta . . . 'Farewell . . . greatness': 'enough'; from Shakespeare's *Henry VIII*, III. ii. 352.

Fair waved . . . pleasant land: hymn by J. Hampden Gurney (1802–62).

164 *'Whither . . . sails crowding?'*: first line of 'A Passer-By' by Robert Bridges (1844–1930).

the mundane egg: many ancients believed the world to be egg-shaped, or hatched from an egg.

167 *Cézanne*: the French Post-Impressionist painter Paul Cézanne (1839–1906) is treated at greater length in 'Introduction to These Paintings', pp. 261–3, 265–71, 274–81 below.

169 *Platonic Idea*: from Plato's Doctrine of Forms or Ideas (see note on p. 30 above).

170 *Giotto, Titian, El Greco*: accompanying Turner, the greatest English painter, are Giotto di Bondone (*c.*1266–1337), the innovative early Florentine painter; Tiziano Vecellio (*c.*1488–1576), the greatest Venetian painter; and Domenico Theotocopoulos, 'The Greek' (1541–1614), the Cretan-born Spanish painter.

Vox Populi, Vox Dei: 'the voice of the people [is] the voice of God', from Letter 164 of the English theologian Alcuin (*c.*735–804).

a sin . . . a knock on the head: in traditional accounts of the Fall (Genesis 2 does not specify an apple) and the discovery of gravity by the English scientist Sir Isaac Newton (1642–1727).

171 *significant form . . . colour-mass relations*: Lawrence attacks the jargon of art criticism: in particular, 'significant form' derives from Clive Bell (1881–1964) in the opening chapter of *Art* (1914) and 'tactile values' from Bernard Berenson (1865–1959) in *Florentine Painters of the Renaissance* (1896).

Fantin Latour's: the realistic still-life painter Ignace Henri Jean Théodore Fantin-Latour (1836–1904).

rock of ages: from the hymn 'Rock of ag[...] Montague Toplady (1740–78).

pole-star . . . Allons: the star near enough t[...] marker changes because of the precession of the[...]

Rameses: the Egyptian pharaoh Rameses II 'the G[...] 1237 BC).

172 *the fourth dimension*: a metaphysical concept for Law[...] 'time', as in conventional definitions.

ambiente: 'ambience'.

apples of Sodom: also known as Dead Sea fruit, they look good but are full of ashes; hence anything disappointing.

173 *Van Gogh paints sunflowers*: *Sunflowers* (1888), now in the Metropolitan Museum of Art in New York, is one of the most famous paintings by the Dutch Post-Impressionist Vincent van Gogh (1853–90).

fourth dimension: see the previous essay, p. 172.

175 *sins of . . . the children*: from the second Commandment: 'visit the sins of the fathers upon the children' (Book of Common Prayer, after Exodus 20: 5).

176 *the man . . . the old woman*: Raskolnikov does this near the beginning of Dostoevsky's novel (1866).

If Winter Comes: see note on p. 144 above.

177 *the Constant Nymph died*: in *The Constant Nymph* (1924), popular novel by Margaret Kennedy (1896–1967).

178 *This is the King . . . Holy Ghost*: Luke 23: 28; Lawrence sees the Holy Ghost as the 'third thing', the relation between the opposites of Father and Son.

Lead, Kindly Light: hymn (1833) by Cardinal John Henry Newman (1801–90).

179 *Mr Santayana*: the American philosopher and critic George Santayana (1863–1952).

somebody else's: i.e. the Italian inventor Guglielmo Marconi (1874–1937).

Vronsky . . . devoutly to be wished: Count Alexei Vronsky, the heroine's lover in Tolstoy's *Anna Karenina* (1878); Hamlet, III. i. 63–4.

180 *Prince . . . is a muff*: referring to the feebleness of Prince Dmitri Nekhlyudov, hero of Tolstoy's *Resurrection* (1899).

Mother Grundy's: i.e. Mrs Grundy, embodiment of prudery, from *Speed the Plough* (1798) by the English playwright Thomas Morton (*c*.1764–1838).

'As an officer . . . says Vronsky': in part 8, ch. 5.

at the opera . . . on him: it is in fact Anna to whom this happens (part 5, ch. 33).

...lzac ... to E. M. Forster: i.e. encompassing not just the *...pean* novel represented by the nineteenth-century writers Honoré *Balzac (1799–1850)* and Hardy, but the whole history of the novel from *The Golden Ass* to Lawrence's contemporary Edward Morgan Forster (1869–1970).

Salammbô: Flaubert's historical novel (1862) about Carthage, in which Salammbô, priestess of the goddess Tanit, gives herself to Mathô, a Libyan mercenary, in return for the goddess's stolen veil; he is tortured to death and she dies of grief.

181 *Dostoevsky's Idiot*: see note on p. 111 above.

Timaeus: intended as a typical Dialogue of Plato, though Plato himself is not one of the speakers.

rich man ... the poor: Matthew 19: 21: 'Jesus said unto him, If thou wilt be perfect, go and sell that thou hast, and give to the poor'.

Went to bed ... breeches on: popular parody of the traditional prayer ('Bless the bed that I lie on').

182 *Sylvestre Bonnard ... Pan*: *Le Crime de Sylvestre Bonnard* (1881), by the French novelist Anatole France (1884–1924); *Main Street* (1920), by Sinclair Lewis (see above); *Pan* (1894), by the Norwegian novelist Knut Hamsun (1859–1952). (For *Lord Jim, If Winter Comes*, and *Ulysses*, see notes on, respectively, pp. 113, 144, and 142 above.)

accomplis or manqués: 'perfected or would-be'.

Green Hatted Woman: in *The Green Hat* (1924), popular novel by Michael Arlen (Dikran Kouyoumdjian, 1895–1956).

Constant Nymph: see note on p. 177 above.

Jesus harrow Hell ... bonne heure: in the legend popularized in the Middle Ages by the fourteenth-century poem *Harrowing of Hell*; right', 'very good'.

peccante: 'sinning'.

183 *frère et cochon*: 'brother and pig', suggesting an unwelcome closeness.

Quien sabe: 'who knows'.

convict girl: Katerina 'Katusha' Maslova, convicted of murder.

184 *War and Peace*: the characters referred to in Tolstoy's novel (1863–9) are Count Pierre Bezuhov, Prince Andrei Bolkonsky, and Natasha Rostov.

Attila ... saddle-cloth: as Lawrence writes of the Huns under Attila (d. 453) in *Movements in European History* (1921), ch. 6.

Lenin ... social sausage-meat: i.e. after the Communist revolution in Russia.

lion lie down with the lamb ... the limerick: cf Isaiah 11: 6: 'The wolf also shall dwell with the lamb, and the leopard shall lie down with the kid; and the calf and the young lion and the fatling together'; the usual form of this limerick is 'There was a young lady of Riga, | Who rode with a smile on a tiger; | They returned from the ride | With the lady inside, | And the smile on the face of the tiger.'

185 *bifurcation . . . radish*: alluding to man as 'a forked radish' in Shakespeare's *2 Henry IV*, III. ii. 335.

Honour thy . . . as thyself: Exodus 20: 12; Matthew 19: 19.

cunning of serpents: as in Matthew 10: 16: 'wise as serpents'.

The Goat and Compasses: name of many public houses, possibly from 'God encompasses'.

Beatrice: 'worshipped' in his *Vita Nuova* (1292) by Dante Alighieri (1265–1321).

186 *Laura*: the woman addressed in the poetry of Francesco Petrarca (1304–74).

Dante's Commedia: Beatrice also appears in the poet's most celebrated work, the *Divina Commedia* or *Divine Comedy*.

187 *He could . . . thunder-bolts*: cf. Maxim Gorky in his *Reminiscences of Leo Nicolayevich Tolstoy*, trans. S. S. Koteliansky and Leonard Woolf (1920), section 36.

old-Adam manhood: i.e. before the second or new Adam, Christ, there is unregenerate man, as in the service of baptism in the Book of Common Prayer: 'the old Adam in this child'.

188 *'last infirmity of noble minds'*: from Milton's *Lycidas* (1638), line 71.

Pan: 'all', the name of the Greek pastoral god of creation.

189 *Mrs Eddy . . . Annie Besant*: Mary Baker Eddy (1821–1910), founder of Christian Science; Ashtaroth, Semitic fertility goddess; Annie Besant (1847–1933), theosophist. (For Amon, Ra, and Jupiter, see note on p. 155 above.)

Holy Roller: a religious enthusiast, so named from rolling on the floor.

wind bloweth . . . listeth: John 3: 8.

abandoned the girl: Katusha was seduced and left pregnant by Prince Myshkin.

191 *Him With His Tail in His Mouth*: a serpent forming a circle by devouring its own tail is an ancient symbol of infinity, immortality, eternity.

Answer a . . . his folly: Proverbs 26: 5.

Purusha, Pradhana, Kala: in Hindu philosophy, these Sanskrit words represent the primal man from whose body the universe was created, primeval matter, and infinite time.

Bergson: the French philosopher Henri Bergson (1859–1941) presents creative evolution' (from his book *L'Évolution créatrice*, 1907) as the result of a life force for which he coined the expression *'élan vital'*, which Lawrence translates later in the essay as 'life-energy'.

191 *His Own Image*: Genesis 1: 27.

 Plato . . . ideal: see note on p. 30 above.

 Logos: the 'Word', especially in the opening of St John's Gospel, 'In the beginning was the Word, and the Word was God.'

 ugly and venomous . . . in his head: cf. Shakespeare's *As You Like It*, II. i. 13–14.

192 *the rose would be just as scentless*: allusion to *Romeo and Juliet,* ii. ii. 43–4: 'A rose | By any other name would smell as sweet.'

 One, two . . . go again': Lawrence's punctuation of this traditional children's rhyme reflects the rhythm in which it is chanted.

 vitamines and proteids: outdated forms of 'vitamins' and 'proteins'.

 capital X of all our knowledge: i.e. the supreme unknown quantity (by analogy with the mathematical symbol).

 all in all: 1 Corinthians 15: 28.

193 *'He asked . . . and ever'*: Psalm 21: 4.

 fiumara: a flooded river or its dry bed.

 Allons: 'let's go'.

 Life is real . . . not its Goal: Longfellow's 'A Psalm of Life' (1838), lines 5–6.

194 *'Teach me . . . Judgment Day'*: conflated version of the third verse of the 'Evening Hymn' ('Glory to thee, my God, this night') of Bishop Thomas Ken (1637–1711): 'Teach me to live, that I may dread | The grave as little as my bed; | Teach me to die, that so I may | Rise glorious at the awful day.'

 We can't . . . life, alone: cf. Matthew 4: 4: 'Man shall not live by bread alone.'

 'Oh man . . . the Sphinx: referring to the riddle of the Sphinx in Greek mythology ('What goes on four feet, and two, and three?'), solved by Oedipus as 'man' (crawling in infancy, then walking, and with a stick in old age).

 Susan: Lawrence's cow at his ranch in New Mexico.

 cock . . . Peter . . . liar: alluding to the cock crowing when Peter denied Christ (Matthew 26: 73–5).

195 *monistic*: of theories of being that reject dualism or pluralism and maintain there is only one ultimate principle.

 Mundane Egg . . . fourth dimension: see above, pp. 164 and 172 respectively.

 The Greeks . . . their goal cf. their motto, 'Nothing too much', ascribed by Plato (*Protagoras* 343) to the Seven Wise Men; however, Lawrence's equation of 'equilibrium' and 'relationship' later in the essay suggests a reference to the doctrine of the philosopher Heraclitus (fifth century BC) that equilibrium comes from the strife of opposites.

196 *Jonah . . . whale's belly*: Jonah 1: 17.

197 *'vir' . . . 'vis'*: 'man', 'energy'.

connaissance: 'understanding', with the suggestion of familiar acquaintance.

198 *anthropos*: 'human being'.

Praxiteles Hermes: *Hermes with the Infant Dionysus* is the only surviving original statue by the greatest Attic sculptor of the fourth century BC.

statues of Pharaohs . . . soul of the man: information probably derived from the French Egyptologist Gaston Maspéro (1846–1916), in *New Light on Ancient Egypt* (trans. E. Lee, 1908): 'The statues . . . according to Egyptian belief . . . were imperishable bodies to which a soul . . . was attached' (p. 192).

Rodin's re-merging: probably referring to the attempts of the great French sculptor Auguste Rodin (1840–1917) to restore the 'soul' to sculpted figures by giving them powerful emotional and symbolic force.

sparky: 'lively' (or 'speckled' in dialect).

Sekhet-cat: 'cat' because the goddess of war in Egyptian mythology was usually represented as a lioness, or a woman with the head of a lioness.

199 *Altamira . . . Ajanta*: caves rediscovered in the nineteenth century in, respectively, northern Spain (near Santander) and the Indian state of Maharashtra (near Aurangabad); the Spanish cave-paintings are prehistoric and the Indian ones date from the second century BC.

Burne Jones: leading Pre-Raphaelite painter, Sir Edward Burne-Jones (1833–98).

Wells' History: Lawrence wishes to reverse the view of Herbert George Wells (1866–1946) in *The Outline of History* (1919) that man progresses.

G. F. Watts . . . Physical Energy: sculpture by George Frederick Watts (1817–1904) for the Rhodes memorial in Cape Town, with a second cast (1904) in London's Kensington Gardens.

200 *Baron Corvo*: Frederick William Rolfe (1860–1913) so styled himself; *Hadrian the Seventh* (1904) is his best-known novel.

'Huysmans's': Joris Karl Huysmans (1848–1907), French novelist of Dutch origin, who wrote in a contorted, mannered style.

Yellow Book . . . Simeon Solomon: icons of the 1890s, a 'decadent' decade summed up by the notorious periodical *The Yellow Book* (1894–7), devoted to literature and art, including illustrations by Aubrey Beardsley (1872–98), initially its art editor, but dismissed when the Oscar Wilde scandal broke, and Simeon Solomon (1840–1905) the Pre-Raphaelite painter.

201 *those amazing chapters . . . Then the description*: i.e. the introductory 'Prooimion' and chs. 2–3 (elaborated in ch. 6).

202 *old Adam*: see note on p. 187.

203 *unwinding the antimacassar . . . gorgonzola teeth*: Hadrian in ch. 9; Mrs Crowe, his would-be lover; describing a minor figure in ch. 10, but probably Lawrence intends Jerry Sant, Hadrian's assassin.

Rampolla: Cardinal Mariano Rampolla del Tindaro (1843–1913), a liberal force in the pontificate of Leo XIII.

President Wilson . . . Roosevelt: Lawrence intends the idealistic Woodrow Wilson (1856–1924; President 1912–21) as a contrast to the tough Hernan or Hernando Cortés (1485–1547), the Spanish conqueror of Mexico, and Wilson's Republican rival, Theodore Roosevelt (1858–1919; President 1901–9).

The time . . . for stripping: in ch. 8.

Lord! be . . . a judge: in chs. 3, 22, and 24 (slightly adapted).

some old writer: unidentified.

204 *Mens sana in corpore sano*: Juvenal, *Satires* 10. 356 ('a sound mind in a healthy body').

205 *Better a live dog . . . la vie*: from Ecclesiastes 9: 4 ('a living dog is better than a dead lion'); 'that's life'.

206 *St Francis . . . the years'*: Lawrence's version of St Francis of Assisi (1181/2–1226) apologizing to 'Brother Ass', his body, for his rigorous asceticism.

no wafer . . . to eat: as in the Mass.

207 *burning bush . . . tablets of stone*: Exodus 3: 2–6 and 32: 15–19.

old Adam: see note on p. 187.

'The grass . . . for ever': Isaiah 40: 8.

renews its youth like the eagle: Psalm 103: 5.

208 *wine, woman, and song*: attributed to Martin Luther (*'Wein, Weib und Gesang'*).

210 *John Galsworthy*: English novelist and playwright (1867–1933), author of *The Forsyte Saga* (1922), comprising *The Man of Property* (1906), *Indian Summer of a Forsyte* (1918), *In Chancery* (1920), *Awakening* (1920), and *To Let* (1921); Lawrence also refers to characters in his other novels *The Island Pharisees* (1904), *The Country House* (1907), *Fraternity* (1909), *The Dark Flower* (1913), and *The Apple Tree* (1918).

Sainte Beuve . . . Macaulay: contrasting the French critic and novelist Charles Augustin Sainte-Beuve (1804–69) with the English critic and historian Thomas Babington Macaulay (1800–59).

211 *Pater's . . . Gibbon*: Walter Pater (1839–94), critic and aesthete; the historian Edward Gibbon (1737–94), famed for his *Decline and Fall of the Roman Empire* (1776–88).

these Forsytes: the 'Forsyte' characters to which Lawrence refers in the essay include 'Old Jolyon', tea merchant, his brothers James and Swithin, and his sisters (the 'old aunts'), Ann, Juley, and Hester. James has a daughter, Winifred, and a son, Soames, who is divorced by his first wife Irene Heron, marries Annette Lamotte, and has a daughter, Fleur. Irene, whose previous lover Philip Bosinney is killed in an accident, marries Soames's cousin, 'Young Jolyon', son of Old Jolyon, and they have a son, also Jolyon, known as 'Jon'. By an earlier marriage, Young Jolyon has a daughter, June, who is engaged for a time to Bosinney. By the end of the saga, the love between Fleur and Jon has been destroyed by the revelation of their parents' histories, and Soames has learned that Annette was unfaithful and Irene, whom he still loves, is lost to him.

Sairey Gamp . . . Meredith's Egoist: in Dickens's *Martin Chuzzlewit* (1843–4); Sir Willoughby Patterne, in *The Egoist* (1879) by George Meredith (1828–1909).

slave moral: as in Nietzsche's 'slave-morality', opposed to 'noble-morality', in *Beyond Good and Evil* (1886), ch. 9.

212 *Mr Worldly Wiseman*: in John Bunyan (1628–88), *The Pilgrim's Progress*, part 1 (1678).

give away . . . the poor: cf. 1 Corinthians 13:3 ('though I bestow all my goods to feed the poor') and Matthew 19: 21 ('sell that thou hast, and give to the poor').

Oedipus . . . Phaedra: see note on p. 19 above; tragic hero of the *Hippolytus* of Euripides (480–406 BC).

213 *Pendyce*: George Pendyce, leading character in *The Country House*.

the road-sweeper . . . in the head: Lawrence conflates (and confuses) the story of Hughs in *Fraternity*, chs. 24 and 38.

214 *Goneril and Regan*: the wicked daughters of King Lear in Shakespeare's play.

215 *manqué*: 'would-be'.

Hilarys and Biancas: Hilary and Bianca Dallison in *Fraternity*.

'having' . . . Mr Stone says: in *Fraternity*, ch. 2, he describes the poor as 'shadows' of the rich; Lawrence takes 'having', which he quotes towards the end of the essay, from *The Forsyte Saga* (see below).

216 *Dark Flowers . . . George Pendyce*: Lawrence refers to love affairs in *The Dark Flower*, *The Man of Property*, *The Apple Tree*, and *The Country House*.

model in Fraternity . . . Big fleas . . . Island Pharisees: Ivy Barton (in ch. 4); adapted from 'On Poetry: A Rhapsody' (lines 337–40) by Jonathan Swift (1667–1745); Louis Ferrand (ch. 1).

217 *a 'hunger' for her*: in ch. 2.

pieds truffés: truffled (pig's) trotter.

basta: 'enough'.

'Welsh farm-girl . . . hero: Megan David and Frank Ashurst.

'My King' . . . Wellsian: Beatrice Normandy, in H. G. Wells's novel, *Tono-Bungay* (1909), calls George Ponderevo 'my prince, my king' in bk. iii, ch. 3, section 6.

218 *drowned Ophelia*: see *Hamlet*, iv. vii. 167 ff.

221 *promised end, of the Forsytes*: there were in fact a number of sequels.

Fleur . . . 'having': *To Let*, part ii, ch. to.

'Didn't she . . . bob up. *To Let*, part iii, ch. to.

222 *name is legion*: Mark 5: 9.

223 *Introduction to Mastro-don Gesualdo*: this is the Introduction to Lawrence's own translation (1928) of Verga's novel (1888).

an Alfred de Vigny or a Maupassant: the French romantic writer Alfred de Vigny (1797–1863) and realist fiction writer Guy de Maupassant (1850–93) both had aristocratic (and other) liaisons.

Tigre Reale: 'Royal Tiger', an early sentimental novel (1873).

Matilde Serao's novels: the Italian novelist (1856–1927) wrote 'morbid' romances set in Naples.

224 *Pirandello*: Luigi Pirandello (1867–1937) became a leading practitioner in the 'grotesque' modernist school of Italian drama, next to whom Verga seemed outdated.

Silas Marner: the novel (1861) by George Eliot (1819–80) is a suitably sentimental Victorian companion to *A Christmas Carol* (1843).

Les Misérables: the novel (1862) of Parisian low life by Victor Hugo (1802–85).

226 *stale, flat and unprofitable . . . Novelle Rusticane*: *Hamlet*, 1. ii. 133; the sketch is in *Cavalleria rusticana*.

228 *Tchekov*: Anton Chekhov (1860–1904), playwright and short story writer.

Dmitri Karamazov: the eldest brother in Dostoevsky's last novel, *The Brothers Karamazov* (1879–80), and the one who interested Lawrence most.

230 *à terre*: 'on the ground'.

231 *Persephone . . . bringing back spring*: returning each spring from Hades as Greek goddess (the Roman Proserpine) of the changing seasons.

233 *Achilles . . . Pericles . . . Alcibiades*: three Greek exemplars of 'individual splendour': the hero of the Greeks in Homer's *Iliad*; the statesman (*c.*490–429 BC) responsible for the greatest buildings of Athens; the ambitious Athenian general and statesman (*c.*450–404 BC).

Hector: the hero of the Trojans in the *Iliad*, slain by Achilles.

Myshkin . . . Pierre: see above, notes on pp. 111 and 184 respectively.

235 *Wordsworth . . . a primrose*: there are many primroses in Wordsworth's poems; perhaps the most famous (and certainly known to Lawrence) is the 'primrose by a river's brim' in *Peter Bell* (1819), line 248.

primavera: spring, seen as represented by 'nothing but' the primrose.

236 *Chariot of the Sun*: the essay was written in 1928 as an introduction to this then unpublished book (Paris, 1931) by the American poet Harry Crosby (1898–1929); all Lawrence's quotations are from poems in this volume.

Paul Valéry: French writer (1871–1945) of modern symbolist poetry.

238 *God in his own image*: reversing Genesis 1: 26 ('God created man in his own image').

240 *dead-sea fruit*: see 'apples of Sodom' on p. 172 above.

'cinquain': five-line stanza.

243 *Athos . . . Byron*: Mount Athos in Turkey, a monastic centre of learning; Robert Byron (1905–41), English writer on travel and architecture, *The Station* (1928) being his first book.

the Sitwells: the Sitwell siblings—the poet Edith (1887–1964), satirist Osbert (1892–1969), and, to a lesser extent, art critic Sacheverell (1897–1968)—upset the conventional.

Gregorovius: Ferdinand Gregorovius (1821–91), German historian.

244 *stone . . . philistine*: alluding to David and Goliath (1 Samuel 17: 49).

245 *Williams-Ellis . . . the Octopus*: anti-development tract (1928) by Clough Williams-Ellis (1883–1978), champion of the preservation of rural England and Wales.

246 *Baring's . . . Comfortless Memory*: minor novel (1928) by the prolific Maurice Baring (1874–1946).

Heine: the German poet Heinrich Heine (1797–1857).

247 *Somerset Maugham . . . Ashenden*: spy hero of the popular novel (1928) by the prominent English writer (1874–1965).

dirty dog . . . dead lion: revising Ecclesiastes 9: 4 ('a living dog is better than a dead lion').

248 *Aretino*: the Italian poet Pietro Aretino (1492–1557) wrote 'bold' bawdy sonnets and plays.

'mortal coil': *Hamlet*, III. i. 67.

Oedipus: see note on p. 19 above.

Orestes: see note on p. 25 above.

249 *Donne . . . 'Drink to me . . . honour more'*: Lawrence refers to the love poems of John Donne (1572–1631), later Dean of St Paul's; 'Drink to me . . . thine eyes' is a lyric by Ben Jonson (1572–1637), who influenced

Cavalier poets like Richard Lovelace (1618–58), the last two lines of whose 'To Lucasta, Going to the Wars' (1649) are quoted.

249 *Old Adam*: see note on p. 187 above.

Fielding . . . Richardson . . . Sterne: the novelists Henry Fielding (1707–54), Samuel Richardson (1689–1761), and Laurence Sterne (1713–68); for more on Swift going 'mad with sex and excrement', see the next essay below.

Swinburne's 'white thighs': Swinburne is fond of the adjective 'white', and uses it of many parts of the body (hands, feet, limbs, breasts, shoulders, etc.) but seems never to have applied it to 'thighs'.

250 *Darnley*: Henry Stewart or Stuart, Lord Darnley (1545–67), second husband of Mary, Queen of Scots.

wisest fool in Christendom: James I was reportedly so described by King Henri IV of France (1553–1610).

253 *Charles*: Charles I, beheaded in 1649.

254 *Giorgione . . . Baedeker*: Giorgio Barbarelli (c.1478–1511), Italian painter; Karl Baedeker (1801–59), German publisher of guidebooks who starred significant tourist attractions.

Botticelli Venus: see 'Study of Thomas Hardy', p. 27 above.

255 *Ils n'ont pas de quoi*: 'they don't have the wherewithal.'

256 *crétin*: '(of a) cretin'.

Maria Edgeworth's tales: 'improving' moral fictions by the Irish novelist (1767–1849).

hero of Paradise Lost . . . Satan: as William Blake (1757–1827) and Shelley believed.

257 *Watteau . . . Chardin*: the French painters Antoine Watteau (1684–1721), Jean Auguste Dominique Ingres (1780–1867), Nicolas Poussin (1594–1665), and Jean Baptiste Siméon Chardin (1699–1779) hardly seem a coherent grouping, chronologically or stylistically.

Hogarth . . . Gainsborough: the English painters William Hogarth (1697–1764) and Thomas Gainsborough (1727–88); for Reynolds, see 'Study of Thomas Hardy', p. 56 above.

Sargent's: the fashionable American portrait painter John Singer Sargent (1856–1925).

Velasquez: the Spanish painter Diego de Silva y Velázquez (1599–1660), often considered the greatest of all painters. (For Titian and Rembrandt, see above, pp. 170 and 29 respectively.)

258 *Lawrence or Raeburn*: the English portrait painter Sir Thomas Lawrence (1769–1830) and the Scottish portrait painter Sir Henry Raeburn (1756–1823).

Etty's . . . Leightons: the English painters William Etty (1787–1849) and Frederic, Lord Leighton (1830–96). (For Watts, see p. 199 above.)

259 *Wilson, Crome, Constable, Turner*: the 'great landscape-painters' Richard Wilson (1714–82), John Crome (1768–1821), the chief representative of the 'Norwich School', and John Constable (1776–1837), perhaps most popular of all. (For Turner, see note on p. 47 above.)

Hetty Sorrell's 'sin' . . . *eyes burnt out*: Hetty Sorrel betrays the hero of George Eliot's *Adam Bede* (1859); Mr Rochester is blinded in ch. 36 of *Jane Eyre* (1847) by Charlotte Brontë (1816–55).

Millais: the Pre-Raphaelite and popular painter Sir John Everett Millais (1829–96).

260 *Ça fait du bien au corps*: 'it does the body good.'

Puvis de Chavannes: the French decorative painter Pierre Puvis de Chavannes (1824–98).

Renoir . . . *my penis*: the French Impressionist painter Pierre Auguste Renoir (1841–1919) is quoted by his son Jean Renoir, in *Renoir, my Father* (trans. R. and D. Weaver, 1962) as replying 'With my prick' to a journalist's question as to how, with his arthritic hands, he managed to paint (p. 185).

Daumier . . . *Courbet* . . . *Dégas* . . . *instrument*: of these French painters, Honoré Daumier (1808–78) is famed for satirical caricatures, Gustave Courbet (1819–77) for realistic paintings of peasants, and Edgar Dégas (1834–1917) for paintings of dancers.

261 *plein air and plein soleil*: 'open air' and 'full sun'.

262 *Matisse* . . . *Braque*: Henri Matisse (1869–1954), leader of the 'Fauves' ('wild beasts'—hence, perhaps, Lawrence's 'howling cats'), a school of painters including André Derain (1880–1954) and Maurice de Vlaminck (1876–1958); Georges Braque (1882–1923), a founder of Cubism. (For Gauguin, see p. 118 above.)

263 *Claude Lorrain*: the French landscape painter Claude Lorrain (Claude Gêlée, 1600–82).

Hail, holy light: Milton, *Paradise Lost* (1667), iii. 1.

Primitive Methodists: the term for those church members who broke away in 1810 from the main body of Methodists is punningly applied by Lawrence to those who use or admire primitive methods in art.

the elect . . . *Ruskin* . . . *Calvin*: John Calvin (1509–64), the Protestant reformer associated with the theological doctrine of predestination, by which 'the elect' or 'chosen few' were to be saved, the rest damned; the great art critic and social critic John Ruskin (1819–1900) was the opposite of this, in trying to extend education to the working class, but perhaps Lawrence is thinking more of Ruskin's 'ecstatic' responses to art and architecture.

263 *Significant Form*: for Clive Bell's coinage, see 'Art and Morality', p. 171 above.

264   *Ravennese*: i.e. of Ravenna, the city of northern Italy famous for mosaics dating from the early Christian period.

    Rudolph Valentino: film star (1895–1926) who was the leading screen lover in the 1920s.

265   *Behold . . . of God . . . Washed in the Blood . . . Jerome*: John 1: 29; Revelation 7: 14; the monk and scholar St Jerome (*c*. 342–420).

266   *'willed ambition'*: a phrase from Roger Fry (see p. 270 below).

    stone from . . . the tomb: as at Christ's Resurrection, Matthew 27: 1–2.

267   *Plato's Idea*: see note on p. 30 above.

    it stinketh: see note on p. 113 above.

268   *the dead . . . bury their dead*: from 'Let the dead bury their dead' (Matthew 8: 22).

269   *Friesz*: the French painter Othon Friesz (1879–1949), influenced by Cézanne.

    hommes . . . femmes d'esprit . . . Laurencin: usually 'men/women of wit', but also literally 'men/women of spirit', ghosts; the French painter Marie Laurencin (1885–1957).

270   *Paul Veronese and Tintoretto*: the Venetian painters Paolo Caliari 'of Verona' (*c*. 1528–88) and Jacopo Robusti 'the Little Dyer' (1518–94).

    Fry: the art critic Roger Fry (1866–1934), champion of Cézanne; see his *Cézanne: A Study of his Development* (1927), from which Lawrence's quotations are taken.

    M. Geffroy and his books: Roger Fry (see previous note) writes of this portrait (*c*. 1895) as 'the most celebrated'.

275   *The Pasha . . . La Femme*: the painting also known as *Une moderne Olympia* (A Modern Olympia', *c*. 1870); possibly *Femme au miroir* ('Woman in Mirror', 1866–7).

277   *connu*: 'known', or 'that's an old story'.

278   *Madame Cézanne . . . red dress*: *painting* (*c*. 1890) now in the Museum of Art, São Paolo.

    Card-Players: five versions of this subject exist, three of them with two figures.

282   *Winsor & Newton . . . Lefranc*: respectively, English and French makes of artists' paints.

283   *become . . . as little children*: Matthew 18: 3.

284   *Caractères . . . pattes de mouches*: the *Characters* (1688) or character-sketches of Jean de la Bruyère (1645–96); literally 'legs of flies', normally meaning bad writing or 'scrawl', but here evidently referring to flourishes or arabesques separating items on the printed page.

285   *'In the beginning . . . with God'*: John 1: 1.

ischial tuberosity: humorous coinage roughly equivalent to 'pelvic tube'.

Augean stables: so filthy that Hercules, the Greek mythological hero of prodigious strength, had to divert a river to cleanse them.

286 *ladies in the Voltaire story*: some ladies have their buttocks cut off in ch. 12 of *Candide* (1759), a satirical tale by the French author François Marie Arouet de Voltaire (1694–1778).

poem of Swift's . . . Celia shits: 'The Lady's Dressing Room' (1730).

288 *Dufys . . . Chiricos . . . Ito*: the French artist Raoul Dufy (1877–1953); the Italian artist Giorgio de Chirico (1888–1978); Lawrence himself could not remember the name of this unidentified Japanese artist, then in vogue in Paris, and asked for it to be added when he sent the essay to the *Studio*.

289 *Friesz . . . Laurencin*: see, notes on p. 269 above.

Maria Huxley: Maria Nys (1898–1955), wife of Aldous Huxley, donated canvases (started by her brother) in November 1926.

290 *Minerva . . . Dying Gladiators*: the stern Roman goddess of wisdom, identified with the Greek Athene; the most famous sculpture known as 'Dying Gladiator' is the copy in Rome of an ancient Greek statue more properly entitled 'Dying Gaul'.

291 *'Blessed are the pure . . . heaven'*: cf. Matthew 5: 3 ('poor in spirit').

the Ramblas: a popular promenade, this series of tree-lined avenues in the centre of the old part of Barcelona has many flower-stalls.

Leader's . . . Girtin: Benjamin Williams Leader (1831–1923), landscape painter; Sir Frank Brangwyn (1867–1956), most famous for his murals; Peter de Wint (1784–1849) and Thomas Girtin (1775–1802), English watercolourists.

Paul Sandby: the English painter (1725–1809) known as the father of watercolour art.

Brabazon: the English watercolourist Hercules Brabazon (1821–1906).

292 *'Flight into Egypt . . . Lorenzetti's . . . Carpaccio*: painting of *c.*1451, now in the San Marco Gallery in Florence; the picture known as *La Tebaide*, in the Uffizi, attributed in Lawrence's day to Pietro Lorenzetti *c.*1280–*c.*1348); the Venetian painter Vittore Carpaccio (*c.*1455–1522).

Rubens . . . Peter de Hooch . . . Vandyck: apparently referring to the expansive nudes of the Flemish painter Peter Paul Rubens (1577–1640); the Dutch genre painter Pieter de Hooch (*c.*1629–*c.*1684); the Flemish-born portrait painter Sir Anthony van Dyck or Vandyke (1599–1741).

'Death of Procris' . . . 'Wedding' . . . Giotto from Padua: masterpiece of the Florentine painter Piero di Cosimo (*c.*1462–*c.*1521); possibly *The Marriage at Cana* (*c.*1583) by the Florentine Andrea Boscoli (*c.*1560–1607), as a more famous 'Wedding' picture with 'scarlet legs',

Raphael's *Marriage of the Virgin* (1504), is not in the Uffizi but in Milan; Giotto (see p. 170 above) painted frescos in the Arena Chapel in Padua.

293 *Piero della Francesca or Sodoma or Goya*: the Italian painter (*c.*1420–92); sobriquet of the Italian painter Giovanni Antonio Bazzi (1477–1549); the Spanish painter Francisco José de Goya y Lucientes (1746–1828); all produced paintings that could be called 'sad'.

El Greco: see p. 170 above; the qualities Lawrence describes seem to come from the distortions of his elongated figures, cold colours, and surreal intensity as well as some gruesome subjects.

294 *Aristophanes*: the satirical comedies of the Greek playwright (*c.*448– *c.*388 BC) can still shock audiences.

Vox populi . . . Odi profanum vulgum: see p. 170 above; Horace, *Odes* III. i (opening words), 'I hate the common herd.'

296 *laying the golden egg*: in the Greek fable of the goose that laid golden eggs.

297 *Rabelais . . . Boccaccio*: the French satirist François Rabelais (*c.*1494– *c.*1553) and the Italian writer Giovanni Boccaccio (1313–75), author of the *Decameron* (1358), have both been accused of being pornographic, as was Aretino (see p. 248 above).

298 *'Annie Laurie'*: song by the Scottish poet William Douglas (1672–1748), set to music by Lady John Douglas Scott (1810–1900).

Michelangelo . . . phallic acorns: as seen with male nudes below God dividing light from darkness on the ceiling of the Sistine Chapel.

Pamela or Clarissa Harlowe . . . Tristan and Isolde: *Pamela, or Virtue Rewarded* (1740–1) and *Clarissa, or The History of a Young Lady* (1747–9), novels by Samuel Richardson (see p. 249 above); opera (1865) by Richard Wagner (1813–83).

The Sheik: see p. 142 above.

British Home Secretary: William Joynson-Hicks (1865–1932), later Viscount Brentford, Home Secretary 1924–9, waged a campaign against books he considered immoral; Lawrence quotes him again towards the end of the essay.

300 *on the side of the angels*: phrase coined by the politician and novelist Benjamin Disraeli (1804–81) in a speech at Oxford, 25 November 1864.

301 *The Mill on the Floss*: novel (1860) by George Eliot.

Lasca: the Florentine writer Anton Francesco Grazzini (1503–84), one of whose racy satirical novellas was translated by Lawrence as *The Story of Dr Manente* (1929).

305 *One of my . . . critics*: unidentified.

Who is Sylvia, what is she?: song from Shakespeare's *The Two Gentlemen of Verona*, IV. ii. 40.

Du bist wie eine Blume . . . Jawohl: 'You are like a flower', first line of an untitled poem by Heine (see p. 246 above); 'yes'.

so pure, so clean and beautiful . . . so clean and pure and beautiful: Lawrence's variations nearly match Heine's reversal of the second line (*'So hold und schön und rein'*) in the last line (*'So rein und schön und hold'*) of his poem.

'sadness strike through the heart': from lines 3–4 of the poem (*'Wehmut Schleicht mir ins Herz hinein'*).

306 *My love is like a red, red rose:* from Robert Burns (1759–96), 'A Red, Red Rose' (1796), line 1: 'O my Luve's like a red, red rose'.

lilies . . . festering: alluding to the last line of Shakespeare's Sonnet 94: 'Lilies that fester smell far worse than weeds.'

Dr Marie Stopes: (1880–1958), pioneer of birth control in such books as *Contraception: Its Theory, History and Practice* (1923).

311 *The Decameron, Benvenuto Cellini's Life, and Burton's Arabian Nights:* three famously 'indecent' works by, respectively, Boccaccio (see p. 297 above); the Florentine goldsmith, sculptor and engraver (1500–71), whose autobiography was not translated into English until 1822; and the English orientalist and explorer Sir Richard Burton (1821–90), who translated *The Arabian Nights Entertainments*, or *The Thousand and One Nights* (1885–8).

'Let it be . . . public support': both quotations from 'Censorship of Books' in *Nineteenth Century and After*, 106 (1929), 207–11 (p. 211).

312 *You can't fool all the people all the time:* attributed to Abraham Lincoln (1809–65).

Thou still unravished bride of quietness: opening line of Keats's 'Ode on a Grecian Urn' (1820).

my picture show: the exhibition at a London gallery of Lawrence's paintings was raided by the police on 5 July 1929.

314 *Introduction to . . . Frederick Carter:* Lawrence wrote this Introduction for a work by Frederick Carter (1883–1967), artist and astrologer, to be entitled *The Dragon of the Apocalypse*, but Carter changed it to *The Dragon of Revelation* (1931), which was published without Lawrence's Introduction.

317 *And I saw . . . white horse:* Revelation 19: 11.

Pilgrim's Progress . . . Dante: see, respectively, pp. 212 and 185 above.

318 *Mr Facing-both-ways . . . Janus:* a character in Bunyan's *Pilgrim's Progress* (see p. 212 above); the Roman god of gates and beginnings, represented with two faces looking in opposite directions.

Chronos: also Cronos or Chronus, youngest of the Titans in Greek mythology; he was the father of Zeus, who later overthrew him.

319 *Sanahorias:* properly *Zanahorias*.

320 *sodom-apples*: see 'apples of Sodom' on p. 172 above.

Chaldean: of a part of Babylon anciently associated with astrologers, as in Daniel 4: 7 and 5: 7.

321 *Euphrates, Mesopotamia*: between the rivers Tigris and Euphrates lay Babylonia or Mesopotamia, ancient cradle of civilization (modern Iraq).

strong man to run a race: Psalm 19: 4–5.

Belshazzar's: the last king of Babylonia, 562–538 BC.

322 *Artemis and Cybele*: Artemis, Greek goddess of nature, became associated with the Roman goddess Diana, and with both virginity and the moon; Cybele, the Phrygian fertility goddess worshipped as the Great Mother by the Romans from 204 BC is more an earth-goddess than a moon-goddess.

323 *Astarte*: the fertility goddess of Phoenicia was represented with cow horns, later mistaken for the horns of the crescent moon.

324 *Band of Hope . . . Christian Endeavour*: a non-denominational Christian temperance association that encouraged children to renounce alcohol; a nonconformist church association.

I was . . . and Omega: Revelation 1: 10.

325 *'Alleluia . . . omnipotent reigneth'*: Revelation 19: 6.

'And he treadeth . . . Almighty God': Revelation 19: 15.

Moffatt's: James Moffatt (1870–1944), Scottish-born theologian whose translation of the Bible into modern English was published in 1913 (New Testament) and 1924 (Old Testament).

Seleucids: the dynasty that, starting with Seleucus Nicator (*c.*358–280 BC), ruled Syria from 312 to 65 BC, subjugating much of western Asia.

Pompey and Anthony: the Roman generals and triumvirs Gnaeus Pompey (106–48 BC) and Mark Antony (*c.*83–30 BC).

Ur . . . Nineveh . . . Sheba . . . Tarshish: ancient cities of, respectively, Sumeria, Assyria, Arabia and Spain.

Mithraic: of the Persian sun-god Mithras, whose secret worship spread throughout the Roman Empire from the first century AD.

Index

The Oxford World's Classics Website

www.worldsclassics.co.uk

- Information about new titles
- Explore the full range of Oxford World's Classics
- Links to other literary sites and the main OUP webpage
- Imaginative competitions, with bookish prizes
- Peruse *Compass*, the Oxford World's Classics magazine
- Articles by editors
- Extracts from Introductions
- A forum for discussion and feedback on the series
- Special information for teachers and lecturers

www.worldsclassics.co.uk

American Literature

British and Irish Literature

Children's Literature

Classics and Ancient Literature

Colonial Literature

Eastern Literature

European Literature

History

Medieval Literature

Oxford English Drama

Poetry

Philosophy

Politics

Religion

The Oxford Shakespeare

A complete list of Oxford Paperbacks, including Oxford World's Classics, OPUS, Past Masters, Oxford Authors, Oxford Shakespeare, Oxford Drama, and Oxford Paperback Reference, is available in the UK from the Academic Division Publicity Department, Oxford University Press, Great Clarendon Street, Oxford OX2 6DP.

In the USA, complete lists are available from the Paperbacks Marketing Manager, Oxford University Press, 198 Madison Avenue, New York, NY 10016.

Oxford Paperbacks are available from all good bookshops. In case of difficulty, customers in the UK can order direct from Oxford University Press Bookshop, Freepost, 116 High Street, Oxford OX1 4BR, enclosing full payment. Please add 10 per cent of published price for postage and packing.